YANKEE STRANGER

CHART OF FAMILIES

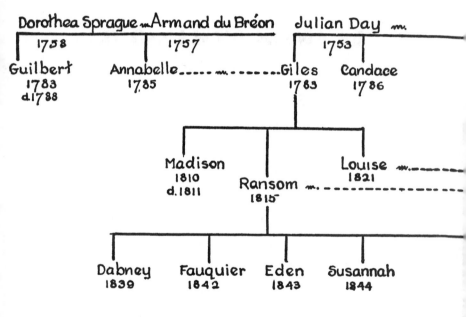

Dorothea Sprague m. Armand du Bréon   Julian Day m.
   1758   1757   1753

Guilbert   Annabelle ....m.......Giles   Candace
1783   1785   1783   1786
d.1788

Madison   Louise m.
1810   1821
d.1811 Ransom m. .
        1815

Dabney   Fauquier Eden Susannah
1839   1842   1843   1844

AND RELATIONSHIPS

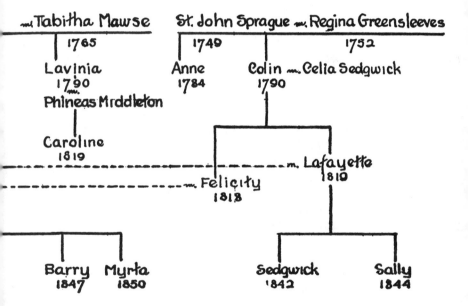

m. Tabitha Mawse   St. John Sprague m. Regina Greensleeves
1765   1749   1752

Lavinia   Anne   Colin m. Celia Sedgwick
1790   1784   1790
m.
Phineas Middleton

Caroline
1819
      m. Lafayette
      1819
m. Felicity
1818

Barry   Myrta   Sedgwick   Sally
1847   1850   1842   1844

ALSO BY ELSWYTH THANE

Fiction

RIDERS OF THE WIND
ECHO ANSWERS
CLOTH OF GOLD
HIS ELIZABETH
BOUND TO HAPPEN
QUEEN'S FOLLY
TRYST
REMEMBER TODAY
FROM THIS DAY FORWARD
MELODY
THE LOST GENERAL
LETTER TO A STRANGER

The Williamsburg Novels

DAWN'S EARLY LIGHT
YANKEE STRANGER
EVER AFTER
THE LIGHT HEART
KISSING KIN
THIS WAS TOMORROW
HOMING

Nonfiction

THE TUDOR WENCH
YOUNG MR. DISRAELI
ENGLAND WAS AN ISLAND ONCE
THE BIRD WHO MADE GOOD
RELUCTANT FARMER

Plays

THE TUDOR WENCH
YOUNG MR. DISRAELI

Yankee Stranger

ELSWYTH THANE

Foreword by Leila Meacham

CHICAGO
REVIEW
PRESS

This edition published in 2017 by
Chicago Review Press Incorporated
814 North Franklin Street
Chicago, Illinois 60610

ISBN 978-1-61373-816-0

Cover design: Sarah Olson
Cover image: © Malgorzata Maj / Arcangel Images

Printed in the United States of America
5 4 3 2 1

Foreword

Yankee Stranger is the second in the sequence of Elyswyth Thane's output of seven historical novels known as the Williamsburg Series. Published in the 1940s and '50s, the collection begins in Williamsburg, Virginia, at the dawn of the American Revolutionary War and follows the lives of two families over a period of 170 years to the beginning of World War II. The generations begin with the Day and Sprague clans, whom we first meet in *Dawn's Early Light*, which focuses on the relationship and marriage of Julian and Tibby Day. Several generations have passed when we pick up with the families again in *Yankee Stranger*, with Tibby Day, at ninety-five, the sole survivor of their stories and the connective element that binds the two novels together.

A word of advice: Not only have generations passed, but numerous children, grandchildren, and great-grandchildren have arrived and intermarried within the families. So a printed copy of the Chart of Families and Relationships provided at the beginning of the book would be wise to set alongside the novel for easy reference as one reads.

In this novel we meet the present generation of the Southern Days and Spragues on the eve of the Civil War. Into the loving throng of family members gathered to celebrate the ninety-fifth birthday of their beloved matriarch, Tibby Day, strides Cabot Murray, the Yankee stranger of the title. He is a tall, dark, handsome, cynical, and brooding Washington war correspondent impervious to the wiles of the beauties of his acquaintance until his eye falls upon Eden, Tibby's beautiful great-granddaughter. It's love at first sight, though the situation is complicated by the misfortune that each is from warring sides of the fence. A forbidden romance ensues, and the rest of the events of that tragic time revolve around it.

The title in some ways is a misnomer, in that the narrative moves far beyond and involves so much more than just a Romeo and Juliet–esque love story. A student of the Civil War (or the War of Northern Aggression, if the reader prefers) would be hard pressed to find a history text offering as authentic an account of the period as Elswyth Thane's *Yankee Stranger*, not to mention one so readable and enjoyable. As in *Dawn's Early Light*, we board a magic carpet, and with stunning accuracy, scholarship, and speed, the author spins us back to October 29, 1860, when America is once again on the brink of war—this time, as a nation divided against itself. When war is declared, we are whisked through each of the five years of conflict with its victories and defeats, famous battles, illustrious and infamous historic figures, politicians and generals, ordeals and survivals, losses and gains—life on both sides as it was lived through the horrors of war—to the same date in October 1865 when the guns are silent and the South lies defeated. It is once again Tibby Day's birthday. She is one hundred years old. After the celebration party, attended by the survivors of her family, Tibby lies abed "dreaming of Julian in his youth." Her thoughts ramble. *If only Julian could have seen them all at supper tonight—one didn't want to live forever—one left too much behind, till finally one only wanted to get back to all that was gone. . . .*

By the time the carpet ride is over, in *Yankee Stranger*, Elswyth Thane has taken us back to all that was gone. Through irreproachable research brilliantly incorporated within the narratives of the families, we have lived through the Civil War. Enjoy the journey.

LEILA MEACHAM

TO

JACQUES CARTIER

Acknowledgments

G REAT care has been taken that the whereabouts of the fictitious soldiers in the two armies are always subject to those of the specific regiment or commanding officer to which they have been assigned. With regard to the standing of Special Correspondents a generation before Richard Harding Davis, the following is quoted from "Four Years in Secessia," an account of his own adventures as a "Special" by J. H. Browne, published in 1865.

> "The Correspondents have figured in the casualties again and again; have been killed and wounded and captured; have perhaps had quite their share of the accidents of war. . . . They usually enter some officer's mess, on taking the field; have their own horses; pay their proportion of the expenses; and live exactly as the officers do, except that they are not subject to orders. . . . If they have any fondness—and many of them have—for fighting, they can always be accommodated. I have more than once seen them in the field, musket in hand and frequently trying their skill as sharpshooters. They very often act as voluntary aides on the staff of general officers and have in numerous instances played a conspicuous and important part in engagements."

Again I owe thanks to the same patient people who assisted during the research for "Dawn's Early Light"—notably, Miss Mary McWilliams of Colonial Williamsburg, Dr. E. G. Swem, Librarian at the College of William and Mary, Mrs. F. G. King and the staff of the New York Society Library, and Mr. F. F. Van de Water. In addition, gratitude is now due Mrs. Eudora Ramsay Richardson of Richmond, and Mr. Frank Browning, the latter even lending me, a stranger, valued books from his own library.

E. T.

Contents

YANKEE STRANGER

I. OCTOBER 29, 1860

I

It was her birthday, and she was ninety-five.

She sat at her window, looking out into the quiet street beyond the white picket fence and box hedges of the front garden; waiting, like a good child, for it to be time to dress for her party. It was a pretty street, in the soft autumn sunlight of Virginia. But Williamsburg was old too, now, it had never been the same since Thomas Jefferson made them move the capital up river to Richmond, back in 1779 when he was Governor. (To make the Legislative body safe from capture by a sea-borne army, he said, and even then the British nearly caught Jefferson.) It was lively enough for a while after Yorktown, while the French were still there. The Comte de Rochambeau had come to her wedding, and paid her French compliments while they danced. Julian had taught her such good French, and so much of it, that she missed no nuances of Rochambeau's compliments, and found them a trifle embarrassing. All the French soldiers were very oncoming people. . . .

She sat smiling out into the noonday sun from her big chair in the window. Her age was always quite incredible, especially to herself. It seemed only the other day that she had stood before the altar in the brick church in the Duke of Gloucester Street and heard those grave words so gently spoken—*"I, Julian, take thee, Tabitha, to my wedded wife—"* And yet the wealth, the fabulous riches of life the years since then had bestowed on Tibby Mawes! Three children they had had—it was not enough, but she was so small and something went wrong when Lavinia was born—there weren't any more after Lavinia. They had had Giles first—Julian's son—you couldn't ask for better than Giles. And now there was Giles's son Ransom, and you couldn't do better than Ransom either, if it came to that; always biddable and good-tempered, ruling his household as firmly and tactfully as ever Julian himself had done. One was very fortunate to live with a grandson like Ransom, and his wife Felicity, so truly named, and his children who were one's own great grandchildren. . . .

And yet it seemed only the other day that Julian was still alive, going a little grey, but carrying himself just as tall as he had done the first day she ever saw him—only a little while since Julian's death, swift and kind, by a fall from a new horse he had not allowed them to gentle for him. She was only sixty when Julian died, though, and they never let her forget, either, that she had had a proposal of marriage within the year. And that was more than thirty years ago. . . .

They said that Richmond was very gay these days, in spite of all this slavery talk—abolition—secession—she could remember when it was Massachusetts that was going to secede instead of South Carolina. But who would live in Richmond when Williamsburg still sat here in the sun, a little shabby, perhaps, a little down at heel, and the lovely Palace all burnt to a shell when the troops used it for a hospital after Yorktown, and even the Raleigh not what it was—the balls they used to have in the Raleigh, and the gay dinners in the Daphne Room— the glitter was all gone to Richmond now. Archer Crabb, who had asked her to marry him before her widow's year was out, had had a big house in Richmond and was in the Legislature and did a lot of entertaining. She supposed if she had married Archer she would be living there in Franklin Street now, with his grandchildren from his first marriage—they preferred it to their Williamsburg house, except for holidays. But one would be lonely in a big place like Richmond where one never knew who might be passing by, instead of here where everybody looked up at the window to wave, and people ran in and out all day long with flowers, or letters to read to her, or a dish of something they thought she might fancy. They said she knew the whole town by its given name, and probably she did. One wasn't ninety-five for nothing——

"Felicity! Where are you? Eden! Somebody come here at once and tell me who this man is Sally has got by the arm! Never saw him before in my life, and she making eyes as though he was the King!"

"Whose King, Gran?" But Eden came with a swift rustle of silk to look over the high back of the chair into the street.

"They're stopping at the gate, Dee. Is she going to bring him in?"

"Not if she can help it! She wouldn't give Sue and me a chance at him for worlds!"

"Do you want a chance? Who is he?"

"He's a Yankee named Cabot Murray. He is visiting President and Mrs. Ewell at the College."

"Know anything more about him?"

"He's very tall, dark, and handsome, with a cleft in his chin and the devil in his eye, and Sally is simply terrified that somebody will get him away from her before she can make him fall in love with her."

"Is he likely to?"

"I don't see why not, Gran, Sally is very pretty."

"Not so pretty as you are, Dee."

"Now, Gran, would you have me set my cap for a Yankee just to prove that?"

"What's wrong with a Yankee if he's got long legs and would make a good husband, I'd like to know?"

"That's heresy these days! Uncle Lafe would throw him out of the house if he tried to marry Sally. Besides—I'm not sure Cabot Murray would make a good husband."

"How long have you known him? Why have you all kept so mum about him? Why haven't I seen him close to?"

"I don't know him at all. There has been no reason to discuss him. And you haven't seen him because Mrs. Ewell hasn't brought him to call."

"Why hasn't she——"

"Because he's a Yankee, no doubt, and she knows he isn't welcome everywhere. Look—he's going on and Sally is coming in. Now you can quiz her about him to your heart's content."

The tall stranger had lifted his hat and bowed over Sally's hand, which lingered in his as she backed reluctantly away from him and through the open gate behind her. Her head turned after him while he walked down the street, very long in the leg, it is true, very broad in the shoulder and narrow in the hips, with a spring that was almost a swagger in his step.

As Eden was about to whisk away from the window she felt herself caught and held by a small firm hand on her wrist.

"How do you know," demanded her great grandmother, "that he has the devil in his eye?"

Eden flushed.

"I can't tell you now," she whispered. "Later!" And she freed herself and ran out of the room to call a greeting down the stairs to her cousin Sally, and ask her to come up at once because Gran wanted to see her.

Tabitha Day, whose husband had called her Tibby and had had very long legs himself, leaned forward to catch another glimpse of the Yankee as he turned the corner towards the Duke of Gloucester Street. (Her eyesight was as good as new, except for fine print.) Young, she decided, with that walk. A horseman, with those hips. Bowed like a gentleman, hat in hand. And there was something Eden hadn't told.

2

Sally Sprague was fair and high-bosomed and a beauty like her great grandmother Regina. She was spoilt too. But she could not hold a candle to her cousin Eden Day, whose hair was golden red and whose eyes were greenish, and whose chin was round and sensitive and always quivered pathetically just before she cried. The hair she got from Giles, who had got it from Julian's mother. The eyes were her great grandmother Tabitha's. The chin was Eden's own.

Sally was still wearing a rather guilty sparkle when she came into the square white room, bright with chintz and needle-point, where Grandmother Day had lived as long as anybody could remember. In this fourth generation of Williamsburg Days, relationships were very closely knit. Sally and Eden were double first cousins, for Sally's mother and Eden's father were sister and brother, and they had married Lafayette and Felicity Sprague, who were brother and sister. The middle generation of Days and Spragues had been more than pleased, for the bonds of friendship were already old and strong, and the two families had grown up in each other's gardens and nurseries almost as one. But Grandmother Day had thought at the time that for Louise and Felicity it must be rather like marrying their own brothers, rather like something forbidden in the Bible—and had told herself to mind her own business, because Julian was no longer there to tell her himself. Neither of the boys had ever courted another girl. Felicity, it is true, had led Ransom a dance, but Louise and Lafayette had been in love in their cradles. Louise was allowed to marry at sixteen in order to make it a double wedding, when Felicity suddenly made up her mind to take Ransom after all, and he was afraid to give her time to change her mind, he said. But the worst flirts always make the best wives, the saying goes, and Ransom's marriage was a very happy one. As for Sally's parents, Louise and Lafe—they were sweethearts still, till it made your heart ache for your own lost love to see them together.

Sally's veil was laid back over the brim of her bonnet and her blond curls shone on either side of her glowing face. Her teeth were white and even in her wide smile, her dark blue eyes were candid and gay.

"Hello, Gran," she said gently, and bent with swooping grace for her kiss. "Mother said I mustn't stay long because there will be streams of people later on to say Happy Birthday and you mustn't be tired. I just had to see your dress, is that it on the bed? May I look? Oh, Gran, it's perfect!"

The dress lay there, full spread by Mammy's loving hands, in its pride of lace and taffeta—too lilac to be grey, its yards of narrow velvet ribbon trimming a rich lavender. She always had a new dress for her birthday party, and it was always exquisitely right, ever since the day when it had been rose and white, as became a seventeen-year-old bride, down to this cheerful compromise with dignity and old age.

"We'll none of us ever have a waist like yours!" sighed Sally, reflecting enviously for the hundredth time on her grandmother's distant girlhood. "I'll bet Grandfather could get his two hands right round it with room to spare!"

All three of them glanced instinctively towards the portrait above the mantelpiece—Julian Day looked back at them from the gold frame, the deep corners of his generous mouth hinting at the smile which also lurked behind his eyes.

"Mother says she can remember him carrying Gran about the house as though she was a doll, one time when she hurt her foot getting out of the carriage," said Eden.

"Does she really remember that?" Grandmother Day was pleased. "She couldn't have been more than five at the time."

"I wish *I* could remember him!" Eden stood before the portrait, looking up. "He looks as though he'd never said an unkind word in his life. Did he ever lose his temper, Gran?"

Julian's widow smiled.

"Not with me," she said.

"How dull!" said Sally, and her eyes were shining and reckless. "I like a man who is a bit of a brute, I think!"

"Have you seen one like that?" queried Grandmother Day, and added with the lightest possible stress—"lately?"

Sally's eyes went to the window above the street, and she caught her lower lip between her teeth. Very deliberately then she came and sat down on the footstool beside her grandmother's chair, and laid one arm across her grandmother's knees.

"Eden, dear," she said in the artificial sort of voice grown-ups sometimes use towards children who are in the way, "didn't I hear Mammy calling you a minute ago?"

"As a matter of fact, you did not," said Eden with entire good humor. "But I have no desire to hear about your Yankee, if that's what you mean!" And she marched out, her nose well up.

Sally hunched her shoulders with childish amusement, and laughed, and looked slantwise to see how her grandmother took it. The eyes which met hers seemed as young and knowing as her own.

"Why don't you bring him to the party?" said Tibby Day.

"Oh, Gran! I wouldn't dare!"

"It's my party. I'll ask whomever I please to come to it!"

"The Ewells aren't coming, though, because Mrs. Ewell has been ill."

"I'm sorry to hear that. But he can come with you, then."

"F-Father says he won't have a damn-Yankee in the house any more," Sally remarked uncertainly.

"This isn't your father's house, Sally, it's Ransom's."

"You think Uncle Ransom wouldn't mind?"

"I don't see why he should. Any guest of the Ewells is surely welcome here."

"Well, you see, Gran, President Ewell went to West Point and all, and—and he seems very much opposed to Secession, and—and besides, nobody seems to know quite who Mr. Murray *is.*"

"Don't the Ewells know who he is?"

"Oh, *yes*—that is, I suppose they must, but they don't say, really, except that his father was at West Point too, and has left the Army since, like President Ewell."

"Isn't that good enough?"

"Well, I don't think you quite realize, Gran—since that dreadful business about John Brown last year, people are getting awfully worked up against the Yankees. Father says if Lincoln is elected he really doesn't *know*."

"Know what?"

"Oh, Gran, you don't think there's going to be a war?"

"War—between the States?" Her grandmother's clear eyes darkened and sought, as they always did when she was troubled, the face of the portrait above the mantelpiece. What would *he* say to this foolish quarrel between men who spoke the same language and believed in the same religions and principles of government? He hated war, but he had fought under General Greene and Lafayette to establish this union of States, which had grown from thirteen to—how many were there now?—Texas had come in—was Texas the last? What would he think about Lincoln? "No!" cried Tibby Day, with sharp conviction. "No, they will find some way! We have been through too much together, just a little while ago—there was no North and no South at Valley Forge and Yorktown! They are sure to find some way, Sally, never fear."

But Sally was looking frightened.

"It would mean Sedgwick—and Dabney—and maybe Fauquier— going off to get shot! It doesn't seem possible that one's own family should be in a war. I thought we had finished with all that!"

"Yes, dear—we hoped so. I'm sure we have. Feeling often runs high at election time. They'll quiet down again when that's over."

"But Lincoln, Gran—they say he's like an ape!"

"Who says? That Yankee?"

"N-no. Mr. Murray thinks Lincoln can hold the country together if anybody can. He says——"

"Has he seen Mr. Lincoln, then?"

"Yes. Well, I don't know, for sure. One can't tell."

"Can't you ask him?"

Sally fidgeted.

"You—don't ask him things straight out, like that. He's so—he's a strange man, Gran."

"Is that why you like him so much?"

"I'm not sure I like him—so much."

"You'd better let me see him, don't you think?"

"If you do, you mustn't give him any impression that I—" Her wide blue eyes came up, and dropped again.

"My dear, I wasn't born yesterday. You bring him to the party."

"Can you manage Father?"

"I think so," said Tibby Day, and smiled.

"He'll yell," warned Sally, for Lafayette Sprague's moods were ebullient and noisy.

"Not at me, he won't!"

"H-how shall I——"

"Just run round to President's house on your way home, and tell them I sent to enquire about Carrie Ewell, and to say it would give me pleasure if she would lend me their guest today. Then tell your father I asked you to bring Mr. Murray with you."

"It sounds simple, but——"

"And if your father has anything to say," added Grandmother Day, "tell him to save it up and I'll listen tomorrow. I haven't time now before I dress."

3

When Sally had departed, with a last rather doubtful wave at the window from the gate, it soon occurred to Grandmother Day that Eden was avoiding her. She rapped with her ebony stick on the floor beside her chair—which for some reason always seemed to her a less peremptory summons than ringing the little bell which stood within her reach—and Mammy's starched white turban came round the door.

" 'Tain't no need to git dressed yit, Mistis, honey—I ain' fergot you!"

"I want Eden first."

"Miss Eden doin' de flowers now."

"Ask her to come here. Sue can do the flowers."

"I tell her you say so——" It trailed away unwillingly as Mammy dis appeared.

Eden came in briskly, wearing a white apron and trying to look as though she had been interrupted in the midst of important affairs and had only a moment to spare.

"Yes, Gran?"

Grandmother Day pointed with her ebony stick to the footstool where Sally had sat, and Eden placed herself on it docilely and smiled up into her grandmother's face, trying to look as though she had no recollection of any previous conversation which might be considered unfinished.

"Isn't it almost time you got dressed?" she enquired.

"Sally is going to bring Mr. Murray to the party," said Grandmother Day. "I'd like to see a real live Yankee, we never thought much about them one way or the other in the old days."

Eden's fingers went to her mouth in a gesture of half-shocked excitement.

"Gran—*really!*"

"It's my party, isn't it? Now, what was that about his eyes?"

"They're very dark—very—bold."

"And how do you know so much about them?"

"It's rather a long story—don't you think——"

"No, I want it now, before he comes."

"Well, you remember that thunderstorm we had last Tuesday? It broke just as I was coming home from the Creswells', and the rain started in sheets. It was too far to go back, so I ran towards Gloucester Street and come round the corner bang! into Mr. Murray, who was hurrying too. The wind was blowing a perfect gale, and I had my head down, trying to keep my bonnet on, and I was carrying my sewing-bag and that jar of marmalade Mrs. Creswell sent you and a letter to post for her. Mr. Murray was trying to hold an umbrella up, and I ran full tilt into his chest! He's very tall."

"What did he say?"

"He looked as though I'd knocked the breath out of him for a moment. I think I spoke first."

"What did you say?"

"I don't think I know, exactly, I must have said 'I'm so sorry,' and 'Did I hurt you?' and 'It's this dreadful wind—' The sort of thing you *would* say if you'd nearly knocked a stranger down! So then the jar of marmalade slid out from under my elbow and landed on the ground which was fortunately getting muddy so the glass didn't break. He picked it up, and with it dripping in one hand and the umbrella in the other and the wind blowing my hoop practically into his teeth, and the rain simply lashing at us, he laughed and said, 'What a lovely day! May I see you home?' "

Her grandmother was delighted.

"Did he know it was a pun?" she asked, and added at Eden's stare—"Your name, stupid! Did he know your name?"

"Oh, Gran, I *am* stupid! He didn't then, I think, but later on he said——"

"Tell it right end to. Why didn't you let him see you home?"

"It was too wet then. And I had Mrs. Creswell's letter to post. And it's difficult to think straight with your feet in a puddle. Anyway, I said I was going to the Post Office, and as we were right in front of it, he held the umbrella over me as far as the door, when there was a terrific thunderclap and he came inside too, to get out of the storm."

"Naturally."

"Old Mr. Weeks came out from behind the Post Office grille and gave us chairs—there was no one else in the shop—and they shook out my shawl and hung it over the grocery counter to dry, and wiped my shoes with a duster, and Mr. Weeks said we must stay cosy where we were till it stopped raining and then he went to opening crates and things with a lot of tactful hammering and banging about in the back of the store. Mr. Murray couldn't seem to get over being surprised that I wasn't frightened. Apparently all the young ladies of his acquaintance scream and hide their faces during a thunderstorm!"

"Lots of people do," smiled Grandmother Day.

"Well, I think it's very silly. Thunderstorms are bound to come every so often, and one might as well get used to them. Besides, if lightning does strike you, you never know it!"

"Did you say that to Mr. Murray?"

"Yes, I did. And *now* I see what he meant when he said, 'I still think it's a lovely day'—because Mr. Weeks called me Miss Day when we first went in!"

"He's one ahead of you there, Dee. You'd better do something about that while he's here today."

"What would you suggest?" Eden looked a little mutinous.

"Big girls like you should know how to manage their own beaux," her grandmother rebuked her.

"He's *not* my beau, Gran! We only sat in the Post Office store till the storm stopped! We've never even been properly introduced. Old Mr. Weeks' idea of hospitality was to come out with a fresh box of peppermint lozenges he'd just unpacked and pass it round—so Mr. Murray and I conversed, each of us with a bulge in one cheek and smelling like a nursery! And half the time we had to shout because of the thunder. What's romantic about that, I want to know! Gran, what are you thinking about?"

She was thinking about her own first meeting with Julian, to whom she had not been properly introduced either. She was thinking that this was the way it was likely to start, by accident, with shock or surprise or comedy—likelier this way, she was thinking, than formally, in a drawing-room, or at a ball, or coming out of church. She was wondering how Sally had met Cabot Murray. But mostly, she was remembering that summer evening 'way back before the war that brought Cornwallis to Yorktown—'way back when Julian first came to Williamsburg. . . .

"Gran, why do you look so—so beautiful? How did you and Grandfather Julian meet? In a thunderstorm, by any chance? Please tell, Gran!"

"I was nine years old," said Gran. "My step-father sometimes got rather drunk, and one night he knocked me down in the street outside the Raleigh and broke my arm—just as Julian and St. John Sprague were coming out of the door. Julian picked me up unconscious and carried me inside. I came to in his arms."

"Oh, *Gran!*" It was an envious whisper.

"Washington was there that night—and Thomas Jefferson made them give me brandy and water to drink. I can see Julian's face now as it looked in the candlelight—I thought it was the kindest face in the world—the only face in the world from then on, for me. Sometimes it happens that way——"

She drifted, smiling, looking as Eden said very beautiful. Tibby Mawes, child of disgrace and poverty, had grown up to marry the young schoolmaster from England—it was likely to happen that way, suddenly and forever, with a man you'd never seen before—love at first sight—the best kind, she always thought, even though her own children, except Lavinia, had married their life-long playmates and been happy with them. But there was surely something about a stranger— an odd, sudden meeting—it struck a spark—it kindled a flame—something that was surely lacking if you had grown up in each other's pocket, day by day—if there were no surprises, no discoveries to make, no mysteries to solve. . . .

She sat, a beautiful old lady of ninety-five, and pondered love. One would think she had learned nothing at all in her time, to find it still so puzzling. One would think, at her age, she would *know*. Perhaps you couldn't call her own childhood idolatry of the schoolmaster love —there was twelve years' difference in their ages—but it had become love, and for all any other man had ever meant to her it had always been love. He, like this Cabot Murray, had come to Williamsburg a stranger. And yet—and yet—there was her granddaughter Louise, who had never known a time without Lafe's guardian presence in her background, ever since he guided her first staggering steps, himself a whole two years older. Louise seemed to inhale strength and happiness from Lafe's mere presence, as though he were the sun. When he was absent, she drooped and was listless and depressed. Even when they were children, their devotion had had a frightening, fatal quality which was almost unnatural. And from this strange marriage had come Sally, spoilt and perhaps a little shallow, a flirt and a beauty; and Sally's brother Sedgwick, who must be eighteen by now——

Just as she was groping after something connected with Sedgwick which seemed important to her train of thought, just as she seemed about to turn some sort of mental corner into some sort of conclusion to her whole reverie, Mammy bustled into the room saying, "Time to put on yo' fix-ups now, Mistis, honey, an' make yo'self grand fo' de party! Miss Eden, yo' ma say effn you don' go watch Miss Sue like a hawk she'll try an' git herself laced too tight agin, she so wild 'cause Marse Sedgwick took an' teased her 'bout still havin' some o' her baby-fat, an' her sixteen last birthday!"

"Oh, Gran, Sue *is* a monkey! She's getting a lovely little figure, and all she can think of is a seventeen-inch waist!"

"She won' nebber have it, an' I tol' her so myself!" said Mammy with cheerful resignation. "Yo' sister Eden cain' git herself less'n twenty, I says to her, an' you's lucky wid twenty-two, I says, any less'n dat fo' either one o' you an' we'll have you in faintin' spells ever' time you run up stairs, I says. 'Tain't as if you was built like yo' gran'-mammy when she was a girl, I tol' her——"

"Nineteen," said Tibby Day, and rose unaided to don her party dress. "Nineteen and a bit, Mammy, since the children came!" She noticed suddenly that Eden was at the door. "Dee, come back here. There's something I want to know."

'Yes, Gran?"

"Why didn't he see you home?"

Eden eyed her impudently from the threshold, her round chin tilted, her eyes narrow with laughter.

"Because I knew if you saw him from the window you'd ask questions!" she said, and sped away down the hall towards the bedroom she shared with her sister Susannah.

It was rather an absent-minded argument she had with young Sue about the size of a sixteen-year-old waist—her mind kept fumbling around something her grandmother had said. *The only face in the world from then on, for me—sometimes it happens that way. . . .* Ah, but Grandfather Julian looked so kind. One couldn't count on Cabot Murray always to be kind. Or could one? Besides, he was a stranger. A Yankee. One couldn't fall in love with a Yankee these days. Or could one?

His eyes were pitiless, even while they laughed. They looked at her hair beneath the bonnet-brim—and saw it down, free and shining, to her waist. They looked at her fingers, accepting a peppermint lozenge, and it was as though he had taken them in both his hands. They looked at her lips—and it was as though he had kissed her. If he had chosen to strip her naked with a glance, she would have had no defense. . . .

"There's Sedgie now!" cried Sue at the window. "He said he'd be the first—it's his turn to take Gran down stairs——"

She ran out of the room and you could hear her happy voice all the way down the stairs, chattering to Sedgwick at the bottom.

Eden stood before the long mirror in her hooped petticoats, for Sue, who was already dressed, had forgotten that she was about to drop the dress over her sister's head and fasten it up behind. She would have to wait for Mammy now.

Eden's own eyes looked back at her gravely from the mirror. *Sometimes it happens that way.* Had it happened to her, last Tuesday in a thunderstorm? Perhaps when he came today she would be sure. She wondered what Gran would think of him. Gran set such store by kindness. And why was one so doubtful of Cabot Murray's kindness? Because Sally called him a brute? He wasn't that. But he had hard edges, his face was rocky and used-looking, there were sharp lines at the corners of his eyes and mouth when he laughed, his lips were carven and very masculine, his jutting chin had a cleft—a rugged, uncompromising, fighting face he had—swarthy, as from the sun, black-browed, a terrible face, no doubt, in his anger—but if the mockery once left it, if it could be tamed and softened, if he could be taught to smile more *lovingly*——

Standing before the mirror in her spreading petticoats, Eden Day hid her face in her two hands from the eyes in the mirror. He was a stranger, and he was a Yankee, and he was a bewildering, bantering, ungentle, ruthless-seeming man—but he had invaded her heart, possessed himself of all her thoughts, and imposed himself upon her every waking hour since that day in the Post Office store. She was seventeen, and everyone was beginning to wonder when she was going to make up her mind to marry. She had had plenty of chances. Grafton Crabb, grandson of the man who had wanted to marry Gran in her widowhood, had proposed three times and was quite prepared to try again. And there were two or three other boys at least, boys she had known all her life—she had only to risk an encouraging smile to bring any one of them to the point. And all of them were kind, soft-spoken Virginia men, like her father, like Grandfather Julian—too kind, perhaps?—too much like a member of the family—too *usual?*

4

Borne in the strong, careful arms of her great grandson Sedgwick—who, though he was a Sprague, was going to have Julian's height—Tibby Day descended the staircase to the drawing-room. She was perfectly able to walk down stairs, and sometimes did it all alone. But the ceremony of carrying her down before her birthday party had originated some ten or twelve years ago when she had had an illness and was still convalescent. Since then, the men of the family took turns in the order of precedence, and carried her down. It entertained them, and she liked it.

Sedgwick moved majestically, admonished by Sue at every step, and lowered his grandmother as though she was made of glass into the armchair which awaited her. Sue and Mammy fussed around her, spreading the lilac-grey skirts, fetching her ebony stick, setting the little bell within reach. Then Felicity rustled in, wearing amber watered silk, kissed Sedgwick affectionately, approved Sue's hairdress which was a matter of green satin ribbon and coppery curls, asked Grandmother Day if she was pleased with her new dress and said it looked charming, and rustled away again, her wide hoop swaying, to see about the tea-making.

Ten-year-old Myrta appeared next, Ransom's youngest, and hurled herself at her cousin Sedgwick, whom she extravagantly adored, and was persuaded to make a sober pirouette in the middle of the room while they all admired her new party frock and her first hoop.

"Eden is waiting for Mammy to hook her up," she remembered suddenly, and Mammy sailed off to wait on her favorite of Ransom's six children. "None of us counts for anything with Mammy if Dee wants her," Myrta remarked philosophically. "Not even Gran."

"She's not Gran's mammy, she's mother's," Sue reminded her loyally. "What became of your mammy, Gran, did she die ages ago?"

"I never had a servant till after I was married," was the unexpected reply.

Sue and Myrta stared.

"Why not?" Myrta asked incredulously.

"I was too poor." Tibby Day looked slowly round the bright, cosy room, remembering a cabin by Queen's Creek Landing and a thin weary child who worked at the laundry and candle-making and sewing jobs that kept the little household from starvation. It had seemed like a fairy story at first, to have a house like this. "We haven't always lived here, you know," she told Myrta. "When I was first married we lived in the room above the old schoolhouse. Your grandfather Giles was born there. Then old Mrs. Fields died very suddenly and this place was put up for sale, the year before Lavinia was born. Your great grandfather St. John helped us to buy it—he lent us money to start the new school too. But it paid him, in the end. He got it all back, along with our everlasting love."

"How many grandfathers did I have?" queried Myrta, fiddling with her hoop. "I get all mixed up!"

"It's the great grandfathers that mix you up, honey!" Sedgwick explained. "We've all got the same ones because we're all related. Some day I'll write it out for you. Gran is the only one who really knows how it goes, aren't you, Gran!"

"It's very simple, really, there were just the six of us to start with," she murmured, thinking how true the Sprague strain ran, and how except for his leggy height and a too-sensitive something about his mouth, Sedgwick might be St. John back again. His father, Lafe, was the original battle-ax type of Sprague, irrepressible, full of spirit, loving a fight, tender with women. Sedgwick had got, perhaps through Louise, a more contemplative approach to life. Sedgwick could be hurt, he was less armored than most Spragues, it made one uneasy for him. His sister Sally, now, could be trusted to look out for herself. Sedgwick must have the right wife, or else——

Once again, just as she was coming to a conclusion about Sedgwick it was snatched away from her, this time by Sedgwick himself.

"What are you looking at, Gran?" he demanded, and his hand went involuntarily to his cravat.

"I was thinking how you had grown," she said, to put him in his place. "Those are very handsome roses in that blue vase. Who sent them?"

"Sedgie brought them," Sue told her promptly, jealous of his dignity. "They're straight out of Uncle Lafe's greenhouse."

It was Lafe's privilege, as it had been his father's and grandfather's, to make up her own bouquet himself and present it in its little silver holder, on his arrival—always early—at the birthday party. She looked forward each year to Lafe's bouquet, and held it proudly while she received her guests. Ransom had no greenhouse, to grow roses out of season. It was one of the many small evidences of the difference in fortune which still existed between the Spragues and the Days, though Julian's school had flourished from the beginning and they were moderately well off by the time Giles was grown.

"I never saw your eyes so green, Gran—you look beautiful today!" said Sedgwick.

She smiled at him. The Spragues could always turn a compliment.

Myrta, who was unduly excited by parties, rushed out of the room screaming that Uncle Lafe was coming in at the gate with the bouquet.

Soon after that the party began in earnest, and for an hour Tibby Day held court for the people who came in genuine affection, many of them devoted to her all their lives, to wish her a happy birthday. Some of them who were grandfathers now had been little boys in Julian's new school back in the '80's, and they held by the hand little boys to whom Ransom was now the schoolmaster. Women with grown-up daughters in their teens had been babies when Louise and Ransom were babies, and their grandmothers had been her friends when she was a young matron. She knew them all, and made no mistakes about their names, except sometimes when the fourth generation confused her by looking exactly as the third had looked only a few birthday parties ago.

And all the time her eyes kept going back to the door to look for Sally and President Ewell's guest. Lafe had not mentioned the Yankee. Either Sally had said nothing at all, or Lafe was lying low. In any case, Gran had no doubt that she would hear from him tomorrow if Cabot Murray came to the party.

He came, with Sally hanging possessively on his arm, and he made his bow before the erect small figure in the armchair with an almost Virginian grace.

"It is very kind of you, ma'am," he said gravely, "to include a stranger in so intimate a festivity as this."

With a quick, impulsive gesture of welcome, she offered him her hand, and felt his powerful fingers close on it without regard to its fragility. He bent as impulsively and kissed it—with astonishment she felt his warm lips move against it—kissed it as though it was a girl's. His dark head, with its thick, well-brushed black hair, was level with hers—he wore his hair cut shorter than the Virginia men. Their eyes met as he raised his head, and she said simply, "I hope that after today you will not feel yourself a stranger in Williamsburg, Mr. Murray."

"That is quite the kindest speech I've heard since I came here, ma'am."

"Why, Mr. Murray, how you talk! And here I've been doing my poor little best to make you feel at home!" cried Sally, just a trifle too archly.

"Well, now at last you have succeeded," Cabot Murray told her, and his smile showed his white teeth and drew sharp lines at the corners of his eyes and round his rather heavy, chiseled lips, but somehow did not change his eyes.

Heavens, thought Tibby Day, I see now what they meant about him—he wants gentling. Somebody's taught him manners—but somebody else has made him a sure 'nough outlaw inside.

The crest of the party had passed by then, and people were grouped about the refreshment tables, and arrivals were less frequent. With a

single look around, Grandmother Day saw Grafton Crabb gazing towards Eden who was behind a tea-urn, and by sheer force of character
she drew his glance to herself and signalled him to approach.

"Get Sally a cup of tea," she commanded, rather abruptly for her. "I
want to talk politics with Mr. Murray."

As Sally, who was too surprised to find an adequate protest, moved
away with a willing Grafton towards where Eden sat, her grandmother
indicated a chair close to her own, and Cabot Murray, also surprised,
folded himself into it. His dark eyes were wary, his lips smiled. Julian
would have known how to handle him, she thought—he's like an un-
backed colt. What ails those Yankee women, I wonder!

"Sally hates to hear politics," she remarked experimentally, and received a sardonic glance.

"I wouldn't wonder," he assented.

"I'm sorry Carrie Ewell has been unwell," she went on. "Tell her
that we missed her today, won't you."

"I will, with pleasure, ma'am."

"I trust it's nothing serious?" she prodded, watching him.

"I trust not. The weather has been unseasonable—they tell me. And
a sensitive woman like Mrs. Ewell, whose sympathies are divided on
the political situation, feels the stress in the air these days and it affects
the nervous system—I am given to understand."

"Why do you dislike women, Mr. Murray?"

He looked at her, straightly, as he had done when he kissed her
hand. Then suddenly he laughed—but not as he had laughed at Sally.
This time his eyes squinted with mirth, his whole face crinkled into
laughter lines, and he reached to lay one large brown hand protectively, apologetically, on hers in her lilac-grey lap.

"But I don't dislike you a bit!" he said, which was no answer.

"And poor Carrie Ewell? What has she done?"

"Nothing, I assure you. She has been most hospitable."

Even as he said it, he closed up again. She could guess, though. A
man like this, in rugged health himself, would have scant patience
with Carrie's war megrims.

"And Sally—why are you so hard on her?" she pursued, watching
him.

"Am I? Miss Sally is a very pretty girl."

"And Eden?" she murmured.

That brought him out in the open, which was what she was trying for.

"Did she tell you?" He seemed surprised.

"About the storm," she nodded. "And about the peppermints. And even why you didn't see her home."

"I wasn't permitted to. It was supposed to be a secret. We are not supposed to have met." His voice was flat, as though in distaste for the subterfuge.

"I'll introduce you. Later."

"It will be a privilege, ma'am, to meet any granddaughter of yours," he assured her gallantly, and they laughed together, without much reason but with understanding, like old friends. Eden, catching sight of it from across the room thought, There, Gran's done it—Gran's got the kinks out of him—I knew it could be done, thought Eden, behind the tea-urn—I wonder what she said to make him look so *unbent*—if ever he looks like that with me, Eden thought. I shall be past praying for. "In fact," he was saying to her grandmother, so that nobody else in the room could hear, "if ever I found a girl I could be absolutely certain would be just like you all her life long—I'd throw up my hands and surrender so fast it would make her head swim!"

"I fancy it would, at that." Tibby Day's gaze travelled slowly from the top of his crisp black head to his well-polished boots and back to his bold, waiting eyes—he was so confident of the verdict as to be almost indifferent to the form it took; so accustomed to feminine appraisal as to be almost impudent under it, no matter whose. "All the same, it's a job I'd think more than twice about taking on, myself," she decided. "At any age."

"Are you refusing me, ma'am?" he inquired, grinning.

"Regretfully," she nodded, well pleased with him. "But quite finally. It will be useless to ask me again."

He leaned towards her, as though she was the only woman in the room, in the whole world.

"Why don't they make 'em like you any more?" he asked, very low.

"My dear child, the room is full of women like me," she told him, choosing her words with care. "Only not so old."

"You lie in your teeth," he said deliberately. "And you know it."

Well, at least he had stayed out in the open this time. At least she had another try coming.

"Who raised you?" she asked recklessly.

"My father."

Apparently it was the wrong thing to ask, for he looked away from her, rocky and withheld, watching the people who chatted in groups round the refreshment tables. She thought she saw his eyes catch Eden's and pass on without recognition; with, in fact, a monstrous indifference.

"I understand your father was a West Point man," she insisted wilfully. "Did you go there too?"

"I went to Princeton. I wanted a year at Oxford, but that was out of bounds. I was allowed three months to see the world after I graduated." He shot her a dark, resentful glance, as though she had been to blame. "It's not long enough," he said.

"You went abroad." She was still groping.

"For three whole months!" His lips were scornful. "Then my funds were cut off and I had to get home as best I could."

"How was that?"

"I shipped from Liverpool as an able seaman."

"You mean your father took that way of forcing you to return? He sounds a hard man."

"There's no love lost between us," he said briefly.

"Still, three months abroad is more than I ever had," she sighed, and he turned to her with a smile.

"I've got money of my own now. Let's elope."

"If you'd asked me thirty years ago——"

"Don't rub that in!" he interrupted almost roughly.

"Talking to you is like blind man's buff," she remarked. "One never knows what one will lay hold of next."

"I suppose it's time I apologized for my manners. I usually have to, sooner or later."

"It is not your manners I object to, Mr. Murray, it is what they are supposed to conceal."

Just at that point the Creswells came up to take their leave of her, and Cabot Murray rose and stood beside her chair, jealously, while they did so. Then he sat down again, drawing his chair still closer to hers. But he did not reopen the conversation, and she was sure that he was covertly watching Eden, who had risen and was moving among the guests with Grafton Crabb at her side.

"Where were we?" Tibby Day asked at last, gently nudging his attention back to herself.

"You were saying that I myself am even worse than my manners," he reminded her, without even turning his head.

"I didn't mean to say that," she objected meekly. "I think you are very nice indeed—when you let yourself go."

"Thank you, ma'am. I have been called many things by your sex before now, but I don't recollect that a lady has ever told me that I was nice!"

"You are much too young, it seems to me, to be so—embittered."

That drew him.

"I'm twenty-seven," he said.

She thought of Julian at twenty-seven—the summer she said good-bye to him on the bridge at Queen's Creek Landing before he went away to the war. Odd how the years closed up as she grew older, so that Julian at twenty-seven seemed clearer to her than Julian at seventy-two, when he died. She remembered every detail of that evening at the Landing—the fireflies and the peepers, and the size of him in her unaccustomed arms, and the scent of the pomade on his hair—she had said him a bit of the Ninety-first Psalm—*For He shall give His angels charge over thee, to keep thee in all thy ways....*

"You are thinking of your husband," Cabot Murray said unexpectedly. "What was he like, at my age?"

"As tall as you," she said, looking back, "but narrower. Thoughtful, but not—disillusioned. Easier to talk to—gentle with children——"

"I don't as a rule trample children under foot," he said, nettled.

"But you wouldn't know how to talk to them."

"How do you know? Hey, missy—" He reached a long arm and caught Myrta by the sash. "Come and protect me, your grandmother is tearing me to shreds."

"What did you do?" asked the logical Myrta with interest.

"Not a thing. I'm just sitting here, a harmless guest under her roof, minding my own business and paying her compliments in my clumsy Yankee way—and whang! she went for me like a chicken hawk!"

"Did you criticize Eden?" Myrta inquired shrewdly. "Gran won't ever stand for that."

"On the contrary, I am willing to go on record that I think Miss Eden is a most attractive young lady."

"Gran won't let you marry her either," Myrta warned him. "Not if Eden would have to go up North to live."

"Well, now, whoa, is it all right if I just go on admiring her from a safe distance?"

Myrta considered him a wit.

"I should think Eden would hate that, though!" she said through giggles. "If anybody was admiring her she would want to *know!*"

"Good heaven, femininity starts early" Cabot Murray's mouth went wry. "I beg your pardon, missy, that is exactly the sort of thing your grandmother was objecting to."

"Oh, I'm used to swearing," Myrta said, to put him at his ease. "Uncle Lafe does. Shall I tell Eden you're admiring her?"

"By all means. And make sure that the gentleman on her left hears you."

Myrta was again convulsed with giggles, and withdrew importantly on her mission.

"Myrta is not my favorite grandchild," remarked Tibby Day into a silence. "I don't recall that Eden was ever so silly."

"I have a sister about that age," he said unsentimentally. "They're all pretty much alike, I guess—at any age."

She rejected in quick succession several things she would have liked to say regarding cheap cynicism and the sort of remarks he should have outgrown by now—after all, he had spoken to Myrta as an equal, which is the right way to speak to children. Myrta was obviously taken with him.

"It occurred to me to wonder," she began, elaborately circuitous, "how you happened to meet Sally."

"Coming out of church. With the Ewells."

"Ah!" It was a little crow of satisfaction, but he seemed not to notice.

"Who *is* that fellow?" he demanded, tacitly confessing that his eyes and his thoughts dwelt on Eden.

"Grafton Crabb."

"Any good?"

"The Crabbs have always been rich as Croesus. His father was in the Legislature at Richmond—died last year. The pretty girl in yellow is his sister Charlotte, and his mother is just beyond. They have a big house in Richmond and a family place here, and the children grew up with ours."

"Money, eh! Slaves too, I suppose—hundreds."

"None at all."

"What? Are they Abolitionists?" He said the word with loathing.

"Oh, no. His grandfather freed all his slaves by his will, just as my own husband did. It makes very little difference to the Negroes, of course, except that it's likely to hurt their feelings. They go right on living in the quarters, unless you turn them out, but nobody does that."

"Then—these girls here—?" He indicated the two white-turbaned maids who were serving the guests under the Negro butler's direction. "They're not slaves?"

"All our servants," she told him with a faint stress on the word, "are free."

"I knew that a few people like George Wythe had freed their slaves, of course. But I didn't realize it was a general practice."

"Mr. Wythe impoverished himself to give each freedman a competence. When St. John Sprague inherited his wife's property, the plantation called Farthingale, he gave all the servants the ownership of their cabins and enough land to make a living on—and then soon found he couldn't afford to keep the big house going for even part of the year. So Farthingale is closed, except for a care-taker, and as a consequence none of the blacks on the place now is living as comfortably, and certainly not as merrily, as when they were beholden to the Spragues for everything."

"That's very interesting." She had caught his attention in a different way—keen, impersonal, searching attention—all insolence, all languor, all mockery had left him. His questions came like a lawyer's, quick, crackling, boring towards the facts. "You don't think, then, that freedom betters the lot of the slaves?"

"I think in most cases it worsens it."

"How?"

"They don't understand it, you know. The first thing a slave says when he is told that he is free is, 'Do I *have* to?' And the second is, 'Who gwine take care of me now?' It robs them of their childlike pride of belonging in—they wouldn't say *to*—a beloved household. And it imposes a far greater financial strain on their masters, with exactly the same obligations, to feed and clothe and doctor them. Negroes take no joy in shifting for themselves, and they are terrified at the idea that they might be sent back to Africa. All they want, as a rule, is to be allowed to stay on as they are, *in spite* of being free."

"That presupposes that they are happy in their masters, of course," he put in. "Have you, personally, ever known of cruelty to slaves here in Williamsburg?"

"A few instances—mostly dealt with very promptly by public opinion. In most households there is an unwritten law that no servant shall be whipped."

"But further south—in the Cotton States?"

"Ah, well—there you have a different situation. Two, in fact. The labor down there is largely gang labor in the fields—and the majority of slaves are field hands, many of them half wild."

"I realize that—yes. Go on," he urged.

"Secondly, the white population in the Cotton States is mostly very come-by-chance—Northerners, of the wrong sort, out to get rich quick in cotton—or people from other parts of the South who have made a mistake at home and had to leave."

"Well!" he said triumphantly. "For the first time since I came south of the Mason-Dixon Line I have got a simple answer to a simple question! May I come back and talk to you about this, some other day?"

"Certainly. I don't say my ideas aren't a bit old-fashioned——"

Late comers eddied into the room, presented their compliments to Grandmother Day, acknowledged her introduction of Cabot Murray rather coolly, and drifted on towards the refreshments and Felicity's efficient hospitality. As he resumed his chair he said thoughtfully, "It's just barely possible that you would do better not to devote yourself so exclusively to the only Yankee in the room. Ought I to go away?"

"Nonsense, I'm old enough to devote myself where I please. I've known these people ever since they were born, and I see some of them every day. The Crabb boy isn't getting anywhere, if that's what you wanted to know." She smiled as his glance snapped back to her, revealing his surprise. "He's just like his grandfather," she said, remembering with indulgence Archer's endless, uncomplaining devotion which, though Julian was a quiet man himself, had seemed to her so *tame*. The Crabb women were always pretty and charming and the Crabb men were dull, and there it was.

"It's none of my business anyway," he conceded, and then the shutters swung back open a crack—"Now, if it was *you* he was beauing around I'd sail in and cut him out!"

"Eden is part of me," she reminded him.

"So is Sally!" he replied, with that wilful twist of his lips.

"Just what is it that you can't forgive Sally for?" she inquired curiously.

"*Proverbs*, 1-17," he remarked tersely, and gazed in astonishment when she uttered what in a younger woman would have been called a peal of laughter. "I thought you'd have to look it up after I'd gone," he said, chargrined.

"*Surely in vain the net is spread in the sight of any bird,*" she quoted with relish. "I learned my Bible very thoroughly when I was a child, Mr. Murray. You think Eden is less—obvious, then," she pursued, fascinated.

"Eden has no more guile than a kitten," he agreed, and added, "Bless their sharp little claws!"

A general leave-taking began then and they had no chance for further conversation. He seized an interval in the good-byes and said he must find Sally and take his own leave.

"Sally will be staying to supper," she said. "The family always does. I would like you to join us, Mr. Murray, if you have no other engagement."

His pleasure was a heart-catching thing, she thought, but it clouded quickly with the inevitable gibe.

"Do you think the family would be pleased with that?" he suggested.

"I am not accustomed to consult the family when I give an invitation. Besides, you haven't had a chance to talk to Eden."

"You're very good to me," he said with a sudden touching humility. "I shall try to be deserving."

Felicity approached them then with a group of departing guests, and was informed that Mr. Murray was staying to supper. Felicity took it very well, under her grandmother's eye, and her response was cordial. Before the last guest had been sped it was candle-lighting time, and Cabot Murray found himself, a little incredulously, making one of the group round Grandmother Day's chair like a son of the household.

5

They sat down fourteen to supper, and during the meal what had been to him just a confusion of Days and Spragues, most of them with a strong family resemblance to each other, separated themselves into personalities and formed a family pattern.

There were only four Spragues—Lafe and his wife Louise, who had been born a Day, and their two children, Sally and Sedgwick. And there were nine Days, beginning with the eldest, who had placed him on her right hand, ousting from his usual place her grandson Ransom, who was next in seniority. Eden was on their guest's right, and with her help he sorted out the rest of them: her mother Felicity, who had been born a Sprague; her eldest brother Dabney, twenty-one and something of a dandy, just home from a year at the American Legation in London and a Continental tour; her second brother Fauquier, eighteen, a "rat" in his first term at the Virginia Military Institute at Lexington, out on very special furlough for the occasion; Eden herself was the third child; then came Susannah; then Barry, thirteen, and very envious of Fauquier's tight-fitting uniform; and lastly Myrta.

With Gran's eye upon them, they accepted the outsider graciously as one of themselves, not singling him out for special attention, but paying him the compliment of letting him alone. Mrs. Ewell's illness during his visit had so far curtailed the hospitality of the President's household, and this was the first time Cabot Murray had dined *en famille* in Virginia.

He was finding it a new experience. His hard, hooded eyes went from face to face along the festive, candlelighted table with its low centerpiece of hothouse flowers. They were a handsome family, but the thing that interested him more than their good looks or the obvious ease in which they lived, was the undisguised, unself-conscious affection they had for each other. That they should all adore Grandmother Day was natural enough. It was doubtless natural too, Cabot reflected, that Ransom should be devoted to the still beautiful fair-haired wife who had borne him this engaging brood of healthy children. And there was no reason why those children should not cherish an extravagant love for such charming parents. Cabot did not know that Lafe Sprague had courted Louise all his life, but their tenderness for each other was always noticeable even to the most casual stranger. Sally—well, perhaps of them all only Sally thought first and last of Sally. Her brother Sedgwick was seated next to Susannah Day and they kept up a constant lighthearted tomfoolery which drew Cabot's glance again and again, until Eden said, smiling, "Those two never let up. Most of the time they might as well be talking Cherokee, for all the sense it makes to anyone else, but it amuses them all day long!"

"Mr. Murray is not quite sure how to take us," remarked Tibby Day on his other side. "Any of us."

"Perhaps he is not accustomed to such a large and noisy family," Ransom suggested from across the table on his grandmother's left hand. His thin, kind face broke into its irradiating smile as Cabot looked back at him searchingly.

"Is it always like this?" Cabot asked, with a nod towards a burst of laughter at the other end of the table. To the three who heard him it was as though he wanted to believe and could not.

"Like what?" said Eden gently, trying to come at the cause of his apparent bewilderment.

"Yes, Mr. Murray, tell us what we are like, to you," Tibby Day encouraged him quietly.

He took his time about it, as though hunting for words. He looked away from them, down the row of happy faces in the candlelight— Sedgwick was now weeping with laughter, his hand held up as though to shield his eyes from Susannah's childlike mirth, while the others joined in enjoying some hilarious point she had scored in their endless tug of war. Susannah had a misplaced dimple close to the upper corner of her mouth—her teeth were small and straight—her hazel eyes were pansy-dark in the soft glow from the candles, her throat rose small and young above her round young bosom, her springing curls shone like the satin ribbon which threaded them. She was dainty and sweet as a porcelain shepherdess, but she was alive—terribly, pitifully alive. . . .

"You are all so—so fond of each other," Cabot got out inadequately.

"And are you accustomed in the North to families who hate each other, Mr. Murray?" Eden inquired, voicing what was to her an absurdity, and was startled by the way his face closed in, black and bitter, and he said, not looking at her——

"I have heard of such things."

Eden glanced at her grandmother, then at her father, in swift appeal for them to say something to cover her blunder. Ransom spoke too quickly, and only made things worse.

"It takes a family occasion like this one," he said, without looking ahead into his sentence, "to bring home to a man how empty a life of single blessedness can be."

"Does it?" said Cabot coldly, and added, devoting himself to the food on his plate, "You talk more like a parson than a schoolmaster."

"Ransom means," interposed Ransom's grandmother, "that he enjoys feeling patriarchal and smug. He takes himself very seriously as head of the family, since his father died a few years ago."

"I agree that it is a very serious business," Cabot replied, ostentatiously civil. "To be responsible for the welfare and happiness of so many helpless, delightful creatures would worry me into an early grave. If we have war between the States, Mr. Day, and I do not see how we are going to avoid it, I shall have only my own skin to think of. Whereas you will have to see your sons march away and your women weep. I would not change places with you then."

The word had been said—the small and terrifying word that carries such a weight of dread. War. Nobody wanted to hear the word, no one wanted to think beyond this pleasant moment. But Ransom never shirked words, and he had been wondering what the Yankee viewpoint would reveal. It should have waited till the men were left alone in the dining-room to smoke—but since it had come now he met it with quickening interest.

"Then you think Lincoln will be elected," he said at once.

"Sure to be. Not so much because a true majority wants him, as because his opposition is hopelessly divided."

"If only one knew more about him!" Ransom said impatiently.

"Such as what?"

"Well—what he is really like, without exaggeration—and what he really believes in, apart from politics."

"I'll try to answer both those questions, I think. He isn't like anything you have been led to think, you can take my word for that. He is a simple, humble, almost bewildered man, driven by destiny. And he has no politics, except to preserve the Union."

"Have you seen him?" demanded Eden, breathless. "You sound as though you had talked to him!"

"I have. You won't like to hear this, sir—perhaps I shouldn't say it in your house at all—but I believe, for reasons I would be put to it to get into words, that Abraham Lincoln is a great man, even as Washington was great." In the silence of their incredulous surprise, Cabot looked round at them defiantly under his brows. "I have probably said the wrong thing," he surmised, without apology.

"You have said a very interesting thing," remarked Ransom without animus. "I would very much like to hear more."

"But Washington was a gentleman born," said Tibby Day unexpectedly. "He had dignity, he had presence, he had a great kindliness."

"Oddly enough, so has this man Lincoln—all three," Cabot told her, and leaned forward, his alert curiosity awakened as she had seen it when they spoke of Emancipation. "Would it be tactless to inquire, ma'am, if you ever really saw Washington?"

"I saw him many times," she said simply. "We all did, here in Williamsburg. He was kind to me when I was a child."

"I envy you that," said Cabot from his heart. "But do you know, I have a strange feeling that some day—if any of us lives to tell it as you have done—we who have spoken with Lincoln will be as enviable as you are."

"Are you a friend of his?" Ransom's question was academically keen. There was an odd absence of sectional feeling in the discussion which was developing between them.

"I don't know that one could safely say he has friends, in the intimate sense you mean. I have had access to him, informally. I have seen him off guard, for whatever that may be worth."

"And you believe in him?"

"Yes. But don't ask me why, because I don't know."

"Lafe." Ransom's voice cut into the chatter beyond, causing a silence to fall on the whole table. "Lafe, Mr. Murray is qualified to speak about Lincoln. I think we should listen."

"That ape!" cried Lafe, bristling. "If he's elected we shall have to secede. No other course left to us!"

"On the contrary," Cabot began, and they could see that he weighed his words, "if Virginia stood out for patience—for moderation——"

"Politics!" cried Sally, and made a face. "Not politics, for pity's sake, at Gran's party!"

"Be quiet, Sally!" commanded her brother Sedgwick, and at the same time his hand came down on Sue's arm, suppressing protest from her. "We're going to get Lincoln, we might as well know about him!"

"I'd rather know about his wife," said Sally perversely. "Is it true, Mr. Murray, that he is sorely hen-pecked?"

Cabot's eyes rested on her sardonically. It was the sort of thing he would have expected from her, that was plain to see.

"I think it would take real talent," he said drily, "to hen-peck Abe Lincoln—successfully."

"Have you ever seen her? Tell us what she's like!"

"I have dined with them in Springfield. But I am no judge of women, and must beg to be excused from expressing an opinion."

"That means you didn't like her!" crowed Sally. "Is she a good hostess? Was it a good dinner?"

Cabot's eyes went from her pert prettiness to the serene, mellow beauty of Felicity Day, across the table from him, sitting next her husband as the custom was at these family parties. She was roundabout forty, he supposed—she would have to be, with that great galumphing Dabney for a son. But her lips were wide and tender, her broad brow was smooth, and her eyelids, weighted with long curving lashes, gave her the look of a drowsy, brooding child in the candlelight. He knew that he had judged Mrs. Lincoln, and he knew a sudden swirl of re-kindled anger against her—why?—because she was not Felicity Day, soft and kind and soothing, for a man to come home to? He knew with a sort of savage surprise that he wanted a woman like this one for Lincoln, who was most certainly going to need sanctuary in the months to come, instead of——

"Mrs. Lincoln greets a guest," he heard himself saying flatly, "as though she hoped he had wiped his feet before he came in."

The table gasped, then broke into pleased laughter. Cabot permitted himself a rueful smile, and looked apologetically at Tibby Day.

"You see, ma'am, already your Virginia hospitality leads me to make unkind comparisons. If Lincoln lived here—" He left the sentence unfinished in his own astonishment at having begun it. If any man had the good fortune to live here, would not his viewpoint on the world undergo drastic changes? And yet, to Ransom it was the usual thing. Ransom already had that viewpoint. To Dabney and Fauquier and young Barry—to the fire-eating Lafe and his tall son Sedgwick, it was the stiff, chilly house in Springfield which would seem strange.

Lincoln would never know what he had missed. But Cabot Murray was beginning to know, though he was still unable to accept this Virginia household as anything but the exception. "I wish first of all you could manage not to think of Lincoln as an Abolitionist," he went on slowly. "He has no convictions about slavery, so far as I can tell—only about the Union."

"But surely——"

"But can you be sure——"

"But then why——"

"Quiet!" yelled Sedgwick, watching their guest, his face alert and grave, his fingers still lying, half caressing, half warning, on Susannah's arm. "Let the poor man hear himself think, can't you? How does he propose to save the Union regardless of slavery, Mr. Murray?"

"He will go to war to save it."

At the low, simple words pandemonium threatened again, but Lafe's voice topped them all, crying hotly, "Compulsory union is a contradiction in terms!"

"I know that, sir. So does Mr. Lincoln, no doubt. But if the South cannot mediate—cannot come to some kind of terms with Emancipation, it will have to——"

"If your Mr. Lincoln cannot stop the Government in Washington from meddling in our private affairs, the South will secede!" shouted Lafe.

"And be damned," Cabot agreed softly.

"Don't be too sure about that, Mr. Murray! The best officers in the Army are from the South—we may send them up to West Point to learn their trade, but by heaven they still belong to us and not to that gang of politicians in Washington! They will resign their commissions, you see if they don't! They will come back home and organize an army of the South——"

"And how will they equip it, sir? The guns and ammunition are all manufactured in the Northern factories. The supplies are endless, but the South will have only what it has got on hand at the time of Secession. With a blockade of Southern ports, it would be difficult to bring in more. The war would soon be over because the seceding States would have to cease firing."

"Virginia will never secede," said Tibby Day, and every head turned towards the small erect figure at the end of the table. "Virginia *made* the Union. I saw it done. If the Cotton States want to go, let them go. They are riff-raff—black sheep. We can do without them."

"Why, Gran——!"

"*Gran,* darling, really——!"

"I don't see what you are all staring at. You all know very well that Virginia will emancipate in her own way. I remember when the Legislature here at Williamsburg passed the law that made the importation of any more slaves illegal. It was the New Englanders who kept it up —they owned the ships, they made the money out of it. Tom Jefferson, passed that law—he hated slavery, and he always said it would have to go, 'way back when I was still a girl. Julian agreed with him. But it can't be done just by passing a law in Washington. It can't be done by a war, either. You'll have to give us a little more time," she said, looking at Cabot Murray.

They all saw his face soften as he met her confident, confiding gaze —saw his big brown hand come out to rest reassuringly on hers where it lay beside her plate—heard the affection in his voice as he said gravely, "And I am convinced that Mr. Lincoln would see eye to eye with you, ma'am."

"How on earth can you say that, man?" cried Lafe, unable to contain himself even though Mr. Murray was their guest. "Mr. Lincoln is the fellow who said two years ago that this government cannot endure half slave and half free, and reminded us that a house divided against itself cannot stand!"

So close on his last word as to be almost an interruption, Cabot's hard Yankee voice dominated the attentive table.

"'*Wrong as we think slavery is, we can yet afford to let it alone where it is, because that much is due to the necessity arising from its actual presence in the nation,*'" he said, and looked from Lafe to Sedgwick to Fauquier to Ransom in one swift black glance. "Mr. Lincoln said that too, more recently, in his speech at New York."

"But that would mean he has no desire to interfere with us at all!" said Eden incredulously.

"Which is what I am myself trying to convey to you," Cabot assented.

There was a bewildered silence.

"B-but I thought—" Eden began, gazing at him with a puzzled frown.

"But you *don't* think," Cabot cut in. "You guess—and assume—and dash off at tangents, even the best of you! I tell you again that this man Lincoln is not an Abolitionist. He himself has told you so over and over again. But you don't hear. You listen to everybody but him. Has any one of you at this table read the speech he made last February in New York? No, I thought not. Yet four newspapers printed it in full, the *Tribune* reprinted it as a pamphlet, and it was pamphletized again as a campaign document last summer. It was one of the greatest speeches ever made in this country. I heard it, and I'm not ashamed to say I yelled as loud as anybody at the end."

"Now, wait a minute, let's be calm about this." Lafe was being calm with a visible effort, open-minded by main force. Louise's loving brown eyes rested on him knowingly, amused at his unhabitual mildness of approach. "Where was this speech? Tell us about it."

Cabot looked again round the table, this time at the women's faces —Susannah sweet and serious under Sedgwick's hand, beautiful Felicity polite but not really interested in politics, Sally frankly bored— and came to the bright, watching eyes of the elder Mrs. Day.

"I hope you will forgive me, ma'am—I had no intention of creating an issue——"

"Tell us about the speech," she said gently. "We all want to hear."

"How did the fellow *get* to New York?" demanded Lafe. "Illinois is his stamping ground!"

"They were turning out the political cupboards in search of a man to beat Seward and his machine. They thought Chase might do it. But just so as not to overlook anything they offered Lincoln two hundred and fifty dollars to address an audience at the Cooper Union. After that we didn't hear much more about Chase."

"What happened?" Ransom was the first to voice their question.

"They damned near—excuse me, ma'am—they very nearly tore the hall apart and gave it to him when he finished."

"*Why?*" That was Lafe, simmering.

"It's hard to say why, in a dozen words."

"Take hundreds," said Tibby Day on his left. "But tell us how it was."

He turned to her, with that prompt softening of face and voice she always won from him. And as though he spoke to her alone, as though she were a beloved, intelligent child, with no other listeners around them, he began.

"It was snowing that night in New York," he told her, "and they said that would keep people away. The admission was twenty-five cents, to hear what Seward calls 'the prrrairie statesman'—and they said that was too much. Anyway, the auditorium wasn't full—only about fifteen hundred people, waiting to hear the wild man from the back woods make a fool of himself. It was a very select and high-nosed Republican audience. The one and only Horace Greeley himself was sitting on the platform, and William Cullen Bryant, no less, was to introduce the speaker. I'm not notoriously tender-hearted myself, but I was feeling pretty sorry for him before he appeared. It was a den of lions he walked into when he followed Bryant on to the stage, and his suit was new and didn't fit very well, and a black broadcloth coat musses anyway if it's rolled up in a carpet-bag for a two-day journey. He could have had it pressed at the Astor House where he was staying, but he hadn't thought of that. He looked just about the way they expected him to—fairly wild and woolly, and all hands and feet. I'm a tall man, myself, and I know how that feels—Bryant was brief and not very helpful, and the applause was businesslike and cool, and Lincoln stepped forward into it and began to talk." Cabot was not looking at any of them now, and his right hand was busy turning the stem of his wine glass slowly against the pattern of the handsome tablecloth beneath it. He watched the play of the circle against the linen scrolls absorbedly, his head down, and they all watched him, fascinated by a simplicity of utterance and emotion as naked as Lincoln's own. "His voice was too high for such a big man," Cabot was saying slowly in his own rough, burly tones, so unlike the cadence of the gentle speech habitual to that table. "They might have tittered at that, but they were waiting for something funnier. They were so sure that something funnier would come soon, even if it was only one of the raw stories he was supposed to let off every chance he got. But he didn't make any jokes. He started right in talking sense to them—facts about the founding of this Republic, and the men who framed its Constitution. He flattered them by assuming that none of the sound research behind what he said would be new to them. In no time at all he made a monkey of Douglas and his airy statements about the founding fathers intending that slavery should be universal in this country. Lincoln had the chapter and verse. He argued like a lawyer—a brilliant lawyer. And they listened. They couldn't help themselves. And pretty soon they applauded something he said. And then they cheered something else. His voice had got back into a normal register, he had forgotten his hands and feet and the creases in his black coat. He spoke for two hours. At the end they stood up and shouted and waved their hats and handkerchiefs, and began to push towards the platform to congratulate him and shake his hand. The reporters went crazy. I heard one of them say that no man had ever made such an impression on a New York audience. And it was just Old Abe Lincoln in a mussy suit that didn't fit, speaking the truth that was in him."

"Then—you believe he can save us," Tibby Day murmured into the silence.

"So help me, ma'am, I believe he will try," he affirmed very low. "And that is more than I can say for the rest of 'em!" He raised his head and his eyes sought Felicity's sweet, drowsy stare, and he gave her a smile more disarmed and friendly than anyone but Tibby Day had yet won from him. "I beg everybody's pardon," he said lightly, "for introducing such a dull note into a happy evening. But this is the first time since I arrived in Virginia that I have seen any hope of reaching an understanding with the inhabitants. You have all been very patient with me—" His smiling gaze ran on to Susannah, who instantly smiled back at him as though she had known him all her life and shared with him a secret no one else knew. "—and I hope you will ruminate over what I have said. Virginia's weight will mean so much in the balance between peace and war during the days to come—and your own attitude here in Williamsburg must be of great consequence." His eyes came now to Lafe at the other end of the table. "I cannot help hoping that you will all throw your influence on the side of patience—give Mr. Lincoln a chance to solve this thing without stacking all the cards against him before he can deal. And now, Miss Susannah, I have quite finished. Aren't you glad?"

6

When the gentlemen returned to the drawing-room they found the chairs set back against the wall, leaving a cleared space in the middle of the room. Again there was a place between Eden and her grandmother awaiting Cabot, and it occurred to him to wonder how Sally felt about having what she doubtless considered a new conquest snatched away from her by her grandmother. After all, he had come to this party as Sally's beau. A glance at her perfect, rather expressionless face told him nothing. She flashed him no provocative message, nor did she appear to be sulking. Merely she accepted the fact that Gran had pre-empted him and apparently bore Eden no malice either. For all his wayward, cynical knowledge of her type, he did not comprehend that once a man's attention wandered from Sally he ceased, so far as she was concerned, to exist. Already Sally, the professional Southern belle, was developing some of the less pleasant attributes of the female spider —she would have all of a man or none of him. If Cabot allowed himself to be enticed away from her by any means at all, Sally was not sufficiently interested in him to lift a finger to bring him back. Besides —she suspected him of laughing at her, though she couldn't think why, and that was not a thing she was accustomed to, and she didn't like it. She decided, before the evening was over, that she didn't like Cabot Murray anyway.

After everyone was seated Susannah stepped forward, her dimple much in evidence.

"Ladies and gentlemen," she began formally, "as you all know, it is our beloved Grandmother Day's birthday, and we are gathered together in celebration of that very happy event. She thinks she has had all her presents, but there is one more still in store for her. Some time ago she was heard to express interest in this shocking new dance called the Waltz. And so—if Mrs. Lafayette Sprague will kindly oblige at the pianoforte, Mr. Sedgwick Sprague and I will demonstrate—a waltz." She curtsied deeply, impudently, and went to where Sedgwick waited at the doorway, and they disappeared hand in hand into the hall, as Louise started towards the piano.

Eden said hastily to her grandmother and Cabot——

"They've worked at this for days, and we must all applaud like anything. Aunt Louise says they nearly wore her fingers to the bone, getting every step and every turn just right." She finished with a glance at Cabot which appealed to him not to scoff at the performance and the music began, and Sedgwick swung his green-clad partner lightly into the room, his every move designed to show her off from each exquisite angle as they circled slowly across the carpet.

They danced without self-consciousness, absorbed in the dip and sway of their own young bodies, moving together as one. Sedgwick held her devotedly, a half smile on his lips, seeming to regard his own graceful presence in the dance as mere background, seeming to eliminate himself as a performer so that attention should rest entirely on the girl in his arms. And she, surrendered to him with such confidence, her small satin slippers lighting so surely within what appeared to be millimeters of where his own foot would fall, was lost to everything but the rhythm they kept and the touch of his guiding hands.

Ransom was soon conscious of an ache in his throat as he sat watching, and Felicity saw them through a blur, and even Eden's eyes were grave and tender—they were so young, so gloriously, obliviously young, that it hurt to look at them. Lafe, who had assisted at some of the endless rehearsals in his own drawing-room, was observing the finer points with satisfaction. Dabney, who had waltzed in all the capitals of Europe, looked on with indulgent approval, Fauquier with admiration, Barry and Myrta with envy. And Grandmother Day, even while she delighted in her latest birthday gift, was plagued by trying to remember what it was about Sedgwick. . . .

When they finished, the applause was spontaneous and hearty. Then Dabney sprang up and caught his cousin Sally by the hand.

"Play it again, Aunt Louise!" he called. "Let's have the same one again. I heard it last in Vienna."

The music began again. Eden dared to steal a look at Cabot Murray's face and found it unguarded and smiling, his eyes still following Sue and Sedgwick who had begun the new waltz almost without a pause, laughing at each other in high satisfaction that the surprise had gone off so well, entirely willing that Dabney should do better if he could. And so Susannah too could take the kinks out of him just as Gran had done, Eden thought, and teach him that smile without a dagger in it.

"You are still looking at our darling," she said softly. "We think, quite fatuously, that there was never anybody anywhere so perfect as our Sue. It's a wonder she isn't completely spoilt and conceited, but she doesn't even *know*."

"They are so pathetically in love with each other," he said, as though to himself, "that one can hardly bear it for them."

"In love!" she repeated, laughing. "Oh, nonsense, they grew up together! They're cousins, you know."

Grandmother Day smothered a small sound of dismay which was covered by the music anyway. Cousins. It was what she had been trying to come at in her own mind. Sedgwick mustn't be in love with Sue because they were double first cousins. And that wasn't all, either. Giles Day had married St. John Sprague's niece only the generation before. It was one of those family intricacies which so baffled Myrta. Dorothea Sprague and the French husband she married after Yorktown had sailed for France in 1788 to settle his estates after the death of his father. They expected to return within the year, and though they took with them their first-born, a son, little Annabelle was considered too small for the voyage and was left behind in the household of her uncle St. John, who had a baby daughter too. The ship never reached France and was never heard of again. When Annabelle was seventeen she married Giles Day and became the mother of Ransom. So because of Annabelle and Giles, Sue had Sprague blood three times over. It would never do again. Such a possibility had not occurred to anyone in the family, of course—it took this observant stranger to see how they felt about each other and bring her own vague forebodings to a point. Not even Eden took him seriously now, simply because he was a stranger. But he was right, and this was what she had been feeling in her bones lately. Eden mustn't be allowed to think twice about it. Not yet. If only Felicity had not noticed—if only no one said anything —if only Sedgwick himself wasn't jostled into realization—but to what end? If it went on as it was everyone would be aware of it soon. Postponing that wouldn't help much. Or would it? Couldn't she think of something, at her age? Should they send Sue off to that school in Richmond after all? Shouldn't Sedgwick be made to go abroad, now that Dabney had come back in such form? But she knew in her bones that all this anxious scurrying would be futile and too late. Cabot Murray had seen what the rest of them were blind to. It had already happened.

All this had gone through her mind with the speed of lightning, and she spoke before Cabot could reply to Eden.

"If I were a few years younger," she remarked, with her eyes on the two revolving couples, "I would see to it that Mr. Murray asked me to dance."

"Oh, but Gran, I—" Eden was blushing.

Mr. Murray gathered in his long legs, rose, and made her a bow.

"Will you do me the honor—?" he suggested, and extended a formal elbow.

"A—a waltz?" Eden faltered, looking up at him helplessly.

From under a lifted eyebrow he glanced at the other four.

"It's all in the family," he said, and his white teeth gleamed beneath eyes which were—yes—quite friendly and kind.

Eden stood up, a little diffidently, for she had never waltzed with anyone but Dabney and Sedgwick, and she was not even wearing gloves— She felt Cabot Murray's right hand go behind her waist and caught at his shoulder as he swung her masterfully into the waltz. Their hands met in mid air. She looked up at him, as though to ask for quarter, and found his dark face very near, looking down. He danced well, with a strong lead and a pronounced rhythm which made him easy to follow. Eden was unable to take her eyes away from his, now that they were so near.

"Thank God I'm not a cousin!" she heard him murmur, just above the music.

"Why—Mr. Murray! That's an odd thing to say!"

"Is it?" He reversed her expertly so that her swaying hoop brushed Myrta's knees where she sat enthralled at the edge of the floor. "Is it odd to be glad I start with a clean slate tonight and my own way to make? It's to our advantage, I think, that you never slapped my face when I wore petticoats, and I never saw you with a front tooth out!"

Eden laughed, her eyes on his.

"Perhaps. But if I had known you in petticoats I should never have let you grow up to be so—" She stopped, looking over a brink of words, breathless in his arms.

"So—?" he insisted curiously.

She laughed again, and felt the warm blood flooding up to her hair.

"I can't find the right word for you," she admitted. "I don't understand you, I think."

"Good," he said with satisfaction. "I can see right through you. But I like it. All of it. You're the first woman I ever knew that I liked all the way through."

"H-have you known a lot of women?" She could not resist the question.

"Quite a lot," he said, grinning. "But I never saw one before that I wanted to marry." Her startled eyes went absolutely round, and he tightened his hand possessively on her waist, and laughter shook him silently. "Scared, aren't you!" he noted. "Well, don't be. It might not be so bad."

Eden was speechless. They danced all the way down the room without speaking again, and her heart was beating somewhere up at the back of her throat, and her head was going round, and the warmth of his ungloved hand which held hers tingled all up her arm, while her feet followed obediently the pattern set by his.

"Maybe I shouldn't have said that," he offered at last. "All right, then, cross it out. I take it back. Feel better now?"

She looked up at him briefly and away again. She was not altogether sure she wanted him to take it back. At least—he might have left her time to refuse. Well, yes, she had had time for that, while they danced. Perhaps he was afraid she would accept. Didn't he know that one was supposed never to accept the first time one was asked? Maybe you had to be quick, up North. Not that she would ever accept a Yankee. At least not the way things were now. And certainly not such an unpredictable, confusing, domineering sort of Yankee as Cabot Murray. And yet—he knew how to behave with Gran. And he knew that Sue was sweet.

"And you are the first woman I ever knew," he was saying beneath the music, "who won't talk unless she knows what to say." A smile touched Eden's lips, but she kept her head averted from him. "Look at me," he demanded softly, and his fingers tightened on hers. Against her will she obeyed, and endured his probing, pitiless stare without flinching. "It was time I came to Virginia," he said then. "High time. I had begun to think there wasn't anybody like you."

The music stopped. They stood still where they were and his hands left her reluctantly.

"Why are you so—bruised?" she whispered.

"That's a queer word to use," he said.

"It's a queer way to be."

"Yes, I suppose it is—in your experience. That's why I take back what I said a few minutes ago. You'll be better off without me. We'll let it go at that, shall we? And thank you for the waltz."

He made her a bow. She had no choice but to take his proffered arm and let him lead her back to the chair at her grandmother's side.

7

In not much more than a week's time the last doubt about the election vanished. Many would have said the last hope. Mr. Lincoln was going to be the next president.

In the late afternoon of the eighth of November Eden sat alone in the drawing-room with her knitting. It was a grey, cloudy day and a small wood fire had been lighted. The house was very quiet. Felicity was making calls and had taken Sue and Myrta with her. Dabney had left two days ago to visit the Charleston cousins, Fauquier had gone back to the Institute, Ransom and Barry were at the school.

Eden was just wondering if Gran would like a cup of tea to keep the chill out when Pharaoh, the black butler, opened the door gently and announced, "Mr. Murray callin' to see you, Miss Eden."

She had encountered him several times since the birthday party—at church, in the street, and when he had called again to hear more about slavery from Gran. Lafe had not asked him to the big house in England Street where the Spragues lived. President Ewell was well known to have no sympathy with Secession and was therefore out of favor in some quarters—and now his guest was said to be an out and out Lincolnite. It distressed her that prejudice should close some doors to Cabot Murray. She wanted him to like Williamsburg and feel at home there. She found herself being a little extra nice to him always to make up, though perhaps he had not noticed any lack of hospitality in the town. At least he gave no sign. She rose now to greet him and gave him her hand with an unself-conscious warmth of welcome.

"How very nice of you to come today," she said. "I'm all alone and boring myself to death!" And then she wondered if she should have called attention to the fact, like that, that she was alone, and took her hand back rather suddenly, and motioned with her knitting to the armchair on the other side of the fire from the sofa where she had been sitting. "Sit there, and toast. Uncle Phare, bring us some tea, please, and something good to eat." She resumed her place on the sofa with a rustle of spreading skirts, and Cabot sat down obediently where she had indicated, with his feet towards the fire.

There was a moment's silence while her needles flew. His eyes rested thoughtfully on her hands, small and white and busy, with a tight white wristband between them and the ballooning sleeves of her blue merino gown. A narrow white crocheted collar framed her slender throat, her hair gleamed ruddy in the grey room.

"And I find you knitting socks," he remarked.

"For Fauquier. I sometimes think the Institute must drill them without their boots on, the number of socks a cadet needs! Gran thinks she is the only one who can knit socks good enough for Father, but I notice she's quite willing to leave Fauquier to me!"

"It seems to me that the men of this household must be outrageously pampered," he said with what sounded like envy, and Eden's curiosity stirred as it always did at any hint of what might be the background of his own life.

"Gran said you mentioned a sister," she suggested cautiously. "Doesn't she knit your socks, or isn't she old enough?"

"I should have said half-sister. She's twelve or thirteen. I don't think she knows how to knit."

"That's very remiss of somebody," she said lightly. "I could knit quite well when I was twelve."

"Could you, my dear? That must have looked very charming."

She glanced up quickly to see if he was jeering, and was quite unable to read his face as he sat watching her, lounging in the armchair, his legs stretched out towards the fire. Her eyes retreated at once to the sock. The silence drew taut between them.

"Eden," he said softly. "I want to say it once before I go. Eden, my dear."

"Before you go?" The needles had faltered. She bent her head above them. Of course he would go. Some time.

"Charleston. There's going to be trouble there."

"Do you—look for trouble?"

"I'm afraid I do."

"You could have travelled down with Dabney. He went two days ago. We have cousins there."

"More cousins?"

"My great aunt Lavinia married a Middleton, no less. And then her daughter married a Rutledge. They have a big house on the Battery and entertain a great deal—ever so much grander than we are. Dabney is such a snob he couldn't wait to pay his respects to them!"

"Don't you ever go to Charleston?"

"I haven't since I was a child. We went to a wedding there once—I've forgotten whose."

"And didn't you like being grand?"

"No. I like our way better. When do you go?"

"Tomorrow."

Again the silence.

"I've dropped a stitch," she said, her head bent, her fingers not quite steady.

"Even tomorrow is too late. I never thought to feel about any woman as I feel about you—today. I'm not going to make love to you, Eden —I'm not going to ask you to marry me, do you hear? But you've got a right to know, I guess, what you've done for me. I don't know quite how to say it, either. There were things I didn't believe in. I do, now. I'm not very good at words, and I haven't got any sort of farewell speech prepared for you—I had no idea I'd have a chance like this to make one, I came mostly just to look at you once more, I guess——"

"Oh, please don't sound as though you were never coming back!" she cried, and dropped the knitting and put her hands up before her face.

For a moment he stared at her from his chair, his expression a mixture of regret and tenderness. Then he got his long legs under him and rose and crossed the hearthrug and pushed aside her skirts so that he could sit down on the sofa.

"I can't come back," he said. "I'm a Lincoln man, and before long I shall be very unwelcome anywhere in the South. This thing is bound to get worse before it gets better."

"Then why do you go to Charleston?"

"Because I must." He took her wrists in his big fingers and drew her hands away from her face. "I shan't ever forget you, Eden, whatever comes. You're not like anybody I ever saw before—or am likely ever to see again. But you're not to think of me, I tell you."

"That seems a very—one-sided arrangement."

"You'll be better off without me," he said doggedly, his hands holding hers.

"You said that before. Why do you say that? Why are you so sure?"

"I know myself. I'm not for you, Eden. I'm not your kind." He bent his head. She felt his lips hard against her hands. He laid her hands back in her lap and rose, with a long sigh. "Besides—there are bad times coming."

"Gran says maybe it will blow over."

He shook his head, and walked away from her on to the hearthrug.

"Sooner or later," he said, "somebody's got to be licked. South Carolina has been spoiling for a fight for years. She's going to get it—one way or another."

"Why don't you go home, then?"

"Home?" He looked at her oddly, as though the word had no meaning for him.

"Where do you live?"

"Trenton. New Jersey. It's not a very cheerful place." He hunched his shoulders in a derisive sort of shudder. "Let's not think about it. I'm leaving now, Eden—before it gets any harder. I've seen you by candlelight, and midday, and firelight—and in a thunderstorm. And if I were struck blind as I stand here I would see you till I die as you are now, with tears on your cheeks, because I don't take you in my arms and fight the whole boiling lot of them for you! It's not because I don't want you, Eden—I want you till I can't eat or sleep—I want you morning, noon, and night—and in the dawn, that's the worst time, Eden, but you wouldn't know about that. I've no right to talk to you like this, have I—I never meant to, it isn't the way a Virginia man would tell you that he loved you, is it! Maybe it's not what I'd be saying myself if I stood a dog's chance of having you for my own and damn the war! But we're done for, Eden, right here, right now, and will you for God's sake try to forget me, for your own sake, and as soon as ever you can! Promise me that, before I go."

She sat very still, very straight, her hands lying together in her lap and tears on her cheeks.

"I shall never hear a thunderstorm again," she said quite steadily, "that I don't think, 'What a lovely day!'"

The door opened gently after a soft double tap.

"Ole Mistis says will you all gib her de pleasure o' takin' yo' tea up stairs wid her," said Pharaoh.

8

She had seen him from her window, as he came through the gate. She knew that he would find Eden alone today—the first time they had ever been alone together. And for a little while she sat frowning at the dreary day outside, trying to sort herself out on this Cabot Murray.

Why had she taken to him so, she asked herself. What was there in him that she responded to, not instinctively, as Eden did, but deliberately, wilfully, enjoying the sensation? He was a difficult man, an unruly, contrariwise, suspicious man—none of them things she was accustomed to. He was also an unhappy man. Well, there were lots of those, probably. She couldn't at her age go round gathering up miserable people and dusting off their knees and telling them they weren't really hurt. And yet she had definitely gathered up Cabot Murray and kept him to supper with the family and made him waltz with Eden. And now she was pleased, obtusely pleased, that Eden must receive him alone and deal with him somehow, unless she herself chose to interrupt or unless Eden fled to her for protection. It would do Eden good, she heard herself thinking, with surprise. And suppose Eden fell in love with him, what then? Do her good, she thought again, and was astonished at herself.

The man was a Yankee. If there was a war, he would be on the wrong side. Well, she had seen all that before. Julian, of course, had ended up on the right side. We're wrong this time, she thought. Not him. *We're* wrong if we take to acting like South Carolina. But we won't. Washington is part of Virginia State, after all. I remember when they made it. He's not a New Englander, anyway, not by the look of him. Why do I like him so, she ruminated, frowning. He's nothing like Julian. And yet—I wonder. Julian had no people, nothing to love, when he came here. And this man is loveless too. How do I know that? In my bones. He takes it differently from Julian, that's all. He minds it worse, and he hates minding. Julian was sort of—resigned to it. This man is fighting it, he wants something he hasn't got, and he despises himself for wanting it and tries to think it's not worth having. Well, why hasn't he got it, I wonder. He said he had a sister, so there must be some kind of home. What's his mother about, I wonder. Or is she dead? A dead mother wouldn't turn a man sour like that, though, not unless there was something else. A love affair? It could be, I suppose. Some woman who wasn't worth caring about, perhaps. He's got his knife into Sally's kind, all right. But he knows Eden is different, that's the queer part. Felicity would think I am throwing Eden to the lions, but I'm not so sure——

He would be a fine, masterful man to love, if you could tame him, she thought. More like St. John Sprague than like Julian, I suppose, but nothing had ever hurt St. John, he was a darling of the gods. This man has been knocked down and rolled in the dust by something, and he's all hurt pride and prickles, he doesn't *trust* you. Julian never quite lost his trustfulness, somehow, I hadn't such a hard job as Eden will have. Eden has got to give him back his faith in—something. If I was a good, careful grandmother, I'd shoo him away before she falls in love with him. Only I'd be too late now. The harm was done that first day in the thunderstorm. It happens that way sometimes. This will mean losing Eden, when he takes her up North. How can I be so sure he wants to? I feel it in my bones.

But I'm not to blame for it, any more than I can stop it now, she thought. Ransom will try to stop it, I imagine. Ransom and Felicity won't be able to see how Eden can be in love with a man she hardly knows. But my Lavinia did it, down there in Charleston. Lavinia never looked back, it was beautiful, you couldn't be sorry to see her go when she had got what she wanted. Where will he take Eden, I wonder. He *will* take her, I feel it in my bones, it's no good trying to keep her now, she's already as good as gone. I must make Felicity see that somehow. And he will be good to her, too. How can I be so sure, and he such a headstrong, high-strung, passionate man—like a colt that's been brutally broken. Who's to blame for that, I wonder. Because he can be tender too, if you know how to come at him—Eden knows how—Eden is the first to know how—I feel it in my bones. . . .

After a bit she roused herself and rapped with her stick and gave her orders about tea. Felicity and the others would be home soon. The two in the drawing-room would be better off up here with her.

They came very promptly, and Eden left her no time for conjecture.

"Mr. Murray has come to say good-bye, Gran," she announced rather breathlessly as they entered the room. "He's off to Charleston tomorrow to see the war."

Cabot's eyes met Tibby Day's as he bent to kiss the hand she held out to him—he looked guilty to her, and the hard lines around his mouth were etched deep. Eden was decidedly pale. Refused him already, thought her grandmother. Cowardy-cat. Her sympathy flew instantly to Cabot Murray and wrapped him round with jealous indulgence while she dispensed tea and hot biscuits with honey and told him all about her daughter Lavinia who had fallen in love at first sight with Phineas Middleton once when they were all visiting in Charleston, and had never even come back home to Williamsburg before the wedding because she simply couldn't bear to part with him at all, and now she had a married daughter Caroline and lived with her in a big house on the Battery.

"You remember your cousin Caroline, Eden," she prodded, for neither of them seemed to be attending very well. "You were quite a big girl the last time we went to Charleston—the year before Myrta was born, wasn't it?"

"Yes, Gran, I remember."

"Caroline was very lovely then," she went on, pretending not to notice their preoccupation. "Dark—not much like the rest of us. Dark, with a heart-shaped face. Dear me, she's been married ten years now, I wonder what her two little boys are like. You must go and see Caroline, Mr. Murray, so you can tell me how everything is when you come back."

"Mr. Murray isn't coming back here, Gran. His home is in New Jersey."

"Is it," she said placidly. "I felt it couldn't be in Massachusetts, in spite of his Christian name."

"I believe I was named, ma'am, not for the Boston Cabots but for the English navigator Sebastian. My father has made a hobby of the Northwest Passage story—he's been writing a book about it for the last thirty years or so."

"My husband wrote books," she remarked approvingly. "I used to copy them out for him. I wrote a very fine hand in those days. I daresay your mother helps with the copying too?"

"I have no mother, ma'am," he said briefly. "My father has married a second time—his housekeeper. Her duties leave her very little leisure, it appears, to spend at a desk."

"I see," she said. "In those circumstances, you must be a comfort to him."

He gave a short, hard laugh, as though it had been jerked out of him against his will.

"As a family," he said, and the old, black look was on him, "we don't seem to comfort each other much. Poor Melicent—that's my sister by his second wife—would hardly know what to make of the free and easy way Myrta behaves with her father."

"What a pretty name," she said. "Melicent."

"It was my mother's."

"Your—" She sat a moment, contemplating this fantastic glimpse into his life. The child of the housekeeper was named for the first wife —and she was afraid of her father. They were all afraid of him. How do I know, she wondered. In my bones.

"You see, ma'am," he went on with some difficulty, looking down into his teacup, "as I was trying to tell Miss Eden downstairs—coming to this house has been for me rather like being at a play. Something that never really happened to me at all. Something I saw, from outside a fourth wall, for a few hours, until the curtain dropped. Something I shall always remember with pleasure and—and gratitude. But something I have no part in—any more than I would have among the actors in that make-believe world on the stage."

"Dear me," she murmured, seeming not to notice the stricken look Eden turned on her, a look which said so plainly, *Do something— don't let him feel that way*. "Dear me, that sounds very—final."

"I put things badly, I know," he said restlessly. "Either I say nothing at all, or else I sound as though I was making a speech. Up where I come from we haven't the gift of putting our feelings into words." He set down his cup and rose, and took one of her little hands in his. "You have been very kind to me, ma'am—I can't think why—and I only wish there was some return I could make."

She laid her other hand on his and squeezed them together.

"Come back and tell me how things are in Charleston," she coaxed. "I will give you a letter to Lavinia—Pharaoh will bring it round this evening. Promise me to go and see her, and take her my love."

He hesitated.

"Does it occur to you, ma'am, that a Yankee will be even less welcome in Charleston just now than here? Mightn't she find me a trifle embarrassing?"

"Nonsense, she will be glad to see anyone I send her! And Dabney will vouch for you. How long do you expect to be in Charleston?"

"It's hard to tell. Perhaps until I am kicked out. I have no plans, except to go to Washington for the inauguration in March."

"What about Christmas?" she inquired, looking up at him, holding both his hands in hers. "Won't your family expect you at home, or don't you keep Christmas in New Jersey?"

"I'm afraid I never thought much about it, one way or the other," he confessed. "Melicent just says she wants a book or a doll or a muff, and her mother buys it for her, and that's the end of it."

"What a *wicked* way to do!" she cried, and flung his hands away from her reprovingly. "I never heard of such a thing! You come back here for Christmas, Cabot Murray, and see how it is done—and mind you bring me a gift from Charleston!"

He stood above her, half laughing, half puzzled, and his eyes sought Eden's inquiringly. She nodded, smiling.

"If you never saw a Virginia Christmas, it's high time you did," she said.

"I've half a mind to take you up on it," he murmured.

"I shall be very displeased if you don't," Grandmother Day told him severely. "Mind you, it isn't as though the Spragues still kept open house at Farthingale and we could do it in plantation style as we used to when I was young. And Lavinia will try to keep you in Charleston, but don't you take any notice of her. We still do it better in Williamsburg. Promise?"

"If I keep Christmas at all," he promised, "it will be here with you."

9

It wasn't much to go on, but it was better than she herself had been able to do with him, Eden reflected as the November days crawled by. She never told Gran what had been said that afternoon in the drawing-room, but she had a comforting suspicion that Gran guessed how things were and sympathized.

She had plenty of time now to contemplate what had happened to her. Suppose there wasn't a war after all, and Cabot Murray came back from Charleston at Christmas time and asked her to marry him—she would never have the will power to say No to him, but how about the courage to say Yes? What did he mean, about not being her kind? What dark things was he hinting at when he said, *I know myself.* Had he—her innocent mind fumbled among elusive dreads—had he done something to be ashamed of, something like, well, like forging somebody's name for money or—*stealing?* Or was it something dim and disgraceful about a woman? Her good sense indignantly rejected all such things. He was honest and he was honorable, she was sure. Gran was sure too, or she would never have opened her heart to him. What then? What had made him the way he was, moody and grim and solitary, but—this was the strange part—so quick to see and to need what he apparently lacked?

What sort of life would it be, she wondered, in Trenton, New Jersey? Would he expect her to live in the mysterious household of second wife and half-sister, with no Christmas presents and no—no comfort? Even Gran seemed to sense something—*unusual,* something almost sinister in the house which had obviously never stood for the things her own home stood for to its children. But other people's mothers died and their fathers married again. Could it be that the housekeeper wasn't, perhaps, quite *nice?* Again her maiden thoughts came to a blank wall of ignorance and swerved aside. Even if he asked her, could she bear to leave Gran, and Sue, and the rest, and go out into the unknown with a man she hadn't yet seen a dozen times, but who when he went away to Charleston had taken all the sparkle and the zest of life with him? You couldn't miss a man you scarcely knew. And yet she missed Cabot Murray, desolately and drearily, so that things which had heretofore been enlivening and important were now as dust and ashes, and all the young men she knew bored her, especially Grafton Crabb.

Dabney's letters from Charleston indicated that he had been badly bitten by Secession now, and his father began to look grave and worn. Everybody said President Buchanan was simply muddling along until he could dump the whole mess into Lincoln's lap next March and escape all responsibility. Then they would see. It would be up to Lincoln then.

Early in December a letter came from Caroline to Gran, who sent for Eden at once and handed it to her silently and sat looking into the fire while she read it.

"Your Mr. Murray is very presentable, for a Yankee," Caroline had written, "but I must say, Gran, it is asking a good deal to expect me to take him under my wing in Charleston just now! In the first place, he hobnobs continually with the garrison at Fort Moultrie, and while they are of course received everywhere in town that is largely because Major Anderson in command at the Fort is from the South himself and is known to sympathize with our Cause, even though he is in the Federal Army. Whereas Mr. Murray is so unwise as to try to preach the gospel of Lincoln and patience—patience for *what?*—and has the sublime impudence to imply that even if we do start a war, we can't win it!

"But it really was the last straw when Madeleine Morell—who is just back from Washington a few days ago—showed me the enclosed article in an old Philadelphia paper, *signed* by CABOT MURRAY! Your protégé, Gran, is a *journalist,* did you know? Of course I told Madeleine I was sure you had *no idea,* and she said she thought I ought to tell you, before he abuses your confidence further. And I may as well tell you also that *Yankee journalists* are regarded here as just next door to *spies,* and I really feel very uncomfortable to think that I have introduced him at several of my receptions and dinners to my most intimate friends, even though I did so in good faith and because you had sent him to us.

"I am sure you will quite understand, Gran darling, and Mother entirely agrees with me, when I say that I really cannot ask the man inside the door again, and I have had all I can do, as it is, to prevent Dabney from trying to call him out with pistols. Of course that is perfectly absurd, as it is well known that Northerners won't fight duels anyway, and he probably couldn't hit the side of a house if he did, but all the same I had to *squash* Dabney very firmly and try to hush the whole thing up. No one will ever learn from *me* who and what he is, but I don't at all trust Madeleine, it would be just like her to give it away. And *anyone* may see his hateful name signed to something *more, anywhere,* ANY MINUTE! . . ."

And so on.
When Eden had come to the bottom of the last page, her grandmother reached out and took the letter from her with the tips of her

fingers and tore it daintily into shreds and leaned forward to toss them into the fire. Eden said nothing, but sat watching the blaze, her hands lying idle in her lap, her knitting on the sofa beside her. Her shoulders drooped, she looked drained of life and hope. She looked very young, her grandmother thought with a twinge of pity, and her own needles began to click briskly on a sock for Ransom.

"It's easy to see," she remarked, "that Caroline is a goose. But I must say I am surprised at Dabney going off half-cocked like that."

"Aren't you surprised at Mr. Murray?" Eden inquired, and nothing but her lips moved as she spoke.

"Are you going back on him, just because he writes for a Philadelphia paper?"

"Have you—did you read the article she sent?"

"I did. It's there on the table."

Eden made no move towards it. Then she seemed to change her mind and reached for it, and read it in silence to the end.

"I don't see anything so very terrible about that, do you?" her grandmother remarked then. "It's exactly the sort of thing he said when he was here—and most of it makes very good sense."

"Yes, I suppose it does." Eden picked up her knitting. "Gran—why do you like him so much?"

"Blessed if I know," admitted Tibby Day cheerfully. "But I do. I don't care what he does for a living, I like him. Don't you?"

"Yes," said Eden faintly, knitting.

"We needn't say anything about Caroline's letter, I suppose," her grandmother reflected. "And we could burn the clipping too."

"Dabney knows," Eden reminded her.

"That's right, he does. I reckon he'll raise a rumpus about having Mr. Murray here for Christmas now, by the time Caroline has finished with him. And that will start your father off. Lafe is bad enough already. I never could see why a man's politics should affect his social life. Lots of perfectly charming people were Tories when I was a girl, and you'd have thought they were suddenly turned into thieves and murderers overnight to hear the Patriots talk! Your grandfather Julian was a Tory once," she observed above her needles. "But it never made any difference to the way I felt about him."

"But he was with Lafayette!" Eden objected, surprised.

"Finally. Anyway, that was a different thing altogether from this.

You can't dress Secession up and call it Revolution, it's plain anarchy. It couldn't happen with a man like George Washington in the White House. South Carolina is just working itself up again. We all know that slavery is wrong. And South Carolina wants to fight just to prove she's got a right to go on doing wrong!"

"Why, Gran, you sound exactly like Mr. Murray!"

"Most of the time he knows what he's talking about, Dee. And those new Cotton States are worse than South Carolina, even. They moved heaven and earth to get themselves into the Union, I can remember! And now, because they can't have it all their own way they want to get back out again and set up for themselves. But where will all this seceding stop? Pretty soon South Carolina will want to secede from Alabama, and then Charleston will be seceding from South Carolina—it will make us a laughing-stock abroad if we don't hang together now."

"Well, I wish Uncle Lafe could hear this!" cried Eden. "Why don't *you* write articles for the Philadelphia paper?"

"Maybe I could," she said complacently. "Wouldn't Dabney be surprised!"

A few days later Dabney wrote to say that if his father permitted he would like to spend Christmas in Charleston this year. And a few days after that came a brief note from Cabot to Gran, regretting that he would be unable to come back in time to see a Virginia Christmas after all. In the house in Williamsburg they looked at each other with anxious, questioning eyes. What was going on down there in Charleston? They had done without Dabney last year because he was in London. But Ransom sighed and refused to order him home. Dabney was old enough, said Ransom, to decide things for himself now.

And so, on the twentieth of December Dabney rushed into the Charleston drawing-room waving a flimsy placard. "We've done it!" he shouted at the two women who sat there. "We've begun!"

As he spoke all the churchbells in Charleston began to ring wildly, and scattered shouts were heard in the street outside the house, and running feet, and then the stutter of drums.

Caroline snatched the paper from him. *THE UNION IS DISSOLVED,* it said in tall black letters.

"We've seceded, mother," she announced quietly, and her face was white. And, "Oh, God help us all!" moaned Lavinia, and burst into tears.

Dabney stared at them.

"But I thought you'd be glad!" he said stupidly. "I thought you all *wanted* to secede!"

"The forts," said Caroline, staring at the paper in her hand. "What about the forts? They belong to us now. What will Major Anderson do?"

"Anderson will submit gracefully on any terms he can get," said Dabney. "What else can he do? He can't fight all Charleston with sixty men and a brass band! It's only a point of honor with him to hold Moultrie anyway, if you ask me—he's on our side!"

"A soldier's honor, though," said Caroline. "I'd hate to be in his shoes now. Heavens, what's that?"

"Cannon," grinned Dabney. "Oh, just for fun! They're firing the guns at the Citadel. Did you think the Yankees were bombarding us already?"

The windows rattled with another salvo and Caroline covered her ears.

"It sounds like war," she said, white-faced. "Where's Jonathan? Have you seen him? What's Jonathan going to do? Why doesn't he come home?" Her voice rose hysterically. "I want Jonathan here!"

"All right, all right, I'll go and find him," Dabney soothed her. "He's perfectly safe wherever he is, nobody is going to shoot at him! He's probably turning out the company for parade."

He tore out of the house without his hat—Dabney, the dandy, running down a street in Charleston in broad daylight without his hat! As he passed the Mills House he saw Cabot Murray standing quietly near the entrance, watching Charleston celebrate Secession.

"What will Lincoln do now?" he called, and saw that Cabot heard, and ran on towards Tradd Street where the bright militia uniforms were mustering in the December sunlight.

But it was his friend Anderson that Cabot was wondering about.

Major Anderson was a Kentuckian, married to a Georgia girl who, unlike the wives of most of the other officers at Fort Moultrie, had not followed her husband to Charleston. Mrs. Foster, wife of the engineer officer, was there, living in a charming little house at Moultrieville near the Fort, and some of the men housed whole families inside the fortress itself. Mrs. Foster was giving a party on Christmas night which a number of prominent Charleston people had promised to attend, and out of the kindness of her heart she had asked Major Anderson to bring along his Yankee friend, who must not be left to the dreary hospitality of the Mills House on Christmas. Cabot was wondering too, while Charleston shook with cannon fire and resounded with bells, what effect today's news might have on Mrs. Foster's party.

While he stood there a clod of dried horse manure struck the shoulder of his coat, and two half-grown boys ran by, looking back over their shoulders with rude gestures and yelling some insult which was drowned out by the bells and the music of a martial band. Cabot brushed off his coat, and one of the hotel servants—an Irishman, for the Mills House departed from custom in that it did not employ colored help in the dining-room—stepped close to him and said, "I'd go inside, sir, if I was you, before that happens again."

"What did they say?" asked Cabot. "I didn't hear."

"Something about a damn-Yankee, sir."

"Children," said Cabot, and strolled off in the direction Dabney had taken.

In the first block, two women he had met at Caroline's cut him dead from their carriages, and a very young man in a fancy uniform, hurrying to join his company, said at the top of his voice, "I wonder you dare to show your face today, sir!" and waited for no reply. At the corner Cabot ran into Anderson's orderly, who greeted him cordially and offered to walk along to the Mills House with him.

"I've just come from there," said Cabot, and the orderly raised his eyebrows.

"I'd go back if I were you, sir. Things may get rather rough."

"What about yourself?"

"I'm in uniform."

"That's no safe conduct now," said Cabot, and they went on together through the town.

There were ugly looks and rude remarks, but no one attacked them. When they parted an hour later the noise showed no sign of dying down, and the orderly made himself heard above it to say that he would see Cabot at Mrs. Foster's on Christmas night, no doubt.

During the next four days Cabot went about Charleston unmolested, but a good many people let him very severely alone. On Christmas morning he received a note from Mrs. Foster to say that Major Anderson was coming to Moultrieville direct from the Fort and had arranged for Mr. Murray to come out by boat at six o'clock, with directions where he would find the craft.

It rained throughout Christmas Day, and the short passage across the bay was chill and choppy. He arrived to find a family party, or combination of family parties, well under way. Children scampered and squealed and squabbled under foot, one of the rooms was cleared for dancing, and the punch had already begun to circulate. No one seemed to have a care in the world.

Anderson met him with a quizzical smile.

"I don't mean to sound inhospitable," he said, below the chatter all around them, "but I almost hoped you might have cleared off by now."

"You know why I'm here," Cabot said briefly.

"Devotion to duty," Anderson nodded ruefully. "I've got it too. The only thing is—I'm under orders."

"So am I, in a way."

"You mean as a special correspondent? I suppose your father would fire you from the newspaper if you retreated now!"

"He'd fire me twice as quick as he'd fire anybody else, just because he is my father. Besides—I think it matters a good deal what sort of impression is sent North just now."

"You're a great believer in the power of the Press, aren't you!"

"For good or evil," Cabot told him seriously. "And the dignity of the Press, too. I would like to see that upheld a little better than it is!"

"You know, in the event of military operations, you newspaper fellows could make a lot of trouble for us poor devils of soldiers if you start telling all you know," Anderson observed thoughtfully. "Now that every crossroads has a telegraph office, almost, you'll have to take care not to tip off the enemy to every move we make—just by sending in your daily article."

"In careless hands, the telegraph could certainly be a nuisance to you," Cabot agreed. "I'll remember what you say about that. Anyone reporting from the field should always show his copy to the commanding officer, probably, before he sends it off."

"As your commanding officer," Anderson said gently, "with a campaign on my hands, I should probably tell you to go to hell."

"You probably would. Well, perhaps they'll have to set up some sort of clearing house in Washington for news." He drank from the glass in his hand. "Where's your toddy, sir?"

"I'm not drinking tonight," Anderson murmured, his eyes travelling idly from face to face around the room. "Been having a little trouble with my insides. Have to be careful for a bit. How long do you expect to stay in Charleston?"

"Haven't decided. Waiting for things to break, I guess."

"Have you tried to use the telegraph office lately, by the way?"

"Yesterday. Why?"

"No trouble?"

"No trouble."

"That's good. I thought maybe now that the cat is out of the bag— that you write for the newspapers, I mean—you might find yourself a mite unpopular."

"No more so than usual."

"Who gave you away on that? I didn't."

"Somebody saw an old signed article of mine. It was to be expected. I should have travelled more incognito, maybe, but I didn't think it would matter so much. Too late now." He shrugged. "Well—how do we stand?"

"Oh, no, you don't!" said Anderson in all friendliness, even with affection. "Trying to pump *me* for your no 'count rag of a paper, eh! I'm surprised at you."

"Not for publication, sir. I'm just asking."

"Oh, in that case—and not that it's any secret—I have sixty-one men and a band to guard fifteen hundred feet of ramparts, which are entirely overlooked from Sullivan's Island. A mob could overrun us from the sand banks in no time, and I am not allowed to raise fortifications there until after I see them coming, for fear of offending South Carolina. Forts Sumter and Pinckney, on the other hand, are defended by one ordnance sergeant each, armed with worsted epaulets and stripes down their pantaloons."

"Incredible."

But Anderson only smiled, and his eyes followed a chain of laughing children which wound in and out among the guests.

"You'd be better off out at Sumter, wouldn't you?" Cabot asked after a minute.

"Oh, yeah, Sumter," drawled Anderson inattentively. "But it's all boarded up. And the worst of it is," he added half to himself, "my heart isn't in this war. It seems to me ridiculous and childish that a young, fearless, intelligent nation like this one cannot come to terms with itself. War is no remedy for what ails us, Cabot. I'm a soldier by trade, and yet I say that to go to war on this question of slavery— which doesn't really come into it at all—is simply ridiculous. A fine thing if you took *that* to the telegraph office!"

"We're going to get a war, aren't we, sir."

"We're going to get a war," Anderson assented wearily. "But how few can see that yet!" He shook his head, and sighed. "Somebody is going to take an awful whopping," he sighed.

"Better have a drink, sir. You'll feel better," Cabot suggested.

"No, thanks, not tonight. Those little beggars are going to be sick as dogs before morning, eating all those ices. You know, I didn't get a Christmas gift sent off to my wife up North. She'll think I forgot it, but I couldn't seem to get away to come into town lately."

"She'll be just as glad to see it if it comes a little late," Cabot comforted him. "Come and have dinner with me at the Mills House and we'll choose her something. I have to buy a gift myself. I'd like some advice."

"Courting a girl at last, are you?" said Anderson with interest.

"She's the sweetest thing in the world, sir. And she was ninety-five last birthday. How about dinner tomorrow?"

"No, not tomorrow, I'm afraid."

"Well, let me know the first time you are in town, then."

"Yes. I'll let you know."

10

The party broke up about midnight.

Early on the morning of the twenty-seventh, the inhabitants of Charleston saw smoke rising from Fort Moultrie. Crowds of citizens, their breakfasts untasted on the tables, rushed to the Battery or perched on the roofs of their houses, gazing seaward and speculating uneasily as to the meaning of the fire at the Fort. Some said they had heard gunfire during the night. Some said the garrison had burned blue-lights as signals. Finally from some workmen returning from Moultrieville they learned with astonishment which mounted rapidly to in-dignation that at dusk on the twenty-sixth under the very nose of the guard-boat the entire garrison had removed itself successfully to Fort Sumter, which could not be overlooked and which could not be mobbed from the shore. Fort Moultrie was left without flagstaff or officer, not even an ordnance sergeant in striped pantaloons, its guns were spiked, and its gun carriages set afire. Charleston called it an act of aggressive war against the sovereign State of South Carolina, and before midday the streets were full of militia uniforms.

Major Robert Anderson, of the United States Army, has achieved the unenviable distinction of opening civil war between American citizens, by an act of gross breach of faith, said the Charleston *Courier* hotly. *He has, under counsels of panic, deserted his post at Fort Moultrie and under false pretexts has transferred his garrison and military stores and supplies to Fort Sumter.* "Bob Anderson has opened the ball," said Caroline, smiling with white lips at her Jonathan, warlike in a red sash and sword worn with his frock coat, and a palmetto cockade.

Cabot was tickled. He couldn't help it. He had known Major Anderson in Trenton before Anderson was sent south in November—to take charge of the fortifications in Charleston harbor—and on Christmas Day the fellow had looked him in the eye and worried about sending a present to his invalid wife. *I'll let you know,* he had said, about coming to dinner at the Mills House. That was a good one. Trouble with his insides, like fun. He'd had an all night's job in front of him, getting ready to evacuate. And he had stood about till twelve o'clock, cold sober and looking blank as a new slate, enjoying the party at the Fosters'. I mentioned Sumter, Cabot thought, chuckling, and he never batted an eye. Boarded up, he chuckled. So it was all boarded up, the old fox! Well, that's one story the paper didn't get till afterward!

By evening on the twenty-seventh the militia in their new uniforms had stormed and occupied the unresisting forts Moultrie and Pinckney, and taken over the Post Office and Custom House building on Broad Street. Cut off from most of his acquaintances in the city, and owning no real friends there except Anderson and the Fosters, Cabot spent the day observing the endless excitement in the streets and pondering the events it would now be his duty to report to the daily paper which his father owned and edited in Trenton, and the other publications he served occasionally as a roving correspondent. He knew that he was seeing history made—tragic history, it seemed to him, as he watched the arrogant, noisy Charlestonians preparing so confidently for the war they never doubted their ability to win before it had even begun.

He returned to the Mills House at twilight for a meal and to write up his notes. But during the evening a new outburst of cheering and a torchlight procession with a band attracted him into the streets again and led him to the vicinity of the Custom House where some sort of oratory was going on.

He set his back against the corner of a building at the fringe of the crowd and began to listen. The speaker, who had obviously been tippling, thundered on, his discursive theme the unfair and ill-informed hostility of the North to South Carolina, who wouldn't hurt a fly; the iniquities of the Abolitionists in general and the Black Republicans in particular; and the abusive language used by Northern statesmen and Northern newspapers against the courteous, soft-spoken, unexcitable, unprejudiced people of South Carolina—suddenly at the finish of a sweeping gesture which nearly overbalanced him, his glance fell on Cabot, tall behind the crowd, and recognition glimmered in his bloodshot eyes.

"*There's one of 'em now!*" he cried, and his voice rose a notch triumphantly. "There's a Yankee now—*spyin'* on us down here—and telegraphin' back his lyin' drivel to be printed and enflame 'em against us some more—listenin' to every word I say, mind you, and takin' *notes* on it, no doubt, lookin' on at an honest man in that toplofty Yankee way of his—*eavesdroppin'*, that's what he's doin', *spyin'* on us——"

Too late Cabot recognized the dishevelled orator as one of the clerks at the telegraph office. Heads turned in the crowd, and it began to mutter—where?—who?—which one?—where was the spy? Cabot brought his weight firmly to both feet. He remembered subconsciously having passed the dark mouth of an alley further down the block at his back—blinded by the torches, he could not tell how far away it was —if he could just recede unnoticed beyond the edge of the glare and duck up the alley——

"*Yankee spy!*" some one yelled shrilly from the middle of the crowd. "Lemme at him! Show *me* the damn-Yankee spy!"

Cabot took several cautious steps backward, his eyes on the wall of faces. A man broke through the fringe and made a lunge at him.

Cabot threw him off easily, and he stumbled and fell and the crowd yelled. A tall figure loomed at Cabot's shoulder and he whirled defensively, his fist ready. It was Dabney.

"Steady," said Dabney coolly. "Some of them are pretty drunk. Look out!" They both dodged. Something whizzed past their heads and shattered against the wall. "Back up and to the left," said Dabney, moving with him, their faces towards the mob. "I'll try and stay with you, but if we get separated—stand away, you little rat, keep your filthy hands off me!" He knocked a small rumpled man backwards into the front ranks with a well-placed upper-cut, and the crowd's clamor rose to a roar. "If we get separated run for Caroline's stables and take the first horse you see. Get out of town—this is no joke——"

The crowd was throwing anything it could pick up now, as they retreated before it. Just as they reached the entrance to the alley something cold and sharp struck Cabot's head, knocking his hat off and starting a trickle of blood at the edge of his hair.

"Now *run!*" said Dabney, and they ran headlong into blackness, with the howl of the mob behind them.

After what must have been the length of a block they came to an opening between the outhouses and stables which lined the left hand side of the alley, under a gleam of light from an upstairs window. Cabot staggered dizzily, and applied his handkerchief to the cut, for it was bleeding into his eyes. He felt dazed and sick. As they paused, torchlight showed at the mouth of the alley, and the mob turned into it towards them, baying as it came.

"Down!" said Dabney, and pushed Cabot to his knees in deep grass which stank and was full of briers, and flung himself flat beside him. " 'Way down—now crawl—put that white handkerchief away—round here to your left—it's a henhouse and the stupid things will squawk if we're not careful—round this corner—keep crawling—keep *down*——"

Torchlight streamed through the narrow alley, and the tramp of feet and the strange unhuman sound a mob makes when it hunts a man both grew louder. The window above their hiding-place went up, and a head looked out.

"What is it?" yelled the head. "What's going on?"

"Spies!" came the answering yell from the mob, and a huge, bearded fellow capered drunkenly with a rope from which a noose dangled. *"Yankee spies!* Come and see the hanging!"

"I'll be there!" The window banged.

With Dabney's arm heavy across his shoulders, Cabot lay still in the shadow of the henhouse, his face smothered in the rank grass, and strove with nausea. His head was singing till he could not be sure where it left off and the noise of the mob began. But gradually the tumult did recede down the alley away from where they lay, and the light in the upper window went out, and they sat up in a blessed, spreading silence.

"You all right?" Dabney whispered.

"Yes, thanks. You're not in very good company, you know. Better leave me here and— Don't think I'm not grateful, but——"

"Rats!" said Dabney the elegant one. "I'm not doing it for you. I'd catch hell from Gran if I didn't get you out of this!"

"I'll be all right now. It needn't be your funeral too."

"You don't know Gran the way I do!" said Dabney, and got to his feet rather stiffly. "They caught me one on the shin with something. I *did* have a hat—here it is—come on, we'll get you a horse."

They retraced their steps cautiously to where they had entered the alley. The mob could still be heard in the next street, and people were hurrying to join it, and hanging out of windows, and shouting questions. Dabney set his own hat, a broad-brimmed felt with a blue Secession cockade, on Cabot's head and pulled it well down.

"All right, here we go—we've both had a little too much to drink, d'ya see, and I've lost my hat, but you still have yours—quite a load on, we must have—" He linked his arm to Cabot's and they started unsteadily down the street. "Could you bring yourself to sing *Dixie?*" he inquired, and began in a carolling tenor: *"Then I wish I was in Dixie —Hooray—Hooray——!"*

Cabot joined in in a fruity baritone. Their progress was erratic and apparently without direction—but slowly they gained on Caroline's stables.

"I had no idea you could sing!" said Dabney with admiration. "Let's join a choir some place. *In Dixie land I'll take my stand, To live and die in Dixie—Away—A-way—Away down south in Dixie!"*

Two boys ran out of a gate and blocked their way, staring—fugitives from an unwatched nursery.

"Where's the hanging?" one of them demanded. "Are we too late for the hanging?"

"You two sh-should be in bed," Dabney told them thickly. "You're sh-shure to catch it if they fin' out you want to—*what* hanging?"

"Yankee spies!" piped up the smaller of the two. "We want to see the Yankee spies!"

"Well, they aren't down thataway," said Dabney with authority, pointing in the direction of the alley and the mob. "Because we just came from there and *we* didn't shee—see—any s-spies."

"Jack*ee!* Benjamin! Goodness, what a fright you gave me!" Light poured out from an open door beyond the gate. A young woman ran down to the gate and caught the children by the hand. "What *do* you think you're doing, the minute my back is turned!"

Dabney swept her a gallant bow.

"Good evenin', ma'am," he said. "Excush my not havin' a hat, ma'am, but I lef' it—I l-left it in the café. Got to go back for it now. My friend, here, is a lil bit drunk, and tha's how I came to leave my hat—excush me—" He bowed again, and they staggered on, followed by her laughter.

On, towards Caroline's stables, unhurried, unsteady, very drunk indeed, apologizing to the amused passersby they met, many of them somewhat under the weather themselves, who beheld Dabney's elegant disarray with indulgence. Cabot kept silent, lest his speech betray him, and Dabney was endlessly loquacious in an affable stream of slightly thickened words which would have done credit to a professional actor in a well-conned part, building up the history of his incapacitated friend who had no head for brandy, and the forgotten hat in the café which stood in some street whose name had slipped his mind and which seemed to have mislaid itself while he wasn't looking.

Thus they traversed the city, arm in arm, the broad felt brim shading Cabot's face, the trickling stream of blood stealthily staunched and wiped away whenever they came to a good patch of shadow between lamp-posts. Thus they reached Caroline's stables from the alley at the rear, and found them unlighted, empty of coachmen and horse-boys, who had all run out to see the drilling on the Battery.

Dabney felt his way in with no trouble and began jingling harness. "Never saddled up in the dark before," he muttered. "Have to take my time about it. Hullo, Ladybird, don't you bite, now——"

Cabot leaned against the doorpost, feeling giddy and gone at the knees, while Dabney fumbled, cursed, and caressed the mare he saddled blindly. Finally he led her out of the stall and put the bridle in Cabot's hand.

"Well, there she is," he said. "Be good to her, she's been pretty well coddled all her life. I'd make for Georgetown if I were you, and——"

"I can't—can't take your horse," said Cabot dizzily, and Dabney bent forward to try and see his face in the dark.

"Say, are you all knocked up?" he asked anxiously. "Why didn't you tell me?"

"It's this crack on the skull," Cabot said fretfully. "I can't seem to— see straight." He leaned against the door-post again, the reins slack in his hand. "Be all right in a minute."

"Stay right where you are," Dabney ordered, and there was another period of jingling and fumbling and mumbling, and the creak of leather. "All right," he said, appearing again at Dabney's side. "I'm going with you. Safer anyway, with two of us. Know my way around."

"Please don't bother about me," said Cabot, rousing himself. "If you'll just give me a leg up, I'll manage——"

"All right—here you go—" Cabot mounted heavily from Dabney's bent knee. "Let's have your reins."

"I'd really rather you didn't——"

"Hand over your reins."

They moved out into the alley in single file. When they came to the street, which was nearly empty now, Dabney drew Cabot's horse alongside.

"Catch hold," he said, and Cabot took the reins again. "They're down that way still," Dabney said, listening. "Which means we go up this way. All right now?"

"Yes, I'm all right."

"Sure you are. Need some fresh air."

They set off side by side at a circumspect trot. After what seemed to Cabot like miles of almost deserted, ill-lighted streets they came to the edge of the city and a hard-surfaced turnpike. By then the frosty air had cleared his head a little, and he was feeling better.

"Let her out," said Dabney, and they took the turnpike at a canter, by starlight. When he finally drew rein, both men and horses were breathing hard, and dawn was greying the rim of the world. "This is the Georgetown road," he said. "Go to the inn there and go to bed. Say you were thrown, though it's an insult to Ladybird. I'll ride over tomorrow and see how you are. Don't come back to Charleston till I've seen you."

"It's useless to try and thank you——"

"Rats!" said Dabney. "I'd have done the same for any beau of Gran's!"

"Be sure to tell her you saved my life."

"Come and tell her yourself," retorted Dabney, and they shook hands in the dawn.

II

Caroline lost no time in reporting an affair which both Dabney and Cabot would have been quite willing to have forgotten. And as her letter arrived in Williamsburg before Dabney's return there, he couldn't just try to pretend that nothing had happened at all.

> "Your Mr. Murray," wrote Caroline the first week in January, and with no attempt to tone anything down, "was taken for a Yankee spy, or should I say *mis*-taken, and but for Dabney's interference might very well have been hanged to the nearest lamppost. It is impossible to get the whole story out of Dabney, of course, he shuts up like a clam, but it's all round town that Dabney was seen with him that night, ran away beside him with the mob after them, and somehow succeeded in getting him out of town in time to save his neck. Dabney was mysteriously absent from the house all day on the twenty-eighth, and Madeleine Morell—who *loved* knowing more about my own cousin than I did!—told me her husband heard that during the next evening Dabney brought Mr. Murray back to the Mills House, went up to his room while he packed and settled his account, and saw him on to the train for Wilmington. And only a few days earlier Dabney had been wanting to shoot Mr. Murray at sight! I shall *never* understand *men!*"

"Obviously, she never will, at this rate," nodded her grandmother resignedly, reading the letter aloud to Eden.

"I'm not quite sure I do myself, Gran," Eden admitted. "Why do you think Dabney changed his mind?"

"Probably because Mr. Murray behaved well in rather trying circumstances."

"You mean he wasn't afraid?"

"Any man is afraid of a hanging, Dee."

Eden shivered.

"I mean," Tibby Day went on gently, "that a man can be scared
stiff and still behave well. The best soldiers are always frightened, they
say. But they go on, just the same."

"Oh," said Eden faintly. "Is there any more to the letter?"

"Nothing but Caroline's version of the political situation. Charleston
seems to have just one idea, and that is to get possession of Fort Sumter. If Lincoln tries to reinforce Anderson, Charleston will fire on the
ships, she says. A fine thing!" Gran folded the letter disdainfully and
tossed it on to the silver-table beside her chair. "Let's hope Dabney will
make a little more sense—about everything—when he comes."

During January five more states seceded, followed by Texas on February first. The Secession Congress met at Montgomery on the fourth,
and elected Jefferson Davis as President of the new Confederacy. Virginia was not, of course, represented there, and maintained a watchful
sort of neutrality, as her own State Convention met at Richmond in a
last desperate effort to find a way of preserving the peace and the
Union. It was composed of committees of men from both North and
South who were willing to unite in the effort, which if it failed left
very little hope of anything but civil war. At the same time Virginia
was determined, as Lafe put it, not to be driven by the North nor
dragged by the Cotton States.

All four of the Spragues went to Richmond in February, as Lafe was
a delegate to the Convention and Sally demanded a season of gaiety
after a depressing Christmas, marred by apprehension over South Carolina's act of Secession. Once ensconced in the Spotswood Hotel, Sally
found it fashionable to be a rebel, and linger in the hallways of the
State House and flirt with one's favorite delegates as they came in and
out. Louise went to Richmond because Lafe would never have dreamed
of going without her. Sedgwick went because war between the States
would be to him the most dreadful calamity the world had ever seen,
and he was unable to stay away from the speeches and debates and the
forlorn hope of some inspired solution.

But as the days passed, Sedgwick saw with a sort of creeping horror that nobody was going to be able to solve it like this. The sessions of the Convention seemed to him an orgy of loose declamation and purposeless resolutions—the Convention was talking itself to death, he wrote Sue, and the sands of time were running out.

Sue knew only too well what worried Sedgwick most. If war came, every man in the South would be expected to take up arms against the North. The Spragues were a fighting family, they never held back. Even Lafe at forty-one would expect to serve in the field. But Sedgwick, especially since the visit of Cabot Murray, whom he had liked and admired, saw no sense whatever in shooting at his fellow Americans. Sue knew that Gran backed him up in this extraordinary viewpoint. She knew too that to Lafe it was inexplicable, wrongheaded, and humiliating. And she even wished in her secret heart that with regard to the war Sedgwick could be a little more like Dabney, who had come back from Charleston to join one of the volunteer companies that drilled on the Palace Green—Dabney wore, until the new uniforms were ready, his grandfather Julian's red sash and sword, which had seen Yorktown.

It was never that Sedgwick was a coward, she knew. Sedgwick wasn't afraid to fight, even though it might look that way. If some foreign power had menaced Charleston, or Boston either, Sedgwick would have been the first to join the defending army. But he had a rational conviction that America was all one family, and that for one section to take up arms against another was as fantastic and unnecessary as it would have been for Dabney to go gunning for Fauquier because they had started some kind of brotherly wrangle. Sedgwick didn't use any of the familiar arguments against war between the States. He didn't consider it worth while to mention that the South would be hopelessly outnumbered and outgunned from the start, or that slavery ought to be done away with anyway, or that Lincoln had won in a perfectly fair and legal election in which the whole country had participated equally. He simply said that war between the States was silly. And that wasn't a very good argument, because it was a dead end.

Sue knew that Sedgwick himself would look silly if Dabney and Fauquier and Grafton Crabb and all the others joined the Southern army and went away to fight without him. Fight where, she would wonder, lying in bed at night with Eden asleep beside her and the moon coming in the window. Where would the battles be? Down at Charleston, of course, that's where the forts were. She pushed away from her, night after night, the disturbing knowledge that there was a fort in Virginia too—Fortress Monroe, down at the end of the Peninsula beyond Yorktown, was full of Federal soldiers. Would there be fighting at Fortress Monroe as well as at Fort Sumter? If there was, or if the Yankees at Fortress Monroe started to come up the Peninsula, Sedgwick couldn't possibly stand by, because Williamsburg would lie right in their path. Once the British had come to Williamsburg, Gran could remember. The militia couldn't stop them, but it tried. Sedgwick would have to try....

Sue would go over and over it after the light was out, losing sleep till she began to lose weight as well, and one night Eden, who wasn't sleeping any too well herself, roused to feel her sister lying rigid with the concentrated stillness of the wakeful.

"Sue—aren't you asleep?" she whispered, reaching out a hand.

"Not yet."

"Why not?"

"I got to thinking."

"What about?"

"Dee—do you think there's going to be a war?"

"I don't know. I'm afraid so. We must try not to worry, they're doing all they can in Richmond."

"Sedgie says that's no good."

"Well, he's got no right to say that yet. With men like Uncle Lafe there they ought to find a way."

"Tell me honestly, Dee, do you think Sedgie ought to join a company and drill, the way Dabney does?"

"Well, I—I'm a little surprised that he doesn't, aren't you?"

"Do you think Uncle Lafe minds dreadfully?"

"Well, I—think he may begin to mind soon, if—if things go on like this. You see, the Spragues have always——"

"Has he said anything? How do you know how he feels?"

"Only what Aunt Louise said to mother when Dabney joined the company."

"What was that?"

"She only said she hoped Sedgwick would do the same soon, because it seemed to be the thing to do and—and Uncle Lafe couldn't understand why he had refused, and——"

"They think Sedgie is a coward, don't they!" cried Sue fiercely in the dark.

"Oh, no, Sue, it's no question of courage! At least not yet. It's rather as though Sedgwick just wouldn't take the trouble, or as though he— You see, dear, if the boys drill now and there isn't a war, there's no harm done. But if there is a war, then they can be ready a little sooner. It will save time if we have to—have an army suddenly."

"Sedgie isn't afraid to fight!" Sue said passionately, lying on her back, staring up at the ruffled tester of the bed with hot, dry eyes. "Sedgie isn't afraid of anything! It's just that he thinks it doesn't make any sense. Do *you* think it makes sense, Dee, for Sedgie to join a company that is drilling to learn how to fight people like Mr. Murray? Look at Dabney in Charleston—he took quite a lot of trouble to save Mr. Murray's life! Well, there you are! That's what Sedgie means! The Yankees are just like us. We don't want them killed. Suppose Dabney and Mr. Murray met on a battlefield now—would they have to kill each other? If it was Sedgie instead of Dabney, would *he* have to kill Mr. Murray? Would Uncle Lafe *want* him to?"

"Honey, I don't know," Eden moaned, and drew Susannah's taut little body into her arms. "Let's not think about it. Let's go to sleep."

"It doesn't do any good not to think about it," Sue said, muffled in her hair. "The next time you look it's still there, getting worse all the time. Fauquier says all the older boys at the Institute will be officers at once if the war starts. Fauquier wants to fight. Even Barry talks about it. What will Mr. Murray do?"

"I haven't an idea."

"Where do you suppose he went after Charleston?"

"Back home, perhaps. He meant to be in Washington for the inauguration."

"Will he come here again?"

"Oh, honey, do let's try to go to sleep!"

"You liked him—didn't you, Dee."

"Yes—very much."

"Would you marry him?"

"Well, I—I'm not likely to get the chance."

"He's nice. I liked him too, and Gran was positively *smitten* with him! If Yankees are like that, I don't see why we can't get along with them without a war."

"We'll find some way, Sue—we must. They'll work out something at Richmond."

"Sedgie says all they do there is egg each other on. You know how excited Uncle Lafe gets. It's almost as though Dabney were Uncle Lafe's son and Sedgie were father's, isn't it."

"It might have been better that way."

"Imagine Sedgie being my brother!" said Sue, amused, and fell asleep with the feeling that in some dim, unexplored way she was very glad he wasn't.

12

"In your hands, my dissatisfied fellow countrymen, and not in mine, is the momentous issue of civil war," said Mr. Lincoln in his inaugural speech. "The Government will not assail you. You can have no conflict without being yourselves the aggressors. You have no oath registered in heaven to destroy the Government; while I shall have the most solemn one to preserve, protect, and defend it."

That was the first real forecast of his policy, and the prospects of peace did not brighten as the telegraph wires carried his words to Richmond and Charleston and Montgomery. As Lafe had predicted, Southern officers in the United States Army were resigning their commissions and returning home to await events. The Confederate Government was therefore able to order General Beauregard to Charleston, and it looked as though South Carolina was going to try to take by force what she regarded as her own property. There were rumors that the garrison at Sumter would be withdrawn, and other rumors that it would be reinforced at whatever cost.

"Guess who is here now!" wrote Sally to Eden from Richmond. "Mr. Cabot Murray, no less! He has come to see the Convention, and when I asked him what paper his articles would appear in, he showed his teeth at me the way he does, and said—'The same ones as usual'—as though that was any help! People like him here, and because of his Washington connections he has come with introductions to some houses it is very difficult for Yankees to get into any more. I am quite popular because I knew him even before the Charleston episode, which everyone talks about, so it's no good my pretending it's a secret! Whatever hit him on the head that night has left quite a fascinating scar, near his temple on the right side. He and Sedgwick are thick as thieves, and I think Father is afraid Sedgwick will be corrupted even further into the Yankee viewpoint! Mr. Murray says poor Major Anderson is destined to be the scapegoat no matter what happens—though Anderson is married to a Georgia lady and is very Southern in sentiment, he has a stern sense of duty. Everybody says if only his sense of duty had not run away with him, he would never have gone and put his head in a hole, and made everything worse than it was before! Our Washington friends are all wondering what Colonel Lee will do—the man who settled John Brown's hash at Harper's Ferry— he is home on leave at Arlington now, and they say he is very depressed and very much against Secession. They also say he is the handsomest man in the world. . . ."

"Lee," said Tibby Day thoughtfully. "Robert Lee, that must be. I remember. He married into the Washington family—Mary Custis, her name was. His father was Light Horse Harry Lee, in our war. Now who," she demanded suddenly of Eden as though she had been meaning to ask some one for some time, "who is this man Jefferson Davis they have dug up down there in Alabama?"

"He was a senator, wasn't he?" said Eden doubtfully.

"Was he, indeed!" said Tibby Day, and her needles clicked angrily. "A fine thing! Where was he born, then?"

"I'll have to ask Father. I think he comes from Mississippi."

"Aha! Very likely! Not a Virginian, you can be sure of that!"

"Shall I read you the rest of the letter?"

"Sally is a goose," said her grandmother. "Is there anything more there about Mr. Murray?"

"No."

"Then I think I've heard enough."

On the fourth of April a test vote in the Virginia Convention showed a majority of two to one against Secession, and there was a popular outcry that the conservative element was overbalancing the young blood and leading them into undignified compromise.

A few days later Tibby Day got a note from Cabot to say that if she would permit him to pay his respects on Saturday the thirteenth he would come and bring her her Christmas present from Charleston.

"And about time, too!" she remarked, looking pleased all the same. "I'm glad he will see Williamsburg looking so pretty, in the spring." And she added, after a moment—"I wonder what he has got for me."

II. APRIL 13, 1861

I

She had forgotten, because she so seldom went beyond the garden gate any more, that Williamsburg no longer looked quite as pretty as it had done in her youth. She forgot that the Palace had burned down, that the Raleigh and the Capitol were deserted shells, that even the College was shabby and patched up, and many of the fine houses wanted paint and sheltered only the remnants and relicts of the proud families who had lived there in the days which were so much more vivid to her now than recent times since her world had shrunk.

But Williamsburg did look very pretty when Cabot returned to it that Saturday in mid-April. The mulberry trees which lined the wide, unpaved seven-eighths of a mile which was the Duke of Gloucester Street were a new, tender green, and flowers showed bright in the dooryards, and the air was soft and sweet and scented with spring, and the women were wearing light dresses. To anyone fresh from the crowded confusion of the Spotswood Hotel in Richmond the bygone town seemed a little lost paradise of dignity and leisure.

Cabot had promised himself that he would not come back to Williamsburg. Even in the very act of buying Tibby Day's Christmas present on his way out of Charleston, with Dabney at his elbow, he had told himself that the thing to do was to leave the parcel with Dabney—that way she would get it sooner, and his responsibility for it would be ended. Instead, he paid for it in a rather embarrassed silence and when they left the shop Dabney was still trying not to wonder who the lady was for whom this unsentimental-seeming Yankee took so much trouble and chose such an expensive and unusual gift. Now that he heard Cabot was coming to bring Gran a belated Christmas present he wondered some more, and knew that if it was the same purchase he had seen, Cabot's taste and tact were irreproachable.

To receive him, she wore her lilac-grey silk gown, and Eden, after turning out her wardrobe and changing her mind half a dozen times

73

and anxiously consulting the weather, which remained warm and bright, chose a light blue lawn with white lace at the neck and wrists, and enormous angel sleeves. Once she had got it on she felt uncomfortably that she had "dressed up" too much for a solitary afternoon caller, but Gran, placidly wearing her own best, said that one might as well give the poor man something pleasant to look at these days, he must be very tired by now of women who wore cockades and talked politics.

He arrived with no less than three neatly wrapped parcels under his arm, and was conducted at once to Gran's room, where Eden too awaited him, in what she secretly termed a state of idiotic twitters. No one else had ever made her feel like that before. No one, she was sure, but Cabot Murray could ever do it again. But her eyes and smile were so steady as she gave him her hand that he was surprised to find her fingers cold with what could only be nervous excitement matching his own, and his long first look was rueful and kind.

Cabot too had had time now to contemplate what had happened between them last autumn, and it did not fit in with his plans. He was no less in love with Eden in Washington than he had been in Williamsburg, but less than ever at that distance could he see any way to join that new absorbing emotion to the pattern of his life. Besides, he still mistrusted it a little, because he had never believed such a thing could happen to him. This headlong, consuming, sobering, and enduring desire was a very different thing from the casual, skilfully conducted flirtations with the Washington belles he was accustomed to know, or the dull, chaperoned acquaintance with marriageable misses who fluttered their eyelashes at him in modest attempts to interest so famous a catch as Cabot Murray. He laughed in the faces of the pouting belles, and the misses bored him. He believed that he understood both types, and he gave each of them what they seemed to expect—audacious, disconcerting, sometimes quite fascinating advances to one, and a more or less polite indifference to the other.

He had been amused, and sometimes stimulated, and once or twice rather attracted, but he had never been stirred as this honest, laughing Virginia girl had stirred him, with her level green gaze and her odd little dignity, and her sweet reposefulness which was just her breeding. Once he had admitted to himself that he wanted her for his own, he was so drunk with surprise, and whatever else, that he had recklessly admitted it to her before his conscience, or whatever it was, reminded him that it would never do. His was no life to offer a woman brought up as she had been. He lived at the end of a telegraph line, he was off at the drop of a hat for Chicago or Charleston or Boston or far less suitable places. His best friends were a professional journalist's friends, the like of whom she had never imagined—men like himself without roots or ties or illusions, often without manners or morals, women who —never mind. He had lived like that deliberately, wilfully, making a rude gesture at his own upbringing now that he was clear of Trenton, New Jersey, and all it had stood for during his suppressed, rebellious boyhood. Until last autumn it had satisfied him to live like that, but it was nothing to offer Eden. Therefore Eden must be only a dream—a sort of mirage, forever beyond his reach.

During the past winter he had striven thus to convince himself that he could not afford to think of Eden, except as a fragrant episode which was finished. He had seen her once upon a time, and she was sweet. But that was all. No more Eden for him. Even if there was not going to be a war—and there was—but even if no war had threatened, there was no place in his life for Eden. Even if he tried he could never tone himself down now to the sort of fellow Eden ought to marry. Even though he loved her with all he had to give, it was not enough, he was not her kind, she would be lost and unhappy and bewildered in his catch-as-catch-can existence. Besides—he never meant to marry....

Thus he reasoned the winter away, while the war fever rose, and the States seceded one by one, and the little garrison at Sumter held out in its dreary sense of virtue, and Washington waltzed and whispered and waited to see what Lincoln would do. Then he was sent to Richmond to report the Virginia Convention for the newspaper. And there he met Sally again, and became friends with Sedgwick, and heard enchanting stories of Gran, and the need to see Eden once more grew and grew. He knew that he had said things to her that he had no business to, and he told himself that the least he could do was to remove himself once and for all from her life....

And so here he was, on that Saturday in April, and his big fingers closed crushingly on the slim cold ones surrendered to him, and his eyes lingered in spite of him even after he had let her hand go.

"Always wear a blue dress, Eden," he said as his only greeting. "I always seem to think of you in a blue dress."

Eden flushed and glanced at Gran to see how this easy use of her given name would be received, knowing quite well that Felicity's eyebrows would have risen.

"That's because you've never seen her in a pink one," said her grandmother.

"I thought redheads couldn't wear pink," he remarked with interest.

"She's not really red," Gran pointed out without reproach. "She doesn't freckle."

"Titian," he suggested, grinning, and she nodded, while Eden found it impossible to say anything at all in this ridiculous conversation which ignored her presence as though she were a child, or a picture. With relief she saw him lay one of the parcels in Gran's lap. "There's your gift from Charleston," he said affectionately. "I suppose you know that without young Dabney you might never have got it?"

"So I hear," she murmured, her fingers already busy at the cord. "Dabney knows how much I like gifts!" And their eyes met briefly with laughter.

Inside the wrapping paper was a box, and inside the box was a folded fan. She lifted it out and spread it carefully in her two small hands—a French fan painted on silk in the manner of Fragonard, with a rose-clad lady bestowing coquettish fingertips on a bowing youth in blue knee breeches, a skirted coat, and a sword. Both wore their hair powdered and they stood in a classic grove with a broken column and a marble bench beyond. The colors were as fresh and dainty as they had ever been. The sticks and guard were mother-of-pearl, pierced and gilt. She who so loved presents held it in a silent rapture for a long moment and then said softly——

"It's the loveliest thing I ever owned. Regina Sprague had one, when I was a girl—she brought it back with her from London. I never thought—" She looked up at him, brimming with happiness. "I never thought I'd have one!"

"As soon as I saw it, it belonged to you," he smiled.

"It must be very old," she said, awed. "It must be older than I am."

"By fifteen or twenty years at least. And it wears its age as lightly."

"Thank you," she whispered. "Thank you for my lovely gift. Look, Eden—I told you—they wore their hair powdered—I can remember——"

"Yes, Gran, it's beautiful." Eden became aware of a white-wrapped parcel extended towards her.

"Yours isn't from Charleston," he was saying. "I got it in Washington."

"Th-thank you." Eden took the parcel in her cold little fingers and opened it rather fumblingly. Embedded in white satin inside a jeweler's case which was marked with the famous name of Galt lay a silver filigree bouquet-holder with an inlaid mother-of-pearl handle.

"Merry Christmas, Eden," he said gently while she stared at it.

"It's—the loveliest one I ever saw, but—" Her eyes sought Gran's, and his voice cut in decisively.

"But mother would never allow me to accept jewelry from a gentleman," he finished for her.

"Nonsense," said Tibby Day. "It's not to wear. No more than my fan, that is. Of course she can accept it."

"Gloves wear out," he explained, looking savage and sulky. "Sweets get eaten up. Flowers fade. Books pall. That's the list of acceptable presents, isn't it? I wanted this one to be something more permanent, I guess. It is for your gay times, Eden—mind you carry it while you're waltzing, won't you."

She looked up at him helplessly.

"But we have no gift for you," she mourned.

"Ah, but we have." Tibby Day laid down the fan and rose from her chair and took a polished wooden box a little longer and deeper than a book but no wider from a table by the window and carried it back to where Cabot stood and put it in his hands. "It came from England with my husband in 1774. It held his pens and the penknife and the ink and the sand-box. Since you are a writer too, you will find it convenient when you are travelling, as he did. I want you to have it." Thus magnificently did she erase from him the stigma of journalism. Moved beyond speech, he was too wise to attempt to refuse so precious a gift. He bent and kissed the hands that gave it. "And now tell us what's in the other parcel," she commanded, returning to her chair with a resolute matter-of-factness.

"Bonbons for Myrta from Gautier's," he replied, striving also for lightness. "They are all done up separately in silver paper with lace and artificial flowers, and are very highly regarded by my sister Melicent, so I thought——"

"Myrta will be quite beside herself," remarked her grandmother gently. "I think we won't give them to her just now. I'm glad to see that you are soft-hearted enough to make your little sister a present sometimes, Mr. Murray."

"She had been ill," he said defensively before he thought, and then caught the gleam in her eyes and grinned. "I guess she nearly died of surprise, at that. But after I had been here and seen how this family treats its young, I—well, I felt sort of sorry for her. Not that she's any Susannah," he added, glancing up at them under his brows. "I took a good look at her the last time I was home, and good Lord, I never saw a plainer child!"

"She probably only wants bringing out," said Susannah's grandmother. "If you took a little interest in her it might make all the differ-ence. Are they teaching her properly?"

"I haven't an idea. She goes to a little day school, I believe, and is learning to play the piano and sing *Home Sweet Home*. I found that rather funny, as my father can't bear the sound of music, and so she has to do her practice scales when he is out of the house."

"That's very odd," she remarked, treading carefully now that she was on the trail again. "I never heard before of a man who hated music. Has he any reason?"

"Well, yes, he has a reason." The words fell coldly one by one, as though he forced himself to utter them against his will. "You see, his first wife, who was my mother, ran away with a tramp violinist."

There was a silence in the room. Then she said slowly——

"Melicent is her child—not the housekeeper's."

"How did you know?"

"In my bones."

"Sent back to us when she died. Named for her, not out of senti-ment, but to remind us both, my father and me, of the perfidy of women. I am only just beginning to see how wrong he is to take it out on poor Melicent. I've just suddenly realized that the child of my mother's shame is a human being like the rest of us. She can thank you for that—and Eden here—and young Susannah."

"Does she know why she has been punished all her life?"

"No. At least I don't think she does. She was only a few weeks old when she came to us. She has always called the housekeeper Mother. But her eagerness to learn music—that must come from *him*. If my father knew, he would stamp it out of her. I felt like doing it myself."

"No, no." She laid a quick hand on his sleeve. "Let her have the music if she wants it. She will need it. Be kind to her. Because you can be kind, you know, when you like. Never let her know the rest. That is—if she is fond of the woman who stands in her mother's place."

"They seem to get on all right together. I guess they have to. They've nobody else."

"And your father—can't he ever forgive——?"

"I sometimes think my father is a little mad," he said briefly. "I suppose in his place I should be."

"Yes," she nodded, and her fingers moved caressingly, soothingly on his sleeve, as though she had forgotten they were there. "Yes, I can see that. But it's hard on the child. It's been hard on you too. I can see that."

"On the contrary, I have always considered it a useful lesson," he said steadily. "You see, I can remember my mother quite well. And she wasn't the kind of woman you would expect it of. She was as sweet and honest to look at as—as your grandson's wife. Not so beautiful, of course. But not—not a light woman, you would have said."

"Now you're talking like a New Englander," she took him up sharply. "How do you know what drove her? How old were you when she went?"

"About twelve."

"And was she happy, before he came by? Was she cherished, was there laughter in the house, and was she made to feel that it could not get along without her?"

He looked surprised, a little shocked.

"My father was devoted to her. He says himself he had never looked at another woman."

She made a small, derisive sound.

"That's the wrong end of the poker," she said. "If a man has married the right woman for him, the more he sees of other women the better he likes his own."

Cabot looked still more surprised.

"I never thought of it quite that way before," he admitted.

"You have a lot to learn about women, Mr. Murray."

"Yes," he agreed humbly. "I begin to think so." His eyes sought Eden's, and she gave him a small brave smile with her heart in it.

"You have come to the right place, though," Tibby Day consoled him. "Eden can teach you how to trust a woman."

He shot her one of his quick, suspicious glances, and then relaxed as though resigning himself to her mindreading.

"It is useless to go on saying that this is the most extraordinary family I ever saw," he sighed. "I suppose you felt it in your bones too that I am in love with Eden—but why you are not going to raise Cain about it is still beyond me."

"I don't say that Ransom won't raise Cain about it," she qualified at once. "But I'm on your side, for whatever that is worth."

"That is mighty good of you, ma'am." He looked down at his strong, fine hands knotted in front of him. "But I have already told Eden that she must try to forget me. Anyway, it's out of our control now. Just as I was leaving Richmond they gave me a telegram from Washington. Those fools at Charleston have fired on Fort Sumter."

"Ah's me!" cried Tibby Day. "What will that mean?"

"My dears, it means that I have come to say good-bye," he said very gently. "Virginia is sure to secede now. The South is going to try to take Washington with an army. The North will meet them more than half way. All hell is loose, that's what it means. But I had to see you both once more before it starts."

"Are you—going to fight?" Eden got out faintly, for most of all she had to know what war would mean to this man whose life was more important to her than all the garrison at Sumter.

"I'm a Special Correspondent," he told her grimly. "Unless I get fired for coming here today instead of camping in that telegraph office at Richmond, it will be my job to write this war, not fight it."

"Shall you—does that mean you will be under fire?"

"Naturally. Would you have me report a battle with my feet on a desk in the Trenton office?"

"What will Anderson do?" brooded Tibby Day. "Will they all be killed at Sumter?"

"It seems likely, if they try to shoot it out. Anderson has about sixty men, and Beauregard has about seven thousand roundabout Charleston, armed and spoiling for a fight. Fort Sumter was designed for a garrison of six hundred and fifty, and its strong side is towards the sea. Sumter is no good if the rest of the harbor is held by an enemy. It points the wrong way."

"I knew his father," she brooded.

"Whose father? Anderson's?"

She nodded.

"Dick Anderson was one of Lafayette's aides at Yorktown. My husband liked him. He came to dinner at the Raleigh. Such a *little* time ago," she sighed. "How have things gone so wrong? What will Lincoln do about it?"

"I think Lincoln will put his foot down, as he threatened to do last February when I saw him in New York. He is convinced that to abandon United States property now to insurgents on any plea whatever of necessity would be misconstrued by the very element he is trying to control. He is prepared to fight the South to prevent national destruction."

"Won't it come to the same thing in the end?"

"Not if the North wins."

"Even then, he can't force the South to be friends."

"He hopes to force them to come to their senses first of all, I think. But I am afraid, from what I have heard in Richmond, that once the bloodshed actually begins, Virginia is bound to secede. Which is one of the reasons that Charleston is yelling for blood."

"Then you won't be safe here," Eden said. "You must leave at once."

"Oh, I'll get kicked out of Richmond very soon now," he agreed. "What's more, you won't be allowed to speak to me at all, once war is declared."

"Must you go back to Richmond?"

"Tonight."

"But—at Charleston they tried to—" Her lips quivered.

"Tried to hang me, yes. May I have the loan of Dabney to Richmond as a bodyguard?"

"Oh, please don't joke about it, why can't you go straight back to Washington?"

"And hide behind a printing-press? For shame, Eden, your brothers are going to be in this thing, you know. Are you going to try to hustle them to the safest place there is—or is it only that you think a Yankee is a mollycoddle?"

"Don't tease her, Mr. Murray, she's never seen a war and it frightens her. It frightens me, and I've seen two or three. You'll be allowed to carry arms, I suppose, even if you are not in the ranks?"

"I don't know what my status as correspondent will be. Except for a few men who went to the Crimea for the London newspapers, nobody has ever reported a war before as I would like to. I've been working on it in Washington for weeks, and I think I can get a Staff appointment which will give me leeway in the field and some usefulness as well. You see, ma'am, I believe in the power and the freedom of the Press. I believe that reporting a war, or a political convention, is a solemn responsibility. Our free educational system is teaching a great mass of people to read. Well, then, it seems to me we ought to be damned careful, begging your pardon, what we hand out to them for a penny or two, to read. Newspapers are being read like the word of God by millions—and who writes them? A collection of cranks and paid agitators and down-at-heel hacks with an occasional genius like Greeley or Wise, and even then they have an ax to grind. I say the whole system is wrong. I say we want a corps of trained, educated, decently paid observers to write our newspapers. Men with a policy, certainly, but not crackpots or political henchmen or brilliant bums. And it looks as though I'm going to have a chance to justify my ideas on a rather large scale, pretty soon. But you can see, can't you, that it's not going to make me very popular in this section of the country from now on, if I am attached as a Special Correspondent to the Northern Army!"

"But I'm still on your side," insisted Tibby Day, smiling at him confidently, and he laughed and took her two hands in his.

"God bless you, ma'am! If I could only believe that nothing would ever change that, no matter what comes! Can you manage never to think of me as an enemy, even in the midst of a bitter war?"

"War isn't going to make you any different."

"War always makes a difference. For one thing, I can't lay claim to Eden as things are now." He shut his teeth on it resolutely. "I shall be with the wrong army, God knows where. I can't even ask her to wait for me till it's over, in the circumstances—I expect to be in it, up to my neck, from now on, and my chances of coming out of it whole enough to be worth waiting for are—not very good. It's bad enough, what a woman must endure in a war, if her man is on the same side as her brothers." His grip on the frail hands in his was that of a man in pain. "I'm trying to do the right thing for Eden, no matter what it costs me now—so maybe I ought to say, never let her be an old maid on my account, will you."

"Eden would like to say," broke in a rather decided voice on their left, "that she is sick of being talked about as though she was some-·where else, or had gone stone deaf. And this is the third time you have refused yourself in my name, Mr. Murray, without giving me a chance to say No on my own account, and I'm getting a little sick of that too!"

His sombre face broke all up into laughter, and he rose suddenly, seeming to fill the quiet room with the magnetic masculine vitality they both found so irresistible.

"Oh, heaven, sweetheart, don't go back on it now and say you'll have me after all!" he cried, as though he had again gracefully accepted a dismissal, and she looked up at him defiantly, her chin out.

"Gran will bear witness," she said steadily, though her hands were cold and shaking, and her heart beat thickly, "that you behave very much like a man who is frightened to death he will be accepted before he can get out of the house!"

His laughter went as though she had struck him a blow—surprise, anger, humiliation, and a kind of incredulous pain brought the dark blood surging up to his hair, so that the small scar stood out livid on his temple, and the old harsh lines settled deep around his arrogant lips. Before he could speak, Tibby Day stood up with a soft rustle of lilac-grey silk.

"It is time you learned that you will never get any thanks for trying to cheat a woman of tears she has a right to shed," she informed him severely. "If Eden was as old as I am, she would be able to see that you have tried to spare her. That was your mistake, Mr. Murray. I am going to leave you to retrieve it in your own way now." She swept royally towards the door. "I promise not to listen at the keyhole, but I must warn you I'll come back in five minutes." With the knob in her hand she turned on him again where he stood motionless, towering, apparently paralyzed, in the middle of the room. "Don't you be afraid of her," she advised sternly. "And don't forget, either, that no war lasts forever."

The latch clicked behind her.

2

Thirty seconds of their five minutes went by in silence before he moved. Then in what seemed a single stride he was across the space between them and had lifted Eden by the shoulders out of her chair so that she stood against him, shaking and weak, feeling the sharp bite of his fingers as part of a new delight, her eyelids down against the blinding nearness of his searching gaze. As usual, he said the last thing she looked for.

"How old are you, Eden?"

"I'm—nearly eighteen," she announced stoutly.

"Oh, God help me, that's *too* young! It's robbing the cradle for sure!" His lips came down on her cheek, travelled upward gently and spoke in her hair. "Never say I didn't try to do the right thing for once, my darling—and never doubt it was killing me with every breath I drew!"

"Gran's not so young," she whispered, and her cheek found his and rested there, warm and confiding, and he felt her smile. "Gran always knows what's best for me."

His arms crept round her slowly, and then tightened with a sudden crushing possessiveness which made her gasp.

"You're trembling," he discovered, and she felt the labor of his heart. "Eden, I'm a clumsy sort of fool, what makes you think I can ever make you happy?"

"Perhaps because you can make me so miserable," she murmured, and he eased his hold a little to try and see her face.

"When have I ever done that?"

"When I thought you might never come back to Williamsburg."

"Lord knows I tried not to. But only for your sake, Eden, not because I didn't want you."

She caught at his shoulders with both hands, giving herself more completely into his embrace, as her confidence grew a little with the knowledge of her own power to move him, believing blissfully that now he could never frighten or confuse her again.

"Hereafter you will not lie to me for my own good," she commanded. "How could I be better off thinking you didn't love me than——"

"But I told you that I loved you!" he interrupted roughly.

"Not like this," she insisted, nestling, and he shook with laughter while his arms cradled her.

"You're a very forward young woman, Eden," he remarked with delight. "No really nice girl takes to lovemaking quite so fast."

"How do you know?" she murmured, holding to his shoulders, her face against his shirt ruffle and cravat. "Would you really have gone away and left me to love you forever all alone?"

"Will you, Eden? Will you love me forever?"

"And a day," she promised solemnly, and he found her chin with his fingers and tipped back her head to his kiss.

She was still in his arms when the latch turned slowly, and they stood apart, unembarrassed but grave, as Eden's grandmother re-entered the room.

"Well, now you *have* done it," Cabot told her accusingly. "What becomes of us now?"

"Ransom has just come in down stairs," she said. "He's heard about Fort Sumter."

"But has he heard about Eden, that's the question," Cabot remarked.

"Well, yes—I did mention it."

"I suppose he's waiting on the stairs with horse pistols?"

"He's in the drawing-room with Felicity. I think you had better go and speak to them."

"Yes, I think I had." Instinctively his fingers sought his cravat in a nervous gesture.

"Eden will stay here with me. You must tell her good-bye now." She picked up the flat wooden box from the table where he had laid it, and handed it to him with a smile. "And don't be forgetting your gift, either. God bless you, Cabot Murray."

He looked down at her, so small, so straight, in the spreading lilac grey gown.

"Let's not say good-bye," he said. "Let's just say—good-night." She received his kiss on her cheek, and turned away towards the window, while he kissed Eden once more and backed away from her to the door. "You'll hear from me now and then, no matter what happens," he promised. "Even after I leave Richmond, I'll find some way to communicate——"

"We can wait," said Tibby Day. "I had to wait, when I was Eden's age."

Cabot took the stairs nimbly and brought up against the drawing-room door with a feeling of schoolboy panic. Suppose they threw him out. They had every right to. Suppose they forbade even letters. Suppose—if it was a long war—they talked her into marrying some one else. . . . After having screwed himself up for months to live without her, the idea of losing her was now completely intolerable.

"Come in," said Ransom, and the Yankee stepped over the threshold. Felicity sat with a bit of white work in her hands, and Ransom had placed himself behind her chair.

"Yes," Cabot said at once in answer to their eyes. "I want to marry Eden. How it happens that she is willing I don't pretend to know, but that's the way it is."

"If this news about Sumter is true," said Ransom slowly, "we may be in for a long war."

"I think that is very probable, sir."

"And we shall find ourselves on opposite sides, I'm afraid."

"I'm afraid so, sir."

"Your intention is to wait till it is over before you marry Eden?"

"I am simply unable to make any plans at all until I have returned to Richmond and learned what the next few days will bring forth, sir. If the whole country doesn't catch fire from Charleston, I would—would hope to take Eden with me to Washington, where I spend most of my time now. As to—finances," he struggled on against their silence, "I can truthfully say that she will be very comfortable. My father owns the Trenton *Enquirer* besides his steel mill interests, and I am his only heir. I am at present on salary as Special Correspondent. I live at Willard's Hotel. Of course if things should go radically wrong in Washington I could always send Eden to my father's house in Trenton. It is much admired as a residence, though she might find it a trifle gloomy."

Ransom nodded, his face impassive.

"Then you wish to consider that an engagement exists between you and Eden," he said, picking his words.

"If you—with your consent, sir." Their blank, studious courtesy seemed to baffle and infuriate him. "Oh, I know you don't like the idea, and I can't say I blame you!" he cried, looking black and badgered again. "I know I'm not what you'd choose for her! I wouldn't have chosen myself for her! I've lived an odd sort of life, maybe, and I wasn't raised to behave the way you're accustomed to, ma'am, where women are concerned. My father hates them all, with some reason, and until I came here I guess I never saw much need to argue with him about that. I don't really know much about them, first hand—any kind of women. I tried to stay away from Williamsburg, I tell you, but I had to see Eden again. The best thing to be said for me is that I want her so much more than any other man possibly could, that I shall try just that much harder to make sure she's happy with me, if anyone can be happy in the times that are ahead of us. Will you make an effort to believe that, sir?"

"We shall try not to stand in your way if Eden loves you, Mr. Murray," said Ransom politely. "But I would be very grateful if you would wait just a little while until we can see the result of this Charleston business."

"If I did what I liked, I'd take her with me today," Cabot assured them patiently. "But if I am sent straight into the field with the Army she will be better off here with you than alone in Washington, and she's going to stay here, till we know."

Ransom seemed to breathe a little easier.

"You are very considerate," he murmured, and Cabot stared at him resentfully.

"Considerate?" he repeated. "And why in God's name shouldn't I be considerate of the woman I love? I'm not an Apache, sir, that woos by capture, even if I am a Yankee!"

"You must forgive us, Mr. Murray," said Felicity, speaking for the first time, "but it comes as rather a shock to lose our eldest daughter to a man who—who is after all a stranger. We don't want to seem unfriendly, but you must admit, Mr. Murray, that we know very little about you——"

"I admit all that, ma'am. I come from the wrong part of the country, and I've had a lot of wrong ideas. There's one thing I'm proud of, though—Eden's grandmother trusts me. And you know as well as I do, she's a hard one to fool!"

Ransom smiled tardily.

"You're right about that," he conceded, as the street door banged and Dabney arrived in the drawing-room. He stopped short at sight of Cabot.

"Here *you* are again!" he cried, staring. But he held out his hand with a grin, and Cabot took it gratefully.

"You'll never be rid of me now," he said. "I've just asked permission to marry Eden."

Dabney took it without blinking.

"Well, it's a relief to me you don't want Gran instead," he remarked. "We couldn't spare her. I suppose you've all heard about Sumter?"

"Yes. I'm starting back to Richmond at once. Eden thinks you should come along to protect me."

Dabney laughed and examined the scar critically.

"Marked you, didn't they! Why Richmond, just now?"

"Convention still sitting," Cabot reminded him briefly. "Secret session. Secession. War."

"Yankee journalist, rope, and lamp-post!" Dabney added cheerfully. "I can't spend my life getting you out of town, you know! Got other things to do now."

"Thanks, I'll manage this time."

Dabney turned to his parents, his hand resting on Cabot's shoulder.

"This fellow's a Yankee," he said casually, but with purpose. "You don't like Eden marrying a Yankee, do you. Neither do I. But all the same, she's picked herself a man, I can promise you that. And you may as well give in gracefully, because he'll have her anyhow!"

3

Fort Sumter surrendered on the fourteenth, with no bloodshed except one soldier killed and several injured in an accidental explosion of ammunition during the final salute by the garrison to the flag. Anderson and his men were allowed to embark for New York, and the South celebrated this initial victory with no apparent thought of the consequences of the war entered on so lightheartedly.

On the next day Lincoln's call for seventy-five thousand volunteers "to suppress combinations and cause the laws to be duly executed" had a slightly sobering effect. To demand of Virginia her quota of eight thousand troops was in the eyes of men like Lafayette Sprague a fatal blunder on the President's part—and yet, as Ransom reasonably pointed out, to omit Virginia's name from the roll call of loyal States would have been to accuse her prematurely of intention to secede. Lincoln's proclamation gave the Southern forces mustered at Charleston and other points twenty days to "disperse and return peaceably to their respective abodes." This was taken to mean that he would wait till May fifth before putting the Federal Army in motion to invade the seceded territory.

Confronted with the bitter choice of furnishing troops to be used against sister Southern States or refusing point blank to do so, the Virginia Convention announced Secession on the eighteenth, and there were wild demonstrations of delight in the streets of Richmond, and a general rush to join the Richmond Greys and the Light Infantry Blues by young men of wealth and family who were all followed into the ranks by their faithful colored body servants. "On to Washington!" was a battle-cry heard everywhere.

The cadets from the Virginia Military Institute were sent to Richmond to act as drillmasters, under the command of Major Thomas Jackson, a veteran of the Mexican War who was their professor of natural science and the theory of gunnery. Louise wrote that Fauquier was among them, carrying himself like a fighting cock in his smart uniform with *inches* added to his chest measurement—and that it was a both comic and touching sight to see burly, bearded volunteers from the back country diligently marching, wheeling, and tossing muskets about at the shrill but patient commands of striplings whose voices had hardly changed. Every train brought more recruits and ill-equipped companies to Richmond, she said, until the whole countryside round-about the city had become one vast encampment dotted with white tents.

On the twenty-second of April Colonel Lee came to Richmond to see the Governor—having refused the command of the Federal Army by handing in his resignation. That same night he went to bed at the Spotswood Hotel a rather lonely and oppressed general in charge of the military and naval stores of Virginia. And the following morning he opened a modest office with neither adjutant nor clerk in the Post Office building. The Richmond *Dispatch* said of him with enthusiasm —*His reputation, his acknowledged ability, his chivalric character, his probity, honor and—may we add to his eternal praise—his Christian life and conduct make his name a very tower of strength.*

A delicate situation was created by the fact that Virginia was not yet a member of the Confederacy established at Montgomery. Virginia had come out on a point of honor only, with no real grievance of her own. But she was aware that by that magnificent gesture she offered herself as a battleground on the way to Washington, and that an alliance with the States to her rear would be necessary.

The first collison was expected at Harper's Ferry, where a handful of Virginia volunteers had driven out the Federal garrison and now held a wolf by the ears. The Institute's Major Jackson was soon promoted to a colonelcy and sent off to take charge there. At Norfolk too the volunteers were in perilous possession of the harbor and shipyards. But all Williamsburg was speculating anxiously about Fortress Monroe, the only piece of Virginia soil left in Federal hands. An informal armistice existed there now, as the Yankee garrison under Butler was too powerful to be tackled by volunteers, but sooner or later Beauregard would try to come up from Norfolk, or Lincoln would attempt to send reinforcements by way of Hampton Roads. And so Virginia began to build a battery at Yorktown, and a defensive line was to be drawn from there across the Peninsula to the James River, running just east of Williamsburg.

"It's like having Cornwallis on the march again," said Tibby Day. And then she sighed, "Young Robert Lee will have his hands full."

Young Robert Lee was fifty-four, with the narrow hips and flat legs of the cavalryman, and he rode the dragoon seat with long stirrups. He had seen thirty-two years of army service, and a Washington wit had recently remarked that God had had to spit on his hands to make Bob Lee. His brown eyes were kind and laughing, and he had a modest gallantry which won the hearts of women. His wife, always an invalid, had remained behind at Arlington when he came to Richmond.

Lafe presented himself at the little office in the Post Office building and was taken on as a sort of amateur aide, reporting as punctually as Lee every morning for the vexatious office work of organizing an army. Louise and Sally sent back to Williamsburg for clothes and possessions they had not expected to need and settled in at the Spotswood for an indefinite stay.

On May third, two days before Lincoln's deadline, Virginia sent out a call for volunteers over eighteen. And Sedgwick refused to go.

There was a terrible scene in the Spragues' room at the Spotswood, with Louise and Sally in tears, Lafe in a ranting rage, and Sedgwick white and determined, reiterating his fantastic decision to return to Williamsburg, where his existence need not be a daily humiliation to his parents, and resume his reading for the Law.

Fauquier had made things worse by his indignation at being required by his father to remain at the Institute at least for the term. Dabney put the lid on it by arriving in Richmond in search of more active duty than drilling with the volunteer company at Williamsburg, and promptly got himself assigned to Colonel Magruder, who was directing the artillery around Richmond. Lafe cried out in haste that he would rather see his only son dead than a coward, and Sedgwick departed on the river steamer for Williamsburg branded a disgrace to the family, uncertain for the first time in his life of a welcome even from Sue. If Sue turned against him too there would be nothing left, he told himself defiantly, but to go North and join the army which was fighting to preserve the Union. And that would mean, if he survived, a lifetime of exile.

He found Williamsburg aflame with Virginia patriotism. Even the College was closing for the duration of the war, as nearly all of its students and professors were entering the Confederate Army. President Ewell himself, always an outspoken opponent of Secession, had now put his State before his country and was organizing a regiment of infantry for the defense of the Peninsula.

Sedgwick reached Williamsburg late in the evening, and Sue received him just as usual, with a family kiss and a frank expectancy of the gift he produced for her—a small silver music box which played *L'Elisire d'Amour*. Sue was enchanted with it, and kissed him again for gratitude. Then they ran up stairs to play *L'Elisire d'Amour* for Gran, who was already in bed, and Eden heard and joined them, and soon he said a quite normal good-night and went home to England Street with no mention made of why he had left Richmond.

He had to have it out with Sue, though, before he could rest. He had to know if Sue thought he was a coward. Their favorite ride was down to Jamestown, where they often picnicked near the broken brick tower of the old church, with the tide lapping at the edge of the grassy bank while they ate.

And so they set off the next morning with sandwiches and fruit and cakes wrapped up in white napkins in Sedgwick's saddlebags, and they left Judah, his body servant and groom, behind.

It was a delicious May day full of fragrance and bird song. Sue wore a brown velveteen riding habit with a green scarf on her postillion hat, and sat her mare Philomel with easy grace. Sedgwick rode a strutting bay named Cherry, horse and man moving together as one creature with one will between them.

They took the turning which led left of the College and plunged into deep pine woods just outside the town, great trees arching black above their heads in the spring sunshine. They chattered of this and that as they rode, avoiding the thing that lay heavy between them, until they came out into the Back River swamp and splashed across the ford to the Island. Near the church they dismounted, and Sedgwick unslung the saddle-bags and left the horses to graze, and followed her to their usual spot under a big tree near the water. He spread a saddle-blanket for them to sit on, and it was all as it had been a hundred times before, until Sue said with a sigh——

"Thank heaven they haven't started digging yet. Father says they are going to raise fortifications somewhere around here."

"Even on the Island?" He laid himself wearily at full length, his face hidden in the crook of his arm. "What a world!" he groaned. "Sue, I'm a blot on the family escutcheon, did you know?"

"Uncle Lafe never said that!" she protested.

"Your Uncle Lafe put it plainer. He said he wished I was dead."

"Oh, Sedgie, he *didn't!*"

"Well, it came to the same thing. Sue, do you think I'm a coward?"

"No!" She sat very straight, looking out across the water.

"Well, then, what *do* you think, Susannah? It's rather hard to tell today." His voice came muffled, he would not look at her.

"Sedgie, I like Mr. Murray too, but—couldn't you do what they want and—and just trust to luck you won't ever have to shoot him?"

"It isn't just shooting Cabot Murray I'm objecting to, you little idiot. It's going against the President—against the nation George Washington and our grandfathers sweat blood to build for us——"

"But if the Yankees are going to want things all their own way all the time——"

"The Yankees are no worse than the South Carolinians and the Alabamans and the Mississippians about that! They're all acting like spoilt, selfish children, Sue—if we behaved like that in the nursery Mammy came down on us like a ton of bricks and spanked it out of us! People have got to learn to get on together, give and take, respect each other's rights. If they couldn't do that there wouldn't be any family life, nor any happy marriages. States can learn the same thing if they try. It's only because the wrong people got together in Congress and started twisting each other's tails, and then the newspapers chipped in and started calling everybody names, and then the

Abolitionists put in their oar—and pretty soon everybody was fighting mad and had said a lot of things they couldn't back down on, and then Anderson played the fool in the name of duty, and Bang! bang! we've got a war on! It's all so *silly,* can't you see how useless it is?"

"It hasn't really turned into a war yet."

"You'd think it had if you saw Richmond!"

"Nobody's been killed. There haven't been any battles. Maybe it will all peter out the way it does when our family starts a fight."

"It *ought* to work like a family, but Lincoln isn't strong enough to knock people's heads together. There's nobody strong enough to do that."

"Not even you, Sedgie. So it doesn't do any good for you to try."

"Then you want me to join the army just like all the rest of them," he said, lying very still.

"I want you to do whatever you think is right, Sedgie, but——"

"But?"

"If only you could do something that isn't fighting, while you feel this way—just something that would satisfy them, like Uncle Lafe working in Lee's office!"

"And have them all dead sure I'm afraid to face gunfire?" He sat up, tight-lipped, very calm, and smoothed his hair with a familiar gesture that pinched her heart. "All right, Susannah. If that's the way you look at it, I'll join the army. But not the army they think. I'll go North and fight *with* the Yankees to keep the United States of America united until they grow up and learn how to behave!"

"Sedgwick!" she cried incredulously. "You c-*couldn't!*"

"They can't stop me. And they can't think much less of me than they do now."

"But Sedgie, if you did a thing like that they'd never let you come home again!"

"That wouldn't matter to me very much if I got killed."

"You mustn't get killed. I couldn't *live* if I couldn't ever see you again!" She broke off with a gasp, her eyes brimming, her lips aquiver.

"Sue——"

"Oh, Sedgie, I——"

"Sue——"

They stared at each other, breathless, while revelation dawned through fright and doubt, dawned relentlessly, overwhelmingly, until their hands caught and clung—while their eyes still held, wide and wondering, and slowly he raised himself and slid along the blanket towards her, her hands in his. And then he knelt above her, breathing rather quickly, seeing all over again the bright beauty of her hair, her steadfast hazel eyes, her petal skin and the odd, dimpled mouth with its full lower lip. . . . But now she was his, she couldn't live without him, she said so, she belonged to him, to love and to cherish. . . . All these years, all their lives, she had been his, and it was only today with the creeping shadow of war across them that he had discovered it, and she was lovely, lovelier than anyone else in all Virginia, and she was his, to have and to hold. . . . His arms went round her and their lips met.

Then he sat holding her above his heart, unable to see beyond the thing that had happened to them. He took off her hat and touched her springing hair with possessive joy, he commanded her to smile so he could kiss the dimple set askew so near her lips, he kissed her hands and spread them on his own big palms, marvelling at their delicate shape—till she told him, laughing, that he had seen her before.

"Never," he whispered. "Never in all my born days before! It's love at first sight, Susannah." And he hid his face against her neck so that she squirmed and squealed softly because his eyelashes tickled.

For a little while longer, because they were so young and had never been in love before, they forgot the war, and all it meant to them. And suddenly they were hungry, and ate their lunch zestfully, gazing with shining, happy eyes above the sandwiches, kissing between courses, feeding each other the best bits of everything.

And then she sighed.

"Well," she said, for she was always the more practical of the two, "Well, what now?"

"Whatever will be easiest for you, I will do," he promised simply.

"You mean you want me to decide?"

"No, that's not fair. I can decide, I think. I will go to Richmond and join the first regiment I come to. That will settle everything, won't it?"

"Will it?" she wondered, frowning.

"You won't have to be ashamed of the man you're going to marry, anyway."

"I couldn't be ashamed of you, Sedgie, it isn't that. But—if you go

North to the other army, I'll have to run away to go with you, and we'd never see Gran again, and—they'd take on worse even than they did about Eden's wanting to marry a Yankee, because you're a Virginian to start with——"

"Honey, I won't go North, I promise. I've given that up."

"You mean—just because——?"

"Just because I love you, Sue. I couldn't do that to you, I realize that now. You come first—I'm not going to do anything that will make things harder for you."

The dimple showed.

"Makes me feel very important," she said.

"You're important, all right, honey, and don't you forget it. Just that much of you—" He measured off an inch of her forefinger. "—is more important to me than the whole State of Virginia."

He laid her hands, palms upward, against his face, and she sat looking down at his bent head, a little disturbed in her soul that he should fling away his principles and his convictions quite so heedlessly for her sake. Mr. Murray, for instance, seemed not to have altered his chosen course a single degree because of Eden. Of course Mr. Murray was a Yankee. Virginia men, she had heard, were more considerate. She did not know that their grandfather St. John had firmly set aside his own headstrong Tory Regina and served for four long years with Washington before she humbled herself and forgave him. But it troubled Sue just the same, as it would have troubled Gran, that Sedgwick could put his love before everything else, to make of himself with a graceful gesture her slave and bondsman—but that was just the way the Sprague blood ran in him, wild and quixotic and afire. It troubled her that she had turned him, without even trying, down the very road he had hitherto flatly refused to take—just because any other course on his part would make things more difficult for her. Dimly she was aware that to Cabot Murray—as to St. John Sprague in his day—no woman was worth the sacrifice of his convictions. But with Sedgwick she came first. It made her feel important, yes—but it made her feel humble too, and responsible. It was very sobering.

"I think," she said while his face was still between her hands, "I think you'd better not do anything at all just yet. Let's wait and see what happens. We needn't tell them right away."

"Not tell them?" He left a kiss in each of her palms and closed her fingers on it very gently. "I'd burst if I had to keep it to myself! We'll tell them tonight, as soon as we get back. And we'll have to be starting, look at the sun!"

She submitted thoughtfully to being lifted to her feet, she watched in silence while he folded the blanket and readied the horses, she allowed his arms to close round her where she stood beside Philomel waiting to mount.

"Kiss me," he whispered, jealous of her thoughts, and she raised her face to him obediently. Long moments passed. "I thought maybe you'd forgotten how," he murmured gratefully.

"Let's tell Gran first," she said. "I'd rather."

4

But they never got past the drawing-room door.

Dabney had come home again, resplendent in a new uniform and sword, a lieutenant under Magruder, who was coming to establish headquarters at Yorktown. Everyone was excited and pleased that the Peninsula was to have Magruder, because that meant that headquarters would be gay—he was a bachelor famous for the parties he gave, and Dabney would be able to get home on furlough with no trouble at all now, and so on and so forth.

At last Eden took Dabney away to tell Gran the news, and that left Sedgwick and Sue alone in the drawing-room with Ransom and Felicity. They exchanged glances, Sue nodded doubtfully, and Sedgwick cleared his throat.

"You'll be pleased to know, sir, that I have changed my mind. I'll go down to Yorktown with Dabney tomorrow and see if they'll take me on there."

"Oh, Sedgwick, I'm so glad!" cried Felicity warmly, and Ransom laid his hand on Sedgwick's shoulder and said with affection, "Good boy! It will be a great relief to your father!"

"He's got no one to thank for it but Sue," Sedgwick told them with a touch of his old defiance. "I still don't see any sense in this beastly war. But I want to marry Sue, and I can't have her heckled on my account."

Ransom's hand dropped from Sedgwick's shoulder and his startled glance flew to meet his wife's waiting eyes. For a moment they looked at each other as though caught in a sort of paralysis, then at some sign from her Ransom spoke.

"But that's impossible," he said quietly.

"Oh, but Father, he's going to join the army now!" Sue pointed out eagerly. "He said he'd join the first regiment he came to. That makes it all right, doesn't it?"

"My dear, you don't seem to realize—you and Sedgwick are cousins."

She looked at him uncomprehendingly.

"Well, so are you and Mother."

"You and Sedgwick are first cousins twice over, Sue. And that's too close a relationship for marriage. Surely you knew that, Sedgwick, what are you thinking of?"

Sedgwick passed a hand dazedly across his eyes.

"I—hadn't thought about that," he said. "I—forgot."

"But I don't see—" Sue began, and something in his beaten attitude and hidden face struck her with panic. She pulled the hand away from his face and held it in both hers protectively, and then, with a sob of rage and fear turned on her parents fiercely. "Why can't you all let Sedgie alone!" she cried. "If it isn't one thing it's another! First he's got to go into the army, and now he mustn't marry me! I'll marry him anyway tomorrow, if he wants me to! I'll run away with him up North, and never come back here again! You and Mother are happy together, you married the person you wanted to, you can't stop me, I belong to Sedgie, I won't ever have anybody else, you know I can't live without him——"

She leaned against him, sobbing, and Felicity came to her pityingly, her arms outstretched, and was gently warded off by Sedgwick.

"Let me handle this," he said. "Please go away, both of you, and let me handle it."

But Ransom in his father's dismay at Sue's anguish interfered.

"You had better go now, Sedgwick," he said, and took Sue from him into the circle of his own arm. "I think it would be better if you didn't try to say good-bye. Now that you have decided to do as your father wishes, perhaps it would be better too if you went back to Richmond instead of to Yorktown with Dabney."

"You mean I'm not to see Sue again, sir?"

"Not for a while. You are both too young to make a tragedy of this. You and Sue have been devoted playmates, I know, but some day you will find another girl who was meant to be your wife."

Sedgwick drew in his breath.

"I don't want another girl, sir. I wouldn't trade the right to see Sue every day for all of Solomon's wives!"

"You think that now, of course. I have no intention of forbidding you to see Sue, but I think you would be wise to leave it for a little while until you are both—calmer."

Sedgwick looked piteously from Ransom to Felicity and saw no relenting. He stepped close to Sue and turned her face up to his with a hand under her chin.

"Good-bye, honey—it's not forever, you know. Don't cry, now—if you love me, don't cry."

Ignoring Ransom, he bent and kissed her cheek, and left the house with the taste of her tears on his lips. They were wrong, he was sure, not to let him talk to her and try to make her understand. He could have dried up her tears, he knew, and brought her some measure of self-control and comfort, if only they had let him talk to her alone. As it was, she might make herself ill with grieving, and he wouldn't be there. They were wrong, he told himself angrily, swinging down the street, blind to greetings on either side, wrong to behave as though he couldn't be trusted to look after Sue. All her life he had known better than anybody else what was best for her. Why, they even used to ask his advice about her presents and her musts and her must-nots. Try to make Sue see that she ought to work harder at her music, they would say to him—she plays better than anybody else in the family, you tell her you'd like her to learn *La Gondola* by heart, she'll do it for you. Or—Show Sedgwick the story you wrote, Sue, they would say to her, with a glance at him to ensure his praise, rather inclined to believe him when he said it was every bit as good as anything Maria Edgeworth ever wrote. For years he had always had the last word on anything with regard to Sue, and now they turned him out as though he was a leper, just when she needed him most. They were wrong. . . .

When he reached the house in England Street he realized that he had left Cherry in Ransom's stable yard. Still in a sort of trance, he shouted for Judah and told him to fetch Cherry home. And then, as he climbed the stairs to his own room and banged the door behind him, the numbness of shock went off like an anaesthetic and he began to swear at himself. For a long time, while daylight faded and lamps were lit down stairs and the long mahogany dining-table was carefully laid with silver and glass and lace and English china for his solitary supper, he walked up and down behind the closed door, cursing himself with a wealth of epithet, invective, and imagery which would have done credit to the great St. John himself. For he, who loved Sue more than ever man loved woman before, had been such a blind, stupid, selfish this-and-that and so-and-so as to forget—*forget,* mind you—the close blood tie which was the family tradition and pride. He, whose sole excuse for living was to see that nothing made Sue unhappy or afraid, had done her irreparable harm by failing to see in time and guard against her own love for him. There were no words bitter enough for his opinion of himself, though he found and employed a great many blistering terms far short of the ideal.

By the time Judah knocked on his door to say that supper was waiting, Sedgwick's anger at himself had faded into an agony of anxiety about Sue and how she would weather the grief, which he, in his criminal idiocy, had allowed her to encounter. Still wearing his riding boots and plain linen stock, he descended to the dining-room and sat alone at one end of the shining table pretending to eat the meal which was as painstakingly served as though the whole family and a brace of guests had been present. It was commented on in the kitchen, however, that he was only pecking at his food tonight, and surreptitious peeks were taken at him through the door of the butler's pantry. Hadn't changed his clothes—didn't speak a word to nobody—didn't even know what was on his plate—not like him—sickening for something, and his ma away in Richmond——?

When he left the table he returned at once to his room. At nearly midnight Judah went up to ask if he hadn't rung, and found his master seated idly in an armchair staring at the wall. In all that time Sedgwick had found no solution, no alleviation, of the situation for which he held himself responsible.

5

Back in Ransom's drawing-room they were doing the best they could to bring their darling to reason, and to convince her that it was impossible for her to ever be anything but friends with Sedgwick. When Dabney and Eden came down from Gran's room and discovered her tears with surprise and questions, and had to be told the cause, she fled from them all, up to the bedroom she and Eden shared, and flung herself across the bed, too exhausted now even for tears. If only they could have got to Gran first—then maybe no one else would have had to know. . . .

Eden found her there some time later, and helped her to undress and tucked her into bed with silent sisterly tact, and brought her some supper on a tray, and made everybody let her alone.

Sue lay still while darkness fell, trying to think again, trying to see her way ahead into bleakness. Sedgwick was gone, or would be in the morning. He wouldn't be allowed even to say good-bye before he went away to the army, and he might be killed. Suppose she never saw Sedgwick again. What point would there be to living in a world without Sedgwick to talk to and laugh with and confide in? Because even if they couldn't live together as husband and wife, so long as he wasn't killed, so long as he was still there in England Street as he had always been, there would be some sort of life to go on with. Even if some day he married somebody else, as her father said he must do, if ever he was to have a family of his own—well, even then she could see him, see his children, even if they weren't hers too. But—*I don't want another girl,* Sedgwick had cried at that mention of his marriage to somebody else. Did that mean that he would deny himself forever on account of her?

Feeling sick and feverish and thick-in-the-throat from crying, she tried to see ahead for Sedgwick, who mustn't have a maimed, one-sided sort of life just because of loving her. Perhaps if she wasn't there to remind him, perhaps if he couldn't see her every day——? She might go to Aunt Louise in Richmond—but they were sending Sedgwick there. There was Aunt Lavinia in Charleston, but probably they wouldn't want her, with the war and all. Perhaps she ought to go clean away, as far as Europe, so that Sedgwick would forget her and be happy. She and Eden had always dreamed of going to Europe some day with their parents, but the war had spoilt that too. There wasn't anywhere she could go, because of the war, and so long as he could see her every day Sedgwick would never marry somebody else and be happy. . . .

When Eden came to bed and the light was out, Sue turned gratefully into her arms. Still Eden said nothing about Sedgwick—just held her close and stroked her aching head with cool, loving fingers, and Sue clung closer and cried a little more, but not for Sedgwick now, because it had come to her, lying there in the dark, what she could do for him —she cried because she loved Eden so much, best of all her family except perhaps Gran, and because of what she had decided she must do. And at last she fell into a heavy sleep against Eden's shoulder, and did not rouse again till she heard Eden moving about next morning and Mammy came in to hook her up.

For a moment Sue lay with her eyes shut, wondering what hurt so, and why she was so ill. Then she remembered. Remembered everything. Lying motionless, she went over her plans for today, and they seemed to her as sound as they had done the night before—if only she had not got to move to begin on them, if only she could rest a while, if only she need never move again. . . . Well, it wouldn't take long, once she started.

"May I stay in bed today?" she asked Eden, for that was part of her plan, and Mammy came and felt of her head and said she had fever, and bathed her swollen, smarting eyes in cool water, and said she would bring up some breakfast on a tray. "I think I'm going back to sleep," she told them, passive under Mammy's ministering hands. "I'll ring for breakfast when I want it. Please just let me rest a while, alone."

It worked. They tiptoed away. And when she was sure they would all be at breakfast she rose quickly and scrambled into her clothes and put on the velveteen riding-habit, which luckily buttoned down the front, and fled down the stairs like a shadow and out to the stables.

There she found only Micah the fourteen-year-old horse boy, as she had hoped, and she got him to saddle Philomel for her.

"No, you can't come with me," she said firmly when she had mounted. "Sedgwick is waiting for me in England Street—I'm late."

She left Micah staring after her, his none too adequate mind bemused by his faithful slave instinct that something was very wrong. He was further upset when he observed, by a private system of crawling and peeping, that she turned away from England Street and rode off towards the College, alone.

"Done tol' me a lie," Micah ruminated. "Didn' look right, neither.

Peak-ed, kinda. Marse Sedgwick have a fit." He pondered the last idea unhappily. "Yassuh, Marse Sedgwick sho' nuff gimme the debbil effen he knowed I let her ride off by herself like dat." He sighed philosophically. "Well, reckon I got to go tell him."

Having once made up his mind, he lost no more time about getting to England Street, where he found his brother Judah, who was Sedgwick's body servant, polishing his master's boots in the sun outside the kitchen door.

"Whereat Marse Sedgwick, Jude?"

"Nem you mind, he fit to be tied dis mawnin', I cain' do nothin' right, seems like. Hey, best you don' go near him till he's et break-fast——"

But Micah kept on doggedly with Judah protesting at his heels, all the way up stairs to Sedgwick's room, where the door stood ajar. Micah knocked on it apologetically.

"Marse Sedgwick——"

"All right, chuck my boots inside and get out of here!"

Micah pushed the door an inch wider and put his head in. Sedgwick was shaved and brushed and immaculate, just exchanging his dressing-gown for his coat. His feet were still in slippers.

"It's me, Marse Sedgwick."

"Hullo, Micah, what do you want?"

"I was thinkin', suh, best you know 'bout Miss Susannah right away, suh."

"What about her? Is she ill?"

"She done gone."

"Gone where?"

"Search *me,* suh, she done tol' me a lie."

"Make sense, Micah, what are you talking about?"

"Miss Susannah. She done tol' me she gwine meet you yere, nen she rid off alone, up College way, like she been sont fer."

"Alone?"

"She *lie* to me, Marse Sedgwick—she say you gwine ride wid her."

Sedgwick snatched his boots from Judah's hand.

"Saddle Cherry," he said. "Hurry up."

Judah fled stablewards.

Sedgwick knew, with the second sight he had for all that concerned Sue, that she had gone back to Jamestown. He knew also that he had no time to lose. And while he put Cherry along the road breakfastless at top speed he knew, against his will and praying that he was wrong, what she meant to do.

All because they had sent him away in such a hurry yesterday. All because they tried to keep her from him, as though he could not be trusted any more. If anything happened to her now, if he was too late, it would be their fault for not being able to see that no one could handle it but him. It would be their fault. But that would not bring Sue back from the river at Jamestown.

He came to the ford and saw that she had crossed it. Cherry was laboring now, but Sedgwick forced him on. Philomel was grazing by the church. He flung himself out of his saddle and ran on across the green turf, afraid to call, his footsteps cushioned in the grass.

Beyond the big tree where they had sat the day before he saw her, up to her knees in the water, the strong ebb tide already dragging at her heavy riding-skirt, so that she stumbled as she walked steadily out into the river. The first sound she heard was the splash of his feet through the water behind her, and then she was caught in his arms, lifted, and carried back to shore. She heard him say, *"Susannah,* I could wring your neck!" and then she fainted.

When she came to she was lying on the grass and Sedgwick had wrung out her skirt and taken her shoes off and was mopping at her stockinged feet with his handkerchief. He looked round and saw that her eyes were open.

"Well!" he said severely. "What good did you think *that* would do?"

She felt very tired. She felt as though she had died and gone to heaven, because the sun was warm on her face, and Sedgwick was here beside her, and she didn't even care if he was going to be cross. She only wanted to lie still and look at him like waking up from a nightmare.

He sat down beside her and took off his boots—with difficulty—and emptied the water out of them and squeezed water out of the toes of his socks and then pulled his boots back on—also with difficulty. She did not know he was fighting his way back, second by second, from an engulfing nausea of horror which had left him cold and shaking inside and with only just enough commonsense to tell him that now was his chance to deal with this thing once and for all, and absolutely not to bungle it. If he let her know how he felt, if he gave way to his need to hold her warm and dry and safe in his arms and sob out his relief at having been in time, he would not be able to hold things steady for her at their parting. He could tell by looking at her that she had cried herself sick already. He was determined that there would be no more tears for Susannah today. He sat tugging at his boots, his face rigid with the effort for self-control, waiting till he dared trust himself to speak, lining up in his mind the things he had devised for her comfort during the sleepless night.

Finally she could bear what she supposed was his angry silence no longer.

"How did you know where I was?" she inquired in a small voice.

"You lied to Micah. He was so outraged that he came straight to me and told on you."

"Are you awfully mad at me, Sedgie? I thought I was doing the best thing." She raised herself on one elbow earnestly. "I thought if it wasn't for me you'd look at other girls and—one of them would be all right for you and—you'd be happy with her."

"Well, you thought wrong," he said rudely, choking back his pity and tenderness for her sake. "Any time I'm happier with you drowned in the river, I belong in the Asylum."

"Reckon I got kind of mixed up," she sighed, for it didn't seem such a good idea after all, lying here in the sun with Sedgwick sitting beside her.

"That was because they wouldn't let us talk," he said. "I knew you were mixed up, I stayed awake all night trying to think what I could do about it, I was even going to try and write you a letter."

"This is better, isn't it."

"Only by the grace of God!"

"What are we going to do, Sedgie? How are we going to bear it?"

"We're going to forget that yesterday ever happened," he said firmly. "We're going to go on exactly as we were, being friends, and cousins, and never think of anything more, just as we never had before yesterday. We're not going to grieve, Sue, and feel as though our lives are over. You're only sixteen, after all. Maybe, if we don't kill 'em all off in the war, you'll done cotch yourself a Yankee some day, like Eden!"

"Oh, *no!* Don't joke about it, Sedgie!"

"I'm not joking, honey. I'm only trying to find a way out of this thing."

"What did they mean about children?" she asked him, frowning. "Couldn't we have any?"

"We could have them, honey—but it wouldn't be fair to them."

"Would they be queer?"

He tried to laugh, managed to keep from reaching for her.

"They might not all be idiots, I don't say that, but it's taking a risk for them, and we have to think of their children, too, and the ones after that. It's bad for the line, we've had all the inbreeding we can stand. There was your Grandmother Annabelle too, you know, she was half Sprague."

"They all do what they like but us," she said rebelliously.

"It was all right for them. And we don't want anyone to say anything like that about us a generation from now, do we? I'm going away now, it's what they want—next time you see me I'll be all got up in a uniform like Dabney's! It will be easier for me, because I'll be camping out and dodging bullets—but you must keep busy too, don't give yourself time to think till by and by it won't hurt so bad. After all, it's only one short day we have to forget——"

"I'd rather have had that day than all the rest of my life put together!"

"No," he said, wincing. "Let's not think of it like that. We must let it go, Sue—all of it—as though it never happened. That's the best way. If I'd had any sense it wouldn't have happened. And if you're going to be unhappy on my account I hope they shoot me quick, I deserve it!"

She raised a puzzled face to him, blinking in the sunlight.

"Sedgie, you're so strange—don't you *mind?*"

That was nearly too much for him.

"Child, it's the end of the world for me, you know that. But I should have saved you from it, somehow. I should have found some way——"

"Some way to keep me from loving you? You'd have had to start the day I was born!"

He could not answer that, and got to his feet and reached down a hand to pull her up.

"Let's go back," he said. "I'll try and get you into the house without their knowing."

"My shoes——"

He knelt and put them on for her. It took him quite a while. His face was white when he rose.

"Come on," he said, and led the way to where the horses grazed. In silence he locked his hands to make a step to help her to mount and gave her the reins. Then he paused, looking up at her, leaning with one hand on the pommel and one on Philomel's rump. "I wasn't really cross with you," he said rather jerkily. "It was just that you gave me the fright of my life. Will you promise me solemnly never to try and do such a thing again?"

"I promise," she whispered. "Whatever happens, if we both live to be a hundred, we'll go through it together."

Without another word he turned away from her and mounted Cherry.

As they rode back under the tall dark pines, they met a company of volunteers and a squad of Negroes with shovels and pick-axes and wagons full of timber and bricks—on the way to begin the fortifications at Jamestown.

III. JULY 21, 1861

Louise was waiting for Lafe in their room at the Spotswood Hotel in Richmond.

She stood at a window above Main Street looking down towards Capitol Square, where a band was playing. There was always a band somewhere in Richmond now, and troops marching, and trains heavy with soldiers moving along Broad Street from the south and going out northwards towards Manassas or eastwards to West Point on the York River. None of the troops stayed long in Richmond. Beauregard was at Manassas, gathering his army for an assault on Washington, unless MacDowell struck first towards Richmond. Magruder on the Peninsula was bracing for an attack from Fortress Monroe.

Richmond had become a camp, by this first week in July, 1861. It woke to a reveille of drums and retired to taps. There were almost no men in citizens' clothes to be seen in the streets. All the women belonged to sewing circles which usually met in the churches, open every day now, where the sewing machines were kept. During the long hot afternoons they worked at heavy stuff like uniform cloth, tenting, and flannel, with swollen, bleeding fingers because there were not enough sewing machines. While they rested, they made havelocks and housewifes, knit socks and scarves. On the porches and under the trees on the lawns, their colored maids sat in white turbaned, brightly dressed knots and worked just as hard but with more laughter and chatter. Lately, as the first big battle drew near, there was more scraping and carding of lint to be done, and a demand for rolled bandages had to be met.

Mosquitoes, bad hotels, and a scarcity of food had driven the Confederate Government out of Montgomery to Richmond. People said the move was a strategic mistake—Richmond being too near Washington. But it had made the city gayer than ever, and very crowded. Spies were supposed to be swarming everywhere, and one of them had been caught and condemned to hanging.

Ransom was in Richmond now, and Felicity and Eden had come with him. Lafe had written him in June to say that if Ransom would only come and fill his post with Lee, he had a chance to get into the field as a volunteer aide on Beauregard's staff. The school was closed, and Ransom was already debating his own usefulness in Williamsburg. A few days later he arrived at the Spotswood, where with some difficulty he had secured a room for himself and Felicity, while Eden shared Sally's.

It took Lafe only about a fortnight to acquaint his brother-in-law with his duties at Lee's headquarters, which were now in the Mechanics' Institute and which had been increased to include a few clerks, several aides, and a secretary. Since the arrival of the Montgomery Government and the merging of Virginia with the Confederate cause, Lee's position had become a little vague. Jefferson Davis was supposed to be in supreme command of the Confederate Army. This left Virginia's General Lee with an empty title and no clearly defined duties. Tacitly he assumed the responsibility of the defence of Richmond, leaving Davis to concentrate on the more active Manassas and Harper's Ferry areas. Richmond's earthworks and river defences were going forward briskly under Lee's direction, but it seemed to Lafe very dull work. Lafe smelled powder up Manassas way. Ransom could take charge now, and this afternoon Lafe had an appointment with President Davis regarding a transfer to field duty with Beauregard. Sedgwick was already there, in Longstreet's brigade.

There had been two months of war, and no major engagement so far, and only about fifty casualties, not counting the sick in the hospitals. Richmond had had a couple of false alarms, and Magruder had come off victorious in a brush with the Federals at Big Bethel, so soon over that Dabney could not even claim to have been under fire, and the Federals had occupied Alexandria on the Virginia side of the Potomac. There seemed little doubt that MacDowell was massing his Yankee troops there, and that a battle was shaping up before Manassas.

Louise leaned her forehead wearily against the windowpane, staring down into the street. A regiment of blue and orange Zouaves went by, on their way to the railway station. She waved her handkerchief at them automatically, and some of them looked up, grinning, and waved back, and a child darted out from the curb and gave one of them a bouquet snatched from somebody's garden. One always waved at soldiers on the way to the front. Some days it seemed as though one did it every five minutes. A little while ago Sedgwick had been among them. Now it would be Lafe. It did not occur to her to object to Lafe's transfer from the comparative safety of Richmond to what might soon be the firing line. It never occurred to anybody that a Sprague wouldn't be in a fight if there was one. Louise had laid her own plans accordingly.

She was still standing there at the window when she heard the clank of Lafe's spurs at the door before he opened it and came in. She turned and smiled at him as he crossed the room to her—so that it smote him again how sweet she was, how frail and young she looked still, with a smaller waist than Sally's and soft, near-sighted brown eyes, and chestnut hair which fell below her belt when it was down, with only a few white threads in it still—they had been married nearly twenty years, and after only the shortest absence from her his first thought was always to kiss her quick, make sure of her again in his arms—his news, whatever it might be, could always wait for that. It was so today. He held her close against him, aware of the hard clasp of her hands behind his neck, his nostrils drawing in the scent of her hair—war, impending separation, uncertainty, made it all the sweeter. Lafe savored his homecoming jealously, with no hasty rushing into speech and commonplaces. Then, with his cheek pressing hers, he whispered their lovers' ritual—"Who loves you best?" he demanded softly, and—"You do!" she whispered back, and offered her lips.

"Well," he said when he had kissed her again, "it's all fixed up, no more sitting around on my backside in an office!"

"When do we start?" she asked, still in his arms, and he looked down at her ruefully, with a little smile.

"Louise, honey—now, don't take on, will you—but it seems you'd better stay here—just for a little while," he added quickly, laying a finger on her parted lips. "Just till I can see where I am up there, hm?" He squeezed her suddenly till it hurt.

She lay against him, passive in the vise of his embrace, biding her time till she could breathe again, till he had had his say. Then she would have hers.

"You wouldn't for one moment suppose that I want to leave you, would you?" he murmured. "You wouldn't by any chance imagine that I prefer Old Bory's company to yours? Probably in just a few days you can come up to the Springs, where lots of the other women are, and I can get leave and come and see you—like a honeymoon again, hm? Sally can stay here with Felicity, she'd rather."

"I'm coming to Bristoe," she said.

"Oh, not Bristoe, honey, it's a terrible place, and hotter than Tophet! Mrs. Cary came back from there with typhoid, didn't she, now, and nearly died! I can't have you frying in Bristoe just to be near me."

"Freda Smith wants to go too, her eldest boy is with Early. We can keep each other company, and anyway Sally says she'll go along, now that she knows young Allen is with Jackson."

"Jackson is in the Shenandoah, nowhere near Manassas. Is Sally serious about that Allen boy?"

"I don't know, really. He's all right, isn't he?"

"I suppose he is. Bit of a show-off, I thought, but Sally seems to like 'em that way! You've set your heart on Bristoe, haven't you?"

"Oh, yes, Lafe, Mrs. Cary says I can drive right out to camp from there and see dress parades and you can give me tea in your tent. She said it was great fun, much more interesting than being stuck at the Springs."

"Fun, maybe, but she got typhoid all the same."

"Well, I promise not to get typhoid, you'll have enough on your mind without that."

He was tempted, to have her so near. But Bristoe, he knew, was no place for her.

"Honey, if anything should happen to you——"

"Well, that's a fine thing to say when it's you that's going to be doing all the fighting!" She tried to laugh at that. She had the delicate, finely cut lips of a child, and beautiful teeth. He cupped her face in his hands, looking down at her.

"The men aren't doing all the fighting in this war," he said. "What a hideous thing it is to have happen to you, Louise—there shouldn't be wars in the same world with you——"

"Reckon there will always be wars," she said bravely. "There always have been. Reckon the Greek and Roman women felt just the same as I do."

"And I would have loved you just the same, 'way back then," he whispered.

"When do you have to go, Lafe?"

"Tomorrow morning."

Her eyelids flickered.

"I've made you a going-away gift," she said quietly, and went to the top drawer of the chiffonier where she had hidden it. "It isn't very much, but—I thought it would come handy when I'm not there to do your mending."

It was a blue flannel housewife, with needles, pins, thread, court plaster and a tiny pair of scissors all ingeniously fitted into the smallest possible space, with an extra pocket for banknotes, inside a delicately embroidered cover.

"My dear," he said, holding it. "Where did you find the time? You've done it beautifully. But those are your scissors that you prize so, for embroidery silk."

"They were the smallest, and I have others I can use. I want you to have them. You must take good care of it, honey, because needles and pins are going to be very scarce on account of the blockade."

"I'll take care of it," he promised, and stowed it away tenderly in his pocket. "I'll never let it out of my sight. Ransom is waiting for me down stairs, we've got to ride down to the Bluff about some new guns —be back for supper. Are you going out?"

"No. I'm going to pack." She smiled at him, and he knew that it was useless to try to forbid her to come to Bristoe, and would only make her miserable.

A short time after he had gone, Sally and Eden came in to find her putting things into a carpet bag and looking surprisingly cheerful about it.

"Your father is off tomorrow," she told Sally briskly, "and I'm going to follow him as far as Bristoe as soon as ever I can, no matter what he says. Are you sure you wouldn't rather stay here, at least till I see how it is?"

But Sally had taken to wearing brass buttons and a military cap, which was the fashion among her patriotic friends, and while she hated to leave Richmond where she had a string of beaux among the aides and secretaries, the idea of queening it near the front appealed to her, and she hurried Eden off to their room to help her start her own packing. "Now, you're not to take a lot of dresses!" her mother warned. "We shall have to live very simply, and it will be very hot and crowded."

With a wistful sort of envy Eden watched Sally laying out her ruffled petticoats and lace-trimmed drawers and unpractical finery to be packed for Bristoe. Sally had a beau with Jackson in the Shenandoah, another in the same regiment with Sedgwick at Manassas. Wherever Sally went there were beaux, and it made life light and gay and perpetually interesting. Eden was not a flirt like Sally, and she had given her whole heart to Cabot Murray—and there was always Grafton Crabb, obstinately devoted, distinguishing himself now as an officer with an artillery battery near Richmond and refusing to take her engagement to a Yankee seriously, though she had felt it necessary to tell him honestly that he need not expect her to change. There were others quite ready to declare themselves, of course, at the slightest encouragement, for Eden's red hair and greenish eyes could never pass unnoticed in a place like wartime Richmond. But Sally was free to receive advances, and Sally had no compunctions about young men's feelings anyway, and it sometimes made Eden feel rather staid and on-the-shelf, like a maiden aunt, to watch Sally's bright butterfly progress.

There was no way now to communicate with Cabot, for the Northern mails had stopped and you could only get a letter through to Washington by influence or the secret smuggling routes, to which she had no access. She had had no word from him since he wrote from Washington to say that he had caught the last northbound train out of Richmond by the skin of his teeth, and would remain in the Northern capital until sent into the field, which he hoped would be soon, as a Special Correspondent. *Have you heard,* he wrote, *about the unfortunate Southern professor of medicine at Philadelphia who was nearly hanged as a spy, and escaping from there arrived somewhat hurriedly in Atlanta, and remarked thoughtlessly that he was fresh from Philadelphia, and before he could complete his sentence was again nearly hanged as a spy? And he wasn't even a journalist!*

Smiling, she had read on with a dim sense of doubt and disappointment, hardly knowing what it was she missed from the letter, until she came to the very last page, when it suddenly turned into a love letter which left nothing to be desired. It is not every young woman's good fortune to be courted by a man who is trained to express himself on paper, for whom words march and maneuver like soldiers, obedient to his need. And Cabot, though he had never written a love letter before in his life, knew his way down a sheet of blank paper with a pen in his hand. She reached his signature breathless and shaken, feel-

ing herself possessed and humble, consecrated to this brooding, passionate, somehow pathetic stranger, who had invaded her quiet life,
kissed her lips, left the marks of his masterful fingers in dark bruises
on her shoulders, and departed again, no one knew for how long, to
serve the enemy.

It was a fantastic position Eden found herself in, in Richmond that
July. Her parents said little about it, and she had not the sustaining
presence of Dabney, who somehow understood Cabot Murray and
sympathized with her, or of Gran, who had been through it all too,
in her day. She felt a little lost, a little sent to Coventry, and she knew
that everyone—except Gran—was secretly hoping that her attachment
to the Yankee would wear off with time, or would receive, as the war
went on, some logical deathblow. It was lonely to be in love and not
be able to mention his name, or hear from him, or even to answer his
letter. She almost wished, as she sat watching Sally pack, that she was
going to Bristoe too.

2

It was a flat, treeless town, dumped down beside the glittering rails
which ran northeast to the junction at Manassas, south to Richmond.
The single street was ankle deep in red clay dust, the sun beat down
on the bare whitewashed walls. The flies were abominable, the drinking water was muddy, and sanitation was primitive.

Louise and Sally shared with Freda Smith a small stuffy room over
the grocery store, which backed on the railway track, over which the
trains rumbled to and from the junction. The room was too hot to
sit in by day, and much too hot for sleeping in at night, and they never
had the relief of rain. There were a number of other families in Bristoe, packed into sordid, cheerless accommodations for the sake of being
near husbands, brothers, and sons in the camp at Manassas. Each time
a train came up from the south everyone rushed to the station platform
to greet it, sure of seeing familiar faces hanging out of the windows—
friends, and the sons of friends, some wearing the new grey uniform
of the Confederacy, some in whatever clothes they happened to join up
in, with gay sashes and badges to lend a military air. The women
would stand bareheaded in the blistering sun beside the track, waving
their white handkerchiefs or the eternal knitting they never seemed to

lay down, and the boys in the cars would wave back, and cheer, and call out in joyful recognition—and then they would be gone, high-hearted, often singing, to join their comrades already encamped along Bull Run.

As Mrs. Cary had promised her, Louise found that the women who owned or could obtain carriages frequently drove up to the camp to see battalion drill and dress parade, and their soldier hosts spread the best fare they could in their tents and brewed pots of tea with gallant anxiety for the comfort of their sweltering visitors, who usually had the tact to refuse the precious goodies the men had received in boxes sent from home, and to declare that they preferred the novelty of eating the raw biscuits and thumping huckleberry pies of the regular mess—and indeed the mess served better food than most of them got at Bristoe.

Lafe had arranged that Louise's carriage should follow her from Richmond, driven by old black Daniel who had brought her to Richmond from Williamsburg in it. On the morning of the seventeenth of July she drove out again with Sally and Freda Smith to the vicinity of the McLean house where Beauregard's headquarters were, near Manassas. Sedgwick and Preston Smith and Sally's beau, Lieutenant Scott, who were all in infantry regiments encamped around Blackburn's Ford on Bull Run, rode over on borrowed horses with a few hours' leave. Felicity had managed to send Louise a basket of food from Richmond, and they made a picnic on the dusty grass beside the lane leading up to headquarters, served by Zekiel, who was Lafe's body servant and Daniel's son.

It was a strange, feverish sort of peace in the midst of war—the group of pretty women in light dresses, the white cloth spread on the grass, the cold fried chicken and melon and cakes, and the priceless piece of ice tinkling in a pitcher of grape-juice—Sally was flirting with Preston Smith and her lieutenant, Sedgwick looked fit and handsome in his well-cut grey, hatless, munching a chicken-leg, Louise and Lafe held hands even while they ate. To Louise, even in her careful pretence that all this was normal and not in any way frightening or oppressive, it seemed suddenly a kind of nightmare from which she would surely wake up in the big house in England Street, with Lafe lying beside her in their chintz-hung four-poster and the small drowsy sounds of a well-run household beginning the day all around her. But no dream could put Lafe and Sedgwick into those unfamiliar grey clothes, it was no dream that she sat here on a carriage cushion laid on the grass, with the unmistakable odor of an army encampment heavy on the sultry air. Lafe's hand on hers was hot and dry, and he was flushed with the sun——

She leaned over suddenly and laid her fingers on his forehead, below the thick straight hair. He turned quickly, burrowing into her small palm.

"That feels good," he said.

"Lafe, have you got a touch of the sun today?"

"Might have. Head aches a bit."

"You must always remember to wear your hat."

"Sweetheart, I have to wear my hat on duty. It's nothing. This heat is far worse than Peninsula heat when you're not used to it. Can't sleep at night. It must be awful in Bristoe, and yet you come here looking as fresh and sweet as though you'd never left home. How do you do it?"

She smiled enigmatically. It was her business to look fresh and sweet for him. It was all she could do for him nowadays.

An orderly came swiftly across the grass, his feet raising a little cloud of dust at every step, and handed a folded note to Lafe, who sat up and read it at a glance.

He murmured an oath. "You boys get back to your post, quick time! MacDowell is on the move." He rose, pulling Louise to her feet in the same movement. "Zekiel, get these things into the carriage quick. Daniel! Put the horses to, you must take the ladies back to Bristoe at once."

There was a bewildered flurry of good-byes. Preston and Sedgwick kissed their mothers, and Sally's lieutenant kissed her hand. Lafe and Sedgwick exchanged a long, grave look over their handshake, the same flicker of excitement in the eyes of each, and the boys disappeared at a gallop in the direction of Bull Run. Lafe delayed just long enough to see the women into the carriage—to kiss Louise as though they were alone within their own four walls, an unhurried lover's kiss, and a last lingering look at her in his arms—and then, almost before the wheels had begun to turn, was off at a run towards headquarters.

They brought the first news of MacDowell's move to Bristoe, and were soon surrounded by a group of anxious questioners. One woman burst into tears and was led away, her face hidden in her hands. Louise left the others, her lips pressed together, and climbed the dark, smelly stairs to the stifling room above the grocery store. Sally found her there a little later, sitting in a hard wooden chair by the window, her clasped hands idle in her lap, gazing out at the fading day.

"He had a headache," she said when Sally came in. "His hand was very hot. I'm sure he's got a touch of the sun."

"He'll forget about that, I bet, if there's a battle," said Sally. "Does it mean there *will* be a battle now?"

"I'm afraid so."

"Well, it will be a sort of relief to them, won't it, since they know it has to come some time?"

"I suppose it will."

"Shall we be able to hear the guns from here, do you think?"

"Very likely."

"There goes another train!" Sally hung out of the window to wave. "I wonder if *they* know MacDowell is coming! I'll bet Sedgwick is excited! Would you be afraid, if you were a man?"

"Terrified."

"I suppose they all are, really, only it would never do to show it. I wonder how it feels to know, for sure, that you have killed a man."

"Oh, Sally, darling, please don't!"

"Well, Father's not likely to have to, being on the Staff, but Sedgwick and Preston and Lieutenant Scott may. Sedgwick looks very well, don't you think? Camp life certainly agrees with him! I swear he's *grown!*"

"The Spragues all love a fight," said Louise patiently.

She knew it was true. She knew that even now Lafe was busy and happy and indispensable, getting ready for a fight. He wouldn't be thinking of her again till it was all over. Unless his head got worse.

There was little sleep at Bristoe that night. Shortly after eight o'clock on the morning of the eighteenth, when the wan, heavy-eyed women in the baking town were pretending to eat breakfast, the guns began.

Scattering napkins, handkerchiefs, and knitting, they ran for the railway tracks and stood staring anxiously towards the belt of woodland beyond which Manassas lay. The dull rumble of cannon increased, until the ground beneath their feet shook. Through the shimmering heat haze which already hung over the bright ribbon of the rails they thought they could see smoke hanging low over Manassas. Soon they were sure. The battle had begun.

In groups of twos and threes they plodded through the red dust back to the dreary railway inn, picked up their scattered belongings, hushed whimpering children, vanished into their rooms to weep or pray in the scanty privacy each could claim.

Louise neither wept nor prayed, as far as anyone knew. All that long, hot morning, while Freda Smith paced the floor of their room with tears running down her cheeks, and Sally ran back and forth with nervous energy from the railway platform to the hotel sitting-room to the room above the grocery store, Louise sat in the hard chair by the window, knitting. Her lips were pressed together, her eyes were dry, her hands were steady. Even when the windows rattled faintly with the artillery duel which began about one o'clock, she did not raise her head nor slow the steady click of her needles. Sally begged her to eat something, but she only shook her head and began to count stitches under her breath.

Early in the afternoon Sally, who had been absent on one of her aimless excursions, rushed into the room crying, "Mother, do come down! There's a wounded man come in from Blackburn's Ford—he's over at the hotel and everyone is asking him questions. And he saw Sedgwick right in the middle of the fight, quite unhurt and yelling like a banshee!"

Louise got to her feet, white as paper. The ball of wool rolled from her lap unheeded, under the bed.

"Your father——?"

"He doesn't know Father, only Sedgwick. He's quite a character, he says majors aren't much in his line! Don't you want to come and talk to him?"

"Yes," said Freda Smith, and took Louise's arm. "Let's go and talk to him."

The man from Blackburn's Ford sat in a wooden rocker on the porch of the hotel, surrounded by tearful, ministering women. His wound was not serious, but they had taken off the dirty sling he wore and cut away his sleeve above a bloody, painful hole in his forearm, and were dressing it and bathing his face while they bombarded him with questions. He could give no very clear account of what had happened on Bull Run except that the Yankees were beaten. He seemed dazed by his experiences, and further confused by the attention he was receiving. "The *noise!*" he kept muttering. "The *noise* them guns made—like a dozen thunderstorms all fightin' it out right overhead— can you hear 'em here, ma'am, or is it just my ears?"

They assured him that they could hear it too, and he seemed comforted. They brought him food and drink, and urged him to go and lie down inside. But he preferred to sit where he was, in the shade of the porch, staring up the track towards the battlefield, muttering about the noise.

Before long two wagons arrived with more wounded, who were laid out as comfortably as possible in the patches of shade cast by buildings, to await the train which would take them to the hospitals at Culpeper or Richmond. Glad of something to do and some outlet for their sympathies, the women of Bristoe knelt in the red dust beside the stretchers with cups of milk or water, and tore up their personal linen to supplement the hasty field dressings on ugly wounds. As the men revived a little, and discovered where they were, they remembered to produce bits of paper torn from soldiers' notebooks, smudged with powder and sweat and blood, which had been entrusted to them by their comrades before they left the firing line. In this way Freda Smith learned that Preston was safe, at least up until noon. There was nothing from either Lafe or Sedgwick, nothing from Sally's lieutenant.

Fresh troops came up from Richmond along the hot, shining rails, cheering as they heard the guns. At nightfall a train came back from Manassas with wounded bound for Culpeper, and those who had waited at Bristoe were loaded into it, while the women went into the cars among the stretchers by lantern light, carrying food and water. Some of the wounded were attended still by their black body servants, who crouched lamenting by their heads, or begged necessities and comforts for their masters.

Just as the brakeman came through the car ordering out all those who did not want to go to Culpeper, Freda Smith caught at Louise's arm.

"Come quick!" she cried. "Here's a man asking for you!"

His left leg was shot away and he suffered in a tourniquet, but he looked up at Louise with a friendly grin as she bent above him.

"In my left hand pocket, ma'am—piece of paper for you——"

She dug with frenzied fingers and pulled out a crumpled fragment. Some one lifted her firmly under the elbows, hurried her to the steps, handed her down into Freda's waiting arms. The train moved out. She stood in the dark, the paper in her fingers, a trembling all through her body. Which of them? She had had Sedgwick only eighteen years. It was Lafe's handwriting she hoped for.

Freda brought a lantern. She unfolded the paper, peered at it in the dim yellow light—*My darling, keep your heart up, we have got them on the run. All safe here. Love. L.* Tears gushed forth, and she leaned against Freda, sobbing. He had thought of her. Even in a fight, he hadn't forgotten that she was waiting. *All safe here. . . .*

3

The eighteenth was a Thursday. All day Friday and Saturday the guns were silent and news was scarce. The affair at Blackburn's Ford had been a lively reconnaissance only. The general engagement was still to come.

MacDowell was bivouacked around Centreville, resting and provisioning his inexperienced troops, some of whom had been thoroughly demoralized by their retreat from the Ford. On Saturday the rumor ran as far as Bristoe that General Johnston had passed through Manassas Junction from the Shenandoah on the way to Beauregard's support, and that Jackson's brigade was following. That evening Beauregard sent a message to Bristoe that an engine and car would be spared early on Sunday morning to move the women to a place of greater safety. Those that were left looked at each other and smiled faintly. The weaker spirits, and the women whose men had been hurt at the Ford, had already departed with the wounded to Culpeper. The rest chose to stay where they were, as tension mounted.

Sunday's dawn was bright and hot, and by six o'clock the dull boom of artillery began, followed by the sharp rattle which was Confederate musketry fire. Before noon the sky was dark with cannon smoke, and wounded stragglers from the field began to arrive, all staunchly maintaining that a Confederate victory was certain, in fact, was already won. Then came the first train full of wounded bound for Richmond, and the women, numb from strain and sleeplessness, forced themselves into action again and entered the cars to continue the anxious search for familiar faces on the stretchers, doling out their scanty stores of food and drink as they went.

"Miss Louise—oh, Miss Louise, honey, I got Marse Lafe right yere, ma'am—" It was Zekiel, beckoning her from the end of the crowded car. She stumbled towards him, between the lines of stretchers. " 'Tain't no gunshot wound, ma'am—he got de typhoid fever—done keel right over wid his boots on, he did, an' de Gin'ral say bring him back in de kyars an' fin' you to take him to Richmond——"

Louise dropped to her knees beside the stretcher where Lafe lay, on the floor of the car. His eyes were closed, his cheeks were sunken and flushed, he breathed audibly—with a little moan, she set down the pitcher of water and tin cup she carried and gathered one of his lax hands into both hers.

"Find Mrs. Smith, Zekiel—she must look after Sally for me, I can't leave him——"

"Mother, the train is going to start—*oh!*" It was Sally standing above her, staring down at the stretcher. "Oh, it's *Father!* Is he dying? Where is he wounded?"

"It's typhoid. You will have to stay here with Mrs. Smith—I'm going with him."

"But you *can't* go like this, without——"

"Why can't I?" Louise settled back on her heels, dipped her handkerchief into the pitcher of water, and began to bathe Lafe's face and parched lips. "You can pack my things and bring them to Richmond when you come—I won't leave him——"

Once more the brakeman's voice rang through the car—*All out that's not for Richmond.* Sally left the train without even saying good-bye to her mother—she would not have been heard if she had—and stood on the platform watching the last car disappear towards Richmond. She didn't matter—Sedgwick didn't matter either—nothing mattered, ever, if Lafe needed her mother.

Crouched on the filthy floor of the hospital car, Louise made the torrid, jolting journey to Richmond. Long before they reached there, her pitcher of water had emptied twice and been refilled by Zekiel when they stopped at a station. Once she had accepted a cup of tea from one of the women who came into the train with refreshment at some stop along the way, dimly aware of Zekiel's gratitude for a sandwich bestowed by the same friendly hand. The quick southern night was falling when at last the train rumbled through Broad Street and halted at the station. All the way Lafe had not opened his eyes nor seemed aware of her presence.

"Get an ambulance," she said briefly to Zekiel. "We'll take him straight to the hotel."

Ambulances, wagons, carriages were waiting in the hot twilight. All Richmond seemed to be waiting, eager to help, urgent for news. Rich and poor alike, women in light, fragile dresses, colored servants in bright calicoes and white turbans, stood together in the fitful lantern light, their faces lifted to watch the pitiful freight removed from car after car. And while it seemed as though a profound silence held the place in thrall, there were sounds—sharp groans, and cries of joy or grief stabbing through the endless shuffle of the stretcher-bearers' feet —aimless, endless questioning from those who could not find what they sought—a murmur and stir of helpful strangers around a woman who had fainted across a coffin with a name tacked to its lid. . . .

Louise stayed where she was in the car, watching Lafe's quiet eyelids, bathing his swollen lips with the damp handkerchief, trying to find the pulse in his hot, dry wrist. The lightly wounded and the dead were to be unloaded first. Finally they came and carried Lafe out to the platform and she followed meekly at their heels and crouched beside him again where they laid him, one of a long row of stretchers, on the ground beside the rails. Zekiel would find them there, she knew. Zekiel's devotion was second only to hers. . . .

"*Louise!* It *is* you! Oh, Lordy, not *Lafe*—!" That was Felicity, kneeling beside her.

"It's typhoid," she said dully. "He—doesn't seem to know I'm here Zekiel is finding an ambulance——"

"My carriage is here."

"A carriage won't do. He has to go on the stretcher——"

Zekiel came at last, with word that there was room for one more in a wagon just starting. She watched them lift him, saw that Zekiel hoisted himself perilously on to the end-gate of the wagon before it could be drawn up, heard him say gently to the driver, "I'll set yere, suh—dat's my Marse Lafe you got dere." The man turned away towards the horses without objecting.

Felicity drew Louise almost by force to where the carriage stood.

"Zekiel's with him," she said. "We'll be at the Spotswood as soon as they are."

The wagon turned into Main Street just ahead of them. They stood at the curb while Lafe was lifted out, followed him into the building and up to the bedroom which Felicity tacitly surrendered to Louise.

Louise washed her face and hands and smoothed her hair while Zekiel put him to bed and bathed his hot, inert body, and Felicity scoured Richmond in the carriage for the doctor who had attended Mrs. Cary. She found him at last, and brought him back to the hotel with her. Already exhausted with a hundred calls for the wounded, he went over Lafe with care, sent Zekiel flying to the chemist's, turned the hotel bedroom into a hospital with a few terse directions. When he had done, Lafe was more comfortable, and showed signs of returning consciousness.

"You must save yourself all you can," the doctor told Louise firmly. "This will be a long fight. It always is."

"But he—you don't think he——?"

The doctor smiled wearily into her upturned, trustful face.

"He's got a lot to live for, ma'am. The chances are he knows that. We'll try."

And so, while Manassas was won by the Confederates and the defeated Federal troops fled headlong into the streets of Washington—while the trainloads of wounded poured into Richmond until every hospital overflowed and private homes were thrown open to suffering strangers, and every woman became a nurse, Louise's world consisted of a room at the Spotswood where Lafe fought what seemed to be a losing battle with delirium and fever and the ghastly complications of typhoid.

She rarely left him for more than an hour at a time, and grew thin and drawn as the long cruel days dragged by. But even at the very worst, even during the endless, steaming nights when his fever mounted relentlessly, she never really took in the idea of his dying. She and Lafe belonged to each other, and one of them could not be left behind. That time years ago, when she missed the bottom step and fell heavily and lost their third child, losing also the hope of having another, even that time she had not dreamed of dying. Each time she opened her eyes and saw him sitting beside the bed she took a fresh grip on life and held on tightly, more tightly than she had had strength to hold to his hand, where it waited on the coverlet. She and Lafe did not die, they had years yet to be together. . . .

Sometimes for a few minutes in the mornings he knew her, and his eyes clung to her face, sane and bright and full of pain, and his parched lips tried to smile. Then as the day wore on and his fever rose, the blank, unseeing stare would return to him, and the aimless muttering of battle orders and commissary details would begin again, with now and then a sharp, unanswerable anxiety about his son. Louise knew now that Sedgwick was safe, but it was impossible to get that knowledge past the mists that had closed on Lafe's brain. His delirium was all of war, and the riddle of a battle he had not seen the end of. But nothing that they told him lasted long, and he was perpetually unaware of victory and the fact that Sedgwick had survived without a scratch.

Near midnight of the twelfth day he seemed easier, and while the doctor watched him Felicity coaxed Louise to leave the bedside long enough to bathe and change her dress and have her hair brushed out. She was sitting at the dressing-table at the other end of the room, refreshed and soothed by the long, steady strokes of the brush in Felicity's hand, when the doctor gave an exclamation as the pulse beneath his fingers seemed to flicker and fade. Louise flew to kneel beside the pillow, pushing back her streaming hair impatiently to look from Lafe's ravaged face to the doctor—who shook his head with a little gesture of helplessness.

"Oh, no—*Lafe, you can't—!*" Her voice rose hoarsely, her face was contorted not with grief but with terror—a child's stark, unreasoning terror at being left alone in the dark. She caught at Lafe's shoulders with small, frantic hands, and shook him against the pillow. "*Lafe, come back!*"

Felicity tried to take her in her arms, murmuring comfort. But the doctor leaned forward, holding his breath. Under his unbelieving gaze the sick man's eyelids moved, he drew a long, tired sigh—and under the doctor's thumb the lost pulse staggered and steadied, fast and faint but almost regular again. Louise lay sobbing against the bed, Felicity crooning above her.

"Let her cry," said the doctor solemnly, for he had heard of such things but had never seen it before. "Let her cry. She knows she won't lose him now."

IV. MAY 5, 1862

THEY were all at Williamsburg again for Gran's birthday in October.
Ransom had gone with Lee into West Virginia at the end of July,
and as soon as Lafe could be moved Louise took him home to England
Street, accompanied by Eden and Felicity, who no longer had any
reason to stay in Richmond. Sedgwick was in camp on the Manassas
Line, chafing at the inactivity of the Southern Command, which had
failed to follow up its victory at Manassas. Johnston had fortified Centreville, only twenty miles from Washington, and the flag on his outposts flew derisively within sight of the capital. The Peninsula defences were well advanced, but Magruder was hampered by lack of
transport and an inadequate commissary.

By October it was seen that Lee's West Virginia campaign had
come to nothing, and he was recalled to Richmond with some loss of
prestige. Ransom was indignant over the whole thing. He said that
Lee had regarded it as a forlorn hope in any case, and that he had been
harried and thwarted at every turn by the fatal mistakes of his sub-
ordinates. Lee made no excuses and prepared no report to lay the
blame where it belonged. But for Davis' personal faith in him, he
might have been shelved forever. A Federal fleet had arrived off the
coast of South Carolina and Davis chose Lee to go down and organize
the defences there. The appointment was not popular with the fire-
eaters of Richmond. They said Granny Lee was too polite for this war,
and added that perhaps he would do better with a spade than with a
sword. The week that Lee spent in Richmond conferring with Davis
gave Ransom leave just in time to come to Gran's birthday party.

Sedgwick too got leave from the dreary tents around Centreville. He
was thin, but had by some miracle kept well in the midst of measles,
pneumonia, dysentery, and typhoid which struck down men on all
sides of him. Sedgwick did not value his life very highly these days,
and so it seemed he was in no danger of losing it. Lafe, whose con-

valescence had been long, with many relapses, took comfort from the dynamic presence of his tall soldier son, and a closer understanding and affection existed between them than ever before.

Sedgwick told them picturesque stories about a young cavalry officer known as Jeb Stuart, a great dandy in his dress, whose hard-riding, hard-bitten troopers sang as they rode, even on the most taxing marches, if silence was not an essential part of the maneuver. Sedgwick had made up his mind to get out of the infantry regiment and become a horse soldier with Stuart. Meanwhile, Sue watched him almost timidly. He was different, there were things about him now which were unfamiliar to her, and she had always known him so well. He had towards her a laughing, almost paternal air which was all he dared allow himself of their lifelong intimacy. And she missed his tenderness, and wondered if it was gone forever.

The birthday party was not very gay. Except for the men who, like Dabney, were serving with Magruder below Williamsburg, the afternoon reception was attended largely by women, and there was a general want of good spirits among them. Even the most ardent Secessionists had begun to realize that the war was not won at Manassas. Those who had clung obstinately to the conviction that England would intervene on the side of the South because of her cotton trade had begun to doubt. The pinch of the blockade was already being felt, till even the simplest necessaries, like hairpins, needles, calico, and sugar, were often entirely missing in the shops. Coffee had gone up to thirty cents a pound, tea was hard to find and was saved for invalids, everyone was trying to devise substitutes for sugar. Gran had been through it all before. Under her prudent guidance, the household had laid in supplies to stock a small shop before the price-gouging began.

Christmas was even less cheerful. Sedgwick could not get leave; the Institute discouraged holiday travel by the cadets, so that Fauquier too was lacking; Ransom was stuck at Coosawhatchie with Lee. Lafe insisted that he was well enough now to resume field duty, and was setting out with Louise for Richmond again directly after New Year's, hoping for an appointment to the staff of Johnston or Longstreet, as Beauregard had gone to Kentucky.

On Christmas morning when Pharaoh unlocked the front door he found on the threshold a square white parcel tied with stout cord. A tag attached to it was addressed to Mrs. Julian Day—that was Gran, and everyone guessed at once who had sent it.

With some ceremony and excitement it was taken up to her room and she sat up in bed to receive it, discarding her half-finished breakfast tray. Eden and Felicity watched her, smiling, while she opened it—Gran did love a gift. It was a heavy cardboard box of goodies from Gautier's, which had run the blockade from Washington—marvels of marzipan and crystallized sugar, almonds coated with chocolate, mysterious gems of silver paper tied with gauze ribbon and little nosegays—Gran exclaimed like a child. It was not until afternoon that they came to the bottom layer.

Gran had come down to the drawing-room in her best dress, in case anyone called, and they were sitting in a group round the fire, and Myrta was exploring the square white box for the single sweet she was allowed to choose, when she cried suddenly, "Oh, look, there's something more!"

The bottom layer revealed two wrapped packages, and one of them was marked with Eden's name. She had to open it there before them all, her cheeks rather pink—a small box with Galt's gilt signature on the lid, and inside it a blue sapphire ring set with diamonds.

"*Oh!*" cried Myrta in an envious ecstasy. "Oh, *Eden,* he must be rich as Crow-sis!"

Felicity's eyebrows rose, and she glanced at Gran, who refused to return her look.

"Put it on, Dee," said Gran, for Eden sat staring at the lovely thing in its box without making a move to possess it.

"Yes, do put it on, Dee, what luck you're wearing a blue dress!" said Sue.

Eden lifted the ring from its white satin bed and slipped it on her third finger. It was a perfect fit. The large, pure stone shone unbelievably, lit by the diamond points which surrounded it.

"*Oh!*" said Myrta again, spellbound. "I wish *I* was engaged to Cabot Murray! What's in your parcel, Gran?"

It was an eighteenth century silver vinaigrette made like a heart-shaped locket with *L'Amitié* engraved on an embossed ribbon scroll across it. When you opened the snap top it revealed a grid exquisitely pierced in a design of heartsease and leaves, and when you sniffed there was the sharp sweet tang of French smelling salts.

"To think of all that lying on the doorstep!" said Sue. "How do you think it got there, Dee?"

"The rivers are full of smugglers," Felicity told her quietly. "It would have been more to the point, I'm afraid, if he had sent quinine and calomel for our poor soldiers."

"But not so much like him," murmured Gran.

That night Eden crept down stairs after everyone was asleep and posted a letter to Cabot Murray on her own doorstep. But when she went down in the dawn to see, it was still there. No one had come back for a message.

"Well, at least he can be sure you won't forget him now!" Gran consoled her, laughing.

2

A Yankee general named McClellan had been given command of the Federal Army in Virginia, in place of MacDowell, who could never live down Manassas. He was an engineer, and had gone to the Crimea as an observer with a Military Commission when he was only twenty-nine. His assignment now, at the age of thirty-five, was to take Richmond. He was hard, vigorous, up-to-date, and conceited, with a liking for personal fame. And during the winter of 1861–62 he built an army of citizen soldiers which was rather like himself. As spring came in, there was uncertainty in the South as to whether he would hurl it first against the troops encamped near the old Manassas battlefield or try to flank them and come at Richmond up the Peninsula.

In March Johnston suddenly withdrew his army from the Manassas Line to south of the Rappahannock, where he could more easily cover all available routes to Richmond, and could in case of need unite quickly with Magruder below Williamsburg. McClellan promptly occupied the deserted camp at Centreville. Then from Alexandria he embarked his army for Fortress Monroe, where he arrived on April second.

Changes had taken place on the Confederate side too.

After undue elation following the Manassas success, the South was now depressed and discouraged by a series of disasters in the West, where Fort Henry, Fort Donelson, and Nashville had all fallen to an obscure Federal general named Grant. They were next briefly cheered

by the exploits of the iron-clad dreadnaught *Merrimac,* but then there
was a rumor that Richmond was going to be given up without a fight.
That came to nothing, but the March enrollment of all men between
eighteen and forty-five for conscription did not raise their spirits.
Davis recalled Lee to Richmond in something like despair, and Ransom wrote disgustedly to Felicity soon after his return from the Carolina coast:

"Things have gone from bad to worse—now let Lee try! And
even now they won't give him a free hand. Davis believes in him
—says he does—but keeps him at a desk at Richmond headquarters and clings jealously to his own rights as Commander-in-Chief
with a deathlike grip. Johnston still commands in the field. People
here are beginning to realize the odds against us—we are 9,000
against 23,000, for one thing.

"Lee expects an attack on the Peninsula as soon as the roads are
firmer. I am of two minds about your safety. You are in the line
of march there, but Richmond is after all their goal, and is now a
very unpleasant place to be, besides. It is full of refugees from the
Norfolk area, which is considered to be in danger, as well as from
the northern part of the State. Food is scarce and very dear. Meat
isn't fit to eat, butter and eggs are never seen any more, coffee and
tea are luxuries of the past. Poor Johnston has lost three small children by scarlet fever. I think you had better stay where you are for
the present. Lee and I are two Spartan bachelors inhabiting the
Spotswood. His wife is at White House on the York River, and he
does not think it wise to bring her here in her present state of
health. Our long hours at the office leave us little time for social
life.

"Sedgwick has been in town on a few days' leave, much elated
over his transfer to Stuart's cavalry, a coveted post. But you know
that, of course, as he has sent home for a remount. He says if you
cannot sing *Oh Susannah* and make up a new and shocking verse
as you go you can't get into the cavalry at all! He looks well, and
is the only person I know who seems to be enjoying this war. I
saw Lafe for a few minutes yesterday—he's not very happy since
his assignment to General Johnston, who is irascible to a degree.
I wish you could persuade Louise to come home, she is as likely

to see him there as here now, and it is lonely for her at the Spotswood, though Sally is anything but that!

"The newspapers nowadays are enough to make you want to cut your throat, and in their zeal to inform the public leak all sorts of the most vital information to the enemy. We need time desperately —time and ammunition, which is endlessly delayed by the blockade. Everyone is calling for reinforcements, even Stonewall Jackson. . . ."

He did not add that there was sickening anxiety in Richmond for Magruder's little force on the Peninsula. And Felicity when she answered the letter did not tell him that the women of Williamsburg were making sandbags for Magruder out of everything from tablecloths to their silk dresses.

On the fourth of April McClellan advanced on Yorktown.

3

For Tibby Day it all had a weird nightmare quality of repetitiousness. She had been there before. But now, in the fortifications made by the British in 1781 and lately improved by modern engineering, Magruder held Yorktown against the enemy, and Dabney was with the men who slept on their arms in the trenches at the other end of the Warwick Line, which ran north and south across the Peninsula along the little river of that name. Magruder's ranks were thin and overworked, and everyone knew that in the face of any real attack he must give ground to the last fortifications, only two miles east of Williamsburg—where he had constructed a fort named for himself, and numerous redoubts and rifle pits, and had felled trees on the far side of open land to form a natural abatis of logs.

It was all improvised and undermanned, but it was all there was. And it brought McClellan to a standstill outside Yorktown on the fifth, and to everyone's surprise he went into camp and began digging parallels and making redoubts of his own as though for an elaborate siege in the George Washington manner.

When this had gone on for days, and still McClellan seemed in no hurry to attack, Williamsburg relaxed a little. Dabney rode into town for a few hours' leave, and told with joyous laughter how Magruder, always theatrical, was stage-managing his outnumbered forces to make them look like more—how on involved, meaningless maneuvers designed only for show he even marched companies in a circle like a stage army, at the edge of dense woods, as though he shifted whole regiments for some obscure purpose hidden by the trees from the watchers only a few hundred yards away. And McClellan, peering through his field glasses, receiving reports from his observation balloon which went up daily, was gratifyingly deceived, and considered his force inadequate for assault, never dreaming he outnumbered Magruder more than three to one.

When Dabney had gone back to the line, tall and confident and swaggering a little in his freshened-up grey uniform, Gran comforted Felicity. "We always win at Yorktown," she said.

The next day, while Eden sat with her knitting in Gran's room after dinner, Pharaoh's soft tap on the door preceded his doubtful entrance with a soiled and rumpled white envelope in his hand.

"Black chile nobody ever saw befo' bring dis-yere to Micah in de stables," he explained apologetically, "swearin' it's for Miss Eden. 'Tain't so written on de outside, but Micah bring it into de house, an' chile done disappear."

Eden held out her hand for the letter with misgivings. From tact or caution the envelope was unaddressed. She glanced at Gran uncertainly.

"Thank you, Pharaoh," said Gran, dismissing him with a placid smile. "Open it, Dee."

Eden broke the seal rather daintily. The paper inside was clean, and the message was brief:

Beloved, I am here with McClellan. When I got the assignment I had no idea it would bring me so near to you so soon. I think of you always, for you belong to me by a law which was not made in Richmond or Washington, nor can it ever be revoked by any legislature yet devised by man. Whatever happens now, I hope with all my heart that it will not bring grief or disaster to your household. Rest assured that my part in the coming campaign will be that of an observer only. I shall not fire a shot.

C.

Eden finished reading it with a little moan and dropped the paper in her grandmother's lap.

"What difference does that make!" she said, and covered her fac with her hands. "Oh, what *difference* does he think it makes!"

"It was all he could say," said Gran, when she had read the messagr through. "He meant it for your comfort." Eden was sobbing, and she reached to lay a small frail hand on the shaken shoulders, but her face was serene. "There, there," she said. "Don't take it so hard, Dee. Wars don't last forever. I know. I can remember the last time before York-town—*how* I cried! But he came back safe. Most of them come back safe. I can remember——"

Towards the middle of the month General Johnston arrived from Richmond with Lafe riding in the group of officers which followed him, and Lafe got nearly an hour to visit Gran and to give them all the news. From him they heard that the Confederates were beaten at Shiloh, after they had so nearly won—that man Grant again, and another named Sherman. The Manassas army, Lafe said, was now en-camped near Richmond, and Johnston wanted to keep it there and withdraw Magruder to the Richmond side of the Chickahominy as well. Lee and Davis were in favor of sending it to Magruder's sup-port on the Peninsula. The next few days would decide.

Ransom had become indispensable to Lee at the Richmond head-quarters, Lafe said, and Sedgwick had been on leave again in his new glory of cavalry boots and sabre. Jeb Stuart was likely to choose his men on whims, and Lafe told the story of Sedgwick's transfer with laughter which did not mask his pride.

Sedgwick had taken his favorite horse Cherry back to Centreville with him for company, after his October leave, Judah riding behind him on a sober little mare named Jingle. Soon after they reached camp again Sedgwick had ridden over to the cavalry camp near by to see the horses, and was standing with his bridle over his arm chatting to a friend when Stuart passed by on his own blood bay. The general's eyes ran swiftly over Cherry's points, and he drew rein. "Whose horse is that?" he demanded. Sedgwick presented himself respectfully as Cherry's owner. Stuart's eyes lingered on Cherry. "I'd like to try him," he remarked. "Would you like to try my Skylark, here?" Sedgwick would like nothing better. Stuart dismounted, tossed his reins to Sedg-wick, swung into Cherry's saddle. Sedgwick was up on Skylark simultaneously. "Come on!" said Stuart, and they were off, trot, canter, wheel, parade walk, full gallop over broken ground—they pulled up at last, far from the camp, and eyed each other with mutual respect. "Did you ever time him over the half mile?" Stuart asked wistfully, and just as Sedgwick replied with regret in the negative a bullet whizzed past their heads, followed by another, and another.

"I think we have ridden towards the enemy outposts, sir," said Sedgwick without blinking.

"Must be we have," Stuart agreed, with a glance in the direction from which the shots were fired, as two more came whining over. "Shootin' high—they always do." He put Cherry to a leisurely trot back towards their own lines, and Sedgwick followed. "Cavalry gallops *at* the enemy and trots *away* from him!" the general advised him cheerfully. "A good man on a good horse needn't ever get into any real trouble, with any luck at all."

They rode back to camp side by side at an easy pace, and exchanged horses again. The next day Sedgwick was ordered to report for duty to General Stuart. It was only a question of time now, said Lafe, until Stuart discovered that Sedgwick had the sort of singing voice derisively known in the family as Negro tenor, and could, of course, play a guitar.

Lafe left Williamsburg with Johnston the same day they came, and Ransom wrote that it had been decided after a stormy conference at headquarters to reinforce Magruder with the Manassas army—which meant that Louise was returning to Williamsburg at once with Sally as both Lafe and Sedgwick would arrive there within the next few days. *Lee is not allowed to fight this war in the saddle,* Ransom added bitterly. *Only to give advice, which as a rule is most ungraciously received. No one but McClellan would have hesitated so long to attack as things are now.*

"Must we tell them Cabot is with McClellan?" Eden inquired of her grandmother.

"I don't see the necessity," was the reply. "We burned the message, didn't we?"

Eden nodded drearily.

"I hate having to burn my love letters!" she cried. "It's—humiliating!"

"You've still got the ring," Gran consoled her.

Johnston made his headquarters at the Vest house in the Duke of Gloucester Street. For days the reinforcements poured through the streets of Williamsburg and out towards Yorktown—Harvey Hill came first with his Carolinians; then Longstreet and Early, Pickett, and A. P. Hill; and Stuart's famous cavalry, who rode into town singing, led by their general's own lusty baritone——

> *"If you want to smell hell—*
> *If you want to have fun—*
> *If you want to catch the devil—*
> *Jine the cav-al-ree!"*

There were veteran troops from Manassas in Johnston's army, and newly organized units as well—a very cheering sight to the inhabitants of Williamsburg. Things perked up there in no time, though Johnston was gloomy and warned Huger at Norfolk to prepare to evacuate if he fell back from Yorktown. Johnston had not wanted to come to the Peninsula, and he did not want to stay there. Meanwhile, he viewed McClellan's complicated siege operations with a disparaging eye.

Lafe could live at home now, and Sedgwick often clanked in to town in sabre and spurs from the cavalry camp. Sedgwick was already sporting the yellow sash of a captain on the Staff, and even as Ransom had said seemed actually to be enjoying the war—as quite possibly he might, for there is nothing like cavalry life for taking a man's mind off himself.

There was daily cannonading to and fro as April wore on, but with scant result on either side. And there was daily sniping at McClellan's observation balloon, which was never hit, and much riding back and forth from the front line to the Vest house by orderlies and staff officers. Johnston's headquarters were nothing like as gay as Magruder's had been—he ranked Magruder, who fell back gracefully before his superior officer—but there was considerable social life all the same, especially where the cavalry went.

Next to horses Jeb Stuart loved music and dancing, loved to sing and hear singing, and kept always with him a sort of personal minstrel, a man named Sweeny who played the banjo and knew all the songs. It was said that Stuart went to any lengths to entice away from any other commander any man with a good singing voice, and that men who were bored in the infantry or artillery moved heaven and earth to get into the cavalry, where the fun was.

Large, laughing, bearded, booted, with a tasseled yellow silk sash and an ostrich plume in his broad-brimmed hat, General Stuart dined out in Williamsburg with great success—and one night with Sedgwick as his host he bowed over Gran's hand, coaxed Eden to play and sing his favorite *Oh Susannah* with him as a joke on young Sue, made Sedgwick sing *Lorena* to the guitar, flirted with Sally, flattered Felicity, and spoke to Louise with simple affection for her son, who, he said, was a fellow after his own heart. When the evening was over they were all agreed that there was no one like General Stuart, and were proud that Sedgwick should be serving under his command. There was just one thing, said Sedgwick confidentially. The cavalry camp was always bone dry. If you wanted a drink you had to go next door to Longstreet's gang.

The weather was foul for spring in Virginia, with a continuous cold downpour of rain enlivened by thunderstorms. On the evening of the first of May Lafe brought home word of the loss of New Orleans—which some felt was the whole war lost, with Farragut in possession of the lower Mississippi and Grant outside Corinth.

While they discussed it, grave-faced, in England Street, Sedgwick's spurs announced his arrival in the hall and he came in looking keyed up and ready for anything.

"I think we're moving," he told his father. "The sick and wounded are ordered out to Richmond. Things are stirring somehow. What's up, do *you* know?"

"Yes," said Lafe cautiously. "We may be pulling out of here."

"Without a *fight?*" cried Sedgwick incredulously.

"You'll get a fight, all right, in the cavalry," Lafe promised him grimly. "You'll get the rear guard action while we drag the baggage wagons through this mud!"

"You mean we're *evacuating?*" Sedgwick demanded. "Then what in the name of commonsense did we come here for?"

"We came to delay McClellan as long as we could—which we have done. Johnston never wanted to come here. He is convinced that now McClellan is about ready to open with his batteries and blow us right off the Peninsula. We haven't got the guns to compete with his, you know, once he turns loose on us."

"But—what about the town?" asked Sedgwick, thinking of his womenfolk, and Lafe sighed with a glance at Louise where she sat sewing within reach of his hand.

"Better than fighting for it, maybe. If we clear out they will march right through it, after us. The fight will come later, in front of Richmond, just as Johnston intended all along."

"Oh, the deuce!" said Sedgwick. "I haven't hung about here for two mortal weeks just to fight a nasty little rear guard action with the whole Federal Army!"

"It's what you're going to get, all the same," said Lafe.

And it was, only a little nastier than anyone expected.

On that Saturday night, May third, Johnston pulled his men out of the Warwick Line under cover of a cannonade, and began to pour them back through Williamsburg towards the Chickahominy and New Kent Courthouse—back towards Richmond. It was still raining. Magruder's men went first, so that Dabney in the vanguard reached the town in the mid-morning hours after slogging through deep mud all night from Lee's Mill, past Fort Magruder from where the spires of Williamsburg were visible in the wet dawn, and into the Duke of Gloucester Street, where people lined the sides of the road under umbrellas and waterproofs to wave good-bye. A halt was made, and the tired men snatched cups of coffee and sandwiches and home cooking from the loving hands of the women who came to see them pass.

The Street was by then a bottomless sink of mud—the wagons sank in it up to the hubs and stalled whole regiments, the officers' horses ploughed through it knee deep, and the whole town had become a scene of shouting, cursing, frantic confusion, with the crack of the long mule-whips like pistol shots and the fluent mule-lingo of the black drivers a profane babel of tongues. It was still raining. And to the east there was the dull boom of cannon and the rattle of musket fire, for McClellan had discovered the retreat at daybreak, occupied Yorktown at once, and organized himself for pursuit.

About one o'clock on Sunday, when the streets were jammed with baggage wagons and the draggled, drenched companies were detouring round them and the whole fifty thousand of the Peninsula command seemed to be packed into the town, the firing to the east grew suddenly quite loud, spreading a new alarm—the Federal pursuit was driving the Southern cavalry in. Johnston was seen to confer with a muddy courier. And then, most unbelievably, a whole brigade was turned and marched back in their own tracks to occupy Fort Magruder and hold up the Yankee advance. There was going to be a battle after all.

4

McClellan's pursuit was much closer than Johnston had counted on, the Confederate progress to the rear much slower than he liked. Johnston himself led the way back to Fort Magruder, flagging in another brigade as he went, and it came to a race for the Fort to occupy it in sufficient force to hold the other army off it till artillery could get into position.

Johnston won by a nose, and the Federals recoiled under a hot fire into the woods. By that time darkness fell and it was pouring rain harder than ever.

At daybreak the main Confederate army began worming its way westward through Williamsburg again, and the Federals opened a sharp artillery fire on the Fort. Johnston, who had caught a few hours' sleep at his Williamsburg headquarters during the night, returned to the Fort and ordered back more men from the retreating files.

The battle for Fort Magruder raged all day long, and the fighting was often intense. Stuart led charge after charge in his favorite column of squadrons formation—the squadrons following each other at a distance of only twelve paces or so, solid blocks of yelling men standing in their stirrups at a pounding gallop, with the white glitter of sabres above them and the gouts of mud from their horses' hooves spattering like bullets all around them.

About midday they charged McClellan's hard-pressed center at the edge of the wood opposite the Fort, and as they wheeled and fanned out and circled back to re-form, Sedgwick saw in his path a blue-coated officer who was just disentangling himself from a horse which had pitched headlong and thrown him heavily. Two or three other mounted Federals had scattered among the trees and escaped. The dismounted man dodged the trooper ahead of Sedgwick and stumbled back, favoring a twisted knee, squarely in front of Cherry, who was at a hard canter. Just in time, Sedgwick saw his face, and Cherry rose on his hind legs, snorting and outraged at the drag on his tender mouth.

"Get yourself out of here, Cabot Murray, do you want to be killed?"

yelled Sedgwick furiously, and thundered on in the wake of the squadron.

Grinning in spite of the pain in his wrenched knee, Cabot made his way back among the trees to where one of General Hooker's orderlies and a man from the New York *Tribune* had hung about waiting for him.

"Well, *that* was close!" said the *Tribune* man. "I thought you were a goner, and I shut my eyes! What did he say to you?"

"Something rude—I couldn't hear," said Cabot briefly, not wishing to claim acquaintance in this company with the man in grey who had refrained from riding him down. "My horse is finished. You'd better go on out of this, I'll get back somehow."

"Rubbish!" said the *Tribune* man. "This beast will carry double for a while. Get up behind me, I think they're going to come in again."

Thus the Press, who had come down to the front lines to see for themselves how Hooker's New Jersey troops were standing punishment, retired prudently from the hottest part of the field.

By twilight the firing had thinned all along the line and the Yankees seemed to have had enough. General Early had been badly wounded in a fracas at the northern end of the Confederate front, and Stuart's cavalry had not been out of fire all day. But Johnston left the field before dark, convinced that he had gained enough time for his withdrawal towards Richmond. Some cavalry and part of Longstreet's men were left at the Fort as a holding force and most of the rest set out again on the bottomless roads which led back through Williamsburg, taking the wounded with them. There were no ambulances, and no wagons could be spared for their transportation beyond the town. Those who could not march would have to remain in Williamsburg to become prisoners of war.

The thunder of the big guns rattled the windows in Williamsburg all day, and some of the citizens went out, wearing waterproofs and carrying umbrellas, to see the battle. Those who took their carriages soon bogged down, adding to the confusion on the roads, and when they tried to pursue their investigations on foot were ridden over and around by profane cavalry detachments and caused splits and fissures in the infantry columns moving up into position as they gathered in bewildered, deafened knots in fancied shelter debating their retreat homeward. Those who rode out on horseback were likely to venture

under fire in innocent curiosity, to the rage and distraction of the officers, who would order them behind the lines only to come upon them
a few minutes later, still in the way.

Just at lamplighting time, when the guns were slacking off, the
Spragues' coachman, Daniel, was shown into the Days' living-room by
Pharaoh. Eden and Felicity sat there together, white and silent, trying
to sew and knit as calmly as Gran did, and to endure until this dreadful day was over. They looked up at Daniel, who was dripping in a
waterproof and panting from his hurried progress through the choked,
streaming streets, each of them dreading to hear his message.

"Miss Felicity, ma'am, Miss Louise sont me to tell you all de wounded
has begun to come in an' dey's a-sortin' of 'em out down at de College,
an' could use mo' help——"

"Is there anyone—has she heard from——?"

"Oh, Lawdy, ma'am, none o' our folks is hurt, leastways far's we
know now—Marse Lafe, he rid off wid Gin'ral Johnston, not a scratch
on him, praise de Lawd, an'——"

"Sedgwick?"

"Marse Sedgwick ain' showed up yit, ma'am—but ain' no call to git
skeered 'bout dat, 'cause Gin'ral Stuart hisself ain' come by yit—an'
you know yo'self de Gin'ral ain' gwine let nothin' happen to dat boy,
ma'am——"

"I'll come along to the College at once." Felicity rose and laid aside
her thimble. "Pharaoh, tell Mammy to fetch my things and an umbrella."

"I'll go too," said Eden, and after a doubtful moment Felicity con-
sented.

Susannah was out in the Duke of Gloucester Street with the devoted
Micah at her heels, trying to hold an umbrella over her while she
watched for the return of the cavalry from the field. They told her
everywhere she asked that General Stuart would be among the last
to leave. But she had already stood for an hour in the rain among other
white-faced women, watching while the long, stumbling lines of exhausted infantry ploughed towards the rear; peering eagerly at each
group of mounted men, in her search for Stuart and his aides. The
mare Jingle had come home to England Street alone in the dusk with
an empty saddle, mired up to her mane and with a deep sabre cut in

her neck above a half-severed rein. And while she was only a remount, and there had been no sign of Cherry or the other horse Sedgwick had with him, Jingle's appearance was alarming, and after she had heard of it Sue could not be kept in the house.

Once while she waited there in the rain with Micah, a woman who stood next her had uttered a cry of joy and run out into the straggling files and been caught up in the arms of a soaking man in grey, and she went on down the muddy road with him, still held in the circle of his arm, to be with him as long as she could—a man who was at least safe, Sue thought enviously, even though he must keep on towards Richmond—but the woman who loved him knew he was alive to-night. . . .

Sue stood where the feeble light of a street lamp above her fell on the men as they passed—their drawn faces were lighted too by an occasional lantern on a foundering wagon or a flare in the hand of a hurrying courier. She had no idea how long she had stood there, nor how long she must wait till she knew about Sedgwick. She wore an old waterproof of Fauquier's which nearly touched the ground, and she had tied a kerchief over her hair, which escaped in little rings and curls around her ears, shining with wet. Her feet were soaked and cold, and Micah in his waterproof and sou'wester shook like a dog with chill.

> *"I had a dream de odder night, when ever'thing was still,*
> *I thought I saw Susannah, a-comin' down de hill——"*

"Hark!" said Micah, and——
"It's them!" cried Sue. "That's Stuart's men, they always sing!"

> *"Oh Susannah! Oh, don't you cry for me!*
> *I've come from Alabama, wid ma banjo on ma knee!*
> *Oh, Su-san-nah!——"*

Five men, riding easy at the head of a splashing column which sang as it came—five men with waterproofs over their yellow sashes, their wide hats pulled low; in the center, the long-legged boy general who was their leader—and then Sweeny, who knew all the words—and the adjutant, who wore a mustache—and two others—but not Sedgwick.——

"It rained all night de day I left, de weather it was dry,
De sun so hot I froze to death,
Susannah, don't you cry!——
Oh Su-san-nah!——"

Before Micah saw her move, Sue was out into the muddy road, dodging between horses' heads, to catch at General Stuart's stirrup. He threw up a hand to halt the column behind him, reined in sharply, and leaned to see who she was.

"Oh, please—have you seen my cousin Sedgwick? His horse came home alone—*is* Sedgie with you——?"

"Honey," said Jeb Stuart gently, "I haven't seen him since roundabout noon-time—second charge we made down to the wood he was right behind me—lost him when we wheeled—he didn't come in to re-form."

She was staring up at him, her knuckles against her mouth. He reached down a hand in its white buckskin gauntlet, coated with mud, and gripped her shoulder sympathetically, while the endless, deafening chorus bellowed around them.

"Now, hold up, honey—lots of hope yet—they're bringing in the wounded to the College, why don't you try over there?"

A mounted orderly floundered up, yelling a message in the general's other ear. Micah had arrived at her side and was pulling her back in frantic anxiety from among the horses' feet. She went with him, dazed, unresisting, docile.

"De bull-jine bust, de hoss ran off, I thought I sure would die,
I shut ma eyes to hold ma breff,
Susannah, don't you cry!
Oh, Su-SAN-NAH!——"

"Where's that girl?" Stuart was demanding of his shadow, Sweeny.

"Gone to the College, I reckon. Should I have hung on to her?"

Stuart glanced about hopelessly into the lantern-lit confusion, and put the column in motion again. The song passed on, with its tireless and terrible improvisations, towards the College and out along the Jamestown road.

When Sue and Micah arrived at the College she found Felicity and Eden at work with the surgeons among the stretchers laid out in rows on the floor. The damp, warm air was heavy with stench, through which curled the sickly smell of chloroform. They assured her that Sedgwick was not there, and Louise turned white at the question even while she shook her head. But Sue passed on doggedly down the lines of wounded men to make sure. The face of one was swathed in bandages, so that she bent above him. "Please tell me your name," she said gently, but there was no answer, and it occurred to her to look at his hands—they were not Sedgwick's hands—she straightened and went on, turned at the end of the line and went back along the other side. He was not there.

Felicity came and caught her by the arm and ordered her to go home at once and change into dry clothes. Sue nodded obediently and left the College, Micah close behind her.

"Where now?" he queried, raising the umbrella above her.

"There must be more wounded," she said dully. "We'll have to find them."

They found them at the schoolhouse, and at the Post Office store, lying in rows on the floor, leaning against the wall because there was no place to sit down, crouched on the steps at the edge of the rain, cradling a roughly bandaged arm or hand until their turn with the doctor came. No one pushed or demanded attention first, no one complained of delay which was added agony, no one seemed to think he was quite as badly off as the next man, very few of them made any sound at all except sometimes under the surgeon's probe. Patiently Sue passed between the dreadful stretchers, viewing unspeakable horrors with unseeing eyes because there was only one thing she looked for— Sedgwick's face. And then they seemed to have come to the end of the wounded, and still they had not found him.

Sue stood on the steps of the store, staring eastward through the streaming night while the army scuffled and scraped and cursed its way past her to the rear. It seemed as though she knew where he was. It seemed as though if only she could get to the battlefield she would find him, at the edge of a dark belt of trees, lying in the mud with Cherry's dead weight pinning him down——

Micah touched her arm fearfully, peering into her face.

"Sho' you ain' gwine faint, Miss Sue? You look awful bad——"

It was gone, like putting out a light—the feeling that she knew where he was. Her feet were wet and cold, she was muddy to the knees, her soaked skirts dragged at her hoop, she was hungry from missing her dinner—but worst of all, that strong, surging certainty that she could find him was driven away by Micah's voice. She had had it, though—for just a few seconds she had known exactly where to look for Sedgie. . . .

"We're going down to the battlefield," she said, starting towards home. "Come on and saddle up."

"Well, 'fore de Lawd!" breathed Micah, following in a trance. "Yo' ma sho' nuff gwine have a fit."

"I'm not going to ask her. Hurry up, Micah, pick your feet up!"

"I's pickin' 'em up an' puttin' 'em down in de wet," Micah mumbled, sloshing beside her. "Ain' had my dinner," he added in an aggrieved aside.

"Neither have I," she reminded him. "Neither has he."

They reached the stables by a stealthy detour of the house, and lighted a shaded lantern there. By comparison with the night outside, the dry, hay-scented air seemed sweet and cosy, and the pampered horses munched contentedly in the box-stalls.

"Saddle Philomel," Sue commanded. "And *hurry,* Micah! Then saddle Firefly for yourself, and we'll take Laurel for him."

"Lordy, Miss Sue, Marse Ransom sho' gwine gib us de debbil 'bout takin' all dis good hoss flesh out on sich a night!"

But Micah set to work, and when he led Philomel out of her stall saddled and ready to start, Sue's discarded hoop lay in a circle of tapes and wire on the stable floor and she stood slim and straight with her wet skirts clinging to her, waiting to mount.

They knew every foot of the way towards Yorktown, having ridden over it dozens of times by daylight. Micah went first with the lantern, leading Laurel, Philomel splashing daintily behind. They took the back roads and private lanes to get out of town unnoticed, and even then they met stragglers and walking wounded and a small troop of cavalry. Once a grey-clad man caught drunkenly at the stirrup of the led horse, demanding a lift in the other direction. Micah pushed him off angrily and he reeled away into the darkness, muttering threats. When the cavalry troop came up, Micah and Sue took to the drenched bushes at the roadside and waited, shivering, till the quagmire which passed for a road was clear again.

Finally the dark shape of the Fort loomed on their left, with here and there a point of light—Longstreet's men were even now abandoning the last posts, and once again Sue and Micah drew back from the road until the weary companies had passed on their way to Williamsburg.

"Reckon we got it all to ourselves now," said Micah lonesomely. "Lookit, dawn comin' up at last."

The lingering drizzle of rain stopped as they rode on in the dim grey light, out across the trampled shambles of open ground before the Fort.

"Gwine git de sun today sho' nuff," said Micah, sniffing the morning air. "Dry things out some. Whereat you think we fin' him, Miss Sue?"

"Trees," she said, frowning after the lost moments on the steps of the store. "Let's go down to the edge of those woods."

The broadening light showed hideous sights on the deserted battlefield. Men and horses lay grotesquely, disfigured in death. Sometimes something stirred or cried out, and Micah averted his eyes, but Sue rode on, aware only of the dark line of trees ahead. When they reached the edge of the felled timber they dismounted and saw that most of the quiet forms which were scattered like broken toys on the ground were blue-clad. They had come to where Hooker's Jersey troops had held against Stuart's pounding charges.

"Should I shout?" asked Micah, awed by the spreading silence under the trees, a silence made louder by the occasional cries and groans of despairing wounded men. "Jude might hear me. Seems like we oughta see somethin' o' Jude, finally."

Sue moved off slowly without replying, groping for the certainty she had felt on the steps of the store, which seemed forever shattered now. There were acres of this battlefield, scores of uniformed bodies. . . . As she went, a hand reached up and caught at her skirt, almost tripping her.

"Help me—somebody help me——"

She stopped, knelt beside the wounded man, motioned Micah down beside her. Together they raised him a little, pushed a knapsack under his head. He was caked with blood from the waist down, and he picked feebly at the bright buttons of his blue coat.

"Inside—pocket—" he kept mumbling. "Pocket—inside—my coat—help——"

She undid the buttons, and the edge of a little leather case showed from the inner breast pocket. She drew it out, put it in the fumbling hand. Before he could open it his head fell back and he died.

They left him there, the picture of his children in his stiffening fingers, and plodded on along the edge of the clearing. Once Micah bent to turn over a grey-clad body which lay face down, and shook his head. They went on, leading the horses.

Suddenly they both halted in their tracks, and their eyes met unbelievingly. While they held their breath, listening, the faint call came again.

"Jude! Judah, are you all right? *Jude!*"

Micah uttered a prayerful sound, but Sue's voice rang out confidently.

"Sedgwick! We're here, Sedgie, call again—louder!"

Silence.

They looked at each other—but both of them had heard it—*both* of them, at the same time. Micah began to look frightened.

"*Sedgie!* Answer me, Sedgie, we've come to find you!"

And when there was still no reply she dropped Philomel's bridle and ran forward towards the fallen trees, her unhooped skirt dragging round her feet while she scrambled over down logs and fought her way through underbrush which tore off the kerchief she wore, and tore down her hair until it lay in short, tumbled curls on her shoulders—but still she ran, half sobbing now, stopping often to call his name and listen, begging him to answer. Micah followed at the edge of the timber with the horses, arguing with her.

" 'Tain' no use in dere, Miss Sue, honey—cavalry cain' work in de woods—he boun' to be out in de open, Miss Sue——"

She came back towards him and stood poised on a slanting log several feet above the ground which gave her a wider view. The sun came up behind her, throwing the long dark shadows of the trees at her feet. The stir of their presence and their voices had raised all round them a feeble clamor for succor among the crumpled figures strewn about the field, who had roused to a hope that the stretcher-bearers had come at last—but Sedgwick, wherever he was, had made no sound to guide her. Then she saw him, not far from where Micah had paused with the horses, saw him lying on the muddy ground at the edge of the timber, with Cherry's corpse across his legs.

Together she and Micah raced the last few yards and fell on their knees beside him. He opened his eyes as her arms went round him, and looked up into her face.

"Oh, Susannah, I—thought I was hearing things—how did you get here——"

"You're hurt—oh, Sedgie, you're *bleeding*—!" The hand that had touched his shoulder came away covered with blood.

"Get Cherry off my leg, Micah—can't move—" He hid his face against her, stiff with pain, while Micah tugged the carcase of the horse away.

"Can you ride, Sedgie? We've brought Laurel for you—can you stay on?"

"I'll stay on. Where's Jude?"

"We haven't seen him. Jingle came home alone."

"He was here. Find Jude—I won't go without him—" He leaned against her, his breath coming fast and irregular with the pain.

"Find Judah quick," she told Micah. "He must be here somewhere. Call to him."

"Ju-dah! Where you got to, boy? Oh, *Jude*—!" Micah's voice ceased abruptly, came again on a different note, from the underbrush beyond. "I got him, suh—he's daid."

There was a moment's silence, and then Sedgwick said, "We'll take him with us," and Micah came back to them, half carrying, half dragging the body of his brother.

"He kin have de Firefly hoss, suh, dat I was ridin' today—we got Laurel yere fer you—time fer us to git movin', too, dem Yankees be 'long any minute now—" Unaided, he got Judah's body across Firefly's saddle and came to bend over Sedgwick. "Now den, Marse Sedgwick, you put yo' good arm roun' my neck an' jus' hang on tight to Micah, we git you into dat ol' saddle in no time—easy, now—rest yo' weight on me, suh—yere we go——"

Sedgwick's right leg was bruised and almost useless, and his left arm hung limp from a bayonet stab in the shoulder. When after a sweating, swearing struggle he was actually up on Laurel, he held a moment to Micah's supporting hands and said, "You're sure—?" and Micah nodded, his black cheeks shining with tears. "He came for me," said Sedgwick. "He brought me Jingle."

With Sue holding Sedgwick's bridle while he clung with his good hand to the pommel, and Micah walking at Firefly's head, they started back in brilliant sunlight towards Williamsburg. And as they drew away, the Federal field surgeons and stretcher men filtered into the haunted thickets behind them, picking up the last of the wounded and carrying them to where the wagons waited. The Federal Army had wagons, and even ambulances, for the transport of its wounded.

It was a little easier going now that there was daylight over the road. But they had not covered more than half the distance to the town, Sedgwick swaying in the saddle, his teeth clenched, when Micah called out sharply, "Yankees comin'!" and dashed into the underbrush at the side of the road, dragging Firefly after him. Sue followed quickly, leading Laurel, and they dismounted, except for Sedgwick, well off the road, hidden from it by the dense foliage, holding their horses' noses and peering through the leaves.

Soon the clink of bit and spur and the creak of saddle leather came opposite to them and a group of scouts went by. Close behind them, at as smart a pace as the condition of the road would allow, came a dozen men in dark blue coats with gold braid and crimson sashes. Sue gave a smothered gasp, and swallowed the impulse to tell Sedgwick what she had seen. Only a few horse-lengths away from her in the morning sunlight, Cabot Murray rode with the Federal officers towards Williamsburg.

5

A detachment of Federal cavalry followed the group of officers, and then Micah, scouting cautiously towards the road, reported the long, inevitable line of infantry on its way.

They dared not return to the road. And so began a sunlit nightmare of beating through wet underbrush and cutting across muddy fields to the outskirts of the town, where they paused again to get their breath. Sedgwick was barely conscious now, and they had to hold him in the saddle, walking one on either side of him.

"Nebber git him home to England Street bang in de middle o' dat ol' Yankee army," said Micah. "Might git him into our own stables, though, round through de orchard."

"Come on, then," said Sue doggedly, and somehow they made it, through the orchard, and Pharaoh came running out of the house as they rode into the stable yard. With exclamations of amazement and concern he helped lift Sedgwick down and support him into the house where they allowed him to collapse on the drawing-room sofa.

Felicity and Eden had not been to bed at all, in their anxiety over Sue's disappearance, and breakfast was just coming in. Eden was up stairs with Gran, who was having her tray in bed as usual. Sue ran up in her torn, muddy dress with her hair down on her shoulders and her hoop missing and her face chalky with weariness and strain, and said—"Gran, I've got Sedgie down stairs wounded, and the town is full of Yankees. What shall we do?"

"Where is he?" asked Gran, for nothing could surprise her any more, and she had told them all along that Sue would be safe with Micah.

"On the drawing-room sofa."

"Heavens me!" said Gran. "He'll get blood on the upholstery. Bring him up here at once."

"Oh, Gran, will they take him for a prisoner? He'll die if he doesn't get good nursing!"

"Tell Pharaoh to bring him up here to me. And go and change your clothes at once and hide the ones you've got on. Eden, take away the tray."

Pharaoh, who was still a young man and had the strength of an ox, made nothing of getting Sedgwick up stairs, but as they reached the top step Micah's voice rose hysterically from the lower hall.

"Unc' Phare, Yankees comin' in at de gate!"

"Bring Sedgwick in here," Gran repeated without hesitation, and added, pointing, "Under the bed, quick." She sat up very straight against the pillows, her eyes bright and dark under the fetching lace-trimmed cap she wore, and her little bed-jacket had frills at the neck and wrists.

They lowered Sedgwick to the floor and rolled him under the flowered chintz valance which reached from the bottom of the mattress to the polished floor.

"Now, don't make a sound, Sedgwick, whatever you do," she said firmly. "All of you leave the room except Eden. Micah, go and get the saddles off the horses in case they search the stables. Sue, get into a dressing-gown and be ready to show yourself as though you had just got out of bed. Felicity, go down to the dining-room and behave as though you were eating breakfast. Eden, give me back that tray.

There's the doorbell, Pharaoh. If they want to search the house **don't** try to stop them."

Everybody scattered, hypnotized by her commands. Gran poured out a rather coolish cup of tea with a steady hand. These were only Yankees, and in her young days she had seen the British come to Williamsburg, and even then nobody ate her.

In a very short time Pharaoh was back again, the whites of his eyes showing.

"*Cap'n* Murray in de drawing-room, Miss Eden," he announced with stately disapproval of the company she kept.

"I c-can't see him," gasped Eden, her hands cold moist paws.

"Of course you can," said Gran. "In fact, you must. Ask Captain Murray to come up here, Pharaoh."

"Yes, ma'am," Pharaoh's back as he turned away was very straight.

"Gran——!"

Tibby Day put milk in her tea, because that was the way she always took it, though it would now be stone cold.

"It's always nice to have a friend at court," she remarked gently, wondering if she would really have to drink the stuff.

Cabot came up the stairs with a clink of spurs and sword-belt. He looked enormous in the unfamiliar blue uniform, and he spoke very quietly, his eyes seeking Eden's across the room.

"I hope you got my message," he said. "Otherwise this must be rather a shock."

A moment more she looked back at him from where she stood—then without a sound she crossed the room swiftly and buried her face against his shoulder with a touching effect of homing and submission.

He held her there, gratefully, and over her head he looked at Gran, sipping her tea in bed.

"Yes, we got the message," said Gran. "I do hope your army isn't going to be a nuisance, we've just got rid of ours."

"That's partly why I'm here," he explained. "There is an order that all Confederate wounded in the town must be listed as prisoners of war and surrendered for medical care, and the search is pretty thorough. I have given my word at headquarters that this is a household of defenceless women and servants, and I don't think you'll be molested in any way. But as a mere formality, there is a man from headquarters downstairs who must be allowed to satisfy himself that I am not mistaken. After that he will post a sentry at the gate until things settle down." He waited a moment as though for her to speak, but her eyes were steady and calm. "Have I your permission for him to just—glance through the rooms in the name of duty?"

"Certainly," said Gran. "Let him come up. Have you had breakfast, Mr.—Captain Murray?"

"Yes, thanks." He went to the head of the stairs. "You may come up, Wilson—and then get out, will you?"

"Thank you, sir." Grinning self-consciously, a very young lieutenant clanked briskly up the staircase and looked in at the open door of Gran's room. "Good morning, ma'am—sorry to disturb you, I'm sure——"

"Go with him, Eden," said Gran graciously. "And open all the doors for him. You'll probably find Sue not dressed yet."

The lieutenant followed Eden from door to door apologetically, averting a tactful gaze from the ruffled confusion in Sue's room, thanked Gran politely, saluted smartly, and retired noisily down the stairs. Cabot stood near the window waiting to see that a sentry remained in front of the gate when the officer moved away with his detail. Then he turned and came towards the bed with a smile.

"Well, that's a relief," he said. "I got permission to come here with him because there was a report that you had—" He stopped, his eyes resting on the floor at the edge of the chintz valance. Across the polished surface of the floor a narrow dark trickle crept from under the bed towards the braided rug under his feet. "Is it Dabney?" he asked.

They only looked at him, speechless.

"Who is it?" he repeated then, more brusquely. "Dabney or Sedgwick, which? Under the bed."

"Sedgwick," admitted Gran, and dropped her hands on the edge of the tray with a little gesture of defeat. "He needs good nursing. You know what military hospitals are, he might lose his arm. Sue went all the way down to the battlefield for him last night."

Cabot knelt and turned up the valance and reached in.

"All right, son," he said kindly. "Come out and let's stop that bleeding."

But Sedgwick was unconscious, as he had been ever since they put him there, and did not move. Cabot laid hold of his grey coat and pulled him across the polished floor, folding up the edge of the rug to save it from staining.

"That's bad," he said after a quick look at the wound. "Let's get him to bed." With no apparent effort of his broad shoulders he lifted Sedgwick's stripling length in his arms and said enquiringly—"I suppose Dabney's bed is empty?"

Eden fled silently before him to show the way, and he laid Sedgwick on a sofa in the room while she stripped back the counterpane and opened the bed, which had yet to be made up for use.

"I'll bring sheets and blankets and send Pharaoh to undress him," she said. "His own servant seems to be—to be missing."

Cabot untied his own sash and laid his sword across a chair and began to unbutton his coat.

"Send up a lot of hot water and bandages too," he said. "And some brandy. And tell them to be quick."

Eden stared at him.

"Are you going to——"

"You're wasting time, my dear," he said briefly, rolling up his shirt-sleeves, and she ran out of the room to do his bidding.

When she returned with the brandy bottle, a maid had brought kettles of hot water and basins and cloths, and was helping Mammy to make up the bed. Cabot worked over the wound with the cool concentration of a surgeon while Pharaoh, also in his shirtsleeves, hung above him obeying orders with silent zeal. The floor beside the sofa was littered with blood-soaked linen.

"Don't want the brandy yet," he said without a glance at the bottle she held. "Leave him in peace a bit longer. This isn't a pretty sight, I'd come back in about twenty minutes if I were you."

"Sue says he was pinned underneath his horse by the right leg and it might be broken."

"We'll come to that later. Got to stop this bleeding first of all. Keep Sue out of here, will you?"

Eden lingered.

"I—didn't know that you——"

"I'm not a doctor, but you can't get one now—and it's only common-sense in the field to know something about wounds. Will you please go away like a good girl, I'm busy."

Eden closed the door behind her with an expression of dazed surprise, and tracked down Sue in Gran's room where, in a pink peignoir, she was drinking hot coffee and eating scrambled eggs under her grandmother's eye. Sue forgot food when Eden came in.

"Is he all right? May I see him now?"

"Not yet, honey. Cabot is dressing the wound."

"*Cabot* is!"

"Just like a doctor," Eden told them, awed. "I never knew he—Gran, could he get into trouble for this?"

"Probably. But I think we can trust him to get himself out again!"

"Yes." Eden stood looking down at the sentry's back, where he stood at ease between the gate-posts. Her round chin lifted proudly. "We can trust him."

When Cabot returned to Gran's room nearly an hour later he was buttoned again into his blue coat with its captain's shoulder straps, his sword hung at his side, and every fold of his crimson sash lay precisely.

"He'll do," he said to the three questioning faces which awaited him. "We've got him into bed and the bleeding has stopped. His leg will turn black and blue and be very painful but it isn't broken." He rested thoughtful eyes on Sue. "And while I'm playing at being the old family doctor," he added, "I'd better order you to bed, Susannah, for the rest of the day."

"Can't I see him first?"

"No. He's full of brandy and doesn't care about anything. You've done your part, and your mother is sitting with him. Bed for you. March."

Sue stood up rather stiffly and showed her dimple at him.

"You're what they call a martinet," she said. "Eden's not used to being bossed around like this."

"I haven't begun to boss Eden yet. It's you I'm after right now. Git!"

Sue got, her eyelids already heavy with sleep. He turned, smiling, to find Gran holding out both her hands to him from the bed.

"Cabot," she said, and it was the first time she had used his name, "this family is going to love you very much—even when you come in brass buttons and a sword."

"Thank you, Gran." He stood a moment looking down at her, her hands in his. and Eden spoke haltingly from beside the bed.

"We didn't—at least, I never thought you'd be wearing the blue!" she blurted, and flushed up to the eyes as he turned to her.

"I mentioned that I would try for a Staff appointment," he reminded her. "And I got it when McClellan took command. I rank as a volunteer aide to McClellan first, and Special Correspondent second. The general combs out all my despatches very thoroughly and tells me I am a better aide than I am a journalist. He means it as a compliment. I suppose you realize that you have got me right up a tree now, with McClellan, if I don't report Sedgwick's presence here."

"Oh, but you can't do that!" Eden flew at him, caught his arm. "Poor Sue, she saved him—you can't take him away now, he isn't able to be moved—oh, please promise to say nothing about it just yet!"

"That makes him liable to arrest for being behind our lines though not a prisoner of war," he pointed out.

"If they find him," said Gran. "We can meet that when he's better."

"I don't like it this way," Cabot objected. "Of course Wilson would swear we didn't see a trace. But after I've gone, suppose——"

"How long—" Eden swallowed and tried again. "How long will you be in Williamsburg?"

"Unless McClellan is completely crazy, which is not impossible, we'll keep hard after Johnston till he turns and fights—somewhere between here and Richmond."

"Another battle?" Eden asked faintly.

"Sweetheart, this wasn't a battle, it was only a rear guard action! The battle is still to come." He held her by the waist, looking down, as though they were alone. "Where's your blue dress?" he asked very low.

"I—" Her chin quivered, her eyes filled. She flung her arms tight around his neck and leaned against him, her face hidden. "How long does this go on?" she demanded fiercely, muffled against his coat. "How many battles do they have to fight?"

"If we took Richmond with the next one, it might be the last."

She was suddenly very still, in his arms. When she raised her face her tears had stopped.

"But that would mean that you had beaten us."

"You—us! North—South! Blue or grey! What does it matter, Eden, between you and me!"

"You say that because you are winning now."

He shook her, not too gently, forcing her to meet his eyes.

"Take that back," he said.

"I—shouldn't have said it."

"Think what you like about McClellan, Eden, he can look after himself. But I am not your enemy, remember that. Somebody has to win this war some time. Better for everyone if it doesn't take too long. I've got to go now. May I come back this evening?"

She nodded, realizing gratefully that he had not used Sedgwick as a lever in that request.

"Unless Sedgwick seems a lot worse I wouldn't call a doctor in the circumstances. It's a clean wound, and nowhere near vital, he was bleeding to death, that's all."

She looked up at him piteously.

"Oh, Cabot, I do thank you! I didn't mean——"

"Shut your eyes, Gran," he said, and kissed Eden long and hard before he went.

6

It was an endless day for everyone but Sue and Sedgwick, who slept through it.

Cabot was no sooner out of the house than Eden discovered with anguish that she had not said a word to him about the ring, which had been on her finger the whole time. In the depths of her chagrin she searched out last year's blue lawn dress—no one had new clothes any more—and Mammy freshened it and sewed in clean lace collars and cuffs. Against it the blue stone in the ring took new fire and Eden was glowing too, Gran thought, as though she herself was set with diamonds.

Felicity and Louise worked at the schoolhouse hospital most of the day and Felicity found an opportunity to tell Louise that they had Sedgwick hidden in Ransom's house, running a high fever and very uncomfortable, but in no danger so far as they could tell. Louise went round to see for herself during the afternoon, and decided against spending the night there for fear of its looking odd to the sentry at the gate.

McClellan had settled himself comfortably into the Vest house vacated only a few hours before by Johnston, and was bringing up reinforcements and supplies from his Yorktown and Hampton bases. The Federal troops who had taken part in the action in front of Fort Magruder went into camp around the town, appropriating the College buildings for their wounded and offices. McClellan was a soldier and a gentleman, and under his eye it was a fairly well behaved army on the whole, and its hosts treated it with icy courtesy.

Pharaoh came back indignant from an excursion through the streets just before twilight.

"Yankee soldier stop an' ax me why I don' jine up wid dem an' fight fo' my rights," he reported to Felicity. "I tells him I done *got* my rights. Don' I live jus' as good as Marse Ransom, I tells him—don' I eat jus' as good, an' sleep jus' as warm, an' don' de same white tailor-man make my clothes outen best broadcloth dey is? Whaffor I go pointin' off hollerin' 'bout rights, I says to him, an' he done look like a sheep sho' nuff!"

It was after dark when Cabot returned to the house, and Felicity had gone wearily back to the schoolhouse hospital, reminding Gran that since it would never do for Eden to entertain him alone in the drawing-room all evening they would have to come up stairs to her.

"I suppose I can go to bed before he comes," said Gran tartly, for she always resented the role of chaperon. "Nothing matters at my age!"

Felicity remarked patiently that it mattered very much at Eden's age, even if the man was considered one's fiancé, and that she wasn't going to have a Yankee think her girls were free and easy, and that as Mr. Murray had found Gran in bed once already that day she could do as she pleased about tonight.

And so she was sitting up against her pillows in the lace cap and frilled bedjacket, and Eden was knitting in the corner of the sofa, when Pharaoh showed Cabot in. There was wailing and chanting in the quarters behind the house where Judah's body lay, and the once quiet streets were churning with couriers and supply wagons and officious young aides as the Yankee army settled itself in. Against the impertinent tumult of war and the untimely festival of death, stood the sweet serenity of Gran's room, where she had ordered a small fire kindled for cosiness, and all the lamps were lighted, and the white dimity curtains at the windows moved in a breeze that was fragrant with the Virginia spring.

"Welcome home," said Gran, as he paused on the threshold as though not quite sure he belonged in so pretty a picture, and his quick glance at her was full of mutual understanding. "Everything is here but your pipe and carpet slippers," she added, indicating the sofa by the fire.

"You both look beautiful," he said sincerely. "I'll see Sedgwick first, and then come put my feet on the fender."

Sedgwick, he told them ten minutes later, would not be very happy for a good many days to come, but would live through it, barring accidents, and must keep very quiet for fear of opening the wound. He sat down on the sofa beside Eden, still looking a little incredulous of his surroundings, and she held out her left hand to him, the ring winking in the firelight.

"There was no way to thank you," she said simply. "And this morning I forgot! I'm very proud of it, Cabot."

He kissed the hand, for Gran's presence never embarrassed him in the least, and then kept Eden's fingers locked in his so that the knitting languished in her lap.

"I let Melicent try it on," he said, turning the ring in the light. "She has good hands, with long fingers—not as pretty as yours, though. She sent you her love."

"We must find her a present," said Eden. "What would she like?"

"Music!" he replied ironically, and shrugged. "Nothing but music! Remembering a lesson I learned here last year, I asked her what she wanted for Christmas, and found she spends all her pocket money for songs to learn. And I must say the poor little beggar's got a voice like a lark when she dares to let it out!"

"I've got lots of music," said Eden. "I'll choose some for her. Can you send it?"

"I can. With my copy for the paper. And she'll like having it from you. You see," he said ruefully to Gran, "I do what I can for her now, and she's so grateful it's embarrassing. In fact, between you and Eden here, I'm a reformed character, haven't you noticed?"

"You aren't entirely, or you wouldn't brag about it," said Gran.

"I'll brag if I like," he retorted defiantly. "What has happened at home is a minor miracle. My father will never change, of course. But with him gone for the day, and Melicent practicing her music—well, it no longer feels as though the body was laid out in the best parlor! I even tried to buy her some pretty clothes the last time I was in New York, but I'm not very good at that, apparently. Her mother—which we will still say for the sake of convenience—said the dress I brought back was meant for a lady of the town, and Melicent is not going to be allowed to wear it."

"She must come to the wedding," Gran smiled. "After the war."

"I doubt if she'd live through it. She's never been anywhere." He sat playing with the ring on Eden's finger, and his face darkened and drew in. "After the war," he repeated. "Must we wait that long?"

"Will it be so long?"

He sighed impatiently.

"It's easy enough to tell the generals where they're wrong and what they ought to do," he admitted. "But nobody has any gumption about this war! It can go on forever, as things are. *You* could have finished it after Manassas, I think—you had us on the run, you could have taken Washington if you'd kept on coming, but you sat down at Centreville for months! You had Shiloh won, hands down, last month, and you let Grant snatch it back again! Oh, we're just as bad! Here we sit while Johnston retreats in good order and gets all ready for us in front of Richmond. If we kept moving and hit him now while he's on one foot we might end it before the year is out!"

"Ransom said we had no transport and supplies to take Washington."

"I know, I know all the reasons and excuses and justifications on both sides!" he said angrily. "It's my business to know. But if I have to wait till this war is over before I marry Eden, I may be an old man with a long white beard! I want her now. I suppose her father wouldn't hear of it?"

"He's in Richmond," said Gran sadly, and shook her head.

"Well, when I get there myself," he said through his teeth, "I'll ask him!"

"And if he says No I'll come anyway," said Eden, her heart beating faster at the thought.

"Would you?" His eyes raked her face with something of the old bold bantering look, from her hair to her throat. "Would you elope with me, Eden, down a rope ladder in the moonlight, with a carriage and pair, and live with me in sin at Willard's till we could get a marriage license? I believe you would, at that! Well, you won't have to. I'll manage things better than that, when the time comes."

Pharaoh came in then with a big silver tray which he set on a table on the hearthrug.

"Coffee, suh?" he suggested softly. "Or Madeira, suh?"

"Coffee, please," said Cabot, making a mental note to send them some from the officers' mess. "Black."

Pharaoh poured it out and took it to him, showing the same loving care with which he served Ransom or the boys. Captain Murray's status had altered with Pharaoh since they put Sedgwick to bed in Dabney's room that morning. Then he poured Eden's cup, half hot milk with a dab of sugar, and set a plate of sponge cakes within their reach. Lastly he carried to Gran's bedside a glass of Madeira wine and a thin sweetened biscuit on a smaller tray. After which he wished them a soft good-night and went away, closing the door gently behind them.

There was no such pleasant nightly ceremony in the great gloomy house in Trenton, and Cabot turned it over in his mind, perceiving that it was not done in his honor only, but was part of a household routine he had never encountered before. Each time he came here, it seemed, he realized anew the infinite possibilities of living with women like these who pampered their menfolk and in turn sunned themselves in masculine tenderness. Once more he contemplated rather dizzily the unending revelations his marriage with Eden would mean. Impatience, longing, a reckless exigency ran through him like a flame. His youth was wasting while they bungled this stupid war. He had much to learn from Eden, and something of his own to teach her. But first they had to take Richmond.

Gran broke the silence Pharaoh left, sipping her Madeira.

"I was thinking this afternoon," she said slowly, "you could do a kindness for our Sue, Cabot, if you would."

"Gladly," he said, rousing himself, supposing at once that like all Southern women Sue wanted something the blockade denied her, something he could obtain for her from Washington or Trenton.

"You own a newspaper, don't you?"

"My father does. It's not quite the same thing. We don't always see eye to eye."

"Sue has been writing stories. I don't mean novels like Fanny Burney, I mean stories—like the ones you see in *Harper's Monthly* and *Godey's*, only I think better than they are. My husband wrote. She gets it from him. If you could print in your paper something that she wrote, it might seem more worth while to her. I don't mean I want you to pay her money for it. I just mean—to see something in print might encourage her to go on."

Cabot groaned inwardly, for he agreed with his misanthrope father that the greatest cross an editor must bear is the literary output of his friends. But he said forbearingly, "I might arrange it. Have you something of hers that I could see?"

"The last one she did is there on my desk. Give it to him, Eden. You see," Gran continued, sipping her Madeira, "Sue has had a shock. She and Sedgwick want to marry, but the cousinship is too close. There is nothing anyone can do, they must make their lives separately. Sue needs something she can call her own. And her stories give her something to think about."

Cabot took the closely written pages from Eden's hand with an unuttered sigh and leaned towards the lamp. He had not much hope of Sue, at eighteen. He supposed it would be possible to give her a column now and then and out of his own pocket provide a small payment for her self-respect. No more.

They watched him glance through the first page, and read the second. Then they saw him go back to the first and read it again, and the second, and the third—slowly, attentively, absorbed and unhurried, to the end. Then he sat staring at the rug under his feet, frowning, silent, apparently puzzled. We shouldn't have asked him, Eden thought unhappily. He doesn't like it, and he doesn't like to say so. We've put him in a very embarrassing position. . . .

"Are there any more of these?" Cabot asked abruptly.

"Quite a lot," said Gran. "Some better—some not so good."

"I want to see them all."

"Do you think you can——?"

"People pay money for things like this. Where did she get it? How does she know how a man feels when he is going to fight a sword duel? How does she know that a fencer's arm begins to ache way up in his back teeth as he tires? *I* know that, because I've done fencing at school, but Sue hasn't! Did Sedgwick tell her?"

"Sedgwick doesn't fence."

"Give me the rest of them."

"I can't now, they're in her room and she's asleep."

He turned to Eden.

"Go and get them," he said.

"But it wouldn't do to raise her hopes until we're sure——"

"Her hopes can go as high as they will," he said. "This thing is as good as published right now. I haven't sweat at a desk for ten years for nothing, I know good writing when I see it! I don't know how she does it, or where it comes from, but unless this story is just a freak, unless all the others are altogether different, Sue has a job if she wants it—she can sell what she writes, beginning now, and I know a dozen people twice her age who would give their ears to say the same!"

"She gets it from Julian," said Gran complacently, and then she sat up very straight and looked at them with wide dark eyes above the wine glass. "Julian was a fencer," she said. "So was St. John Sprague. Two of her great grandfathers were keen swordsmen. It's as though she *remembered*——"

"And that's not all she remembers," said Cabot soberly. "She has laid this story in London. Was she ever there?"

They shook their heads silently.

"I have been. But how does Sue know that you walk *uphill* to St. Paul's and keep left for Cheapside? All right, she saw a map. But how does she know that if you stand in a certain place beside the water in St. James's Park the towers of Whitehall show like minarets against a pale blue sky?"

"It's *Julian!*" said Tibby Day, with conviction. "I've felt it before, with Sue, but I never realized——"

"Now, listen to me, my dears," he said gravely. "Don't let's start Sue thinking about this. Tell her I like the stories and can get them published. Tell her to go on writing more. But don't ever ask her how she *knows.*"

Eden slipped away to rifle Sue's desk, and came back laughing, her hands full of papers, followed by Sue herself in the pink peignoir, her eyes still drowsy, her hair curling on her shoulders—and Cabot as he looked at her was stabbed with pity for Sedgwick.

"Eden said you might *print* something I wrote!" she said to him incredulously.

"What's more, you might even get paid for it."

"*Money?*" she cried delightedly. "Money for what I write?"

"Oddly enough, I get money for what I write," he reminded her, grinning. "And it's not half as interesting. Now, Susannah—listen carefully. I may be wrong about this, but I'm willing to bet myself that

I can sell your story about the man who was going to fight a duel. I don't know about the rest, I can't say till I've read them. I couldn't sell stories about Negroes and the life you lead here in Virginia—not to Northern papers, probably. But this eighteenth century story is worth something."

"There's one about Lafayette," said Sue. "Gran told me."

"I didn't tell you that one," said Gran instantly. "You made it up."

"Well, you told me about Lafayette, and the rest was easy," Sue insisted equably.

"I could tell you another one about Lafayette—" said Gran, looking back.

"You tell me and I'll write it down. That would be a good idea, wouldn't it, Mr. Murray? Because Gran can *remember* things, and I have to imagine them!"

"It comes to the same thing in the end," he said, watching her. "Write another story about London, will you?"

"There seems to be more point to it when they're going to be printed," she nodded. "I don't mean just getting money for them—but putting them away in the desk when they were done, it seemed sort of childish. I wasn't going to do it any more, but now I will."

Gran lay back against the pillows, the empty wine glass in her hand. The Madeira had made her sleepy, and she was content. Between them, perhaps they could save Sue. Now for Sedgwick—in the morning, perhaps—when she had rested—when he was well again—something must be done about Sedgwick. . . .

"Gran's tired," said Sue softly, and came to take the tilting glass from her hand. "I'll go back to bed, and you two can whisper, and it won't disturb her."

Tactful Sue, tiptoeing out the door so that they might make the most of their time together, lying awake herself to plan a new story about London for Cabot in order not to listen tensely for every imagined sound from Sedgwick's room, where Mammy watched beside the bed. The town was quieter now, with most of the army in exhausted sleep, but in the quarters they still mourned Judah, brother of Micah, nephew to Pharaoh, who had died at his post in his young master's service—a woman's voice rose wild and sad in a formless, grieving chant, and was joined by other voices, low, minor, throbbing with pagan sorrow for the first-born—Micah would be there, with his earnest, eager face, and the maids in their white turbans, so silent, so docile, so quick to serve and to please, so *civilized* in their daytime duties about the house, and now— Sue shivered and pulled the sheet higher round her ears. No one knew quite what went on in the quarters when they got to singing like that. It was best not to know. Judah was dead. It might have been Sedgwick, deprived of his own mammy tonight by the mysterious rites for Judah, tended no less devotedly by their own mammy, starched and gentle and solicitous, her round black cheeks wet with tears—for which of them? Judah was dead, and Sedgwick was safe in Dabney's bed, thanks to Cabot who was a Yankee and who some day would take Eden away from them—better to love a Yankee than your own first cousin, Sue thought drearily, and pulled the sheet over her head entirely, and thought her way resolutely back to London a hundred years ago until she fell asleep.

Gran's eyes were closed. Cabot laid his arm behind Eden and she slid into the curve of his shoulder as though she had done it a hundred times before. He held her silently, marvelling again at the unself-conscious confidence with which she received his love, she who had been so wrapped in affection all her life that more was only natural; while to him, from out of that bitter, uncompromising house in Trenton, it was an emotion still new and untried, full of surprises, full of uncertainty, but full too of undreamt-of delight. It shook him beyond all reason that she nestled against him in that quiet room, giving him her hands to hold and her lips to kiss, while her grandmother dozed in the big bed, and the log fell apart, and the clock ticked. This, then, was what men married for—this fireside serenity, and a warm, sweet weight above their hearts. Ah, yes, but married, you need not leave her again and go back to a dreary cell at headquarters with tomorrow's despatch bag to catch. . . .

His arms tightened cruelly and he drew a long sigh against her hair.

"When you marry a journalist," he whispered, "you marry a deadline, and a printing-press as well. It amounts to bigamy on a large scale. The bag goes at daylight, and I still have my despatch to write."

"All about how we licked the rebels at Williamsburg," she suggested, and he could not see her face.

"Eden, do you mind so much?"

"Only when I think of Dabney—and Father—and Sedgwick—and Uncle Lafe——"

"I know," he murmured. "I know. It shouldn't be. This should never have happened to you. I'll make it up to you somehow. I'll make you forget it and be happy, once it's over—I promise."

"Shall I have to live in your father's house?"

"Sweetheart, you won't have to do anything you don't like. Lately I've lived in Washington, myself, most of the time. Would that suit you better?"

"It doesn't seem so far."

With swift insight he was aware of the loneliness she faced, cut off from this large, loving family and the cheerful life she was used to, because she had chosen to love a Yankee, forsaking all others.

"We'll have Sue up often for visits," he promised hastily. "We'll come back for Christmases here. You won't be sorry, Eden, so help me God."

She stirred in his arms, pressing closer to him.

"Who said I was sorry?" she whispered.

That was the sort of thing that shook him.

When they heard Felicity come in from the hospital he rose reluctantly and kissed Eden once more, and kissed Gran's cheek without waking her. And after a few minutes' polite conversation in the drawing-room—Felicity treated him formally still—he went away to headquarters and Eden crept into bed beside Sue and shed a few unimportant tears, just because she loved him so much and the future looked so complex.

Cabot, sweating at his despatch for tomorrow's bag, got no sleep before dawn, and told himself that she was worth it. *Who said I was sorry. . . .* But would he ever be sure. . . .

7

McClellan left Williamsburg going towards the Chickahominy after resting his troops for two days—left Sedgwick safe in bed where Cabot had put him, although in a somewhat anomalous situation behind the Federal lines, as Cabot himself ruefully reminded them before he followed McClellan—for the town was garrisoned, to guard the supply route from Fort Monroe and Yorktown.

Cabot's farewell to Eden was sudden and brief. The battle was shaping up before Richmond. Both as aide to McClellan and as Special

Correspondent his place was at the front, where things happened.

The armies fought at Seven Pines and at Fair Oaks, and the wounded streamed back into Richmond, which shook with the rumble of guns —they fought to an exhausted draw, and paused to pant and bleed and reorganize. Johnston was wounded at Fair Oaks, and Lee at last came into the field as commander of the Southern forces. Richmond was as good as lost, the Federals held heavy advantages—but Lee was in the field.

At the end of June they fought again, and again the windows of Richmond rattled in the cannonade which began at daylight and went on till dark, and its streets were hideous with wounded, and with the open wagons of the dead. Seven days of battle—Mechanicsville, Gaines' Mill, Peach Orchard, Frayser's Farm, Malvern Hill—"I remember Malvern Hill," said Gran. "Julian was there with Lafayette."

And McClellan failed again to take Richmond. On the first of July he fell back to the James with the assistance of his gunboats, and went into camp at Harrison's Landing near Westover, and began to dig fortifications.

A few days later a brief message came through from Ransom.

"Richmond is safe, at least for a time," he wrote, "and Lee is running things at last. There is no jubilation, for it is a city of horrors because of the wounded; full of the sound of muffled drums and the Dead March, played for the officers' funerals. The heat is worse than ever I knew it before, and we smell like a charnel house everywhere.

"Lafe fought under Harvey Hill after Johnston was wounded and distinguished himself at Frayser's Farm. He is worrying about the poor old plantation, which must have been overrun by McClellan in his withdrawal. We hear that many such places in their path have been set afire, either by accident or design, especially if the family was not in residence. So if Farthingale is gone forever, it is a loss many of our friends and neighbors will have suffered too.

"I myself saw most of the action, and both Dabney and I are still whole and well. Cabot Murray is in Libby Prison with a leg wound, taken in the fighting at Gaines' Mill on the twenty-seventh. I will try to arrange an exchange when he is able to travel."

Felicity was not altogether surprised when Eden, looking tragic, said they must go to Richmond at once. But Felicity sighed. Her own love story had run so peacefully, almost uneventfully, to its consummation in happy marriage that she found herself quite baffled by the intransigent, headlong behavior of her daughters. Eden and her Yankee—Sue and her cousin Sedgwick—both affairs so unforeseen, so impossible of accomplishment in a world already topsy-turvy with war.

Felicity's serene, matronly beauty had not been much visited by tears and sleepless nights heretofore. Ransom always knew what to do, and she had only to lay her perplexities before him and they were expeditiously solved by his tact or his commonsense or his domestic diplomacy. But not even Ransom had been able to eliminate the Yankee, and even Ransom admitted defeat in handling Sue's little tragedy. And now Ransom was in Richmond and she had no one even to consult. No one except Gran, who with what Felicity named her periodic perversity, sided each time with the girls. That is, she encouraged Eden in her infatuation for Cabot Murray, and sympathized perhaps unduly with Sue, who Felicity was sure would outgrow this fantastic, immature passion for her cousin Sedgwick. And yet Sue had cried herself to rags for weeks, and now here was Eden with great dark smudges under her eyes, looking like a ghost the morning after Ransom's letter came. Felicity wondered what she had done to deserve such troublesome children. Not even Louise was any help to her, for Louise thought of nothing now but getting back to Richmond herself to be nearer Lafe. And Ransom, the reliable, who was always there when you needed him, had gone into the field with Lee and might get shot any day now. Felicity—serene, beautiful Felicity—sat down and wept.

Eden shed no tears over the news that Cabot was wounded and a prisoner. Eden thought things over by herself and then put on her best dress and her prettiest bonnet and set out alone for the College, where the Federal officer in command at Williamsburg had his office in Brafferton House. Major Cronin had gone to Yorktown for the day, they told her, but his adjutant was in and would see her.

The adjutant was young and wore a smart blue uniform with bright buttons and rose most politely when she came in and placed a chair for her and asked what he could do. Eden, unlike most women he encountered these days, did not by any means hate the Yankees as a separate race, and gave him a friendly smile. The adjutant's head quite swam.

"I have come to—ask a favor," she began bravely, sitting very straight with her gloved hands holding fast to each other in her lap lest he see how they trembled.

The adjutant bowed, and hoped he would be able to oblige her.

"I have just had word that my—that the man I am going to marry is wounded and a prisoner in Richmond."

"In—Richmond," repeated the adjutant, looking surprised.

"He is a—he belongs to your army," she explained.

"I see," said the adjutant, flattered for his army.

"We—we met before the war began."

"Quite," he nodded sympathetically.

"I want to go to him at once," Eden went on, feeling a little happier about the whole thing already, for surely this pleasant young man would put no obstacles in the way of her plan.

"Naturally," he agreed. "You mean you want a pass to leave Williamsburg for Richmond."

"Well—yes, I do. But that's not quite all." Her greenish eyes were lifted to his in a sort of troubled confidence he found very touching. "You see—I have a cousin in the Confederate Army who was wounded at Fort Magruder."

The adjutant murmured his regret.

"And I thought—if the authorities at Richmond were agreeable too —you might arrange an exchange."

"If only this war was run by people like you," said the adjutant admiringly, "how simple it would be!"

"It wouldn't be run at all," Eden said with decision. "If I were President—either one of them—I would go and see the other one and find out how it could be stopped at once."

"The main trouble is," said the adjutant, "that neither of the presidents has anything like your charm of manner."

Eden smiled at him still more broadly, for his was a style which reminded her of Cabot Murray.

"You will try to do something about it?" she said confidingly.

"I will, indeed." He drew a paper towards him and picked up his pen. "Where is your cousin now?"

"In our house."

He glanced up at her sharply under his brows.

"He is listed with us, of course, as a prisoner of war?"

"Well, you see—m-my sister brought him back herself from the battlefield—they have been playmates all their lives—she didn't quite understand the rules of war, and——"

"Are you trying to tell me that you have concealed this man in your home for weeks?"

"He was—so ill," she said faintly. "And you know what the hospitals are. We were afraid they would take him away to Fortress Monroe with the others, or—we were afraid he might lose his arm, without proper care—we always meant to give him up as soon as he was well enough——"

The adjutant's manner had become a shade less cordial.

"I suppose you know that is a very serious offense?"

"I—yes, sir." Her greenish gaze, so hopeful and trusting until now, fell to her hands, clasped tight to hold them steady in her lap. "But as he and Captain Murray were the same rank, I—hoped that an even exchange might be arranged——"

"Murray? Is Cabot Murray a prisoner?"

"Do you know him?" Up flashed that radiant gaze to dazzle him again.

"I do. He is listed missing here. You're sure he's in Libby Prison?"

"With a leg wound."

The adjutant had begun to write rapidly on the paper.

"Your cousin's name?" he demanded as he wrote.

"Sedgwick Sprague. You *can* do something about it?"

He let her wait while he finished the message, addressed it, rang a hand-bell on the desk and gave the paper to an orderly with directions to send it off at once.

"We can do something about Cabot Murray, I think," he said then. "As for your cousin—I'll take it up with Major Cronin when he returns."

"Oh, but—" Her chin quivered. "They're friends," she pleaded. "He and Cabot. It would be——"

"I agree with you, my dear lady, that it would be very appropriate to exchange them," he said, less formally again. "But I have no authority to promise you anything of the kind. Perhaps if everything else fails, Captain Murray himself after he is released might be able to——"

"You mean they might listen to him—about Sedgwick——?"

"McClellan would listen to him, yes. But it is quite impossible for me to guarantee anything now."

"And m-my pass to Richmond?" The wide, piteous gaze waited on his. "My mother would go with me."

An unwilling smile touched the adjutant's lips. With something like a shrug, he picked up his pen again and wrote out the pass.

"And if I were in Libby Prison," he said, "I hope some one would do as much for me!"

8

Almost the first thing Eden and Felicity encountered in Richmond as they drove to the Spotswood Hotel at twilight was the sad pageantry of an officer's funeral bound for Hollywood Cemetery—the coffin crowned with cap and sword and gloves, the riderless horse with empty boots fixed in the stirrups of a military saddle, the soldier escort with arms reversed and crape-shrouded banners, the passersby pausing with bared heads, and over all the solemn throb of the Dead March from *Saul*, played by a military band. Felicity's eyes were wet and Eden could not speak when they descended from the carriage in front of the hotel.

Ransom was thin and fine-drawn, but comfortingly himself, and Felicity went into his arms with a sob of sheer relief. Lafe too came to greet them, hungry for news of Louise, who hoped to follow soon with Sally and Sedgwick when the exchange was made.

In Ransom's room at the Spotswood, the two men listened gravely to Eden's account of the interview with Cronin's adjutant, and Ransom smothered a sigh when she turned to him at the end and added—"And you *will* arrange for me to see Cabot tomorrow, won't you, Father?"

"My dear—it's difficult to get permission to visit the prisoners, and I think perhaps——"

"Where does one apply for permission?"

"To the Provost-Marshal, but——"

"What is his name?"

"General Winder."

"Where do I find him?"

"Eden, upon my word, since that Yankee came in the door I hardly know my own daughter! It's as though he had bewitched you——"

"It's not being bewitched to fall in love, Father. He is the man I am promised to marry. Surely that gives me the right to visit him when he is wounded?"

"I don't think you quite realize, Eden, that Captain Murray is a prisoner of war. If he were in one of our own hospitals, which God knows are overflowing——"

"I don't think it matters much which side a man is on once he's helpless. Who takes care of the wounded at Libby Prison?"

"There is a surgeon, I believe——"

"You mean the good women of Richmond only care for the *Confederate* wounded?"

Ransom spoke sharply then, his overstrained patience snapping, for the problem of caring for the Federal wounded was already a sore subject.

"Every good woman of Richmond is already burdened beyond her endurance with nursing the men who were hurt in our own cause! There are not enough comforts, not enough medicines, thanks to the blockade, not enough food, even, for our own sick men!"

"So the sick men from the North have nothing." Eden's face was white, her eyes were dark and angry. "I never heard of such self-righteousness!"

"Eden, that will do." The schoolmaster's note was in Ransom's voice. "Reduce this thing to cold facts. Would you deprive your brother Dabney to give to Cabot Murray?"

"But Dabney—isn't—?" She looked terrified.

"No, by the grace of God. But he may be wounded at any time. The principle is the same. It's a hard choice, Eden, but it has to be made. There is not enough of anything to go round. And it seems to most of us only just that the men in Libby Prison should be the first to go without."

She looked back at him defiantly, her chin out.

"Mine won't," she said.

"He will go without drugs," he said with finality, "because you can't get them for him in all Richmond." But then, although his nerves were raw with the things he had seen and heard since the Seven Days' battle, his heart smote him, and her white, tearless face made his throat tighten. Wilful she might be, quite maddening in her obstinate devotion to a man who was still to her father a stranger—but she was very young and, till Cabot Murray had claimed her, she was his favorite child. He went wearily to sit on the sofa beside her and took her hands in his. "Dear Eden, we are in the midst of the cruellest war this country has ever seen—anything I say now may sound sententious and futile—but I think that for the love of your brothers, if not of Virginia, you should try to let this man go out of your life. I promise to bring all the influence I can towards his prompt exchange. After that, his own people will nurse him well again. Can't you let that be the end of it?"

She sat looking down at their clasped hands, dry-eyed.

"Not possibly," she said, very low. "What's more, if he'll take me with him when he is sent out of Richmond on the exchange—I want to go."

"*Eden!*" It was a cry from Felicity's heart. She came and knelt by the sofa at Eden's other side, because there was not room on it for both their hoops. Her hands caught hard at Ransom's, which still held his daughter's, so that the four of them clasped Eden's cold fingers, passive in their hold. "Eden, what has got into you, honey? Doesn't your family count for anything at all any more? Think of Gran! You couldn't leave her like that!"

"Gran seems to be the only one who knows what it is to love a man."

Lafe, who had been a silent spectator until now, rose suddenly and came to lay his own hands on Eden's shoulders from behind the sofa, with a sharp, encouraging grip.

"Let her alone," he said unexpectedly. "If it's as bad as that with her—let her see him. You're only making it worse for her like this, and you can't change her. You'd better see Winder tomorrow, Ransom, and get her a permit to visit the prison. Crazy Bet goes in and out every day as she likes, they can't very well refuse Eden!"

"Who is Crazy Bet?" Eden asked, looking up at him gratefully.

"She's a perfectly respectable Richmond lady who is a leetle bit teched in the head." Lafe moved away again, trying to speak lightly. Ransom rose from the sofa and sought his pipe, and Felicity took his place beside Eden, striving for composure. Gradually the tension in the room relaxed, as Lafe told the strange story of Elizabeth Van Lew, who lived in a mansion at the top of Church Hill above Libby Prison

—and who in the midst of wartime Richmond shopped for goodies for the Federal prisoners, going about with a big market basket on her arm, singing little scraps of meaningless song and talking to herself. "She was sent North to school when she was a girl, and it seems to have made her a bit queer," said Lafe. "She was always more abolitionist than the Abolitionists—trying to uplift the Negro and make him our social equal—freed some of her own slaves, bought others in order to reunite families which had been separated. Since the war she seems to have come really unhinged, but is quite harmless, they say. Takes the prisoners novels and books of poetry, and even carries them hot meals in a silver dish—that sort of thing."

"Well, I hope people can agree that I'm harmless," Eden said, "if I take Cabot books and food!"

"As long as they don't say you're a spy," Ransom remarked, lighting his pipe. "Because they say that too, about Elizabeth Van Lew."

"Oh, nonsense, Ransom, she's just a poor witless freak," Lafe objected easily.

"I hope so."

"Besides, what could she spy at Libby? It's the wrong way round—the cart before the horse. The men there don't know anything new—and couldn't transmit anything she told them!"

"True," admitted Ransom.

When Eden went to bed that night at the Spotswood she knew that for all her Uncle Lafe's tact and kindness, her family considered her a disgrace, even worse than Sedgwick when he wouldn't volunteer. But with Libby Prison only as far away as the end of Cary Street beyond Capitol Square, with the hope of seeing Cabot tomorrow morning quickening her heart, she didn't seem to care.

9

Nothing Eden had experienced in Williamsburg so far had quite prepared her for that July day in Richmond.

Shortly before noon she walked down Cary Street in stifling heat at her father's side, to the vast, gaunt warehouse which was Libby Prison. The air was heavy with odors—none of which it was safe to name. Each waft of the sluggish breeze brought an additional smell, and as they went they passed beneath windows which flew the white flag of small-pox, and their feet beat antiphony to the Dead March passing up Main Street. Every other private house had at least one hospital room, and empty dwellings had been commandeered and furnished by donation to make more hospitals. Every woman who passed them was drawn with fatigue or veiled in mourning. It was a city of sickness and sorrow and courage, baking under a pitiless sun.

Libby Prison stood stark and friendless among vacant lots, fronting on Cary Street, its back windows above the stinking canal. The entrance to the commandant's office was the middle one of three doors on Cary Street. There they showed the permit, and were directed to the third door at the far end, which was the hospital entrance. Even there they must pass a sentry and wait while heavy bolts were shot back.

They entered a doctor's office which had been partitioned off with raw boards, with a rough sort of movable screen across the open doorway into the single ward beyond. There was a faint smell of disinfectant here, complicated by much stronger and less pleasant odors. The surgeon himself was a Federal prisoner, gaunt and listless with illness. He received them politely but with visible curiosity, and Eden said quickly, "My father is here out of kindness to me. I came to see my fiancé, Captain Murray. Is he here?"

"Murray," said the surgeon, enlightened. "Yes, he's here." He glanced round the screen into the ward, and then nodded to her. "You may go in. Seventh on the left-hand wall."

Eden passed the screen alone. A wave of fetid air dizzied her. Eyes bright with fever watched her from what seemed to be endless rows of cots—unshaven, unwashed, wretched men, in rags of clothing and soiled bandages, lying on filthy blankets or no blankets at all—spittoons and chamber-pots around which was a roar of flies—uncurtained windows through which the July sun blazed down on to the bodies of the men near the wall. She stood a moment, bracing herself. No one spoke her name to guide her. She turned to the left and counted methodically to seven. . . .

He lay with his eyes closed, uncovered to the waist in the terrible heat, one bare arm hanging over the edge of the cot, which looked too small for him. His thick dark hair was longer than he had used to wear it, and was matted into boyish waves, damp with sweat. Above many days' growth of black beard his forehead was very white, and shining with sweat, and the small scar he had got in Charleston showed livid. There were two bright fever spots of color on his cheekbones. He breathed imperceptibly. He was dirty.

If Ransom had wished for her disenchantment it was here beneath her shocked, incredulous eyes. But for only an instant she stood petrified, staring down at the almost unrecognizable wreck of the highhanded Yankee she loved, before compassion flooded through her, erasing disgust, banishing even pity, in an encompassing tenderness. She moved forward between the cots, which were set so close together that her dimity flounces brushed the man on the other side as she bent above Cabot and lifted the hanging arm in both her hands.

"Cabot," she said quietly. "I'm here at last. What can I do to make you more comfortable?"

Slowly his eyes opened. For a long moment he lay unfocussed looking up without seeing her. Slowly she dawned on him, and he tried to smile with dry, cracked lips.

"I'm dreaming," he said.

"No, you're not. I came to Richmond as soon as I heard you were here. Father is waiting outside. What can I bring you, Cabot? What do you need most?"

"Water," he said. "Enough for a bath."

"I think I can manage that. What else? Is your leg all right?"

"I doubt it. Dr. Cummings does the best he can, but he has nothing to work with."

"Does it hurt?"

"Like hell."

"I can bring fresh bandages."

"Bring lots of them, then. We all need them."

"What do they feed you?"

"Slops."

"How would you like some chicken broth?"

"*Is* there such a thing?"

"There's got to be. Oh, Cabot, I——"

"No, now, don't kiss me, that's a good girl—I'm filthy. You might catch something. You oughtn't to come here at all, you know, I oughtn't to let you."

"You can't stop me. Nobody else could."

His tired eyes glinted.

"Did you have a row?"

"That rumbling sound you heard from the Spotswood last night was Father! He's going to arrange an exchange, though. We saw General Winder this morning. And the man at Williamsburg is working on it too. Cabot, I—I told Father last night that I wanted to go North with you now—when you're exchanged."

"Eden, for the love of God—!" he whispered, and his hot hand crushed hers till the ring drove into her flesh, so that the tears which stood in her eyes were of sheer pain. His fever-bright, bloodshot gaze caressed her face, lingering on her lips. "Did he consent?"

"I'm afraid it doesn't matter any more whether he consents or not. So you must get well fast, and be ready to go when they sign the papers, or whatever they do."

"I'll get well," he said, and she never knew how he had doubted it. "I'm ready any time they are! And now you get out of here, Eden, and don't come back till I'm free, do you hear me? It's a pest-house. Stay away from it."

"I'm coming back this afternoon and give you a bath. You won't be the first wounded soldier I've scrubbed, and I'm very good at it!" She kissed her own fingers and laid them on his lips. "I've got the upper hand now," she said, and left the ward swiftly.

Sixteen pairs of wistful eyes followed the slim, dimity-clad figure with its swaying hoop till the screen hid her from their view.

In the pitiful pretence at a doctor's office she faced the languid, hopeless man in the shabby blue uniform who had had nothing to work with—faced too her father's pleading eyes.

"I am bringing you some bandages later in the day, Doctor," she said. "I've done nursing at Williamsburg. Perhaps we can make those men in there a little more comfortable."

"Make them too comfortable," he said with a faded smile, "and the authorities will revoke your permit to visit the prison."

"But I hear they let Miss Van Lew——"

"Oh, they revoke hers every now and then, but she always gets another one."

"Perhaps I can do the same," said Eden, her chin out. "We can go now, Father, and as you see, I can quite easily come by myself hereafter."

She gave the doctor her hand, the heavy bolts were drawn back, and Ransom followed her out to the hot pavement of Cary Street.

There were, of course, no bandages to be had in Richmond, as Eden soon discovered. In the afternoon she set out, wearing her dimity dress and a wide chip hat and carrying a small parasol, for the Crabb mansion in Franklin Street. Half the house had been turned into a hospital, she knew, and Mrs. Crabb and Grafton's sister Charlotte were nursing Confederate wounded there. Grafton was with the horse artillery now, which travelled with Stuart. Eden hoped he wouldn't be on leave, as so many men were these days, but even if he was she meant to beg bandages from his mother for Libby Prison.

The whole ground floor of the Crabb house had been given over to the wounded, except for the front hall, from which the grand staircase ascended and into which the piano and most of the bulkier furniture had been crowded until it looked like an auction. Eden followed Charlotte's mammy past the open door of the drawing-room, where white cots stood in rows and the air was heavy with the smell of wounds and sickness, while Mammy explained that Uncle Lije, who was the Crabbs' butler, had gone back to camp with Marse Grafton since young Shad had got killed beside his master at Mechanicsville. The rest of the men servants, except for a boy named Jock, were at work on the fortifications down the river—it made fewer to feed, said Mammy philosophically, with no reference to the extra work it left for her and the maids.

She showed Eden into a small upstairs parlor, and pretty Charlotte Crabb, her frivolous brown curls tucked into a fetching cap and a ruffled apron tied round her eighteen-inch waist, came running in.

"Eden, honey, how *lovely* to see you! Grafton will be furious, he left here only yesterday! Is your mother in Richmond too? How is darling Gran? Where are you staying, for heaven's sake, at the Spotswood? Wouldn't you rather move in here with us and help with the wounded? How *sweet* you look, one would think that was a new hat! Eden, are you *sure* Dabney is safe?"

"Perfectly safe, Charl, haven't you seen him?" Everyone indulged Charlotte's endless chatter. Except for her becoming costume, the war seemed not to have touched her at all. She somehow made Eden feel as old as the hills.

"I haven't seen him *once* since the fighting! Oh, your father told me he was safe, yes—but I'd feel better if I could lay eyes on him myself!"

"He'll be in Richmond on leave soon, I hope, to see Mother, and I'll chase him right over here to report."

"*Eden,* now, don't go giving Dabney ideas about me, I only——"

"Charl, I want to beg some bandages, have you got any?"

"None to spare, I'm afraid, we've begun on the best linen now. The grape-vine tablecloth went today, I don't suppose we can ever again give a dinner party large enough to use it anyway!"

"Well, give me some old sheets to tear up. Or give me the best sheets, anything—I must have them."

"Are you working at a hospital, then? Which one? How *naughty* of you not to come here first!"

"I want them for Libby Prison."

"Eden, are you out of your *mind?*"

"Cabot Murray is there, wounded. I want to make him as comfortable as I can, and some of the others who need it worst."

"You and that Yankee! Honestly, Eden, I'd be *ashamed!*"

"Wait till you fall in love, Charl."

"But I *am,* that is, I—think I am."

"With Dabney?"

"Well, now, Eden, don't laugh, just because he's your own brother you can't see anything romantic about him, I know, but——"

"I can, indeed. I think Dabney's very handsome, very kindhearted, very charming, and he'd be very easy to live with."

"Very—very—very! A lot you know! I wish I'd ever seen this fabulous *Murray* man, what's he like, anyway? Honey, do tell—is he handsome? Does he waltz? Would I like him? Whatever I ask, Grafton just *glowers,* and says he hopes you will come to your senses soon, which means marry *him!*"

"Cabot's not much to look at right now, I admit. Father is trying to arrange an exchange so he can go home and get proper care for his wound."

"Where's home?"

"Trenton, New Jersey."

"I should think that would be a *horrible* place to live!"

"It probably is. Will you let me have some bandages, Charl?"

"We-ell, I'll give you one sheet—one of the big ones. And mind you *never* let Mamma know—she's out!"

"Thank you—and be quick, will. you, honey, I promised him I'd come back today and give him a bath."

Charlotte paused on her way to the door.

"Eden, won't it feel awfully *queer* to bathe the man you're going to marry?"

"Well, do you think it will feel any queerer, really, than bathing a man you've never seen before?"

Charlotte retired, baffled, and returned at once with the sheet. Eden kissed her affectionately, promised to ask Felicity to come and lend a hand with their wounded, and hurried away towards Cary Street.

She was not allowed to enter the prison again that day, not allowed even to see the surgeon. They said it was too late, and she would have to come back tomorrow.

Carrying the sheet, she returned to the Spotswood and set about making bandages. The cook at the hotel had promised her, for five dollars, a pint of chicken broth in the morning.

10

Soon after breakfast she set out again with towels, soap, a comb, rolls of bandages and a little tin pail of broth in a basket on her arm. Behind her walked the small colored boy Jock, borrowed from Charlotte, carrying two large teakettles full of hot water and a basin.

The sentry at the hospital entrance was too big for his breeches that day and objected to the little colored boy. He said the permit was for only one.

"You're just being officious," Eden told him curtly, and her critical eyes ran over him, missing no detail of his slovenly appearance. "It is quite easy to see that you have no use yourself for soap and water. Set the kettles down, Jock—and the basin. Thank you. Now go straight home and tell Miss Charlotte you're there." She turned on the sentry. "See that that door is kept open long enough for me to make the three trips necessary to carry these things inside. And don't give me any back-talk about it, either, I've heard quite enough from you for one day."

The sentry never said another word.

When the surgeon had bathed Cabot's wound with the boiled water and put on a fresh linen dressing, Cabot had his broth and his bath, the latter rather piecemeal but deftly given under the admiring and envious eyes of the ward. Then, with the cooling water which was left and which rapidly became dirty but brought refreshment all the same, Eden went down the line washing faces which grinned up at her gratefully.

The hot July days dragged by while they waited for the exchange. News of its likelihood had gone round the ward and everyone was as anxious as though his own name was up as well.

A fortnight or so later when Eden arrived at the prison hospital with nothing to hand round but a few pieces of corn bread smeared sparingly with preserves, she met Elizabeth Van Lew coming out with her big market basket on her arm, singing one of her nameless fragments of tune. For an instant her bright, intelligent eyes met Eden's, then she slipped past and on, chuckling and nodding to herself. But to Eden in that second of contact had come a surprising conviction: *She's not mad.*

Puzzled, she went round the screen into the ward. The men were visibly perked up that day. One of them was reading a letter. One of them had a book. The rest were munching crackers or fruit. Cabot's pillow was a little raised—Eden had brought him her own from the Spotswood—and he was sucking a ripe peach.

"Well!" she said, supplying him with her own handkerchief in place of a napkin. "Everybody seems very cheerful! You know, I think that woman is as sane as I am!"

"That's quite possible," said Cabot blandly, and added, "Nobody who comes here of her own free will can be quite right in the head!"

The man on the next cot snickered audibly and Eden said no more about Miss Van Lew. But when she left the prison an hour later she was still turning it over in her mind. That letter—who brought it, if not Miss Van Lew? And if she brought messages in, might she not also take them out? But what would a man in Libby Prison know that was worth passing on? The guards were allowed to shoot at any head which showed itself near the unbarred windows—and had done so more than once. She began to wonder what she herself might have said, innocently, from time to time, of what went on in Richmond. Would any of that be of interest to— But Cabot would never— Her thoughts faltered on the brink of an abyss. Cabot would never *spy!*

She and Felicity had taken up a nurse's duties at the Crabb house, and more than once Eden deliberately pilfered tidbits there to be smuggled to Cabot at the prison. Her justification was that she believed all wounded men should share what comfort there was. If that was sophistry, she didn't care, and there were a few other women in Richmond who agreed with her. Besides, she denied herself as well, for him, and between the heat and actual hunger she lost weight and color, and soon looked like all the weary women of Richmond who were giving beyond their capacity for the sake of the men they served.

At the end of a month a cartel was signed for the general exchange of prisoners, which suddenly released Sedgwick at Williamsburg and caught Cabot much wasted by fever and with the wound still unhealed. After a conference with the surgeon it was decided that he would attempt to travel with crutches, and he allowed himself to contemplate anew the idea that Eden might come with him, through the lines, to Washington.

When she arrived at the prison that day he was half dressed, in trousers and shirt, his leg still clumsy with bandages, and he had been trying his crutches in the narrow space between the cots. Sitting on the end of his cot, with Eden in the ward's one wooden chair, he watched her face, waiting for her to mention the possibility he had cherished so jealously ever since she had said it the first day she came —dreading for some obscure, intuitive reason to bring it up himself. He noticed again how thin she had got, how the purple shadows lay beneath her eyes. She wasn't getting enough to eat, he knew, and no one could sleep in this heat, and she spent long hours nursing helpless men. Determination rose in him to get her out of Richmond somehow, make her eat and rest and recover her spirits and looks—even if it meant taking care of a more or less invalid husband at Willard's Hotel——

"Cabot—Mother is very ill. I'm—frightened about her."

Foreboding closed down on him. He had sensed something. This was it.

"Typhoid?" he asked.

"They don't say. I don't think they *know*. There is fever, of course, and—dysentery—terrible exhaustion and some pain. They say you get queer things, nursing the men. Today she—doesn't know us."

"I'm sorry, Eden. You hadn't told me."

"I didn't dare," she said, very low. "It means I can't go with you."

He sat a moment, his teeth clenched on despair. There was no privacy in that stifling room with the rows of cots nearly touching each other. They whispered—but even then other ears, however tactfully closed, were bound to hear.

"Are you sure you can't?" he whispered at last.

"Father hasn't done anything yet about getting me a pass—and now I can't ask him to. He's—quite beside himself with anxiety about Mother, and now that Jackson has gone to Gordonsville, Lee may take to the field himself any day—" She caught her breath. "I shouldn't have said that. Please forget that I—mentioned Jackson." Something in his face, something alert and listening, sent a chill through her. "Cabot—that woman with the basket—they say she's a spy."

"Crazy Bet?" He laughed. "They probably say the same of you, had you thought of that?"

"Yes. I had."

"Crazy Bet doesn't care what they say. Do you?"

"No, but——"

"We've got till tomorrow, before I am shipped out. If your mother was better——"

She shook her head. Tears fell on their clasped hands.

"I think she's dying," she gasped. "Even if I could get the pass in time, I'd never forgive myself if——"

He sat holding her hands while her tears dripped down on their fingers. Tomorrow he must leave her here, in this charnel house of a city, and go back to Washington alone. It was the end of a wild dream that he might have her with him there. All the old bitterness surged up in him, darkening his face, drawing the hard, fighting lines around his cracked and swollen lips. What was the good of loving her, what was the good of her promise to him, if he had to leave her here? If Felicity couldn't thwart him any other way she would die, he thought uncharitably, not altogether selfishly, for this meant that Eden must go on starving, tending hideous wounds, for God only knew how long, till somebody won the damned war. She must, that is, unless she too fell ill of something dreadful that no one could name— And everything else was swallowed up in his fear for her, so much worse than any fear for himself under fire; his dread that all this loveliness he held between his hands was doomed to disease or disfigurement or death, and he powerless, not even knowing——

He drew a sharp breath through his teeth and rose clumsily from the end of the cot, staggering till he got the crutch in place. She looked up at him, startled at his sudden move, with tears on her cheeks.

"Come," he said, and hobbled towards the doctor's office where the sad grey man sat at his derelict desk pretending to read an old almanac. "Doc—how about a minute alone with my girl to say good-bye?"

The doctor rose creakingly—glanced at the bolted outer door and the six-foot partition and screen. Silently he shambled into the ward and left them together. Cabot swayed on his crutches and Eden caught his shoulders and guided him to the doctor's chair. He lowered himself into it, while the crutches rattled on the bare floor.

"I'm all right," he said rather blindly, brushing irritably at his damp forehead. "I get dizzy—doesn't mean anything——"

"Oh, Cabot, how can I let you go, you're not fit to travel!"

"I won't get any fitter in this place."

"No. You must go, of course." There was only the one chair. She stood beside him and took his head into her arms, holding him against her breast, his arms around her waist. "Shall you go to Washington, or Trenton?" she asked, trying to see ahead for them both.

"Washington. It's nearer. Just till I get over this."

"Then promise me something. Promise to send for Melicent to keep you company while you're getting well."

"At Willard's? No place for her."

"Her mother would come with her, and you'd have people of your own to look after you. Promise?"

"All right, I'll ask them. But how about you? Will you promise to go back to Williamsburg, where it's safe to breathe the air?"

"If—if only Mother——"

"You must get her out of Richmond as soon as she can be moved."

"Yes."

"You mustn't stop hoping, Eden. She'll get well."

"Yes."

"Besides, if you were at Williamsburg I could send you word now and then. Our fellows are still in possession, aren't they?"

"Yes."

"Give my love to Gran."

"I will."

"Eden, darling, you're crying down my neck."

"I'm—s-sorry."

"I like it."

A moment more they held each other. Then his arms slackened, and he sat up cautiously, but could not look at her, and buried his face in her hands. The doctor came diffidently around the screen.

"I think perhaps you'd better go now," he said with a vestige of his vanished sickroom authority.

The bolts shot back. Gently she withdrew her hands and was gone, and the door clanged shut behind her.

V SEPTEMBER 15, 1862

To MELICENT, the summons to Washington, which came in the form of a telegram from Cabot to his father, was the most exciting thing which had ever happened. The first report that he was missing had caused her an agony of suspense, only a little lessened by the news that he was a prisoner, wounded, about to be exchanged. Now when a telegram arrived and was carried into the library, she hung about in the hall outside, not daring to go in and ask, but hoping, praying, it might be from Cabot himself.

Quite suddenly the library door opened and Mr. Murray stood there, looking angry and upset, the message still in his hand. In spite of herself she took two steps backward and brought up against the banisters, waiting to be ordered up stairs to her room, but determined to ask before she went if the message was from Cabot. His eyes fell on her almost without recognition, he was so preoccupied.

"Find your mother," he said briefly, "and come to the library, both of you."

Melicent felt there was no time to lose. From where she stood she sent her clear, well-projected voice up the stairs.

"Mother! Come quick!"

"Don't bellow like that!" said Mr. Murray irritably, and withdrew into the library.

Anne Murray came down the stairs, moving lightly for so big a woman. She was large-boned, not fat, with a broad, plain, colorless face, an unsmiling mouth, cold blue eyes and mousy hair. Childless, and except for Melicent's lifelong affection, loveless, she had found her niche in caring for a foundling and two self-centered, unnoticing men. She ran the luxurious, gloomy mansion efficiently with a female staff of three, and handled the unlimited funds at her disposal economically, with household books always in order and ready for inspection which never came. The surplus which accumulated under her careful management from each month's housekeeping allowance she laid away for Melicent, with never an idea of using it for herself, though she bore the name of her employer and ranked as the lady of the house.

"It's a telegram," Melicent told her, and grabbed an unresponsive hand in two cold paws. "He wants us in the library. It must be about Cabot!"

Mr. Murray was standing on the hearthrug, reading the message for the sixth or seventh time—a tall, brooding, hawk-nosed man with a greying beard. He looked up at them fretfully over his spectacles, as though the whole thing was somehow their fault.

"Shut the door and sit down," he snapped. "Stop *goggling* at me, Melicent, your eyes are popping out of your head!"

"Oh, please, sir—is it about Cabot?"

"Very well, it *is* about Cabot—he's back in Washington, and apparently parted with his sanity in Libby Prison."

"That's a dreadful place, they say," Anne conceded gravely.

"He was wounded, as we know, and he is still very ill—can't look after himself, has to stay in bed and be waited on hand and foot. He wants you to come there and nurse him, Anne."

"Why, yes, I could do that," she said unemotionally. "Where is the wound?"

"He doesn't say. Just like him, to leave us in the dark about that. Perhaps he's delirious, he says to bring Melicent with you."

"Me!" Melicent bounced on the edge of her chair. Her large brown eyes, already filled with tears for Cabot's wounding, spilled over so that crystal drops rolled down her cheeks and hung on the long, upward sweep of her lashes. "Me go to Washington!"

"It seems a preposterous idea to me." Mr. Murray glanced again at the telegram in his hand, as though hoping that that particular part of Cabot's message might by now have disappeared. But there it was, as incomprehensible as ever: *Please send Melicent too. It will do us both good.* Nonsense.

"Maybe he's lonesome," said Melicent, and the man she called Father looked at her piercingly, as though he suspected her of trying to be funny, or of being an imbecile, one or the other.

"He is probably seriously ill, and what he wants with a child under foot I can't see!"

"I'm fourteen," Melicent reminded him jealously. "I can read aloud to him, and—sit with him when Mother has to go out, in case he wants anything——"

"I've no doubt you will be very useful," he agreed drily. "Well, Anne, I suppose you will have to go—though what will become of things here I can't imagine."

"Jessie can manage," she told him unsympathetically. "She is a very capable girl."

"Who is Jessie? That parlormaid of yours?"

"She is the best maid we've ever had. And the cook knows all your favorite dishes as well as I do. You probably won't even notice we're away," she added, for she knew a certain satisfaction in landing a remark like that sometimes in such a way that it went unchallenged by him.

"How soon can you be ready, then?"

"Tomorrow morning."

"I suppose I must telegraph him. Do you think you had better take the child, as he suggests?"

"I think so. If he is very ill I will need her help. If he isn't, she can amuse him. He's not a patient invalid, as I know very well from the time I nursed him through measles, a few years back!"

Again Mr. Murray eyed Melicent, as though trying to see how she could possibly amuse anyone.

"Very well," he said shortly. "Whatever you think best, of course. Has she the proper clothes for such an expedition?"

"If she hasn't I can get them for her there."

Anne rose. The interview was over. Melicent lingered on one foot when Anne left the room.

"Please, sir——"

"Well, what is it? Don't you want to go?"

"Oh, *yes,* sir, I'm dying to go! M-may I have the message?"

"What's that?"

"The telegram. May I have it—to keep?"

"Why?"

"Well, it—it's got my name in it. I never had a telegram before."

"You didn't have this one. It was sent to me."

She began to back away from him towards the door, looking ready to cry. He glanced again at the paper in his hand—the first word he had had in anxious weeks from the son who was all he cared about in a hated world. He realized he had meant to keep it himself, to look at again, and despised himself promptly for sentimentality.

"Here you are, then," he said roughly, and held it out to her. "Take it."

"Thank you, sir."

She took it, almost with a snatch, and his voice followed her like a whip as she ran out of the room.

"Close the door behind you!"

As she turned to obey, she remembered to drop her curtsy.

She slept that night with the telegram under her pillow, though she knew it by heart then, and woke at dawn to read it once more before she began to dress for the journey.

> Am back at Willard's with nasty wound and fever after month in Libby Prison. Practically bedridden and no nursing available here. Can you spare Anne to look after me. Please send Melicent too. It will do us both good. Yes I will write column on Libby. Give me couple of days. Love to all.
>
> CABOT

He had *asked* for her. She got out of bed to count over again the little pile of her own treasures she had collected to take to him: a deck of cards, to play patience with; checkers, and a board—she could play that with him, when he was bored with everything else; a copy of *Pride and Prejudice,* and a book of Tennyson's poems, in case he wanted her to read aloud; and in her small, childish throat she took him her singing voice and a half dozen new songs he might like to hear, even without the piano. It wasn't much, but it was all she had, and she was consumed with the desire that lives in all devotion to give, to bestow, and to share what she cherished most.

For she was devoted to him now, with a worshiping humility which would have horrified him if he had had any idea of its intensity. Now that she wasn't afraid of him any more, she had centered all her starved heart in this magnificent brother who sometimes remembered to be kind. The thought of being of some use to him, now that he was ill, had kept her awake for hours. And he must have thought she would be of some use. *It will do us both good.* What had he meant by that?

Half dressed, in her plain white chemise and drawers, with no lace trimming on them, she paused to read the telegram again. There was no clue there as to his meaning. She would have to wait, and try to guess by his face what he wanted of her. You couldn't tell much by his face, except that he liked you a little, instead of looking at you as though you were a beetle, the way Father did. . . .

In the train she sat wondering for the hundredth time about the Virginia girl he was going to marry. It was so impossible that any girl should be good enough for him. None of the Trenton girls were, even he could see that. He hadn't said much about his Eden, except that she had red hair and green eyes—then he corrected himself. "Titian," he said, in correction. "She doesn't freckle, and she can wear pink." Imagine wearing pink, anyway. . . . Anne's taste in clothes was sober, even for the young, and if it had not been, Mr. Murray would have seen to it that nobody wore pink in his house. Melicent's travelling dress, even in August, was a sensible brown merino, and the day got steadily hotter as they approached Washington.

The Jersey Senator who lived across the street from them in Trenton was waiting at the station with his carriage. Melicent had always thought him a nice man, square and honest and peppery, and now as they drove down Pennsylvania Avenue to Willard's Hotel he spoke of Cabot with an almost paternal affection. The wound, he said, was in the right leg, above the knee, and the ball had missed breaking the bone by fractions of an inch. It was painful, and slow to heal, but the fever had pulled him down even worse than the wound. If it were not for a truly magnificent physique he might not have survived. It would be some time before he was himself again, even with the very best care. Most of all, he needed feeding up. They starved them at Libby Prison.

Melicent saw very little of Pennsylvania Avenue or the lounge of the hotel through which they passed on their way to Cabot's room. She was intent on the Senator's every word, and she was shaking with nervousness because she was going to find Cabot ill, lying in bed instead of striding about the house more than six feet tall and able to lift you right off the floor with one hand if he had chosen. What would you say, when he wasn't towering above you? How could you act, when he was suffering and starved? Maybe she oughtn't to go in——

"This is the room," said the Senator, and tapped on the door, and Cabot's voice inside yelled, "Come in!" just the way it ought to sound, and the Senator opened the door for them.

"Well, here's your family!" he said cheerfully. "You'll feel better now, you old bear!"

Cabot was grinning at them from the middle of a wide bed. He was thinner and paler, but he was shaved and brushed and very much himself, and had been reading a book.

"Hullo, Anne, I'm glad to see you," he said, just as usual, and Anne, who always knew what to do and did it however grimly, went over to the bed and kissed his forehead, and then began to take off her gloves and bonnet.

"Your room is just through this door, Mrs. Murray." The Senator bustled across to open it. "I had him moved, so you could have connecting rooms. I thought it would be easier if he wanted something in the night. Your baggage is all in there. Perhaps I should have let you take your things off first, but I knew he'd be impatient——"

Anne thanked him, unsmiling and composed, and passed on into the other room, carrying her bonnet and gloves. Melicent started to follow.

"Hey!" said Cabot from the bed. "Come here, and let's look at you."

"Hullo, Cabot." She approached him shyly, and put her hand into the hand he reached out to her. She had never seen him before with even his coat off, and now his night-shirt was unbuttoned at the throat, and the sleeve didn't reach to his wrist——

"What's that thing on your head?" he asked, squinting, and her other hand flew up to make sure.

"M-my hat?" she queried anxiously, feeling of the round straw head-gear with the two flat black ribbons hanging over the back of the up-turned brim.

"It's not a hat, it's a bad joke," he said. "Take it off."

She took it off by pulling up on the front of the brim so that the elastic slipped out from under her curls behind.

"It's—hot, isn't it," she said, her hand still in his.

"Senator, I have a favor to ask of you," Cabot said, and the Senator said, "Certainly, certainly, my boy," and came to lay a fatherly hand on Melicent's shoulder.

"Or rather, of your wife. Will you ask her to take my sister out this afternoon and dress her, at my expense?"

"That is pretty heavy stuff for this climate," the Senator agreed, pinching up a fold of the brown merino.

"It's hideous," said Cabot tersely.

"Oh, but I—I have a blue dress in my bag," Melicent assured them eagerly. "It's a sort of muslin, and much cooler, but it musses, and we thought for the train—my blue dress has a white collar, and it——"

"No, don't tell me," said Cabot sadly. "I can imagine what it's like without looking."

"My wife will be delighted," said the Senator. "We haven't any little girls of our own, and she is always borrowing a niece to take shopping. I'll go and tell her. Will about four o'clock suit you, Cabot?"

"The sooner the better," Cabot nodded, and the Senator went away.

Melicent glanced guiltily at the open door of the room where Anne was unpacking.

"Maybe she ought to go with us—to buy my dress," she suggested.

"She can't leave me. I'm a very sick man. I need lots of care."

"Cabot, does it hurt much?"

"It's not as lively as it was."

"I've been so worried about you. It was awfully good of you to let me come too, and I'll try to be a help—maybe I could read to you, or —something." And she added quickly, because he looked surprised— "I always try to coax Mother to read to me when I'm sick."

"What does she read to you?" His hand drew her down on the edge of the bed.

"Won't I hurt your leg if I sit there?"

"You're on the good side. What have you read, tell me."

"Maria Edgeworth, and Jane Austen, and Tennyson's poems—" She thought he made a sort of face. "Don't you care for them?" she asked anxiously.

"It's been a long time—I liked *Pride and Prejudice,* I remember."

Her face fell.

"I might have known you'd read it. I brought it with me."

"Good. We'll read it again. A man at the prison had a copy of *The Cloister and the Hearth,* and we all read it to shreds, but you wouldn't like that one."

"Was it dreadful at the prison? Were you *hungry?*"

"Hungry all the time, for more than a month. But that wasn't the worst part. Eden almost came with me—well, anyway, we got as far as talking about it—and then she couldn't. I had to leave her there in Richmond, and she's still hungry, it doesn't bear thinking about." He turned his head restlessly on the pillow, and you could see that he thought of very little else. "She came to see me at the prison—you don't know quite what that means, in Richmond, where they hate Yankees like poison."

His hand still held hers on the sheet. She laid her other hand on top of it, longing to comfort him.

"Couldn't we send her something?"

"There's a thing called the blockade." His mouth twisted. "Their army is too much for us, so we hope to starve them out. All for their own good, mind you!"

"Isn't the war ever going to end, Cabot?"

"If I could think of any way to cut it short by one day, I'd do it, no matter what." He was staring past her, scowling at the wall, reading there some dark answer to his own misery. "No matter what," he repeated, and it sounded like an oath.

"I learned all the music she sent me," Melicent offered timidly, trying to bring him back. "Later on if you like I'll sing it to you."

His fingers tightened gratefully.

"I'd like it very much. You know, this was her idea—your coming to Washington while I get well. I'd never have had the brains to think of it. She thought I ought to have a woman to look after me. And she meant you, you monkey, not Anne!"

"I'm fourteen," she bragged, feeling confident and responsible.

"She's only nineteen herself, poor darling."

Anne came in, tying a white apron around her waist.

"Now, then, we'll have you tidied up in no time," she said briskly. "Melicent, I think you'd better go and wash up after the journey, and put on your blue muslin, it will be cooler."

Cabot winked at his sister as she rose reluctantly from the edge of the bed.

"You might as well," he said. "I'll try to bear whatever you have on, it won't be for long."

Melicent hesitated, looking down at him.

"Cabot, do you think—*would* it be too much trouble——"

"Well, what? Speak up."

"Oh, Cabot, could I have a pink dress?"

Just in time he suppressed the impulse to indulgent laughter. Just in time he saw what a serious thing this pink dress was. Somehow he had gleaned that it was a hard color to wear. He rested a thoughtful gaze on her, noting for the first time that her skin was good, her teeth were white, her hair was brushed and shining, and her eyes—good Lord, she had remarkable eyes for such a youngster.

"Sure you could," he said easily. "You tell Mrs. Trimble I said there was to be a pink dress in the outfit."

"Thank you." And before she had time to scare herself out of it she stooped and kissed his cheek, and ran out of the room.

2

Jackson won a victory at Cedar Mountain on the ninth of August and Lee went up to join him. Then there was news that McClellan was withdrawing his army from the James—by water, not overland, which meant that his transports came in at Aquia Creek and Alexandria. That left the whole Confederate Army free to move northward against Washington, and a fresh Federal militia draft began to stream through the city and out across the bridge into Virginia. Furloughs were revoked. Then refugees began to come in from roundabout Manassas again.

Meanwhile as though by sheer will power Cabot was getting well faster than anyone could have believed. Towards the end of August he was on his feet once more, though he limped still and was advised not to ride, and he still slept badly. He had discovered to his astonishment that he enjoyed Melicent's society, and would miss her acutely if she was not there. At the same time, he no longer needed a nurse, and his father was writing peevishly about the shortcomings of Jessie the parlormaid, and Anne spoke of returning to Trenton soon.

The Senator's wife, a lonely woman with one son at the front, asked to keep Melicent a while with her in the big house on H Street. Anne said grudgingly that she thought it would be a good thing for Melicent to have an opportunity to learn how to behave in the social world. And Cabot, with the armies converging again on Manassas, wondered if he ought not to send Melicent out of Washington instead.

The day before Anne was to go back to Trenton they all went to a family dinner in H Street to talk it over. It was Cabot's first outing, and he went with only one crutch, to everyone's admiration. The Senator's wife produced a couple of nieces, highly sophisticated young ladies though not out yet, with whom Melicent had already a somewhat awed acquaintance.

As they sat in the drawing-room drinking coffee, Cabot saw his sister's eyes travel covetously towards the shining piano, and when one of the nieces was invited to play for them he hoped that no one would discover that Melicent liked to sing. The little niece played very badly, but everyone applauded and Melicent gave him a look which said, *I could do better than that.* He shook his head at her, and heard the Senator's wife saying kindly, "And now, Melicent, can't you do something to entertain us too?"

Melicent was dumb, not from shyness, but because Cabot had forbidden her. But Anne had not seen.

"She sings quite well," said Anne, so matter-of-factly as to rob the statement of praise. "Come along, Melicent, you must do your share when your hostess asks you."

Melicent was miserable. Everyone was looking at her.

"I—don't think Cabot wants me to," she gasped, and turned pink.

"Oh, nonsense, my dear, it's all in the family, you give us a song," the Senator insisted indulgently.

It was the one thing she was sure about—her singing. Shy as a bird about everything else, she knew that her voice was a gift from the gods and might make even Cabot proud of her if she was allowed to use it. She wanted desperately to make him proud of her, and to show these lovely people that she too had something to give.

"Please, Cabot, I—I'd like to sing for them."

"Sure, you go ahead and sing," he said unexpectedly, surprised that she was not afraid to try, reflecting that she couldn't do worse than the niece, who had played like a music-box.

Without any embarrassment, Melicent took her place on the piano stool and smiled at him over her shoulder.

"This is one of Eden's songs," she said.

Pure and strong and heartbreakingly fresh and young, her voice flowed out in *The Last Waltz.* The Senator sat up, and his eyes sought his wife's. She nodded impressively. Cabot watched them under his brows, aware of their growing excitement. He had always liked Melicent's voice himself, but he began to perceive now that the youngster must be really good.

When the song ended the Senator went to the piano and kissed Melicent's hands.

"My dear, my dear," he said delightedly. "I have heard Jennie Lind and she's no better! Isn't that so, Lydia? And to think we might never have heard you sing a note! Cabot, you chump, you must have known what a treat she is! Has she got a good teacher?"

"I don't know. Has she?" He looked to Anne, helplessly.

"She has the only teacher in Trenton," Anne said drily, hoping they wouldn't turn the child's head.

"But that voice must be handled with care! Lydia, you must take her to Boldini tomorrow. He'll know what's best for her."

"Boldini by all means, my dear," said his wife. "But she is just what we want for the concert on Saturday. Everybody plays the piano or the harp, but *nobody* sings, so far. Now we have found a songbird for the program. May we have her on Saturday, Cabot? It's a benefit for the wounded soldiers. And may I dress her just as I like?"

"She has never sung before an audience," he said doubtfully. "I'm not sure she wouldn't die of stage-fright."

"We'll risk that," said the Senator's wife. "What else do you sing, child? Give us another one."

Melicent looked at her brother out of the corners of her eyes. There was triumph in that look, and a happiness which was sublime, because he was smiling at her. She hadn't disgraced him after all, and she suspected that he hadn't been sure she wouldn't. Now they wanted her to sing before an audience, and she had to prove to him she wouldn't die of stage-fright. Well, she could do that too. And shrewdly she chose her next song. She sang them *Home Sweet Home*. That time when she finished the Senator blew his nose, and Cabot said, "Don't let her do that one at the benefit, or you'll have them all in tears!"

The nieces were openly envious of her good fortune in coming to stay with their Aunt Lydia, who always gave them a better time than they had at home.

"I suppose you'll sleep in the lilac room," said the one who had played so badly. "It has a four-poster bed with a canopy."

"The green room is nicer," said the other. "It has a bow window.

Won't you be glad to get away from that dreadful Willard place with all the spittoons?"

"Well, it seems kind of heartless to leave Cabot there all alone," Melicent said haltingly.

"Aha, but he isn't going to stay there all alone!" the Senator crowed surprisingly. "He's coming to stay here with us too. There's a—a writing job he has to do and he'll be better off here."

"Both of us?" cried Melicent, radiant, and the Senator's wife quickly covered a look of astonishment with one of hospitable pleasure, but Anne somehow surmised that this was the first she had heard of Cabot's proposed visit.

Cabot gave his sister an affectionate grin.

"I'll race you for the four-poster," he suggested.

"Cabot, I'm so *glad!* When did you decide to leave Willard's?"

"In the library before dinner."

"I knew you two were up to something in there," said the Senator's wife, and received from her husband a glance which caused her to start talking rather fast about the concert.

When they left the house that evening it was all arranged that Melicent and Cabot should move in the next day, and she was to sing at the concert on Saturday, and perhaps later on at a hospital for the wounded soldiers. Going back to Willard's in the carriage Cabot was rather silent, and she asked him anxiously if he wasn't pleased, and he assured her that he was. Then she asked him if his leg hurt, and he said it did, damnably. "Your brother has hatched a swan," remarked Anne from her corner in her dry way, and Melicent wasn't sure what she meant but was too happy to care. Anne had guessed only the half of it. The rest was what he and the Senator had been up to in the library.

That week McClellan was sent to Alexandria to direct the defence of Washington, and Pope was left to fight the coming battle on the other side of the Potomac. Cabot had no great faith in Pope, and neither, for that matter, had anyone else.

On the twenty-ninth Cabot borrowed the Senator's carriage and drove down to McClellan's camp. When he got back the Senator was pacing up and down in the drawing-room in H Street waiting for him, and Melicent was watching out the window. There was a sound in the air over Washington like distant thunder, but a hot sun was shining.

"Well?" demanded the Senator, as Cabot came in the door, and——

"Cabot, is that *guns?*" asked Melicent simultaneously.

"We're going to have another Manassas," he told them quietly. "At least—we'll hope it doesn't end the same way. If they had only held off a week longer I could have been there." He sank stiffly into a chair, with a grimace of pain. His face was white and shining with perspiration. "Damn this leg," he said, and the Senator rang for brandy.

"You should never have gone," Melicent scolded him lovingly. "We said you weren't strong enough. Now tomorrow you'll have to stay in bed all day or you won't be able to come to the concert. —Cabot, *is* that guns?"

"Yes, it is. Guns at Manassas." He was trying to control a trembling weakness which ran all through his fever-ridden body. "If anyone had told me that I'd sit here in Washington with a battle going on just across the river——"

"Give yourself time," said the Senator. "You had a close call. There will be plenty of work to be done when you're fit again. Here, drink this down." Their eyes met over the glass.

"People are leaving Washington by the carriage load," Cabot remarked then, with a glance at his sister. "What do you think, sir?"

"My wife says not. Not yet, anyway."

"Leave Washington?" Melicent cried scornfully. "I've got to sing tomorrow night, and after that Mr. Boldini himself is going to give me lessons!"

All the next day, which was Saturday the thirtieth, Washington could hear the artillery, and towards evening many people were swearing they could smell gunpowder on the breeze from the southwest. In the afternoon the bulletin boards announced a Federal victory and asked for volunteer nurses (male) to go to the battlefield and collect the wounded. Cabot insisted on driving round to the Provost-Marshal's office to see the confusion there as the wagons and ambulances gathered to load supplies and volunteers. There was a shortage of transportation, and the public hacks had been commandeered for service, their unwilling black drivers in every stage of demoralization and fright. When he returned to the house he fainted in the hall and had to be carried to his room. At nightfall the guns were silent.

All that day while the cannon boomed at Manassas the Senator's drawing-room was being made ready for the evening's entertainment. Rows of little gilt chairs were set facing an improvised platform at one end, the buffet arrived from Gautier's with a towering spun sugar centerpiece representing the Ship of State, bales of flowers were suitably disposed, and the professional musicians came to run through the program with the guest performers.

The harpist, whose new husband was at the front, collapsed in tears and had to go and lie down, and the solo pianist had suddenly left town. Composed, earnest, melodious, Melicent added one more song to her list to fill in, and while the caterers and florists milled about her stood cheerfully on the rather unsteady wooden platform singing to the beat of the conductor's baton.

She had never sung with a real orchestra before, and it was an experience that transcended anything she had ever dreamed of. In her enchantment at the way the muted violins embraced and adorned her own clear tone she did not hear the cannon at all, and the conductor, a born musician too, shared her blissful concentration.

Because all the hacks and even private carriages had been sent to Manassas, the guests arrived on foot that evening, the ladies with ruined slippers and flounces, but spirits were held firmly gay because the battle was believed to have been won. Melicent felt no apprehension about singing, it was talking to people that paralyzed her, and answering their well-meant questions about how she liked Washington. She liked Washington because Cabot was there. She would have liked Timbuctoo for the same reason. But you couldn't say that to strangers.

She saw him sitting in the third row as she stood up in the new pink dress to sing. He was white and shaky, she knew, but he smiled, and she smiled back confidently because now he would be proud of her. The orchestra had stopped its incidental music, and the conductor rapped for silence and the chatter of voices died away. It was a hot night, and the long windows stood open to whatever air there was. As the room grew quiet a new sound could be heard in the streets outside—the rumble and clatter of the wagons bringing in the wounded, and even the groans of jolted, tortured men.

There was a swift and deathly silence, and into it, by some trick of the hot wind across the garden, one cry detached itself from all the confused clamor of agony—*"Jesus, stop that horse and let me die!"*

The people on the little gilt chairs sat turned to stone, the conductor hesitated, the pianist bowed his head above the keys, a woman sobbed. Softly at first, unaccompanied, Melicent's voice stole out into the surcharged air, rising, swelling, soaring strong and unafraid, as the stunned conductor gathered his instruments to her support—in a single intuitive second she had thrown away the carefully chosen program they had labored at all afternoon and was singing Schubert's *Ave Maria,* while Washington wept.

3

Early the next morning the Senator appeared at the door of Cabot's room, looking haggard and angry.

"Well, by God, they've licked us again!" he cried. "The wounded are still coming in, and the stragglers. The army is back at Centreville. Two years of war, and we're right where we started from—with dear Lord how many dead!"

"They should have sent McClellan to Manassas," said Cabot, and got up and began to dress.

Hysteria mounted in the streets of Washington as that rainy Sunday dragged on. Rumor ran wild. The wounded poured in till the hospitals overflowed into the City Hall and the churches and vacant buildings.

On Monday afternoon there were torrents of rain, and everybody suddenly realized that it wasn't all thunder they were hearing—it was guns again—nearer. The dripping stream of loaded ambulances never seemed to slacken.

In the lilac room Cabot lay on his bed in a dressing-gown and watched Melicent with curiosity. The Senator's wife was still calm, but that was to be expected. Melicent was the puzzle. Melicent was behaving like a veteran. In order to keep him from limping up and down the floor and cursing and working up a fever she had ordered him to lie down—yes, pointed her finger at him and said in a loud voice, "Cabot Murray, you do as I say!"—so that he was surprised into obedience. "I'll read to you," she announced then. "Maybe that will keep you quiet."

So he lay listening to her voice even more than to the words she read, soothed in spite of himself, drowsing a little, past wondering any more at the sturdy composure of this odd child of whom he had grown so fond.

> " '—and in my dream
> I glanced aside and saw the palace-front
> Alive with fluttering scarfs and ladies' eyes,
> And highest, among the statues, statue-like,
> Between a cymbal'd Miriam and a Jael,
> With Psyche's babe, was Ida watching us,
> A single band of gold about her hair,
> Like a saint's glory up in heaven; but she——' "

A newsboy's shrill call floated up from the street. Cabot stirred, and raised his head. "Listen!" he whispered tensely.

"Battle at Chantilly! Federal army fighting new battle at Chantilly!"

"Is that nearer?" she asked without alarm.

"A little."

> " '—but she
> No saint—inexorable—no tenderness——
> Too hard, too cruel; yet she sees me fight,
> Yea, let her see me fall! With that I——' "

"Melicent. What is it makes you such a good soldier?"

"Am I, Cabot?"

"People have been streaming out of Washington for days. It never seems to occur to you."

"That's just panic."

"Why aren't you afraid too?"

"Afraid of what? Why should I be? You're here."

"I couldn't, even in the best of health, preserve you during a bombardment of the city."

"Will they do that?"

"If they get close enough and it isn't surrendered first."

"Mr. Lincoln is still here."

"Yes, I'd noticed that."

"And Aunt Lydia. She said I could call her that."

"Now that she knows the boy is safe, she'll go any time you wish."

"Cabot, are *you* scared?"

He smiled crookedly.

"I'd like to have two good legs," he confessed. "Well, if you do get a bad fright, I'll never forgive myself. But I like having you here, that's the trouble. You keep me from going crazy and banging my head against the wall."

"Then I'm really some use to you?"

"More than you know, or you wouldn't ask such a silly question."

"Shall I go on?"

"Yes—go on."

She read on, against the thunder and the guns.

The Federals were whipped again at Chantilly and fell back to the Washington defences, which were fully manned. On Tuesday McClellan was in charge again—the army wanted him, if the politicians did not. Government papers were being tied into bundles ready to be sent away in wagonloads, and the Federal gunboats were said to be assembling in the river to shell the town if it was taken by the Southern forces. The rumor also ran that if Washington had to be surrendered it would be first destroyed. A steamer was waiting in the river to remove the President and Cabinet members.

"I won't go till he does," said Melicent. "Not even then, if you don't."

Still the ambulances came, and the gunboats moved up grimly as far as Nineteenth and G Streets. Disorganized, drunken, staggering with fatigue and defeat, the Federal army filled the streets and the bars of Washington, while the awkward incoming volunteers stared at the battle-worn veterans with incredulity. In the midst of demoralization and despair McClellan galloped down the Avenue with his cloak flying and his staff smartly at heel, intent on working the same miracle he had performed in 1861.

Lee fooled them. Instead of attacking the city he slipped past it, going north.

And so, instead of defending the capital behind cosy fortifications, McClellan had now to give chase, and try and catch up, and force a battle on a victorious invader. Except for a small garrison on the Peninsula, the soil of Virginia was now clear of the enemy, and no Federal army would march on Richmond while Lee was on the Potomac flanking Washington. The tables were entirely turned.

Worst of all, for days no word of Lee's exact whereabouts filtered through his cavalry screen. He was supposed to have crossed the Potomac somewhere north of Washington. And within the week McClellan swung a ragged, but spirited and hardened army through Washington towards Maryland and considerable uncertainty.

Cabot saw them go with mixed emotions. His old place was there, with McClellan, who enjoyed figuring in the newspapers and was not pleased to be without his Special Correspondent. But Cabot had found reporting the war not quite what he had expected. Apart from his healthy respect for the 57th Article of War, which provided court martial with possible sentence of death for giving military information to the enemy, either directly or indirectly—and which had already landed one journalist with six months hard labor for a slip—there was also the gentlemen's agreement between McClellan and the eastern correspondents with regard to what they would refrain from printing. Cabot had more sense of responsibility than many of his colleagues, so that whatever the temptation to score a beat, he always dreaded to leak information in a way to jeopardize his commanding officer's immediate plans. He was consequently more than once in hot water with his editors for holding back a story some less scrupulous rival had filed first, often with damaging effect. Before the war had been on very long, several generals, notably Sherman, were in a state of mind to shoot any correspondent at sight, and would not have one attached to their command. On the other hand, too many correspondents became mere press agents for their generals, splashing their successes and covering up their lapses. No dependable censorship rules existed, and yet dispatches sent through Washington by wire were likely to be delayed or diverted by Government caprice or discretion—a condition of affairs which induced some correspondents to deliver their fruitier battlefront news in person by making spectacular journeys on horseback to the nearest railway, and arriving at their offices covered with the mud and blood of combat and in the last stages of exhaustion.

Furthermore, Cabot had some conscience about publicly criticizing his commanding officers and the administration, which he was forced sometimes to consider hopelessly at fault—and this hampered him in what he wanted to write, and ran him crosswise to the convictions of the armchair generals in the editorial rooms. He viewed the New York *Tribune*'s policy of violent attack on the President and McClellan with disgust, and went all the way home to Trenton to quarrel bitterly with his father over an editorial in the *Enquirer* accusing Mr. Lincoln of "languor, blindness, and want of purpose." For an hour the dispute between the two of them raged in his father's office, before Cabot strode out and the door closed behind him with a bang which shattered the already overstrained nerves of the *Enquirer*'s staff, huddled outside in the city room.

Whether Cabot resigned or was fired from the *Enquirer* remained a question to its other employees, but he never wrote for it again. From then on his articles appeared exclusively in a Philadelphia paper which was loyally supporting the administration and not attempting to fight a guerrilla war with Washington on the side. The War Department ruling that all news from the front must be published with a by-line helped to make the reputation of more than one correspondent, and the New York *Times* made him an offer just when he had begun to feel that the less said about this war the better, and the thing was to get it over. The second disaster at Manassas seemed to him to make his decision even clearer. He turned down the *Times*. "I've given up journalizing war from a staff officership," he told McClellan briefly. "Beginning now, I'm going to concentrate on fighting it." "Then 'jine the cavalry,'" McClellan quoted ironically, and Cabot said, "Later."

He was riding every day now, exercising his wounded leg, and the fever had apparently left him for good. Melicent complained that she saw very little of him, and he told her philosophically that it would have to be that way from now on. His room was alongside hers and she noticed by his lighted window that he did not sleep till late. One night she tapped on his door and asked if his leg was bothering. He answered vaguely through the door that he was quite all right.

Accustomed to his invalidism, she opened the door to see if there was anything she could do for him. He was sitting fully dressed at his desk, which was covered with books and papers.

"Oh, I—didn't know you were working," she said, preparing to back out. "You really ought to go to bed, Cabot, you rode all afternoon, and you'll bring the fever back if you're not careful."

"I've just finished," he said meekly. "How about getting a little sleep yourself?"

"Good-night, then." Her eyes caught a carpet-bag, standing open on a chair. "Are you—are you going away?"

He glanced round quickly, and saw the bag.

"Oh, that. No, the books came in that. It's a special job. I have to do some studying first. Go to bed, that's a good girl."

The next day he rode again, and had not returned at midnight. She lay awake listening for him, fell asleep before he came, dreamed of catastrophe, and woke at daybreak feeling uneasy and nightmarish. Tiptoeing to his door, she opened it a crack to reassure herself that he was all right. His bed had not been slept in.

She closed the door and went back to her room, fighting panic. He had fallen during his ride, there must have been an accident, he might be lying somewhere beside the road, helpless—her impulse was to run to the Senator's room, and spread a general alarm. With some instinct of caution, and by a considerable effort, she forced herself to go back to bed and wait till the first possible moment she could dress and go down to breakfast. The next thing she knew the sun was streaming into the room and the breakfast gong boomed through the house.

When she reached the dining-room Cabot was already in his chair at table, freshly shaved and guiltless-looking. He teased her about oversleeping. Oppressed by something she could not name she said nothing of her vigil, and from the commonplace talk during the meal she deduced that no one else suspected the hours he kept.

"The paper says they've caught another one of Pinkerton's men down in Virginia and hanged him," said the Senator's wife. "I don't see what good it does, really, sending spies all the way to Richmond. Surely by the time their information gets back here it's too late to be of any use."

"Pinkerton likes them to wear the grey," said Cabot, and shook his head. "That's a bit *too* low—putting on the other fellow's uniform to pick his brains! Besides—if you're caught it's certain death."

"They're the bravest men we've got, though," said the Senator, handing his cup for more coffee.

"Who are? Pinkerton's?" Cabot asked aggressively.

"Not just Pinkerton's. Any man who goes between the lines, whether he wears the enemy's uniform or any other sort of disguise. It takes twice the guts—excuse me, Lydia—twice the courage it takes to lead a cavalry charge."

"Yes, I suppose it does," Cabot agreed. "In the cavalry, you've at least got company. And they mark your grave too, as a rule."

"Well, of all the depressing conversations!" cried the Senator's wife.

"You began it, my dear," he reminded her.

Cabot slept a while during the afternoon, admitting to a headache, and spent the evening at his desk, and went to bed at a normal hour.

The following morning he remarked that he would be away two or three days, maybe longer. Melicent noticed that he took no luggage.

On the third afternoon of his absence, she began to wonder again, and drifted into the lilac room just for the companionship of his masculine belongings which lived there. It had rained all day and kept her in the house. The Senator's wife had many engagements which did not include a fourteen-year-old guest.

The carpet-bag stood on a chair unlatched, and she yielded to a Pandora impulse—it was empty. The table by the window was piled with his books. She went through them idly, hoping for something new to read. Most of it was heavy stuff—*The Decline and Fall*—a life of Napoleon, a book on cavalry tactics—and *The Cloister and the Hearth*. That was the book they had all read in the prison. She sat down in his easy chair and opened it to the first page.

Before long she noticed that there were words lightly underlined in a way which seemed entirely unconnected with the meaning. She read on, puzzling at it. Cabot didn't believe in marking books, she had heard him say so more than once. And these marks seemed at random. The story bored her, and she left it without regret, going listlessly down to dinner. It was dreadful how you missed him.

In the evening a howling thunderstorm came up, the second that day. The Senator and his wife were at a reception, and except for the servants she was alone in the house. She went back to Cabot's room, lighted his reading lamp, and for lack of anything better went on reading *The Cloister and the Hearth*. The storm banged and rattled on its way, and the wet night grew quieter. Her eyelids were drooping. The clock on the stairs struck eleven. He wouldn't come tonight, and she might as well go to bed——

There were quick footsteps in the hall outside, and the door opened sharply under his hand. For a moment he stood on the threshold, blinking in the unexpected light, the knob still in his hand. Then without speaking he came into the room and closed the door with a snap.

She stared at him silently. He wore a long army waterproof dripping with rain, and a wide-brimmed army hat. But on the way up stairs he had unfastened the waterproof to the waist so that she saw the rough grey butternut suit he wore beneath it—the sort of suit farmers wore, and raw recruits from the hills. Her eyes travelled to his feet—sodden, broken, deplorable shoes, to go with the suit. She was numb with shock, and yet it was as though she had known for hours now what his absences meant. He had been passing between the lines. And if he was caught doing that they would hang him.

She sat frozen, unable to speak, while he took off his hat and beat it in a shower of rain drops against his knee and tossed it to the floor in a corner. Then he shed the wet waterproof, dropping it near the hat.

At last he spoke.

"Well," he said expressionlessly, "I'm afraid I'll have to send you home now."

"Oh, Cabot, I didn't mean to sp—" The word died on her lips. She went weak with horror at what she had said. "You can trust me," she whispered.

"Naturally. I can trust your loyalty, but not your—discretion. Pack up, you're leaving tomorrow. We'll say that Anne sent for you." He came and took the book from her unresisting hand—the book whose underlined words were the key to the cypher he used.

"Oh, Cabot, *please,* I—m-my lessons with Mr. Boldini——"

"I'm sorry, my dear, but I have no choice. You're too intelligent not to see that. I might have known you'd catch on, but tonight was an accident. I missed my half-way station in the storm and had to come on in like this—I borrowed the waterproof from an officer at the fort." He went to a tabouret in the corner and poured out a stiff brandy and drank it at a gulp. His hand was shaking. He had never got his color back since his illness and the whiteness of his drawn face terrified her.

"Please come and sit down, you're—you'll kill yourself if you go on this way! Let's get those wet shoes off." She pushed him into a chair and knelt to unfasten his soaked shoelaces.

"Don't do that, I can manage——"

But she shook her head, picking at the knots while her eyes blurred so that it was difficult to see. She got his shoes off and brought his slippers from the cupboard, and put them on for him. He sat passive, his head against the back of the chair, his eyes closed.

"More brandy?"

"Please."

She brought it to him.

"Cabot—does the Senator know?"

"Yes. That's why I'm living here now. I couldn't come and go like this at Willard's."

"Oh, Cabot, I'd rather you *fought*——"

"I am fighting."

"In the usual way, Cabot. I'd rather you took the *ordinary* risks a soldier has to take——"

"Any fool can do that. What I'm doing takes brains. And nerve. There aren't enough of us, as it is. If we'd known a day sooner that he was pulling out of Frederick——"

"Lee?"

"It's too late now. He's got away again. He always gets away."

She was crying softly, wiping at her wet cheeks with her fingers because she had no handkerchief. He reached out and pulled her to him, so that she sat on the arm of his chair, leaning against his shoulder, crying into her fingers.

"Now, now—you'll spoil your eyes. Don't you fret, they won't catch me. I don't like it myself, you know, but I swore a solemn swear that if ever I got a chance to do anything to shorten the war I'd take it, no matter what it was—and if we could catch Lee now while he's 'way off base—if we could land him with a Sunday punch while his supply line runs all the way to Culpeper—the war might be over. Think of it! The war might be *over!*"

There was a tap on the door and he said, "Come in." The Senator stood there in evening dress, looking horrified.

"It's all right," Cabot said easily. "She caught me—nobody else. I missed Bronson on the road, though. Filthy night, isn't it?"

The Senator came in and closed the door.

"What are we going to do about this?" he asked, looking sternly at Melicent.

"We're going to send her home. Tomorrow. Not that she'd talk if she stayed here—but it's the only way to prevent any possible slip." He rose, and pulled her to her feet. "Go to bed," he said kindly. "I'll see you in the morning." He kissed her, and gave her a little push towards the door.

Before she reached it they had forgotten her. As she closed it behind her she caught one word outstanding in Cabot's lowered voice—Sharpsburg.

VI. MAY 12, 1864

I

Louise and Sally Sprague had returned to Richmond with Sedgwick when he got his exchange, about the time that Cabot was sent north from Libby Prison. Ransom's youngest boy, Barry, came with them too, as he was soon to enter the Military Institute at Lexington which his brother Fauquier was leaving, like many of the upper classmen, for active service in the field. Fauquier was going into the horse artillery, where Eden's faithful childhood beau, Grafton Crabb, was now a captain.

There had been recriminations, transfers, and disillusion in the Confederate command during the summer lull around Richmond when McClellan was beaten back to Harrison's Landing. Lee stood higher than he had ever done, as the savior of Richmond, and was known affectionately to all the army as Marse Robert. Stonewall Jackson was barely second to him. But Magruder, for one, was under a cloud after Malvern Hill, and when he departed to a western command his force was split among several other officers. Dabney was in Pickett's division, which was given to Longstreet, and Longstreet was soon ordered up to Gordonsville to work with Jackson, who was already there. Stuart too was in the field around Gordonsville, and Sedgwick went off at once in high spirits to rejoin him.

Distracted with nursing her mother besides the wounded, Eden was thankful for Louise's gentle, tireless presence, and Sally's rather heartless natural gaiety was in a way a welcome relief from tension and despair. Felicity was still very ill when the time came for Ransom to leave Richmond with Lee, but she seemed a little better and Ransom knew that he could not burden his harassed commander at such a time with a plea for personal consideration. He had not been gone twenty-four hours when Felicity died, serenely and beautifully, as became her, in her sleep.

They buried her in Hollywood Cemetery where the dead soldiers

went, with only women and fifteen-year-old Barry to mourn her at
the graveside, where the roar of the rapids in the river below was loud
beneath the arching trees. And no one had much time to grieve because the wounded from Manassas and Chantilly arrived by the train-
load and there was more work than ever before. They decided not to
return home to Williamsburg after they had seen Barry off to Lexington. Eden could have been in touch with Cabot there, but they would
have been cut off entirely from their men at the front, for Williamsburg was still a Federal garrison, its only communication with Richmond and the Confederate army by the underground mail and smuggling routes. Besides, every woman able to do nursing was needed in
Richmond. And then, just as they began to wonder about going home
for Gran's birthday, the battle at Sharpsburg brought another piteous
harvest of casualties.

So for the first time in anybody's memory Gran's birthday was not
festive, and there was no reception, no new dress, and no one to carry
her down stairs. Sue and Myrta made gifts, and there was even a white
cake to cut, and three generations of Williamsburg women came to
pay their respects and bring their love—but it couldn't be called a
party.

Lee was beaten at Sharpsburg and forced into retreat, his invasion
of the North at a disastrous end. He won the next battle, at Marye's
Heights near Fredericksburg just before Christmas. Although Eden
had already called on the Provost-Marshal to request passes to Williamsburg, they postponed the journey again in order to help with the
new wounded which flooded into the Crabb mansion in Franklin
Street. They were all living there since the men of the family had gone
from the Spotswood—Louise and Sally shared a bedroom, but Felicity's
death left Eden alone in hers and there was some talk of sending for
Sue to make herself useful after Christmas.

Cabot's present to Gran arrived promptly, brought by a smiling orderly from the commandant's office at the College. He sent her a
pound of the best tea money could buy, and in a quaint purple velvet
box a pair of Regency earrings, delicate scrolls set with small yellow
diamonds. She put them on with fingers that trembled with eagerness,
and wore them like a peacock even when there was no one to see.
There was no limit to her love of extravagances like that, and she had
to be ninety-five before anyone discovered it and indulged her.

For Eden he sent lengths of sapphire blue velvet to make a gown, worth a small fortune at blockade prices, with calico at nearly two dollars a yard. There was no way to forward it safely through the lines to Richmond, so Gran enclosed a snippet in a letter by the underground mail, which functioned smoothly now despite the efforts of the provost guard.

Since McClellan's army had departed from Harrison's Landing in August, Williamsburg was the nearest point to Richmond which the Federal troops held, and it had acquired an unhappy importance as a terminal and outpost. The telegraph connected Fort Magruder with Washington. The Press and the Army were established at Fortress Monroe. Confederate detachments from up Richmond way raided Williamsburg one day and Federal troops used it as a starting point for reconnaissance in force the next. Spies of both sides came and went. Smuggling of drugs and luxuries went on in the rivers under the noses of the provost guard, and provoked innumerable small alarums and excursions, usually at night. Gran said it was worse than Cornwallis, for at least he hadn't gone on so long.

The northward and westward doors and windows of the College were bricked up against the Confederate raids, with portholes for small arms. Deep trenches were dug extending from the College buildings in either direction well beyond the Richmond and Jamestown roads, trenches in which ten-foot logs were set vertically three feet in the ground, as a barrier against Confederate cavalry. Back of the College, from road to road stretched a long curving abatis of oak and beech trees with sharpened limbs standing westward and all entangled with wire. The campus itself was covered with the huts of the provost guard where once the white tents of the Fifteenth Virginia Infantry had stood in the early days of the war, and the guard patrolled the streets and preserved martial law. Civil courts were suspended. The Federal soldiers used the bricks from the ruined Palace and Capitol to build foundations for their huts, and burned whatever woodwork they could find as firewood, even at the College.

The regiment in occupation was the Fifth Pennsylvania, composed largely of Philadelphia roughs, and Major Cronin ruled them and the civilians alike with an iron hand. Except when his men got a drinking bout going, or a Confederate raid came down, or a smuggler-hunt was on, something akin to order usually prevailed and the streets were safe for the inhabitants, mostly women, who were left in the town.

It was a grim Christmas—in Williamsburg, in Richmond, and in the bleak shelters the army had thrown up around Fredericksburg; grimmest of all at Washington where twelve thousand wounded lay, the dreadful result of Burnside's useless and costly assaults at Marye's Heights, nearly two and a half times the Confederate losses in the same action.

Cabot had sent Sue's manuscripts north with his copy before he was taken prisoner at Gaines' Mill, and three of them were published during the winter, and paid for by bank drafts, which Cronin's adjutant obligingly cashed for her to a total sum which seemed to her staggeringly large. Early in the year a letter came for her from Trenton, New Jersey. She read it with astonishment and rushed up stairs to share it with Gran.

Dear Sue—[Melicent had written]

Cabot says I may write to you and say how much I have enjoyed reading your stories in *Harper's* and the *Lady's Magazine*. Of course I am used to his having things printed, but it seems to me very exciting that a *girl* can sell things too, and he says you aren't much older than I am. I wonder how it feels to have money that you have *earned!*

All I can do is sing, and I have never had a chance to thank your sister Eden for the music she sent me. I learned all the songs and sang some of them in Washington when I was there, but I had to come back home and didn't get to have lessons with Boldini after all, and it nearly broke my heart.

I sat to a photographer for Cabot's Christmas present, wearing the dress I wore when I sang at the reception at the Senator's house. It's pink. Cabot says I should send a copy of the photograph to you in this letter so you will know what I am like in case you want to answer. It is a lovely dress, but the picture makes me look as though my teeth stuck out, and they don't really, at least I never thought they did. Cabot says if you do write an answer and give it to the adjutant he will send it on to me, but you must leave it open so it can be read and they will know we are not passing military secrets or using a cypher. As though we would know any! [So much for that night in Washington, still a horror to her dreams, when Cabot came home in the wet waterproof and butternut suit and found her drowsing over *The Cloister and the Hearth*.]

I hope when the war is over and Cabot comes down to marry Eden we can meet and really know each other. Perhaps you would let me see one of your stories then, before it is printed, I think it would be very exciting to read it in your own handwriting instead of in type. As you can see, I can't even write a letter very well!

Yours very sincerely,

MELICENT MURRAY

Sue was delighted, and sat down to answer the letter at once, with the photograph propped up on the desk before her. It was, indeed, a lovely dress, and Melicent's childish pride of it was to Sue at eighteen rather touching. Sue had had so many pretty clothes, she had never thought much about them, and now, when it was getting hard to find enough food to eat, clothes mattered to her even less than ever before. All the girls in the family had had well-stocked wardrobes when the war started and were not yet going shabby like so many Southern women who had not had enough dresses to begin with. It was more important to Sue that Melicent's hair looked brushed and shining, and her smile, which parted her lips over small, even teeth, was both shy and radiant. She decided that Melicent was a darling, and longed for the day when she could be added on to the family as another sister.

Dear Melicent—[Sue wrote]

I was so glad to get your letter, and the picture, which I have shown to Gran, and we are both agreed that we could not do better than to acquire you at once as a member of the family.

The war goes on and on, and Eden is still in Richmond nursing the wounded. There has been no way to let your brother know that our mother died last August in Richmond. She was ill when he left the prison. It was some sort of fever she got from the wounded, and the doctors could not get the medicines they thought she needed.

I wouldn't mind the blockade shutting out silks and tea and luxuries, I wouldn't even mind food being so scarce and dear, if only they would let the drugs come through. It isn't going to make our army give up because the men have to bear their wounds without morphine, and even have amputations without chloroform. And now Eden writes that she will always be haunted by the feeling that if they could have got digitalis and opium for mother she might have lived. We always *pray* that the smugglers won't get caught whenever we have a hunt on here, and I would tell the adjutant so to his face—because there is always the chance that they are carrying drugs that will save lives among the sick and wounded. Of course there is a similar chance that they are only smuggling tea or sugar or fripperies, and in that case it doesn't matter, because they are wasting their time!

I hope your brother is well of his wound, and please tell him that when we last heard from Eden she was all right. It seems a lifetime since I've seen her here, but each time she thinks of coming home there is another battle and more wounded arrive. She is working at a private hospital which has been established in the Crabbs' house on Franklin Street. They can take about twenty men there, and the beds are always full. Mrs. Crabb has broken down and it takes a good deal of Charlotte's time to look after her, so that Eden and Sally and Aunt Louise are trying to do all the nursing of the men. We hear nothing from the front, and I suppose I couldn't tell you if we did. All I know is that Father and Uncle Lafe and the boys all must have charmed lives, as they have been in nearly every action so far, and come through safely.

I thought for a while I would go to Richmond myself to do nursing, but it seems best for one of us to be here with Gran—though I must say she is always the calmest of us all when there is a raid! She asks me to give you her love, and tell you to be sure and write again soon and send news of your brother.

Thank you again for liking my stories, and believe me, most affectionately,

Your sister-to-be,
SUSANNAH DAY

2

But Fredericksburg was another barren victory for the South, and Burnside had been able to withdraw his punished army across the Rappahannock. Refugees from the ruined town poured into Richmond along with the wounded and prisoners, bringing terrible stories of the bombardment which had demolished houses and left the old and the sick and the children without shelter in bitter weather. Small-pox came with them too, and there was much talk of spies again, and another sentence of hanging. "Fighting Joe" Hooker superseded Burnside, and Yankee cavalry raids came to the very outskirts of Richmond as the severest winter in years gave way to the spring of 1863.

In February Dabney passed through Richmond with Pickett in the army Longstreet was taking south to forage in the richly provisioned country round Suffolk, which was held by the Federals. Dabney had only a few snatched minutes to spend with Eden in Franklin Street—the first time they had met since Felicity's death, though Ransom had managed to accompany Lee last November on one of his brief visits to the Richmond headquarters.

In the small upstairs parlor the Crabbs had kept for a sitting-room when all the ground floor was given over to the rows of cots full of wounded, brother and sister held to each other while the tramp of marching feet never ceased outside. There was little comfort between them except the warm family contact each stood in need of—their mother's death had been peaceful, but there was no saying she had not suffered—Ransom's hair, they both knew, had greyed, and his youthful carriage was gone forever—the winter was a hard one, both for the troops around Lee's headquarters near Fredericksburg and for the women in Richmond where food and fuel were scarce at any price—Dabney's uniform was worn and muddy, his freshly shaven face was haggard—Eden in her working dress was frankly shabby under the clean white apron, and her soft mouth had tightened at the corners, beneath shadowed, heavy eyes.

They held to each other with tears, exchanging their news—Ransom had sent her his love from Fredericksburg—Sedgwick was well, and utterly devoted to General Stuart, and seemed to have made a life out of soldiering—Pickett was a hero to his men, and Dabney was proud to be one of his captains—the latest word from Williamsburg was that Gran and the family there had kept their hearts high, and the Federal occupation, though inconvenient, was bearable—one could bear anything, it seemed. . . . They clung, cheek to cheek, and then he went down to say good-bye to Charlotte and Louise and Sally in the lower hall and was gone into the relentless tramp of marching feet as the regiments poured through the streets southward.

Jackson was the idol of the Confederacy now. "My troops sometimes fail in driving the enemy from a position, but the enemy *always* fail to drive my men from a position," he said in his dour way, and no one called it boasting. Hooker failed at Chancellorsville in May, but Jackson was wounded there, shot by his own pickets in the dusk by mistake.

The Confederacy was stunned. Even Lee, usually resigned to the will of the Lord, had rebelled during the dreadful week while the beloved life hung in the balance. "Jackson *cannot* die!" he said more than once. "Surely God will not take him from us, we need him so much." But the miracle was not performed. After days of agony, during which his delirium was all of battle and his delusion was always of attack— ("Push up the columns," he would plead with an imaginary staff. "Hasten up the columns—push the cannon forward—")—Jackson came at last to some mirage of green pastures. "Let us pass over the river, and rest under the shade of the trees," he murmured just before he died.

And so the Dead March was heard again in the streets of Richmond, this time for Stonewall Jackson. Everyone wept from the time the signal gun was fired and the distant band began to play the procession towards the Capitol where he was to lie in state. Eden stood with Louise and Sally in the bareheaded crowd that lined Main Street to see him pass, their cheeks wet with tears.

Pickett's men had come north again just too late for Chancellorsville—they led the way down Main Street at the slow step, a ragged, miscellaneously clad escort of mourning men, their arms reversed, their shot-torn banners furled and shrouded in crêpe; the Fayette Artillery came next, their battered, dented gun carriages painstakingly cleaned and polished; and then some cavalry, the gaunt horses groomed within an inch of their lives and still carrying themselves like the thoroughbreds most of them were; then the hearse with its dark plumes and the flower-covered Confederate flag which draped the coffin; the led war-horse followed its dead master, the boots across the saddle; the Staff came behind it with bowed heads, the President and his Cabinet, the officers who could be spared from the field, the Mayor and Council of Richmond, and the mile-long stream of private carriages to do him homage; all moving mutely and patiently in the sweltering heat to the deep throb of the majestic music.

There was no one to replace him, but his command was divided up and Lee drove north again in June with Longstreet and Stuart and A. P. Hill—leaving Harvey Hill in charge of the Richmond defenses, so that Lafe, as a member of Hill's military family, was with Louise again, and Sally moved into Eden's room. Once more Lee passed his army across the Potomac into Maryland and Pennsylvania. Harrisburg was threatened, and even Philadelphia. Lincoln called for another hundred thousand men.

A year ago the South had stood as near to victory as now, and Lee fell back to Sharpsburg and defeat. This time they promised themselves it would be different. This time the supply lines would hold, this time the ragged regiments in grey would have just that last extra ounce of strength that was needed to end the war. This time Lee would not have to retreat into Virginia and begin all over again. . . .

This time they fought at a little place in Pennsylvania called Gettysburg.

Three days they fought in the dust and the heat. And after three days it was plain that Lee was beaten, with terrible losses. He got away, though, across the Potomac, from under Meade's very nose, and took his army with him.

The news came slowly to the anxious, excited crowds outside the War Department in Richmond. The first reports were of a Confederate victory—everyone had been so hopeful, so sure it would be a victory. Then they heard that Lee had recrossed the Potomac, southward. Gradually the disaster grew—Hill had gone in too soon—Stuart had arrived too late—Cemetery Ridge—Pickett's charge—where were the guns which should have covered Pickett?—Pickett was annihilated —a whole division wiped out—where were the guns. . . .

The next day, while Richmond was still reeling, they learned that Vicksburg had fallen—and Charleston was under siege now—but Lee was safe at Culpeper again, and Meade was not crowding him. By the middle of July Richmond rallied groggily in the stupefying heat. A message had come through for Eden from Ransom: *Still here, even Dabney.* A scant fifteen hundred men had come back from that charge with Pickett, but Dabney was among them. Charlotte threw herself into Eden's arms and cried till she got hiccups. She hadn't shed a tear while they thought Dabney was dead.

During August Lee came down to Richmond for a fortnight. His beard was nearly white. Ransom, who accompanied him, said that Lee had offered his resignation after Gettysburg, but Davis wouldn't hear of it; and Ransom said Lee wanted to uncover Richmond and march direct on Washington, at the risk of exchanging capitals, but Davis wouldn't have that either.

Dabney turned up again in Richmond in the middle of September. What was left of Pickett's division was being sent down to Petersburg because of new Federal activity on the Peninsula, and Pickett was going to be married, of all things, said Dabney. Charlotte at once begged him for details.

"She's only a schoolgirl," Dabney told them, sitting in his shirt-sleeves in the little upstairs parlor in Franklin Street while Eden tried to mend his coat to respectability. "He's been waiting for her to grow up, apparently. But Gettysburg jolted him. He's got scared to death if he doesn't get her now he may never have another chance."

"And quite right, too," said Eden, and her brother cocked an eyebrow in her direction.

"But hard on the girl," he remarked.

"Not at all—if she loves him."

"She is supposed to have fallen in love with him at the age of ten, or thereabouts, the story goes."

"You sound as though you don't quite believe it," she accused.

"It seems just a *leetle* bit tall for a story," he said, grinning. "He's a spectacular sort of devil, mind! Long, wavy hair—hands and feet small as a woman's, almost—cuts a dash, you know, can't help it! Romantic soldiers are the *softest* fellers there are, too. He's in a mush about this girl—has been for years, even while he was fighting the Injuns out West. So now he jerks her out of school to marry him. Well, I look at it another way. Suppose he gets the heart shot right out of him— I've seen it happen. She's a widow in her teens. Suppose he loses a leg, or worse—it happens any day. She's saddled with a cripple all her life." Dabney shook his handsome head judicially. "Mm-mm—I couldn't do it. It's cruel."

"But she's got a right to him!" cried Charlotte. "She's got a right to him *now,* while he's whole! Especially if she's been in love with him all her life!" And then she got very pink as Dabney's slow, surprised gaze came to rest on her.

"Well, well," he drawled, and glanced at Eden mirthfully, and back again to Charlotte, who was sitting very straight with her knitting, her cheeks on fire. "Look who's got opinions about love!" Dabney marvelled in his gentle voice, and there was laughter in it, but no derision.

"Any girl has a right to whatever happiness she can snatch these days," Eden reminded him quietly, and——

"Where's Cabot?" he asked at once, with a penetrating look.

"I don't know."

"What's the underground for? Hasn't he sent you any word?"

"Only through Williamsburg. His sister writes to Sue and we send messages that way. She saw him not long ago—he's better of his wound, and—sent his love and his sympathy about Mother." Eden bit off the thread and handed the grey coat back to him. "There, that's the best I can do, I'm afraid. Now it's time for me to relieve Aunt Louise down stairs. Come and say good-night before you go."

She glanced back as she left the room. Dabney's lazy pose had not altered. Charlotte sat erect with scarlet cheeks, knitting very fast. Eden closed the door on them softly, knowing that Charlotte's mother would not have approved.

It was a wonderful wedding Pickett and his Sally Corbell had at St. Paul's in Petersburg on the fifteenth, and there was a big reception for them in Richmond that evening. Mrs. Davis herself gave the cake, though sweets were almost unobtainable, and the plantation servants from Pickett's home near Malvern Hill sent dozens of sora which they had killed for the wedding feast by going out at night with wooden paddles, as there was no ammunition—and gallons of terrapin stew. Little bags of sugar and salt and tea were given as wedding presents. More than a thousand soldier guests came in uniform from the army stationed roundabout Richmond, the President and his Cabinet being almost the only men in civilian clothes. The women wore refurbished and carefully preserved finery, and the dancing went on till dawn, almost as though no war was being fought.

Dabney escorted Eden proudly to the reception and presented her to his general and the blissful little bride who stood beside him to receive their guests. Slight as a boy, with long dark hair and brilliant grey eyes, the hero of Gettysburg bent above Eden's hand. "Your sister?" he said smiling. "I am honored, ma'am. But what about a wife, my boy?" "You sound like the fox who lost his tail, sir," said Dabney, and Sally Pickett's laughter could be heard above the waltz music.

"Yes, Dabney, what about a wife?" Eden asked him while they danced, and he glanced down at her with his lazy, charming smile.

" 'When this cruel war is over'—maybe," he said.

"It's cruel, all right—when she's so willing."

"Who's willing?"

"Don't be dense, Dabney. Poor Charl goes every color of the rainbow every time you look at her!"

"What, little Charlotte?" He seemed genuinely surprised, but pleased. "She's even younger than Pickett's bride!"

"Well, you're younger than Pickett, too."

"Now, wait a minute, Dee, don't rush me. Besides, I've got a war on."

"Pickett found time."

"She *talks* so much, Dee!"

"Mostly when she's nervous. That makes her worse."

"Then she's always nervous when I'm around!"

"Naturally."

Dabney snickered shamelessly.

"I can't help it," he said. "Charl always makes me laugh."

"Not a bad thing in a wife, I should think. Especially these days."

"She's like a puppy," said Dabney, but with affection in his voice. "Or like kittens, with blue eyes and funny little necks. Or colts. Sort of pathetic, but comic at the same time. I don't think I'd have the heart to marry Charl. She might grow up if she got married, and then she wouldn't be Charl any more."

"You wouldn't want her to be an old maid, either, would you?"

"Can't imagine it," he said firmly. "Can't risk some clumsy lummox making her miserable, though, I never thought of that."

"I know one clumsy lummox who is making her very miserable right now," said Eden. "And that's you!"

"*No!*" said Dabney, pleased, but with a lingering skepticism. "I'm just somebody she's known all her life."

"Well, even so, she thinks you're wonderful. Sometimes I find it rather a strain not to set her right on it, but so far I have managed to hold my tongue!"

"Charl thinks I'm wonderful," he said, as though digesting a brand new idea, and then he snickered again. "She does make me laugh," he said.

The music paused, and Eden was claimed by a new partner. When the ball broke up at last, the guests departed under the morning star. Dabney was sleepy, and kept very silent on the way home. Eden hoped he was thinking, but suspected the punch.

3

Dabney was right when he told Eden that Sedgwick had made a life out of cavalry service.

War was to Sedgwick a form of peace—a hard respite from the ordeal of learning not to think of Sue. You had no time to be in love, you had no time to mourn your future, while you were fighting a war. Cavalry forced you to live each day, each hour as it came. Cavalry taught you that the thing you dreaded most might never have time to happen to you. Cavalry took all you had to give and demanded more, until your tired body slept every chance it got and there was no room left in your cosmos for repining. If you were a good cavalryman you couldn't remember ever having been anything else, and you never looked even a week ahead of today because it was likely that nothing would matter to you at all a week hence. So Sedgwick throve and distinguished himself in a life which, before that day on the riverbank at Jamestown, would have been no good to him—a life which was just a little bit harder than sitting still and doing without Sue would have been. And then there was the general.

Like Jackson, whose routes had always been littered with sick or exhausted men who could not keep up, Stuart wore out his horses and wore out his troopers, always cheerful himself and always ready for a fight. It was said that he considered his military problems too serious to be treated seriously—the odds against him were too heavy to contemplate, and so he led his squadrons into battle as to a fox-hunt, hallooing joyously towards the kill.

He seldom set up headquarters, but lived in constant, shifting contact with the enemy, which was his idea of cavalry's proper place. He could ride for fifty hours at a stretch, till the wretched troopers behind him fell asleep in their saddles and the horses stumbled and knocked against each other in the ranks. He never made allowance for man or beast, and removed an officer he considered not sufficiently courageous. He never said "Go" but always said "Come on, boys!"

He was married, and devoted to his Flora, and wrote her frequently from the saddle, beginning *My dear Darling*. But the girls who lived in the country between the armies danced and rode with the grey-coated general and repeated to him all they had gleaned from some unwary blue-clad admirer a few days before. It was no uncommon thing for him to take a delighted rebel miss with him along the picket lines on inspection, detailing an embarrassed trooper to entertain her while he himself transacted military business with the outpost commander, gave his instructions, received reports, collected his lady and rode on.

The legends which grew up around him were no taller than the facts. You could not improve on General Stuart. He said that picking an aide was like taking a wife, it was for better or for worse. He made a clever girl named Antonia his honorary aide-de-camp in a formal written document signed with an impression of his signet ring. He risked himself constantly in little affairs of the videttes like any common trooper. He wore a red rose in his jacket in season, and a red love-knot of ribbon when there were no roses. His wide soft fawn-colored hat was looped up on the right side with a gold star and a curling ostrich plume. He loved charades and ·practical jokes, and wrote bad poetry, and chaffed even the solemn Jackson. Raiding near Alexandria once, he telegraphed the Washington Government over his own signature that if they could not send larger supply trains up to Burnside it was not worth his, Stuart's, while to intercept them. This went so well as a joke that he soon sent another telegram to Washington complaining that the mules he had just captured from their General Meigs were very inferior and please to send better ones next time. On the retreat southward after Sharpsburg his irrepressible troopers swam their tired, gaunt horses across the swollen fords of the Potomac singing *Carry Me Back to Ole Virginny*. . . .

Those were all true stories. Better ones were not invented. This was the man Sedgwick loved like a brother and revered as a commander.

After Gettysburg the Confederate Army lay around Culpeper where good grazing was, while men and horses recuperated and the sick and injured rejoined. By September Meade was jabbing at them again with his Yankee cavalry and Stuart fought back briskly—at Brandy Station, where things went so badly for him that two grey horse-batteries fought back to back on the same knoll, holding off blue troops on either hand; at Auburn, where for a whole night Stuart and two brigades lay on their arms within sight of the Federal camp-fires, almost surrounded and facing certain capture, and got away in the dawn with another good story to tell; at Buckland Mills, where he captured Custer's wagons and personal baggage; and so on through the winter months, while the minstrel Sweeny died of pneumonia and Flora Stuart had a baby daughter.

Furloughs were hard to come by that winter, but Fauquier and Grafton Crabb got off both at the same time for five full days in Richmond, and were made much of there. The night they returned, Sedgwick went over to their camp to hear about it and found Grafton very low in his mind. Fauquier was outspoken.

"Eden is still playing the fool about that Yankee," he said disgustedly.

Sedgwick grinned at Grafton, who lay on one elbow staring into the fire.

"Turned you down again?" he suggested with sympathy.

'Oh, I ought to be used to that by now! Only—if it was some fellow on our side she had in mind, it would be easier to swallow. But you liked him, didn't you."

"We all liked him," admitted Sedgwick. "Especially Gran."

"What's he like, anyway? Or maybe I should say—what's wrong with me?"

"Well, it's hard to say." Sedgwick threw another log on the fire, for the night was frosty and their scanty rations and threadbare uniforms gave them no bodily weapons against the cold. "She's used to you, that's one trouble."

"I know! Like Dabney with Charl."

"*What?*" said Sedgwick, and his eyes widened.

"Played together—grew up together—Dabney thinks Charl is still a yearling. But ever since he came home from England she's been eating her heart out for him. Don't ever let on I told you, she'd skin me sure enough!"

"Well, I'll be damned," murmured Sedgwick, more pleased than not, as he thought it over. Charlotte was pretty cute. "Well, why not?"

"Sure, why not?" Grafton repeated irritably. "Why not Eden and me? The Crabb family just doesn't seem to have much luck with the Days!"

"Oh, I don't know about that," Fauquier said soothingly. "After all, Dabney's pretty busy just now."

"It's now or never," muttered Grafton, throwing pebbles at the fire.

In the spring of 1864 the army was back at Orange and the man named Grant was in possession of Culpeper. He commanded the Federal Army now, ranking Meade. And in May Grant began to move. He moved westward towards the old battlefield of Chancellorsville. He was going to try again, where Meade had failed the year before, through the Wilderness to Richmond.

The battle began on the fourth of May—before Grant expected it to. Lee chose to fight there in the tangled woods among the dogwood and flowering almond, with violets underfoot, and grape hyacinth, and the quail piping their astonishment on every side. The dense undergrowth helped him to conceal how he was outnumbered. It also made his cavalry fight dismounted, which never amused them much.

There were a few small clearings, but no room for cavalry charges, and artillery firing into the thickets where the infantry fighting soon became desperate could do as much damage to friend as enemy, so the big guns were silent and useless. In the maze of stunted pine and scrub oak, the hand-to-hand combat raged all afternoon. The growth was so thick that the officers could not see the length of their own commands, with little idea whether the men in the next brigade were driving or being driven, except by the sound of their musketry. As darkness came on, the position of the opposing lines was revealed only by the flash of their guns and the deep-chested Yankee cheer answering the shrill Confederate yell, and the crash of the companies through the brush.

For two days they fought each other to a standstill there in the Wilderness, with no gain on either side, while the underbrush and even the hasty log breastworks caught fire, often separating the lines by a wall of smoke and flame through which the helpless wounded cried out *in extremis,* and those who could move came crawling with burns more serious than the wounds which had disabled them.

During those two days Ransom at his post in Lee's near vicinity twice saw men from the ranks lay hold of the general's bridle and turn him back from the advanced front line, while the anxious cry, "Lee to the rear! General Lee to the rear or we won't go on!" ran along the

files. And Lee would then sit stationary on the big grey horse Traveller, smiling grimly at their excessive solicitude for his life, the men
who themselves moved forward fearlessly into the inferno. Sometimes
they touched his stirrup or his knee or Traveller's shoulder as though
for luck on their way in; sometimes they cheered him as they went;
one man swept off his hat in silent tribute at sight of his commander
and Lee returned the salute with grave courtesy and the man went on
at a trot into the rain of bullets, his face aglow. Ransom was at Lee's
side when a dishevelled, breathless courier galloped in with a message,
and as he took the paper Lee ran a sympathetic eye over the young
man's winded horse. "Dismount, and rest that horse," he said, and
reached into Traveller's saddle-bag for a biscuit, which he fed the
weary animal.

Ransom was beside Lee too when they rode up about noon on the
second day to see Longstreet's charge along the Plank Road. The
enemy's line was being rolled back, it looked like another Chancellorsville. A Confederate flanking movement had apparently succeeded, and
new columns were moving in at a right angle. Down logs blocked the
artillery, and Lee paused to see the way cleared for the guns. The wild
ardent yell of the Rebel charge had begun up ahead of them, fragrant
smoke from a burning thicket on their right mingled with the dark
acrid smoke of the cannon, shutting out the sun, creating a murky
twilight among the trees which crowded the narrow road. Longstreet
was somewhere up ahead, and there was a smell of victory in the air
—Meade was crumpling, Grant's heavy sacrifice of men the first day
was all for nothing, one more push from Longstreet's well-trained
veterans. . . .

There was a scatter of small-arms fire up ahead, a frantic voice
shouted "Friends! *Friends, you fools!*" And then came other voices
calling for surgeons, for stretchers, for an ambulance—and for General
Lee. It was, in a way, another Chancellorsville. The converging Confederate columns had fired into each other. Longstreet was wounded
by his own men, and a general at his side had been killed.

Lee was there to steady them, and Longstreet's second ranking officer took over, but the columns were muddled. Before the new line of
battle could be drawn the advantage was lost, and the Federals could
not be budged.

Sedgwick as one of Stuart's aides, had seen a hard dismounted action fought with Sheridan's cavalry, also on foot, on the first day, and nothing much the second, owing to sudden caution on the other side. On the evening of the third day they reconnoitred and saw Yankee wagon-trains worming eastward. "Oh, no, you don't!" Stuart told them grimly. "He's trying to turn our right, is he, and get into Spotsylvania! Wait till we tell Marse Robert that!"

So they posted back and told Marse Robert, and the two armies raced for Spotsylvania, and the grey men got there first, and again Stuart's horse soldiers joined the infantry in hot fighting.

About dark on the ninth the pickets brought word of Sheridan moving south by the Telegraph Road, formed up in fours and riding easy, arrogant as fate in his superior numbers, heading straight for Richmond. Stuart knew the roads, which all led to Richmond thereabouts. He cut corners, fighting little rearguard and flanking actions all the way and threw himself between, and they waited for Sheridan at Yellow Tavern, six miles above Richmond. Stuart sent word into the city that he was there, across the road. Richmond took heart, and its old men and boys, and the clerks from the Government offices, went into the entrenchments to hold them till a couple of brigades could come up from Petersburg. Petersburg couldn't spare much, because Butler's Yankees were moving up from the Peninsula now. Richmond lay between two armies, both of them on the march.

That night Stuart and his aides slept under the stars. He had three thousand and two hundred men, hungry, jaded, worn with a week's steady fighting, but ready and willing to fight some more. He knew that if Sheridan had brought his full force with him, which was likely, it would be around twelve thousand.

Sheridan attacked next morning, charge after charge, and they held him. It wasn't until Custer came up with his mounted Michigan regiments, coolly left all cover, took his losses, and got across the Telegraph Road that the Confederate left began to roll back.

Stuart with Sedgwick and another young officer at heel rode straight for the trouble. They left the rest behind, but their own horses were fresh and the aides managed to hold him in sight. The Telegraph Road was thick with smoke and dust, and Custer's troopers were sabering the grey men on foot around the horse-batteries, where Fauquier and Grafton Crabb would be. Stuart galloped up, gigantic on his tall horse. "Steady, boys—form up behind me—off the road, and let them go by

—off the road, boys, form up and face the road—our mounted men will stop them further on—*let them go, I say!*—form up, and fire into their flank——!"

Custer's Michiganders went through them in the dust, taking the flanking fire from the roadside as they passed, and met the First Virginia, mounted, head on a little way down the road. The shock of the collision echoed, merged into a screaming, hacking, blazing tangle of men and horses, fighting hand to hand with sabers and pistols, until Custer's men broke, many of them unhorsed in combat, broke and turned back along the road they had come.

Stuart was still there with his remnants, sitting his tall horse right in the firing line, letting off his pistol into the Yankee rout, and shouting, "Give it to them now! Let them have it, boys, here they come again!" Sedgwick, who had carried a message to Fitz Lee down the line, was just returning to the general's side when he saw Stuart reel in the saddle and his head fall forward. Captain Dorsey, who was nearer, caught the horse's bridle and turned it quickly away from the road. A cry went up from Stuart's men—"The general! The general!" Stuart's horse plunged, and Sedgwick made a flying leap from his own saddle. Together he and Dorsey eased the general down, carried him back into the trees off the road.

"Go on—" Stuart gasped as they held him. "Go back—keep them running—tell Fitz Lee—keep them running——"

The Staff began to collect round him. An ambulance and surgeon were sent for, and arrived down the road under withering fire. Stuart protested that they were wasting time, urged them back into the fight which raged only a hundred yards away. Tight-lipped and silent, they lifted him into the ambulance drawn up in the shelter of the trees, undid his yellow silk sash, found a deep body wound. The pain had increased till he was sweating with it, but he ordered them back to the road, all but three of them, for he was certain that Custer would re-form and come in again, and every man was needed.

Sedgwick stood with the others and saw the ambulance rock away down the road, bullets ploughing the dust around the wheels. A wave of Yankee horsemen nearly engulfed it, but it got away towards the side roads, towards Richmond. All about them rose the banshee Rebel battle cry as Stuart's men passed the word and gathered themselves to avenge him.

Anger seized the Staff, anger above sorrow, so that they all swung into the saddle as with one motion, and rode yelling back to the road, where Custer was coming in again.

They were thrown back, of course, but they had blunted the drive on Richmond, and Sheridan knew he was not strong enough to hold the city even if he could have taken its northern fortifications. He turned eastward that night, in a pouring rain, towards the Chicka-hominy, and they had to let him go.

4

The firing at Yellow Tavern was clearly heard in the streets of Richmond, but the sound of guns was not new to the household of women and wounded in Franklin Street. Louise and Sally had heard them first at Bristoe, Eden at Williamsburg, and Charlotte was a vet-eran of the Seven Days' battle at Richmond's door two years ago.

At first there was no telling what it meant, though it seemed Grant's whole army might be behind it, forcing Lee back step by step on the northern defences of the city. There was no panic now when Rich-mond heard gunfire, the timid ones had all left long ago, and those that were left gathered in knots around the War Department and the telegraph offices and in doorways, waiting, listening, questioning, with anxious faces. The tocsin in Capitol Square rang and rang, calling the militia and the battalions of clerks and invalids to arms.

On the same day that Grant had moved into the Wilderness, Butler had embarked his army from Fortress Monroe and come up the James —"Beast" Butler, infamous for his reign of terror in New Orleans in 1862. If Butler's troops took Richmond, women would be afraid to go into the streets alone. He landed without opposition at City Point below the capital and began intrenching. This put him within easy reach of the Confederate fortifications at Drewry's Bluff on one side and the Petersburg railway on the other.

Harvey Hill and Beauregard were at Drewry's Bluff, and Pickett was at Petersburg. So when the guns began south of the city it meant that Lafe or Dabney or both were seeing action. Louise was white and quiet, but otherwise showed no emotion as she went about her duties among the wounded in her care, while Charlotte chattered endless nothings because she was upset about Dabney.

For days the wounded had been pouring into Richmond from the Wilderness fighting to the north, and morphine and chloroform were running short, ether and opium had vanished entirely, and laudanum was available only in such small amounts that it had slight effect on the agony that filled the hospitals. The Crabbs' little hospital was full, and mattresses had been laid on the floor of the drawing-room ward after the cots had been crowded still closer together to make room for half a dozen more men.

Coming out of the improvised surgical ward which used to be the dining-room, Louise found Eden bent over a basin in the scant privacy of the stair-landing. The whole house reeked of wounds and death. Eden looked up at her piteously, damp and shaking.

"I thought I was getting used to it," Eden said. "You'd think that with food so scarce I could learn to keep mine down, anyway."

"It's their fortitude," said Louise with a weary, understanding smile, for she had by now stopped losing her breakfast after a session in the surgical ward. "One could bear it better if they'd just let go and *groan!*"

"Yes, but if they do, we only long for morphine to hush them up," Eden reminded her.

"I don't know what we are going to do for morphine," sighed Louise. "You can't get it now at all, except for amputations, since the chloroform ran out."

"Isn't there *any* chloroform?"

"A little, perhaps, at the big hospitals. There won't be long, at this rate, we can't get it smuggled in fast enough after battles like these."

"I do think they might let the drugs come through the blockade," Eden said for the hundredth time.

The windows rattled under a new blast of gunfire, and the two women looked at each other questioningly.

"That was to the north," Eden said, and Louise nodded gravely, for things had been quieter there for a while.

"Lee," Louise nodded, and Sally came flying down the stairs behind them, tying on her apron as she came.

"It's begun again up where Lee is!" she cried. Sally hated the gunfire worse than any of them, and complained that it made her head ache. "Why can't he stop them? What do you suppose Lee is *doing* up there?"

"Lee probably knows," Louise told her patiently. "And somehow, even though I know it's silly of me, the nearer Lee is to Richmond the safer I feel!"

But it was Sheridan's guns they heard, when Custer charged across the railway bridge eastward from Yellow Tavern. Lee was still facing Grant at Spotsylvania.

That day Richmond learned that Stuart had been brought in to the home of his sister-in-law in Grace Street and was dying. He was thirty-one years old. Eden passed the house in the afternoon when she went for the brief airing they all allowed themselves, and paused a moment in the weeping crowd gathered in the street to see President Davis emerge from the house with bowed head. They said Flora Stuart had been sent for but could not be in time.

Sedgwick arrived the next day with the rest of the Staff, as part of the funeral escort. There had been dirge and bell and minute gun for Jackson, but when Stuart went without pageantry to Hollywood Cemetery he had instead of the wailing trumpet air from *Saul* only the guns at Drewry's Bluff to play his funeral march.

Like everyone else who had been closely associated with the big, laughing man, Sedgwick was stricken. Zest died with Stuart, and the joy of battle was no more. They would go on fighting devotedly still for Marse Robert, and Fitz Lee was a good cavalry leader, well trained by the best of them all. But they knew now that it was a lost cause. The heart had gone out of it.

Sedgwick managed to get Eden alone in the upstairs parlor and tried out of friendship to smooth Grafton's way a little. He spoke of the hot fighting along the Telegraph Road, and how he had seen Grafton pause in the midst of it to put a merciful bullet through the head of a favorite horse which had been wounded.

"That would be very hard for him to have to do," she said gently. "He's always loved his horses better than anything in the world."

"Except you, Dee."

She flushed and looked uncomfortable.

"Has he been talking about——"

"Oh, shoot, he doesn't have to talk. He came back from Richmond last time pretty crushed. Can't help being sorry for him, that's all."

"Well, I never meant to crush him when he was here, and I didn't, either, I've never had any intention of marrying Grafton and I'd already told him so, even before—" She stopped, rather breathless.

"Even before Cabot Murray. Mm-hm. And less intention than ever since."

"Cabot hasn't made any difference whatever in the way I feel about Grafton. I like Grafton very much. I've liked him all my life, but that's all. You can't marry just anybody you like. If only Grafton would look round him and find another girl, it would be quite easy to do, and I've been telling him so for years!"

"Still going to marry the Yankee, are you."

"Yes. And don't call him that."

"He wouldn't mind. Well, you stick to him, Eden, if that's the way you feel. Don't take second choice, if he's first. Stick to what you want, you're lucky at any price if you get it."

She smiled at him gratefully.

"I'm glad you said that. Charl thinks it's treason to love a Yankee."

"What's this I hear about Charl and Dabney?"

"Who told you?"

"Grafton, no less. Said she'd kill him for mentioning it. Is it true?"

"Yes, it is. Dabney doesn't—well, doesn't seem to take it in yet."

"But has he got a glimmer?"

She nodded and laughed.

"What a pair of gossiping busybodies we are, Sedgwick!"

"Well, I was just going to say, shove him into it the first chance you get, he's wasting time," he said heartlessly.

"And—what about yourself?"

"Me? Oh, I'm lucky too in my way. A man who's got nothing to lose and nothing to look forward to doesn't mind this war so much. It's not robbing me of anything I want, now or later."

Eden glanced at his lean young face, with its tight jawline and sensitive mouth.

"There's a letter from Sue by the underground mail."

"Well, I do think you're a little beast not to tell me before now!" he cried, and his face softened and came alive and was young and vulnerable again, so that her heart bled for him. "What does she say? How are they at home? Can't I see the letter?"

She took it out of her pocket and gave it to him without a word, knowing he would devour it lovingly page by page till he came to what he was looking for, at the end: *Tell Sedgie,* Sue had written at the end, *that it's absolutely no good his getting wounded way over there on the other side of Richmond because it's much too far for me to come and fetch him home again! Not that I wouldn't travel ten times as far on my own two feet just to bring him a cup of water on a hot day.*

On Sunday it was Eden's turn to go to church—only one of them could be spared at a time—and Sedgwick went with her. During the service ammunition wagons rattled down Eighth Street and the iron gates of the Square opposite the church slammed constantly as people hurried in and out. There was a continual mutter and boom of artillery down the river, and a rumor ran that the gunboats were engaged. Sheridan was known to be sidling round the north and east of the city to join Butler on the James.

Just as the Litany began, the sexton came down the aisle and whispered in the ear of a Congressman in one of the front pews, who rose hastily and left the church with his white-faced wife on his arm. The sexton moved back a few steps and whispered again, and a grey-haired woman hurried out, looking blind and frightened.

Eden knew what it meant, because it had happened before. Wounded had come in from somewhere and were being sorted out at one of the depots, and word was being sent to their people as they were identified. This eliminated giving up precious space in the hospitals to those who had some one in the city who could look after them at home. She gripped the edge of the prayer-book with cold fingers, while the now familiar sick heave went through her midriff. Sedgwick was safe beside her today. But Ransom—Fauquier—Dabney—Lafe——

"*From all blindness of heart,*" came the clergyman's voice, strong and steadying, "*from pride, vain-glory, and hypocrisy; from envy, hatred, and malice, and all uncharitableness——*"

"*Good Lord, deliver us,*" murmured the congregation, seeing out of the tail of its eye that more people were sifting down the aisle in the wake of the sexton.

"*From all inordinate and sinful affections; and from all the deceits of the world, the flesh, and the devil——*"

"*Good Lord, deliver us.*"

The sexton was just behind Sedgwick now, who sat on the aisle—but he was going on, to the people just in front. . . .

"From lightning and tempest; from plague, pestilence, and famine; from battle, and murder, and from sudden death——"

The sexton had hesitated, turned—and laid his hand on Sedgwick's shoulder as he bent to whisper.

"It's Dabney," said Sedgwick in her ear. "Wounded. Come on."

Feeling that a nightmare had come true, wondering if her own face looked as stiff and naked as all the others she had seen, she came to the church door with Sedgwick's hand at her elbow and stood blinking in the sunlight.

"In the Square," he said. "Hold up, honey, he's alive."

"There's room at the house," she heard herself saying quite calmly as the iron gates banged behind them. "He could have had my bed, but there's room in the ward because that one-armed boy died yesterday. We can take him straight home—that is, to Franklin Street——"

"Yes, honey, we'll take him home."

The ambulances were coming up from south of the river, and the wounded were being laid out in rows on the grass in the Square till their destination could be decided. It had showered that morning, and the grass was damp and trampled, but the ambulances were hot and hard and crowded, and it was shady under the trees. They passed between the patient, suffering lines, looking for Dabney. Sometimes a blanket had been drawn up to cover the head, but Dabney was alive....

They found him, and he tried to smile without unclenching his teeth, as Eden knelt beside him with a little cry. Sedgwick turned back the blanket which covered the stretcher, looked quickly, and said, "All right—I'll get him moved—stay with him," and went for the nearest driver. Thankful for Sedgwick's steadying presence, she took out her handkerchief and wiped the beads of agony from Dabney's face. His jaws were locked against groaning, but his eyes stayed open, clinging to her.

"It won't be long, dear," she told him soothingly, just as she had spoken to dozens of other men with that look in their eyes, but this was Dabney, this was her brother. . . . "There's a nice clean bed waiting at the Crabbs'—we'll get you comfortable soon——"

He heard, but he could not answer. Sedgwick came back with a driver and they carried Dabney to the ambulance, and she rode in it with them to Franklin Street. Charlotte opened the door.

"Hold tight, Charl, it's Dabney," Eden said, and looked away from Charlotte's face as they carried Dabney past her.

The empty bed was in the surgical ward, and the two girls sat down on the stairs in the hall to wait while Louise and Sedgwick got him undressed and removed the fouled, day-old bandage from the wound. Charlotte for once was silent, but not tearful. She only held to Eden's hand and watched the door of what used to be the dining-room. Her eyes were enormous in her small pointed face.

When Sedgwick came out into the hall his expression was not reassuring.

"I'm going to find Dr. Tracy," he said briefly. "You girls go round to the hospitals and the chemists—ask everywhere you can think of— and find some chloroform. But don't be too long. Don't take more than an hour."

They stood up automatically and followed him into the street— Charlotte was hatless and still wearing her apron. Chloroform meant amputation.

"You go to Kent's and that chemist on the corner," Eden said collectedly, and Charlotte nodded. "I'll try the St. Charles." They separated without another word.

There was no chloroform, of course. The matron at the St. Charles Hospital shook her head almost impatiently at Eden's insistence that there must be some somewhere. "It's all gone," she said crisply. "Used up, hours ago. Can't you tell by this racket that we're working without it now? Come back tomorrow and I may have some morphine." She dropped her voice. "We can get *that,* it's easier to smuggle. It's due now, but Sheridan is in the way."

"How do you get it?" Eden demanded. "Where does it come from?"

"It comes in from the York River, under a brave woman's hoop," said the matron. "She'll get caught some time, and I wish there were a dozen of her! I'm sorry about your brother, have you tried at Kent's? It's no use, of course."

Eden thanked her numbly and turned away. She stopped at a chemist's and several other places and hurried back to find Charlotte there before her, also empty-handed. Sedgwick had brought the doctor, and there was a screen set around Dabney's cot.

"Take Charlotte away," Louise whispered to Eden. "Sedgwick and

I have to help the doctor. Take Charlotte up stairs, *I* think she's going to faint."

The girls went up to the little second floor parlor, and Eden sat down with her knitting, hoping to set an example of calmness and self-possession, although Charlotte was quiet enough, her face an odd greeny-white.

"It might help if you tried to read something," Eden said, steadily. "Take that book off the table, whatever it is, and just read it out loud, one word after another. It will give us something to put our minds on."

Charlotte picked up the book and opened it obediently, turning the leaves.

"It's his left leg," she said. "Shattered to bits below the knee—the doctor says if he's quick he can save the joint, which will—which will be a great advantage—later on—he says if we lose time in the hope of making it easier with chloroform, it will have to be higher—and he says——"

"Sit down and read the book to me," Eden commanded gently, knowing that if she gave way an inch they must both succumb to horror.

Charlotte dropped into the nearest chair and stared at the page a moment.

"I—can't see," she said then. "I can't—see the words—" The book slid off her lap to the floor as she rose and went to stand at the window above the garden, holding to the flowered chintz drape beside it, the sun full in her face. "You think I'm going to faint or do something silly, don't you—well, I'm not, I—I'm going to live right through it with him—the doctor says they often do—the men, I mean, they faint, and miss the worst of it—he's got a tiny bit of laudanum, but he's saving it for afterwards, I don't know why——."

"Charl—honey——"

"No, I'm quite all right, I—I just can't seem to see words on a page, that's all, and—I can't seem to see the sun either, but I can feel it on my face—oh, I don't mean that, *really,* I can see you perfectly well, sitting there, I just—" She looked back into the room, holding to the curtain. They left off their hoops to work among the cots, and Charlotte's little body was slim as a pencil inside the white apron and calico dress she wore. She looked like a child in a pinafore —a twelve-year-old child, except for her eyes. "Why don't you take your bonnet off?" she asked, and Eden realized that she had forgotten to do so, and laid it aside. "It's queer," Charlotte went on in her sweet, chirping voice, "how I *can* see, perfectly well, and yet I—I *can't,* were you ever that way?—and the garden—" She leaned to the open window. "The garden looks *miles* down below, but so fresh and green——"

"Come away from the window, Charl," said Eden above her knitting.

"No, I—there's more air over here—it's very sultry, don't you think? —I can see my vegetables from here, remember how you all jeered at me when I said I was going to raise vegetables right here in the middle of Richmond?—and now my beans are growing, and my corn, and my——"

"We didn't jeer, honey, we only thought there wouldn't be time for a garden along with everything else you had to do these days——"

"Well, I made time for it, didn't I—and won't you all be glad when I go out and pick my own cabbages—do you *pick* cabbages?—especially if Beast Butler gets the Danville Road where all our supplies come from—lucky we laid in some bacon and meal a few days ago, about four hundred dollars' worth—listen to the guns, they're on both sides of us now—you know, I can smell the powder smoke from here, I can, sure enough—the dust must be terrible on the roads—and hot— what can we find for him to eat when it's over, would he like that bit of liver?—it cost a dollar a pound—it's queer, we never used to *think* what things cost when we ate them—and when I *remember* all the clothes we used to have, just as a matter of course, and I never saw the bills for them, did you?—and now it's a question if you can find a pair of shoes to buy even if you have the money——"

A sound went through the house—the unhuman sound, half groan, half scream, that Dabney made when the surgeon's saw bit the bone. Eden's teeth came down on her tongue, and in the hideous, stunned silence which followed the sound Charlotte's broken-off words began again, gropingly, like a blind thing feeling its way.

"—and it—it seems pretty ridiculous—doesn't it—to think of buying—shoes—when you can get—morphine—for three hundred dollars —an ounce——"

Eden got across the room in time to catch her as she slipped to the floor, and knelt on the carpet beside her, shivering in the sunshine, waiting for the sound to come again—but it didn't.

Charlotte was lying inert on the sofa and Eden was fanning her when Sedgwick came in, carrying his coat over his arm and fastening his shirt-cuffs. He was white to the lips and worse gone at the knees than he remembered being since he first heard the guns at Manassas.

"Could you posibly let me have three drops of brandy?" he asked, and sat down limply and put his head in his hands.

"There isn't any," said Eden.

"No, of course there isn't. I forgot." He sat a moment, his face hidden. "He fainted," he said at last without moving. "But not quite soon enough."

"Is he——?"

"Yes, he's all right. A good many other people are living through the same sort of thing." His fingers clenched suddenly in his long brown hair. "God damn them!" he cried, his face hidden. "God damn them, not to let the drugs come through!"

Eden rose.

"Is the doctor still here?"

"Just leaving."

She ran down the stairs, caught him at the front door.

"Doctor—please tell me—the matron at the St. Charles mentioned a woman who brings in morphine."

"She's overdue this time—thanks to Sheridan."

"Doctor, I want to see that woman when she comes. I want to find out how she does it. Next time I want to go with her."

"You!"

"I live in Williamsburg, you know. Some of the family is still there. That would give me a good excuse to travel, and on my way back I could bring something in the way she does—under my hoop."

"It's a risk," he said. She looked so young.

"They won't hang a woman! Not even Butler!"

"Maybe not. But prison life is—very unhealthy."

"I'm not afraid of that. Will you please ask the woman to come and see me? Tell her I can be trusted. Tell her about Dabney today, then she'll know. Tell her there can be two of us now. Won't you?"

"I'll tell her, of course. But promise me one thing, because I shall feel a certain——responsibility. Promise me solemnly—you will bring only the medicines. No messages."

"Very well, only the medicines."

"If you are caught with messages as well, you are liable to the penalty of a spy. If you have only the medicines they might be—lenient."

"Does *she* carry messages?"

"I don't know. I'm afraid so. We can't be sure we'll ever see her again, she's three days overdue."

"But if she does come——"

"If she comes, I'll send her to you. But it costs ready money, you know. You have to carry cash."

"Oh. Well, I'm afraid that settles it, for me. I haven't any." And as she spoke she saw his eyes rest on the sapphire ring she wore. Reluctantly she held out her hand for him to see the stone. "Would that be—worth much?"

"Several ounces," he said grimly.

"Then if I sold it—" For a moment she cradled her left hand in her right, cherishing the ring. "Tell her I'll have the money," she said.

5

Everybody sold things, even wedding rings, she reminded herself many times over during the afternoon and later when she took her turn sitting beside Dabney in the small hours, doling out the precious laudanum Sedgwick had contrived to come by before he left to join Fitz Lee north of the city. General Lee was working southward with the rest of his army. If Grant followed, the next battle would be somewhere on the old ground along the Chickahominy.

Everybody had to sell things these days, usually just to get food to eat, she knew. And although the Crabb fortune was still good for the necessities of life, they had all those sick men to feed. No one had any right to expensive rings any more, no matter what they stood for, surely Cabot would understand that and would be willing that it should go. There was a certain ironic justice in a Yankee ring paying for relief from havoc the Yankee guns had wrought, when the Yankee blockade tried to keep merciful drugs from reaching the Confederate wounded. Surely it was the sort of hard-headed expediency which

Cabot himself could best appreciate. After the way he had cared for Sedgwick at Williamsburg he wouldn't be angry that she had parted with his gift to buy respite for Dabney and the rest. . . .

She sat turning the ring in the light of the single candle that burned by Dabney's cot—candles were ten dollars a pound. Should she try to send Cabot word what she had done—no, wait and tell him later—wait till they could meet again and he noticed that it was gone, cast oneself on his mercy then, and surely he would agree that one had had no choice—perhaps they could get it back again somehow, when the war was over. How often they said that, and how little it really meant, how impossible it had become to conceive a day when the war would be over. When that time came, the South would be beaten, Sedgwick said—but Sedgwick was depressed, sick at heart over losing General Stuart. They had sent the blue lines reeling back from Richmond before, they could do it again. Perhaps if Grant failed too, like Mc-Clellan, on the same ground, they would see in Washington that it was no use, and that the slaughter was no use either. . . .

A shadow moved towards her between the cots—Louise. They exchanged wan smiles in the candlelight. Dabney's eyes were closed, his breathing was regular. The laudanum had helped. Eden wondered if Louise had been able to sleep, after telling Sedgwick good-bye. You did sleep, though, from sheer exhaustion. Her own eyelids were heavy.

"Go and rest," Louise whispered. "Sally will take him at dawn. Sleep till six, if you can."

Before noon of the next day Eden emerged from the jeweller's in Main Street and started towards the market, a basket on her arm. The sapphire ring had been exchanged for a thick roll of blue Confederate banknotes. The money was as heavy as her heart.

Supplies were coming in from Petersburg again after a few days' famine on account of Butler's raid on the Danville road, and the market was crowded. There was no beef to be had, and chickens were thirty dollars a pair. She bought two, with Charlotte's money, and a few potatoes and white beans. The turnip greens in Charlotte's garden were ready to eat, and greens were selling for four dollars a peck—it was like finding money, because she didn't have to buy greens, and she thought wistfully of getting some fantastic delicacy for Dabney, like new peas or strawberries—but nothing like that had come in.

The basket dragged at her arm and she was about to give up and

leave the market when she saw Elizabeth Van Lew buying potatoes
from a tall waggoner just ahead, and wondered idly again if there was
anything in the story that she was a spy who passed on information
to the Yankees, and why nobody did anything about it if they suspected her. When Miss Van Lew moved on into Main Street, nodding
and talking to herself the way she did, Eden was only a few steps
behind her. She glanced at the waggoner's wares as she passed, and
then at the man—and stood rooted, staring into the startled, defiant
black eyes of Cabot Murray.

He wore a rough, disreputable butternut suit such as farmers wore,
and a wide, ragged straw hat, and he had not shaved. For only the
space of a second they stood motionless, while Eden turned faint and
the roof of her mouth went dry and her knees seemed not to be there
at all. Then, with a sketchy gesture towards his hat brim, the impudent parody of a countryman's courteous salute to a lady customer, he
turned away, lounging against the wheel.

Walking as though she was made of wood with very few joints,
Eden went on towards Main Street. There was an empty hitching-bar
near the entrance of the market, and she held to it a few moments,
leaning against the post while the sunlit world whirled around her,
until one or two women passing by glanced at her sympathetically
with some idea of offering help. That frightened her into trying her
legs again, and she went on, carrying the heavy basket, stopping once
more in the shade of a tree, till she reached Franklin Street, where she
set the basket down in the hall and got to her room without meeting
anyone.

It was times like these that made one's overstrained nerves and under-
nourished body go back on one, she thought, lying across her bed
waiting for her heart to leave her throat and go back to its normal
position. Waves of weakness and chill ran through her, her fingers
were damp and icy, her legs shook even after she was no longer trying
to stand on them. Yesterday Dabney, and today— One could not stand
shocks any more, one hadn't enough vitality to spare. . . .

Lying there across the bed, she found with surprise that she could
still think. She wished she needn't. For it seemed that whereas an hour
ago she would have said she desired to see him more than anything in
the world, now that she had done so it was the last thing she ever
wanted to do again. Cabot in Richmond, disguised as a waggoner,

could mean only one thing, even without Elizabeth Van Lew. Passionate, futile negation fought unwilling conviction. No—not Cabot—no. But then, because she remembered everything about him every time she had ever seen him, partly by reason of his vivid strangeness and partly by desperate effort to do so, she remembered how he had looked that day in Libby Prison when she said that Jackson had gone to Gordonsville—alert and listening. Was he, even then—? No. Not Cabot. But Elizabeth Van Lew had been at Libby Prison too. . . .

She lay there, numb and cold, engulfed in a creeping, hopeless lassitude, until Louise came to see why she had not come to dinner. She sat up then, guiltily, conscious of the myriad things she had left undone which some one else must have had to do—sat up too quickly and the room went round and she caught dizzily at the bedpost and said she didn't feel very well and had been—resting.

"It was just too much for you yesterday," Louise said kindly, and put her arms around her niece, who leaned against her gratefully, sitting on the edge of the bed. "I'm worried about Charlotte too. You take off your hoop and lie down comfortably a while. Sally and I can manage."

"I'm not such a baby as all that," Eden said firmly. "You had all the worst of it yesterday. You and Sedgwick."

"I'm tough," smiled Louise. "And I'm wicked, too. It *is* wicked, isn't it, to feel I can bear anything so long as it isn't Lafe!"

"Aunt Louise—has there ever been a minute in all your life—just one minute—when you didn't love Uncle Lafe a bit and hoped you'd never see him again?"

"Heavens, *no!*" cried Louise, and her eyes were soft and shining as they always were for Lafe. "How can you say such a thing?"

"Well, I only wondered," Eden said humbly, and Louise set her small, work-worn hand under Eden's chin and cradled Eden's head against her breast.

"Honey, I think I know—you're afraid it can never come right now for you and Cabot, with him on the other side, and things like what happened to Dabney. But it isn't Cabot's fault, honey, you must try and remember that. Even if he had fired the very shot which hit Dabney, which of course he didn't, it's just war and soldiering, honey, it's not your man's fault."

But Eden couldn't tell her that there was something much worse than soldiering between her and Cabot now, so she kept silent, and tried to eat her dinner, and took her turn of duty in the ward afterward.

About twilight Charlotte came in and handed her a note.

"A little colored boy brought this for you just now," she said. "Dabney knows me tonight—he smiled—almost the way he used to—I'm going to give him his supper——"

When Charlotte had bustled away again Eden went to the window and opened the note in the fading light. It was Cabot's handwriting.

A closed carriage will be waiting at the northeast corner of the street at ten P.M. Please trust yourself to it and come to me.

Her heart lunged in her side. *Come to me.* The words which could have meant the sum of all delight now turned her stiff with dread. What could she say, how could she face him, what could she do if he thought to take her in his arms again? And he, what was in his mind to send for her, what could he offer in his own defence? He took a terrible risk, to put it in her power to lead the way to him. He trusted her. Without question. Sublimely. He had put his life in her hands. Just to see her again? Oh, no, there must be something more, something he could say to—to *explain.* There must be some reason for his presence in Richmond, other than the obvious one. Cabot wouldn't— no, no, not Cabot——

It had never occurred to her not to go to him.

6

The carriage, which was closely curtained, went uphill, she was sure of that. She lost track of the turnings, probably done to confuse her, but they climbed a hill and stopped. The Van Lew house was at the top of Church Hill above Libby Prison.

She sat waiting for the carriage door to be opened, her heart beating thickly. It had been easy to get away from Franklin Street—that came of having the bedroom to herself again. Louise had let her off from night duty so that she could rest. She had brought the key to the garden door, and no one would ever know she had been out. All the way she had held to her naked left hand in a growing terror. What was he going to say about the ring, now that she couldn't give it back to him—if it should come to that, if there wasn't any explanation. . . .

The carriage door opened gently, and the driver's soft Negro voice said, "You come this way, missy, please?"

There had been thunderstorms all day, mingling eerily with the sound of the guns down the river, and the sky was still overcast and starless. The stone carriage block on to which she stepped shone with rain in the light of the lamps. The trees still dripped. There was an iron gate between two tall brick posts. The old colored man opened it with a key, and motioned her inside.

They entered a side door of some big house she could not recognize, and went along a passage and through the dining-room to the front hall. They went up wide, curving stairs—it was a handsome mansion—to a door on the second floor, and the driver tapped three times. A voice said, "Come!" and the door swung open before her. She crossed the threshold, her heartbeats pounding in her ears. Cabot stood there alone, wearing the ragged butternut suit.

She halted, speechless and numb, while the door clicked to behind her and he crossed the room and laid his arms around her—gently, almost with humility, he held her close, and with an odd, clear corner of her brain she noticed that he smelled of horse.

"My darling," he said, very low. "Eden—*you came!*" Because she made no response he shifted to see her face beneath the bonnet brim, loosed her to raise her veil with both his big hands, which went then to her shoulders. "I'm sorry about the beard," he said, and grinned. "But I daren't take it off, even for you!"

She walked out from between his hands, and he let her go, puzzled, but with little dancing flames in his eyes. She looked carefully around the parlor, taking her bearings. It was a small, charming room, rich and comfortable.

"This must be the Van Lew house," she said, just above a whisper.

"You aren't supposed to know that."

"Then it's true!" She stood looking at him with wide, unfriendly eyes. "It's true that she—you——"

"They didn't want you to come here, you know. But it was the only chance I had. I gave them my word—for you." His gaze was grave but confident. He stayed where she had left him, his hands at his sides. "You can't go back, of course."

"I—?" She had no breath for more.

"Didn't you understand? You're to come with me tonight, across the river." And he pointed to a plain homespun gown and a sunbonnet, which lay on the seat of a chair. "As my wife," he added, those dancing lights in his eyes. "At last I can get you out of this pest-hole and see that you have enough to eat, and——"

With some surprise he looked down at her in his arms where she had flung herself. She was transfigured, her fingers gripped his shoulders convulsively, her bonnet was knocked back and hanging by its ribbons, her face was pressed against his without waiting for a kiss, she was laughing and crying both together.

"Oh, Cabot, I'm *so* relieved! I'm so *glad,* I knew you wouldn't come to Richmond just as a spy——"

"Well, that too, of course," he admitted wryly, "or I'd never have got here."

She went very still in his arms.

"That—too?"

"Sweetheart, don't take it too hard, will you? This war has got to be won, it's got to be stopped, the South is beaten, let's get it over as quickly as possible and save as many lives as we can!"

Slowly she withdrew herself from him, feeling the warmth and strength and urgency of him drain away out of her tired body again as she straightened and stood alone. For just a moment she had thought—for just a moment it had seemed as though——

"Eden——"

"I thought you meant—you had come just for me," she managed to say.

"Dear heart, there's a war. There are certain rules to it—certain odds one has to consider. Maybe I should try to pretend that I crossed the lines just for the sole purpose of getting you out of Richmond, but I can't do that, it never occurred to me I could fool a child into believing such a thing. Once you had spotted me in the market today, it became safer to take you with me than to— Oh, Lord, Eden, don't look at me like that just because I'm honest with you, I've never lied to you yet, how can I start now?"

"Then—if I hadn't seen you—you would never have sent the note——"

"Don't you understand, Eden, I didn't dare try to see you, there are too many other people involved in what I'm doing. But once the harm was done and you knew I was in Richmond, I could persuade them— Sweetheart, for God's sake, look at it this way—I work for Butler in these clothes, and the men of your family work for Lee in grey clothes—what's the difference, after all? Except I take more chances than they do!"

"*Butler!*" she said, as though she said Rattlesnake.

"Eden—" His hands caught hers imperatively, and then he stood looking down in a sudden pause at the ringless fingers in his hold.

"I—sold it," she gasped, not looking at him. "We can't get drugs any more—they said the ring would be worth several ounces——"

"Oh, my dear—never mind, we'll get another ring."

"No—you won't have to do that. And I'll pay you back for this one somehow, when the war is over."

"Pay me back—what on earth are you talking about?"

"Because I'm not going with you tonight. It was bad enough when you came to Williamsburg in a blue uniform. I loved you so much I —somehow convinced myself that your being a Yankee officer didn't matter. But I can't quite make up my mind to marry a Yankee spy!"

"But I'm not wearing the grey!" he cried. "I wouldn't do that—not even I would do that!"

"It doesn't matter any more what you wear."

"But my poor darling, you can't mean——"

"I mean I never want to see you again."

There was a dreadful, sickening silence.

"That's plain enough, isn't it!" he said at last. "Wouldn't you care to see me hanged, perhaps?"

"You gave your word, for whatever it's worth. I'll keep it."

"Thanks."

The old reckless mockery was in his face, and behind it a stunned incredulity which she did not see because she would not look at him. The time had come for her to turn and leave this room and all it held for her of warmth and devotion and delight; to forget the hard clasp of his arms and the thing that ran like flame from him to her and back again every time they came within the same four walls. He was a stranger. He had always been a stranger.

"Now, wait a minute," he was saying quietly, as she started for the door. "The carriage isn't there, we'll have to think."

"You can't keep me here against my will!" she cried.

"No, but—are you so sure it would be against your will?"

"You don't belong in my life," she told him steadily. "You said so once yourself."

"I was wrong, I've admitted that. War or no war, you were made for me, and you know it." His eyes held hers across the room. "Come with me," he whispered.

"No."

"You said you would when I was in Libby."

"I didn't know then that you—I thought you were an officer."

"I am. Detailed to special duty, that's all this is. I'll put on the pretty uniform for you again tomorrow. Beloved—think again. Ever since I got out of Libby I've gone nearly crazy because you were still in this stinking city, working yourself to death trying to save other people from dying. What you have done is all very fine—very brave—but it's gone on long enough. I can't leave you here again while it goes on getting worse. And it will get worse, before this summer is over. Eden, I'm a soldier—but I saw what happened at Fredericksburg, and I won't let you go through a thing like that! Even if you don't forgive me the job I'm doing—come out of Richmond tonight, come away with me before we start firing into the town!"

"Now you're asking me to desert," she said.

"Desert! You're a woman, you're *my* woman, and I'm afraid for you! All right, I am, where you're concerned I'm a yellow-bellied coward! I want you safe, I don't want you dying of fever or blown to bits by a stray shell, does that surprise you? This war is going to end some day, and it isn't going to matter, finally, what anybody wore to fight it, we're one nation here, and we're going to stay that way! But what good will that be to you and me if you go down along with Richmond?"

"You're very sure about Richmond, aren't you?" she said after a moment.

"Tragically sure, Eden."

"That means I've got to stay."

"I guess I see what you mean," he said, and his long body sagged to the arm of a chair with a hopelessness that wrung her heart.

"I reckon you do, Cabot. Now may I leave this house?"

"That's not easy either, you know. It's not just me, it's several other people we have to think of. You know where you are, you've guessed too much——"

"Everybody guesses that Miss Van Lew is a traitor, if that's what you mean! I can't think why they haven't arrested her before now."

"Well—you have the evidence for it."

"I have my word against hers, that's all. If I promise to keep silent about tonight, she can trust me to do it."

"I'll have to talk to her. Wait here."

He left the room by an inner door. She stood where she was, adjusting her bonnet, feeling trapped and panicky. Suppose that terrible little woman who wasn't mad at all refused to let her go. Illogically she fell back on Cabot. Cabot would see that she got away. And after tonight she would never see Cabot again. The knowledge brought only desolation. He had been her bulwark for so long, he had stood, hard and strong and confident, at the back of her consciousness through so many horrors, she had been so sure that some day she would go with him, unafraid, into whatever life he chose to make for her. . . .

Almost she wavered. If she put Cabot out of her life like this, there would be nothing left to go on with. But if the Yankees won there would be nothing anyhow. Until now she had believed the South was sure to win, and then, if she wanted to marry a Yankee it was her own affair. But to marry the conquerer. . . .

When he returned, Elizabeth Van Lew came with him. She walked straight up to Eden and stood looking into her eyes.

"If I had dreamed you would want to go back to Franklin Street I would never have had you brought here," she said severely.

"I'm sorry to be a nuisance," said Eden with chilly good manners, resenting what she considered intrusion into the private affairs of Cabot and herself.

"You're sure you won't change your mind?"

"No, I won't," said Eden coldly. Not for her, anyway.

Miss Van Lew sighed.

"It's not that we don't trust you," she said as though speaking to an obstinate child. "But one is so likely to give things away without thinking."

"I'll be very careful to think," said Eden. "Besides, everyone knows about you already."

"But not *enough*," said Miss Van Lew. "It has stopped raining, would you mind going on foot? I'll send my maid as far as your door with you."

"I mind very much," Eden replied, having taken a dislike to her hostess. "The streets are not safe at this time of night."

"I'll order the carriage, then." Without any apparent animus Miss Van Lew drifted out the door to the hall, leaving it open behind her.

"They haven't starved the spunk out of you, have they?" Cabot remarked with satisfaction, and pulled a roll of bills out of his pocket. "Won't you take this? I'm leaving soon and I won't need it. Take it for the hospital, I mean."

She eyed the money in his hand covetously. Morphine—calomel—quinine——

"I'll take it for Dabney," she said suddenly. "He's lost his left leg below the knee."

"I'm terribly sorry——"

"And for the boy in the bed next to him who is dying of blood poisoning," she added, putting the bills into her bag. "They die very slowly of blood poisoning, and—a little morphine helps them off to sleep. And we've got some typhoid cases we might pull through if we could get a little opium——"

"Eden—I'm sorry about Dabney. Is Gran all right?"

"So far as we know. It's difficult to get letters through now, with Sheridan in the way."

"Why don't you go home, Eden?"

"I'm needed here," she reminded him, wondering how much money he had given her, wondering how much it would add to what she had got for the ring, and when the roads would be clear of Sheridan. Cabot needn't know she was going to Williamsburg for a visit. He might do something to interfere with her chance of collecting the drugs, if he knew.

"It won't last long now, my darling. It's almost over."

"I suppose you think that comforts me!"

"It should. I want you to remember what I say, Eden. Are you listening? We're going to take Richmond—I hope without a bombardment, but we're going to take it, and when we do there is going to be a perfect mess, one way and another. Things go wrong at a time like that—things get very nasty sometimes. Will you promise me something—let us say for Gran's sake? Promise to remember that bar-ring accidents I shall be one of the first officers into the city, and I shall look for you at the house in Franklin Street. If you need help then, if there is anything I can do for your comfort and safety, you must rely on me to do it. And if you should leave Franklin Street before I come, will you leave some word for me, so that I needn't go out of my mind with worry?"

"I shan't leave," she said only. "We have to look after our wounded."

"You think you've stopped loving me, don't you?" he said, and his eyes were compassionate and smiling, but she was looking at the floor because that was easier. "You think you've thrown me out for good and all, because you can call me a spy. Secret service agent sounds a little better, but I know how you feel. It won't last, though. I'll have you back, so help me God, I haven't come this far to give up now. I'll have you back, Eden, remember what I say!"

Elizabeth Van Lew stood in the doorway.

"You may come down stairs now, Miss Day. The carriage will be round at once."

A moment more Eden stood facing him, her blood pounding in her ears. Then her chin came up. To go from him now was to tear out something by the roots. But the implacable little figure stood waiting at the door.

"Good-bye, Cabot."

"Au revoir, my darling."

Miss Van Lew shut him into the parlor and he remained there while Eden followed her hostess down the stairs and through the din-ing-room again to the door at the end of the passage which gave on the damp, fragrant night.

"If you betray him," said Elizabeth Van Lew in her soft, low voice, "may God damn your soul."

The door closed sharply.

Eden entered the carriage and it rolled away down hill. Except for the money which weighted her bag, she could hardly believe any of that evening had actually happened. The carriage stopped at the corner where it had waited before, and the old colored man handed her out. She noticed that he stayed there, on guard, until she was safely inside the house.

She undressed by candlelight with cold, shaking fingers, and fell with a sob of exhaustion into the bed. Before the tears came she was asleep, and before she seemed to have more than closed her eyes, Louise's hand was on her shoulder and the room was full of sunlight.

"There's some one waiting to see you," Louise was saying. "A Mrs. Willis from the St. Charles Hospital."

VII. JUNE 1, 1864

EDEN reached Williamsburg towards the end of May, after an uneventful journey from Richmond by the Turnpike which crossed Bottom's Bridge. Sheridan had got down to the James and was at Haxall's Landing conferring with Butler, whose army lay south of the river. Grant was still at Spotsylvania. She passed between the Federal armies on roads empty of soldiers.

She went alone in Louise's carriage with a pass from the Richmond Provost-Marshal in her bag, and old Daniel to drive, and she also carried the old pass with which she had left Williamsburg after the Seven Days' Battle almost two years ago. She had never made a journey alone before, but it went without saying that no one could be spared from Franklin Street to go with her. Eden felt very guilty as it was, for on the face of it she was deserting her post on a sudden, passionate desire to see Gran, and Louise had put it down to exhaustion and homesickness and agreed that it was time Eden had a rest and a change. Mrs. Willis had forbidden her to explain, even to Louise, the real purpose of the journey. Perhaps later, if she went again, she would have to let Louise know. But the fewer who knew, the better, always, as long as possible.

The humiliation of seeming to have cracked under strain instead of standing up to it as the rest of them had was for Eden much harder to bear than the risk she ran. In order that she need not halt overnight on the way, it had been arranged from Richmond that the Williamsburg carriage, driven by Pharaoh, should meet her half way at the change station for the stage-coach, so that she could make the journey in one long day. Daniel would have to wait there, with his equipage at the mercy of stray raids by the Yankee cavalry, until her return. It was not a very satisfactory program, but it was the best that could be done in wartime, and Eden's urgency overrode Louise's misgivings.

Now that she was on the way home again, it seemed impossible that

248

so much time had elapsed since she last saw Gran and Sue. She dreaded the evidence she would meet of those two intervening years. Gran never changed, but Sue's letters sounded much more mature. Myrta would be fourteen now, and Barry was away at the Institute, and Felicity—there would be, pervasively, the knowledge that Felicity was gone forever. They would want to know about her last illness, and about Dabney, who was only just beginning to be out of danger. They would ask about Fauquier, who had fought his gun gallantly at Yellow Tavern; and about Sedgwick, now courier to Fitz Lee; and Ransom, whose hair had got quite grey; and Lafe, under almost daily fire in the fortifications south of Richmond . . . They would ask about Cabot too. . . .

Drowsy with the heat as the carriage rolled on across the swampy Chickahominy land—Daniel had to cherish his horses because they were underfed, like every other creature in Richmond these days— Eden had made up her mind not to tell the truth about Cabot. She would have to say that she had not seen him since he left Libby Prison and did not know where he was. She would say that if he had sent her messages by the underground they had been lost on the way. Perhaps Gran need never know about that dreadful last interview in Elizabeth Van Lew's parlor—about the butternut suit. When the war ended, if it ever did, they would all expect her to marry him, of course, and then some explanation would have to be found. But not the truth, even then. Her own pride demanded that no one in Williamsburg should ever know that Cabot Murray was a Yankee spy.

Even so, the difficult moment was upon her before she was prepared for it. She arrived after they had finished supper, and Pharaoh brought her a tray to Gran's room, where they all sat together trying in a bewildered way to catch up. There was a sort of guilty gladness in her homecoming. Sorrow and anxiety lay heavy on their hearts, but it was still exciting to see each other again after so long, and there was much news that was not tragic to exchange.

Coming back to Gran, she thought, was like taking sanctuary. Gran had been through a war too, Gran knew how bad it could be, and yet Gran had lived through it and here she was, tranquil and safe, proving that one did live through such things, proving that nightmares like Richmond could end, proving that some happy, useful lives did survive wars in spite of everything. It was odd to find oneself clinging to Gran's frail presence as to a life-raft, looking to Gran for strength and toughness to endure, instead of the gentler things she had always stood for until now. But there was no getting round it, Gran was tough. Gran had survived. It was up to her grandchildren now to demonstrate that they could live through a war too and preserve their sense of proportion and their sense of humor and their sanity and faith. Gran had shown them all how.

Pharaoh placed the tray on a little table near the window with many a flourish, for much thought had gone into preparing Eden's first meal at home. Fried chicken, new potatoes and peas in cream, greens cooked with hog-jowl, hot corn bread—and strawberries. Eden, who had stinted herself so long to make the Richmond meals go round, saw that her plate held enough to feed two of them in Franklin Street.

"Are you sure you can really spare all this?" she asked doubtfully as she began to eat.

"We're going to feed you up while we've got you here," Sue said. "You're thin as a rail. Food isn't so hard to get here, because we all have gardens."

"Charl made a garden," Eden told them. "With only little black Jock to help her, he's twelve now. You'd be surprised at how Charl has come on, she——"

Myrta's voice, shrill with surprise, broke in.

"Eden, what *have* you done with your lovely ring? You didn't go and *lose* it!"

What little color there was in Eden's face left it. She sat helplessly, fork in hand, looking down at her plate. Not even Gran was equal to breaking the silence.

"I sold it," Eden said at last.

"Oh, *Eden!* Have you *told* him?" Myrta demanded.

"No."

"He'll *never* forgive you! *I* wouldn't! Not even if you were *starving!*"

"I sold it to buy medicines. The blockade has made them very expensive, and hard to get. After Dabney—was wounded, I couldn't bear it. I gave up the ring so that Dabney, and other people's brothers, could be more comfortable."

Myrta was silenced, but quite uncomprehending. Unless you had been in that house in Franklin Street the day Dabney's leg was amputated, you couldn't comprehend. It was much better that Myrta didn't,

Eden knew, stifling her own sense of injustice. This was only the beginning, she realized, of the things she would have to bear in silence.

"Cabot will get you another ring," said Gran. How well she knew him, Eden thought. But there was one thing she didn't know. Her voice went on quietly, changing the subject so that Eden could eat her meal in peace. "His sister Melicent has been writing delightful letters to Sue, and they've got to be great friends. We look forward to having her come down for a visit as soon as the war is over."

"She was in Washington with Cabot, remember?" Sue took it up eagerly. "They could hear the guns at Chantilly quite distinctly. I think it shows great character that Melicent refused to panic like a lot of people, don't you? Cabot let her stay and sing at a big reception. Honestly, Dee, she *worships* that man!"

"You'd think she'd be jealous of Eden," Myrta remarked. "I wonder if she is!"

"Myrta, that's nonsense!" Sue said firmly. "Sisters aren't jealous, it's not the same thing at all!"

"*I* would be," Myrta insisted. "I shall *hate* the woman Barry marries, you see if I don't, because Barry is my favorite brother. I *wish* he would come home and show us his uniform!"

Eden knew that Gran was watching her. Gran read one's mind with ease. It was going to be difficult to fool Gran, especially when one was so tired and shaky and couldn't think fast.

It was like a dream to go to bed that night in the room she had always shared with Sue. Before Sue had blown out the lamp Eden was asleep, drowned in exhaustion, her mind and body blotted out in the deep oblivion her sense of security and relief from strain had wrought. But she woke with a start at dawn, automatically, jerked back by the habit of responsibility for the helpless men in her care, who were dependent on her for their breakfast and their baths and their clean dressings——

She lay still in the greying room, while her eyes went lovingly from one familiar object to another, and her ragged nerves took comfort from the warmth of her sister's body in the bed beside her and the sweet way Sue always slept, so silently, her face half buried in the pillow, her crisp curls tumbled and gleaming. Eden gave thanks that Sue had not come to Richmond and needn't know how things were there. Gran knew, and she herself knew—Felicity had known. But not

Sue, not their darling. She turned and laid one arm across Sue, draw-ing her close with a protective surge of affection, and Sue roused child-ishly to smile and nestle. "Lovely to have you home," she murmured, and slept again.

Still holding her, shedding a few weak, watery tears, Eden tried to see ahead. There would be only a few days of this, she knew, and she must make the most of it. Her instructions from Mrs. Willis had been quite simple. She was to come to Williamsburg for a visit, and after a few days a message would arrive for her telling her when to start back. She knew where to go then. At Barhamsville beyond the last Federal pickets outside Williamsburg, she was to take a right-hand turn, leading down to the York River, instead of keeping straight on for New Kent Courthouse. From it she must turn right again, till she came to a small brick house with a landing on the river. They would be watching for her here. She must have the money ready. Then with the precious little bags securely fastened inside her hoop she must make all possible speed for Richmond. So far as they knew, the house was not being watched. But if anyone questioned her, she was to say that the coachman must have dozed off on the box and taken the wrong turning. It was not more than a few miles out of her way to Rich-mond, but Pharaoh, who would be driving her the first half of the way, would have to know something of her purpose. She was glad it was Pharaoh and not Daniel, in a way, because he was younger and brighter and therefore more to be trusted not to give things away. . . .

When she woke again, Sue had slipped out of bed and dressed noise-lessly and gone down stairs. The clock said nearly noon.

They spent the rest of the day going over the dresses Eden had left behind, to see which ones could be made use of now. She was required to admire the shining lengths of blue velvet sent by Cabot at Christmas time, and so superfluous in summer. Louise and Sally had each given her a list of things they wanted brought back.

Two days passed—happy, busy, peaceful days, when she was never alone with Gran for more than a few minutes—no time for questions. If only she could get away before Gran said, "And when did you last hear from Cabot?" She knew it looked odd that she said so little about him, but her mind only fumbled at the problem and put it off. Rest and good food were doing much to restore her shattered system. But she was still not able to cope with Gran about Cabot.

On the third day Pharaoh came in with an envelope in his hand and Eden's heart turned over, in case it was the summons from the house on the York River landing. But Pharaoh carried the letter to Gran, who said with pleasure as she opened it—"From Louise!"

They could tell at once by her face as she read that it was bad news. Eden dropped her sewing and went on her knees beside Gran's chair.

"What is it?" she whispered, trying to read Gran's face instead of the letter. "Gran, who is it now? N-not Father?"

"It's Barry."

"But he's at the Institute!"

"The cadets have been in a battle."

"*The cadets!* But they're all under eighteen! Gran, was he——?"

"Killed."

Sue made a little gasping sound and hid her face in her hands. Myrta began to cry rather loudly. Gran leaned towards Eden with the letter, and together they read, dry-eyed, what Louise had written.

"The cadet corps was ordered out against Sigel's Yankees in the Valley a week or so ago. The intention was of course to hold them in reserve unless absolutely necessary, but they wound up in the very middle of the front line, and made a thrilling bayonet charge against artillery and musketry fire. Because they were young and ardent they outstripped the battle-wise veterans on either side of them and for several minutes held their formation alone till the Sixty-second came up. Barry was killed beside the captured caisson where the Institute banner was flying.

"I dread to think of Ransom and am at my wits' end to know how to help him bear the news, which came just after Eden had left Richmond. I have not seen him yet, but presumably he will get a brief furlough soon, as the army moves closer to Richmond. Barry is buried on the field. Poor Ransom, to lose both his wife and his youngest boy! I think Eden should be here, if possible, when he comes. . . ."

Still tearless, Eden laid her face against Gran's sleeve, and in silence, while Myrta blubbered and Sue tried to hush her, her own cheeks shining with tears, Gran and Eden sat hand in hand, absorbing the

fact that Barry, at seventeen, was dead on a battlefield. They had somehow been caught quite unprepared. They had braced themselves for
almost anything but that. They had nursed Sedgwick through his
wound, they had accepted Dabney's mutilation, and they were accustomed to sharp anxiety about Ransom, Lafe, and finally Fauquier. But
except for Myrta, Barry was the baby.

For Gran it brought its own particular wrench, because in Barry,
more than in any of the others, she had seen Julian again—the same
long chin and generous mouth, the same sober, self-contained ways,
the same confiding, radiant smile. She had had a peculiar secret joy
in Barry. And now he was gone.

"Your father will need you," she said gently to Eden. "You must go
back to Richmond now."

"Yes, Gran."

"It's a pity, because you need a good rest here. But perhaps you had
better start tomorrow."

"I c-can't go tomorrow." She could not go till the summons came.
"I haven't seen to all those things for Aunt Louise," she hurried on,
conscious of her grandmother's surprise at such seeming heartlessness
towards Ransom. "It will take Sue and me another day or two to get
them gathered up and packed."

But when that time was up and still no message had come, she was
pressed for more excuses, and Gran began to look at her rather oddly.
It was not her intention to tell even Gran about her proposed detour at
Barhamsville. Mrs. Willis, whose visits along the rivers had begun, she
feared, to create suspicion, had emphasized the need of absolute se-
crecy, and they badly needed a new carrier with an open record. Eden
had never realized before how next to impossible it was to keep things
from Gran.

At the end of the week Sue also had begun to notice that she made
no move to return to Richmond, where she was undoubtedly needed,
and Eden suffered acutely all the pangs of a malingerer. She had no
way to communicate with Mrs. Willis at the St. Charles, of course. She
could only wait. If she went back now, before the summons came, the
journey would be wasted, the pass would be wasted, and the money
was practically useless in Richmond where there were no drugs to buy.
She had to stay in Williamsburg till they were ready for her at the

brick house on the landing. The Federal adjutant at the College was willing that she should return to Richmond now, but would he stay that way as the armies moved southward? Sheridan had gone back across the Pamunkey to rejoin Grant, who was coming down from Spotsylvania, they said, and a sharp action had been fought at Hanover on the twenty-fifth. The roads between the James and the Pamunkey were still open. But for how long? And what about Daniel, waiting at the stage station?

She was not surprised when Gran cornered her one evening in Sue's absence.

"I dare say it's none of my business," Gran said calmly, "but what are you up to, Eden?"

"Well, I—wasn't supposed to tell anyone."

"I thought there was something. Is Cabot coming here?"

"Oh, *no,* it's—nothing like that!"

"I couldn't think of any other reason for your sticking so tight here. And I could tell there was something on your mind."

"Then you didn't think—I'm glad you didn't think I was just *afraid* to go back to Richmond."

"Nonsense. No Day is afraid of anything. I thought perhaps Cabot was contriving to get down here and marry you."

"No, I—haven't heard from him. It's something quite different. I told you I had sold the ring in order to buy medicines. Well, there aren't any medicines in Richmond at any price, after a big battle. I have to—take them in myself."

"You mean run the blockade?"

"Well, it's already been run, as far as the shore. All I have to do is to take the drugs through the lines to Richmond."

"That's all, is it?"

"And so you see, I can't go till they send for me."

"I see. Where do you get the medicines?"

"I'd better not say. It means a short detour on my way back, and I'll have to trust Uncle Pharaoh with that. I have the money with me. They make up little bags lined with oiled silk to be fastened inside your hoop. Quinine—morphine—calomel—that's what I'm getting. I found out about it from a woman at the hospital, but she's run out of excuses to travel and thinks the Maryland route she sometimes takes is being watched. My living down here is very helpful, I can always say I've been sent for—that you aren't well, or something like that. I thought perhaps—it would be better if you didn't know——"

Gran was silent, knitting. Eden watched her a minute, wondering if it had been wise to tell, because Gran might worry now, she might think the risk was too great, she might say that Ransom would never allow it——

"It's not much of a risk, really," Eden added hastily. "I'm no heroine, Gran. I didn't see a single uniform of any kind from the time I left the last Richmond picket behind till I got to the first one outside the town here. You won't have to be anxious about me, what are you thinking, honey?"

"I was thinking what a thing it is to be young," said Gran enviously, above her knitting. "I was thinking how I'd love to go to Richmond."

"*Gran!*"

"They'd never think of searching *me* on the way. Besides, I'd know how to handle 'em."

"I don't expect to be searched myself. And you can't come to Richmond, that's flat, the conditions there won't do for you."

"Don't talk as though I was a useless old woman, Dee."

"Darling Gran, you're not a bit useless and you get younger every day! But you've got to have proper food and rest, and there's no such thing in Richmond. The guns go all day now, on two sides of us. There might even be a bombardment."

"I've been under fire before now," Gran said wistfully.

"Yes, I know you have. You've had your war, and this one is ours. You must let us fight it for you."

"I've had my war, maybe. But I wish I was good for one more."

There was a long silence, filled with the companionable click of knitting needles.

"You haven't heard from Cabot, then," said Gran, for she was not satisfied about that part of it yet.

"No. N-not directly. Not since he left Libby Prison." Eden held her breath now that the lie was out.

"You don't doubt him, do you?"

"No."

"You'd better not. It wants more than a war to turn Cabot from his purpose."

"I—it seems so far away and long ago," Eden said faintly. "As though it had happened to some other girl."

"It will all come back to you," Gran assured her drily.

The message was brought on the last day of May. *Start early tomorrow,* it said, without a signature.

2

It all went just as Mrs. Willis said it would. All but one thing.

Pharaoh turned right at Barhamsville and right again into an overgrown sandy lane where two young girls were loitering, their hands full of wild flowers. They stood still as the carriage approached, and Pharaoh pulled up.

"It's a warm day," one of the girls said with a smile.

And Eden, instructed by Mrs. Willis, replied, "It's warmer in Richmond."

"You'll find something cool to drink at the house," said the girl, and Eden answered—

"Won't you ride the rest of the way with me?"

The two girls got into the carriage with their bouquets and Pharaoh drove on. There were no more passwords and they chatted innocently of the flowers they held and what would best quench Eden's thirst. Soon the little brick house came in sight, with the broad river lying below it.

She was received by a gentle-faced woman in deep mourning, and her white-haired husband, who appeared to be a clergyman. No time was wasted. He opened a cupboard hidden in the wainscot and took out half a dozen small bags and stood weighing them casually in his hands while Eden laid out the money.

"You understand that we have to pay for it as it comes to us," he explained diffidently. "Sometimes they bring more than we can afford. It's hard to see them take it away again, but there's no credit in this business."

A servant brought in a sweating pitcher of grape-juice cool from the spring-house, and the girls poured it out into frail old glass. At the woman's request, Eden untied her hoop at the waist and let it drop round her feet. She stepped out of it and while she sipped the grape-juice her hostess began to fasten the little bags by their draw-strings to one of the hoop rings half way down.

"There's one thing more," said the clergyman, the last bag still in his hand. "In this one, marked Number Two Quinine, there is an urgent message——"

"I promised not to carry messages," said Eden quickly, and flushed under his look of surprise which was tinged, she thought, with contempt.

"There is no one else to carry it," he said coldly. "Reinforcements for Grant have gone up the river to White House—we think they came from Butler's army across the James. We delayed a day in order that you might take this report as well."

"I—couldn't I take an oral message?"

"We have details and figures, written in cypher on jeweller's tissue tucked inside this bag of quinine. All you have to do is take it to the Provost-Marshal immediately, before you deliver the medicines."

He handed the last bag to his wife and Eden watched in silence while it too was fastened to her hoop. Then the woman rose and spread the hoop on the floor. Eden stepped into it and lifted her skirts a little while the woman tied the tape again around her waist inside them, shook down her dress and revolved while it was arranged with deft motherly hands. That was all. They were waiting for her to go.

"Keep to the Turnpike to Bottom's Bridge," the clergyman said kindly as he saw her into the carriage. "The Yankees are all along the Pamunkey now, coming south."

When they were only a few miles west of Barhamsville a Negro boy on horseback crowded past them on the road at a gallop. Eden saw that his animal was a good one and that it was marked with the U. S. brand of the Federal Army. Pharaoh cursed him for the bad manners which raised the dust in their faces.

Daniel was waiting at the stage inn where they had left him, and Eden ate her basket lunch in Louise's carriage while the horses were put to it and the change over of her luggage was made; then they said good-bye to Pharaoh, who would return to Williamsburg the next day.

In the late afternoon as they approached Bottom's Bridge and the railroad which ran from Richmond to White House they heard a growing mumble of guns somewhere ahead. At the crossroads above the Bridge they were suddenly confronted by a line of mounted blue-clad pickets thrown across the road, and Daniel gave an instinctive jerk on the reins.

"Drive straight up to them," Eden told him calmly, while the blood sang in her ears. "Don't look surprised or frightened. I have the passes. It's nothing."

Daniel's conscience at least was clear, as Pharaoh's would not have been. When the noses of his team practically touched the picket's horse which had been wheeled across the road, the carriage stopped grudgingly and a spruce corporal edged his mount in close to the step on the near side.

"Where are you bound for, ma'am?"

"Richmond. Here are my papers."

"Guess you'll have to show 'em at headquarters, ma'am."

"But I—I have been on a family visit. I want to reach Richmond tonight."

"Sorry to delay you, ma'am, but I got orders to bring everybody in today. Take the right-hand road, Rastus. Close up, boys."

With the corporal riding beside the carriage and two more mounted men following it, Daniel drove on, at an angle to Bottom's Bridge and Richmond, towards where the firing came from.

Eden sat paralyzed and speechless, cold with fright under the broiling afternoon sun, wondering if headquarters meant a search which would deprive her of the precious bags. That was what she thought of first—not the possible consequences to herself, but the terror that now the medicines would never reach Richmond. Then after a moment she remembered the message. Had they chosen the best hiding-place for it, she wondered—she had heard of a woman once who carried messages rolled inside her hair, and they had been found there—perhaps in one's shoe—doubtless the first place to look for them—inside one's bodice, next the skin, not even a Yankee would dare—it was too late now. . . .

They crossed the railroad well above the Bridge and drove on westward towards Cold Harbor. It seemed to her that the guns grew louder as they went, but she told herself that it was the wind, though not a leaf stirred. At last they came in sight of the trim white tents of the Federal camp, with the cook fires smoking cosily and the once familiar striped flag on its pole in front of the adjutant's tent, and the cavalry lines in the foreground. As the carriage passed through she noticed a great bustle of saddling up, and a trumpeter who waited, his instrument on his hip, turned to eye her with interest.

The carriage was halted by the corporal outside a large tent with its flaps raised all round to a non-existent breeze. In plain view in its shelter several blue-clad men worked at bare pine tables full of papers and maps. The corporal dismounted and lowered the carriage step and crooked a gallant elbow to assist Eden to alight. There was a purposeful activity throughout the camp which belied the leisurely look of the desk soldiers in the tent. The ground underneath her feet shuddered now and then to the boom of artillery somewhere westward, and a smoky haze was settling.

The corporal escorted her into the big open tent and up to a table where a large, well-fed looking man with a major's shoulder-straps sat reading a little book bound in leather with gilt edges. He laid it aside with apparent reluctance and looked up at them over his spectacles as the corporal saluted smartly.

"Carriage on the Williamsburg Turnpike, sir," said the corporal.

The major took off his spectacles. His prominent, pale blue eyes rested shrewdly on Eden. He did not smile and he did not rise.

"Your name, please?" he suggested.

In hostile silence Eden laid her papers before him on the littered table. Her chin was very high. The major put on his spectacles again and scanned the documents at his leisure.

"On your way back to Richmond from Williamsburg, eh," he said with a sort of ominous satisfaction. "Why did you not take the shortest road?"

"I did."

"Through Barhamsville."

"Yes, sir."

"But you made a right-hand turn at Barhamsville, didn't you?"

"Oh—that. I'm afraid my coachman dozed off—and I wasn't noticing. The first thing I knew the river was in front of me."

"So what did you do then?"

"I called to him that we must be wrong and he turned round."

"At once?"

"Y-yes, sir."

"You didn't stop to enter the house called Bishop's Landing?"

"Oh, well, I—there were two girls picking flowers just where we stopped to turn round, and they invited me to have something cool to drink. I was very thirsty so I accepted."

"Then you did enter the house."

"Yes, sir."

"And you stayed how long?"

"Just to drink a glass of grape-juice."

"Whom did you see while you were at the house?"

"An old gentleman and his wife. They were both very kind."

"I've no doubt. But they did ask you, did they not, to carry a message to Richmond?"

"No, sir."

His shaggy eyebrows expressed disbelief. He swung his spectacles by their gold bows in his pudgy hands while his pale eyes bored into her. In the silence, the cannon boomed. The hot air of the tent was heavy with an acrid odor which was not from the horse lines nor the latrines nor the wood fires near the cook tents. She was aware of a young man at a table near by who wrote busily without looking up, and she suspected that he was taking down the conversation as it came.

"It will save a good deal of trouble and unpleasantness all round," said the major with calculated malice, "if you will surrender the contraband goods you went to Bishop's Landing to procure—without further delay."

"I don't know what you're talking about," said Eden through lips which had gone quite stiff.

"Likewise the message," he added, watching her. "If you persist in this useless pretence of innocence I shall of course have to order a search, both of your carriage and its driver, and of yourself. It makes rather a mess of a carriage, slitting up the cushions and all that sort of thing. And as for yourself, I regret to say that there is no woman available to—spare your feelings."

"I—" she began, while a wave of helpless color flamed up to her hair. "I——"

"I suggest first of all that if you will be good enough to drop off your hoop—" His eyes ran impersonally down her body. "Sometimes there is no need to proceed further."

"I won't," Eden said resolutely. "You can't force me to do any such thing!"

The major spoke wearily over his shoulder to the young man who wrote.

"Appleby," said the major, and the young man laid down his pen and rose, his face a polite blank, and came towards her.

"No—*wait!*" She backed away from him, both hands out to ward him off, and Appleby paused patiently, without expression.

"Kindly don't waste my time, madam," said the major sharply. "If you prefer to do whatever is necessary unassisted, be so good as to do it quickly."

The feeling of trapped desperation which had petrified her ever since entering the tent underwent a sudden transformation. She wasn't afraid of him, this fat man with the unfriendly eyes. She hated him too much for fear, hated all he stood for in this well-dressed, well-fed army with its insolence of unlimited resources and efficient personnel. Because of him, there would be no rest tonight for men with wounds like Dabney's, the typhoid patients must burn up and die, the men with blood-poisoning must rot with their eyes open. And every minute there were more of them, every time one of those guns went off there were more men to suffer for the mercy which was hidden in those little bags tied to her hoop. Eden saw red.

"Very well, I *am* carrying contraband!" she said defiantly. "And it will now be your great pleasure to confiscate it and send me off to one of your filthy jails! I took that risk to myself when I asked to go to Bishop's Landing—because after what I've seen of this war it didn't matter what might happen to me if I got caught, so long as there was a single hope of my getting through just once, or maybe twice, before you could stop me! Well, you have stopped me, *and you can hang me,* but it won't stop other women from trying the same thing, and other women will succeed!"

Her voice had risen hysterically without once losing its soft Virginia cadence, her green eyes swam with tears as she faced the surprised major across the untidy pine table. Outside the tent, which gave no privacy to the scene, her words were audible to a dozen soldiers pursuing their lawful occasions about the camp, and some of them grinned shamefacedly and caught each other's eyes, and some cursed quietly and tried not to hear.

Her voice reached the ears, also, of Cabot Murray, coming from the horse lines leading his favorite mount saddled and bridled for action.

He paused almost on one foot, cocking his head in the effort to sort out the unknown woman's voice from the boom of cannon and the clank of accoutrement and the careless, casual noise of the busy camp. His eyes met those of a nearby sentry who grinned apologetically and shook his head.

"They caught him a red-headed gal this time, and she sure is givin' the Old Man a lambastin'!" he said.

Cabot threw his reins at a passing soldier and approached the tent door, which was more or less blocked by the broad back of the corporal. Eden had not paused for breath.

"You call it contraband! Morphine at three hundred dollars an ounce, and we're forbidden to buy it or carry it to the men who are dying for lack of it! I found the money to pay for it, and I found out where to get it, and every dose of it is needed ten times over, but *you* will have the satisfaction of taking it away from me—that's not war, that's callous murder of sick and helpless men, yes, and women too, because even women fall ill in Richmond, did you ever think of that? I saw my mother die for want of the medicines that might have saved her, but you wouldn't care about that, maybe you never had a mother! Maybe your army has its share of horrible wounds, but do your hospitals have to tie a man down and cut off his leg without chloroform because there's no such thing in the city? And have you heard the sort of sound he makes while they do it? And has it been done to your own brother, as it was done to mine? I was there and I heard! That's why I went to Bishop's Landing, and that's why if you do try to take away from me the little bit of morphine I've managed to scrape together you'll have to do it by brute force, and it will take *six* men the size of that one, because I'll scream the place down and fight you all every way I know!"

She was not crying now, though tears hung on her lashes. She was breathless and chalky-faced, and her chin was up, and her fingers curled like claws, and the major was actually looking nonplussed. Cabot slipped past the corporal into the tent and saluted gravely.

"I beg your pardon, sir, but I thought I recognized the voice. This lady happens to be my fiancée. Eden, darling—" He reached her in two strides, and took her into a masterful embrace. "Kiss me," she heard him whisper, and gave him her lips with a most convincing willingness, while her arms went tight around his neck.

"This is highly irregular, Captain Murray," said the major, recover‑ing quickly, and Cabot faced him with Eden still in the protective circle of his arm.

"I realize that, sir. I had no idea she was in the camp. May I ask——"

"Smuggling," snapped the major. "She visited that Bishop's Land‑ing house this morning and we were notified in time to intercept her at Bottom's Bridge. She admits she is carrying drugs."

"Oh, Cabot, I told you we had to have them!" she cried piteously. "This is what the money was for! Ask him to let me go! Ask him to let me keep the medicines, just this once!"

"I suppose, sir, that it would be quite impossible for you to over‑look—" Cabot began warily.

"On the contrary, I am impressed by the—force of Miss Day's argu‑ment," said the major with the shadow of a smile. "If she will sur‑render the packages for inspection, I will undertake to see that a cer‑tain leniency is observed. I presume you carry the stuff in the usual way," he added to Eden. "If, as I suggested some time ago, you will be so good as to drop off your hoop——"

But now she remembered the message again. Her eyes caught Cabot's easy, confident gaze.

"It—it's only six little bags," she pleaded. "They're all tied up——"

"Let him see them," Cabot said quietly. "That's all. Just a for‑mality."

"No, I——"

"I'm sorry to seem harsh, Miss Day, but this comes at rather a busy time for us," the major remarked crisply. "Either you will surrender the goods at once or I shall require Captain Murray to take them from you."

"Could we—m‑may I see Captain Murray alone?"

"No, you may not. Come, come, Miss Day, it's simple enough to give up your hoop!"

"But—I——"

"Hurry up, Eden," said Cabot, humoring modesty. "We won't look —will we!" And he covered the eyes of the corporal behind him with one hand and his own with the other.

Trembling, she met the inexorable gaze of the major. With a quick, despairing movement she flicked up her skirts at the sides, pulled at the tape, and the hoop weighted with the six little bags slid to the ground. Cabot stooped for it and handed it to Appleby, who began to detach the bags one by one and lay them on the table in front of the major.

The guns were loud in the silence, seeming nearer all the time, louder now than she had ever heard them in Richmond—or was it the pounding blood in her own ears? Then quite unmistakably there came the whine of a descending shell, which exploded with a loud *crrrump* in the direction of the horse lines somewhere beyond the tent. The corporal winced visibly and even Cabot blinked, but the wooden-faced Appleby gave no sign of having heard it.

The major only scowled. He was untying the mouth of each bag as it came and looking inside it and tying it up again. Just as he began on the third one another shell whined over and went *crrrrump* near where the first had landed.

"That's crazy firing if I ever heard it," he said testily. "They're over-shooting our lines like hell. Can't hear yourself think, and it's not do-ing *them* any good! Sometimes I wonder what Artillery uses for brains, half the time they——"

It was the third bag which contained the cypher message written on jeweller's tissue.

The major drew it out and unfolded it slowly. Cabot turned to look at Eden with something like awe. Her face was perfectly white, her eyes rested blankly on the major's fat hands.

"This appears to be the message we're looking for," said the major unemotionally. "Cyphered, of course. Would you be good enough to render it into English for me, Miss Day?"

Eden opened her mouth, but no sound came. Cabot spoke instead.

"It looks to me as though some one had imposed on her, sir. So far as she knew, she was carrying only drugs. I'm sure she had no idea a message was included." His hooded glance signalled her to concur.

"No, I—never saw it before," she said faintly.

"Are you prepared to swear to that?"

"Yes, sir."

"Some day somebody is going to lose his temper and make an exam-ple out of one of these intrepid women who are willing to risk all for their country," said the major, and his voice had a rasp in it. "Some day a woman is going to hang for a trick like this! Personally, I think the time has come!"

"Oh, please, sir—" Eden stumbled forward, leaning with both hands on the edge of the table. "You must believe me, I never meant to trick you! Before I left Richmond it was understood that I would not carry messages. All I wanted was the medicines, and that is the truth, so help me God, I did *not* undertake to act as a spy——"

The major raised his head from contemplation of the cypher, speared her with a glance.

"Will you take your Bible oath that you had no knowledge of this message before I came upon it just now?" he demanded solemnly, and held out to her the little leather-bound volume which he had laid aside when she arrived.

Eden stared at it, cornered. If he had accepted her own wording she could have sworn. The oath he required of her was perjury. Her hand came out—hovered above the book——

"Your *right* hand, if you please," rasped the major.

She glanced at Cabot. And from his quick, waiting eyes the signal flashed—perjury or no perjury, swear. Swear, and go free, perhaps with the drugs as well.

While she hesitated the silver notes of trumpets resounded through the camp, and there was a renewed bustle outside the tent, and the men at the other tables weighted their papers and left, ducking under the raised flaps at the side, so that only Appleby remained—a confusion of running feet, a few words shouted, a laughing reply, and the guns again, nearer, louder . . . A moment more she stood above the book, then covered her face with a little moan, swayed dizzily, felt Cabot's arm hard around her waist, and succumbed to blackness shot with flame.

"Well, what can you expect, you scared the living daylights out of her, sir!" said Cabot, and laid her tenderly on the ground. "Did you have to say that about hanging?"

The major seemed contrite. He sent Appleby for a cup of water, dismissed the corporal, and knelt beside Eden where she lay. Cabot had untied her bonnet and laid it aside and was fanning her with his cap.

"You and your Bible!" Cabot complained, glaring at his superior officer. "Her word was enough!"

"It wasn't a Bible," said the major disgustedly. "It was a book of Tennyson's poems. I thought she'd see that and act accordingly and save everybody's face. Now that young jackass Appleby will have to know I've let her off against regulations!"

Cabot cocked an eyebrow at him.

"I never knew you were fond of Tennyson, sir," he remarked interestedly.

"I see no reason for you to be surprised," snapped the major. "I find it very soothing in a racket like this. How far does he have to *go* for that water?"

"Right here, sir," said Appleby, slopping it in his haste.

The major damped a corner of his blue bandana in the cup and applied it to Eden's temples. She opened her eyes and Cabot raised her against his shoulder.

"It's all right," he said gently, as another shell whined in and landed. "It's all right, sweetheart, you'll be in Richmond tonight."

An orderly appeared at the tent-flap and saluted.

"Beg pardon, sir—Captain Murray is wanted, sir. We're standing to horse, ready to go in."

"Kiss me for luck," said Cabot, and took it without waiting, and gave her into the major's arms. "Look after her, sir—and thank you!"

As the major helped her to her feet she heard the rattle of bit and saber, felt the ground quiver to the beat of hooves, glimpsed beyond the tent-flap the flutter of guidons and dazzle of polished accoutrement as the troop went by towards the guns. They stood together at the tent door and watched the last of them out of sight behind a belt of trees above which black smoke hung low. The whine of the incoming shells was more frequent, and the descending sun hung low and red.

"If I don't get you out of here," said the major crossly, "you may get killed by your own lunatic gunners. Appleby—give me the record on this case." He took the closely written pages and tore them across and across again. "Of course you realize that this whole thing is highly irregular and can't happen twice," he said to Eden as he did so. "Appleby—kindly return Miss Day's hoop and bonnet." Eden took them with a word of thanks and stood holding them and watching while the major sat down at the table, put on his spectacles, and wrote briefly on an official-looking strip of paper. This he held out to her, peering over his gold rims. "Here is a pass to put you back on the Richmond road," he said dourly. "I hope you understand that you are on parole. Now, get out of here and don't ever let me catch you again."

"Th-thank you, sir." A moment she looked at him. Then with a swift snatch she gathered up three of the little bags from the top of the table and dropped them into her bonnet. When her hand darted down for the last three he slapped his own hand down hard on the bit of tissue paper which lay beside them, and she smiled, backing away from him towards the door. "That's not mine," she said. "It never was. God bless you, sir." She curtsied and was gone, bareheaded, carrying her hoop and bonnet.

The major sat a long minute, staring down at the cypher message which remained on his table—and which without much doubt meant that they knew Butler had sent men to Cold Harbor. But did they know how many, and whether cavalry or infantry, or both—and who had written the message. . . . He sighed wearily.

"Appleby."

"Sir?"

"Take this thing to the fellow who knows how to read 'em. And on the way you must contrive to forget how we got it."

VIII. APRIL 3, 1865

I

BUT Grant didn't take Richmond from Cold Harbor.

His obstinate hammering at Lee's army had cost him about seven to one for nearly a month's fighting, and now he was stopped in his tracks where McClellan had stood two years before. Like McClellan, he retreated to the James, with the difference that Butler was there with an army waiting to join him. And the siege of Petersburg began.

Slowly the terrible summer wore away. Sometimes there would be a lull when only the videttes and the artillery would keep up an occasional interest. Sometimes there would be a spell of bitter fighting, when Grant tried a jab here or there to make Lee shift his thin lines and concentrate them anew where the pressure seemed heaviest.

One night in the middle of July bonfires burned all along Pickett's front, and Grant sent out scouts to learn why. They reported that the fires burned in celebration of the birth of a son to Pickett. Grant grunted and fingered his beard thoughtfully. Like Longstreet and Jackson and McClellan and Lee, he too belonged to that old brotherhood of the Mexican War, during which Second Lieutenant George Pickett, fresh from West Point, had recklessly planted the stars-and-stripes on the parapet at Chapultepec under heavy fire. Pickett's good news spread through the Federal camp, and there were other old friends of his there besides the commander. They had all fought for the same thing once. "Well, let's strike a light for the young Pickett ourselves," said Grant, and soon the bonfire salute ran the length of the Federal lines as well. A few days later a baby's silver service, engraved to George Pickett, Jr., was sent across the lines by flag of truce, from Pickett's former comrades in arms to Pickett's son.

Cabot Murray was now wearing a major's shoulder straps at Grant's City Point headquarters, where his ability to get into and out of Richmond undetected was in some demand. But although he entered the town more than once as the autumn passed, bringing out from Elizabeth Van Lew and others information of Lee's dwindling resources and their disposition in the fortifications, and although he lingered dangerously more than once, he never saw Eden even from a distance; while at the same time she never left the house any more without the dread of meeting him again.

At the end of October, after a number of small but costly bickerings around the edges of Richmond and Petersburg, Grant and Butler went into winter quarters, their lines extending in a broad crescent from New Market north of the James across it westward to the middle one of the three railroads which ran south from Petersburg.

Dabney and Charlotte were married at Christmas time, Dabney protesting, Charlotte declared, every step of the way. Dabney's contention was that whereas when General Ewell, for instance, had lost a leg at Groveton they had sent to England and got an artificial one right through the blockade, and the General was up and on it as good as new again before Chancellorsville—now it was almost impossible to get artificial legs and Charlotte would therefore have to marry a man on crutches. Charlotte was understood to say with some indignation and many embellishments that she nevertheless preferred Dabney on crutches to General Ewell on his artificial leg, which so tickled Dabney that almost before he knew it the date was set.

Gran and Sue and Myrta could not come to Richmond for the wedding, but they sent Pharaoh with two enormous hampers which by the grace of God escaped the notice of the Yankee outposts along the road and arrived safely, with the compliments of the Williamsburg adjutant, in Franklin Street. Everyone else came, for the lines were drawn close around Richmond now, and even Lee was constantly in and out of the city, where his wife lay ill in their Franklin Street house.

Ransom had many stories to tell of his general—and most of them were difficult to hear without a mist in the eyes. The army's love for Marse Robert, said Ransom, had become almost a religion, and everything that Lee did in response to it was just right, so that at each encounter the men who worshiped him redoubled their devotion. He told how a backwoods soldier, instead of saluting the impressive figure on the big grey horse as he passed, absent-mindedly greeted it with a respectful "Howdy do, dad," and the general responded with unblinking courtesy, "Howdy do, my man," to the suppressed delight of his scandalized Staff riding behind him. Lee's heart was wrung, said Ransom, by the privations of his men, who lived in rat-holes on wormy rations, burned green firewood, and tried to clean themselves without soap. Then even the percussion caps ran low, which they complained spoiled the pickets' fun. When some one sent Lee a turkey as a gift, or a pound of coffee, or a warm knitted garment, or some other small hard-won luxury, he received it with polite thanks and passed it on to his hospitals. After being very low with dysentery at Cold Harbor, he was in good health now and gave little sign of the gnawing anxiety he must have felt as they approached a winter of growing despair. Books he craved, and would always accept the loan of them. A borrowed copy of Hugo's new masterpiece went the rounds of the whole camp at Petersburg and was read to tatters, being affectionately known to the literate soldiers who thumbed it as *Lee's Miserables*.

Thousands of the best men had been killed in battle, or disabled, and it was evident to all but the very youngest and stoutest hearts that now the odds were hopeless. The troops were starving in their tracks, the horses were feeble skeletons, the conscription barrel had been scraped bare—no food, no fuel, no transport, no reinforcements—but the grey army held on. The front lines were so close together in many places that the pickets could chaff each other without lifting their voices, and traded Yankee coffee for Rebel tobacco by waving a white handkerchief. Many an unofficial truce was made, too, for the gathering of the green firewood in thickets exposed to sharp-shooting fire or for the rescue of a wounded comrade. And many a generous warning came at the end of such arrangements—"Watch yourself, Johnny, we're opening up," or "Low bridge, Yank, here it comes!" It was not a hating war—not any more. Fighting would be bitter again in the heat of battle. But during the winter lull they were still one people, speaking the same language, with the same religions and the same bedrock beliefs. That, said Ransom, was the worst part of it.

There was dancing at the reception after Charlotte's wedding on Christmas Eve, in what used to be the drawing-room, with the cots of the wounded crowded edge to edge into the dining-room beyond and the double doors left open between, so that those who were able could be propped up to see and the rest could hear, and every single one of them had a sip of wine and a crumb of cake. Charlotte hadn't wanted dancing on account of Dabney's leg, but Dabney himself insisted on it, and she was wise enough to realize that the last thing to do was to seem to coddle his feelings.

They were a singularly touching pair, in that city of heartbreak and glory. Dabney stood well over six feet on his crutches, and Charlotte was all of five feet three in her little scuffed shoes, but her tactful care of him was a thing to see. She never hovered nor fussed, but somehow when he was ready to rise from a chair Charlotte was always there to slide the crutch deftly under his arm, doors opened before him by magic, she never dropped things nor needed things done which would require of him the small services he would normally have rendered. Eden was not the only one who noticed that as they left the church together one leaf of the heavy door would have been allowed by the crowd to swing back against him but for Charlotte's small, quick hand braced against it. And yet, with all that, Charlotte could hardly be said to have grown up, and she still made him laugh.

Charlotte's brother Grafton came to the wedding, of course, and during the ceremony Eden felt his humble eyes upon her—too humble —was that it? But anyhow she softened towards him. At least he never took anything for granted. At least——

They had the first dance together. Everyone was waltzing now in Richmond, it kept up one's spirits, they said. And so it did, Eden thought as she circled the room on Grafton's somewhat rigid arm. He danced as he did everything else, efficiently, politely, with an air of distinction and grace. He was breaking his heart over her, she knew, and yet nothing warm and vital and urgent passed from him to her as he held her. What was lacking, she wondered, revolving obediently in silence. Why was it so different from that other waltz in the drawing-room at Williamsburg, when a voice said, so near that the breath of the low words stirred her hair, *It was time I came to Virginia*. . . .

It is time, she told herself severely, that you put all that behind you —time to forget him and make some sort of life with what is left. Why must it be so hard? Why haven't I the decency to love one of my own people, so I can hold up my head in this town and be proud of my man, like Charl?

"It could have been us tonight, Eden," Grafton was saying, below the music, his lips barely moving. "It could have been a double wedding, if only——"

"I know, Grafton. I'm sorry."

"I've got two more days."

"Oh, Grafton, I—" The words ran down to nothing. Perhaps if she took hold of things now with both hands—perhaps if she simply laid hold of life suddenly and *lunged,* it would come out all right. Worth trying, maybe——?

"I don't want to be a nuisance," Grafton was saying humbly. "But look at them, Eden—don't you envy them?"

Dabney was sitting in an armchair at the end of the room and Charlotte stood beside him in her wedding dress, which had once been the drawing-room lace curtains, with her mother's veil. The guests swirled around them, and Charlotte would not dance, but stood radiant at Dabney's side, including him in every word she spoke and every laughing glance she gave. Well, yes, anyone would envy the shining, *blatant* happiness which lighted Charlotte's little pointed face, and the graver, almost spellbound look of Dabney, who had suffered an active man's agony of maiming in body and soul and now found himself shielded and adored and looked up to and *married* . . . in spite of it. But that, Eden knew, was different from herself and Grafton. Grafton was second choice. Worse, he knew it. If only he wouldn't apologize for it, if only he would be a little masterful and sure of himself. Even Dabney, with one leg, bossed Charlotte around like anything. One couldn't marry a doormat. Or could one, if the doormat were good and kind and faithful, and on the right side—the losing side, maybe, but one's own?

"I can't help noticing," Grafton was saying now with his gentle obstinacy, "that you aren't wearing his ring any more. I thought— that is, I wondered——"

"I sold it," and Eden, and——

"Oh," said Grafton, really astonished, and——

"For money to buy medicines, after the Wilderness battles," she explained patiently.

"Will he—mind?"

"I can't imagine that he would—even if he is a Yankee!" She owed him that much, anyway.

Grafton was silent, turning it over in his thoughts, and then the music ended and a new dance began, this time with Sedgwick as her partner. It was a relief to get to Sedgwick.

"Do you think it's ever any good," she asked him, "to try and make do with second choice?"

He looked down at her in some surprise, and she noticed that even his cousinly arm was less impersonal and wooden than Grafton's had been, and his style in the dance was more exciting. Her heart cried out that Grafton was a bore and she couldn't bear him, and her pride insisted that he was very presentable and deserved something of her, more than she could ever give.

"I know what's the matter with you," Sedgwick said in his much too penetrating way. "Dabney and Charlotte look so almighty pleased with themselves everybody longs to go and do likewise. Look out, Eden."

"Then you don't advise me to try and make something out of— out of——"

"Out of Grafton?" He grinned. "Not much to go on, is there!"

"Oh, Sedgwick, really——!"

"Well, you asked me. You wouldn't feel the way Charl looks, Eden. Not with Grafton."

"No," she agreed meekly, and they finished the dance in silence. At the end of it, before she was claimed by the next man, Sedgwick said briefly, "Sleep on it first, whatever you do."

2

That was easy enough to *say*, Eden thought irritably, tossing and turning in the dawn while Sally slept like the dead beside her. Half a dozen of Sally's best beaux had been killed, but there were always more where those came from, and Sally was too kind-hearted—or something—to marry any one of them and disappoint the others.

After breakfast on Christmas Day, as Eden went the rounds of the wards on her duties, young black Jock looked in at the door mysteriously and beckoned her out into the hall. When she got there he opened one hand on a small square box wrapped in white paper.

"Lady brang it early dis mawnin'," he whispered. "Said give it to you when nobody was lookin'."

"What lady?" Eden asked, as she took it from him and concealed it in her own hand.

"White lady, in farmin' clothes—like from de market, mebbe. Come to de kitchen door, she did."

Eden guessed at once—Elizabeth Van Lew, disguised in homespun and a sun bonnet to hide her face, delivering Cabot's Christmas present for him. Almost she guessed what it would be. But not quite. She was not quite prepared, when she opened the box behind the locked door of the bedroom she had to share with Sally now, to find that he had got her the same ring back again, or another just like it.

She hid it from Sally underneath the pile of ruffled petticoats at the back of her bureau drawer and went down stairs again feeling badly shaken. You didn't have to try and make anything of Cabot. He was already there, the complete lover, and a bit more.

She was angry, and amused, and shaken. She couldn't wear his ring, she had sold it. She didn't intend to wear his ring, because she was not going to marry him. He dared her to sell it again, dared her not to marry him. It was unforgivable of him, reckless, risky, and presuming. But she loved it, and she wanted to laugh. Not at Cabot, exactly—but at the impudence of such a gesture from him in the face of what she had said to him. And she was shaken. Yankee he might be, and spy he might be, but coward, no, nor suppliant. And there went Grafton's chances once more, blasted once more, and maybe just in time.

It was a fantastically gay winter in the overcrowded, dilapidated, doomed city of Richmond. With the defending lines so close, all the young officers who had been famished so long for feminine society and music and diversion could get a taste of them again, and thought nothing of doing a dozen miles on horseback through slush and snow to a dance and back again to their posts before dawn. Often they went direct from the ballroom or the bridal bed to some small front line affair which brought their death. Besides the perpetual weddings, almost every night there were amateur theatricals, charades, and contribution parties, where everybody was supposed to bring a bit towards the refreshments and there was never enough of anything to go around. The women wore turned and mended and threadbare finery among the mourning dresses, and there were maimed and invalid men among the dancers, but all wore the grey.

Not a day passed without its dribble of casualties from the trenches to the east of the city or the fortifications to the south, and though the condition of the roads prevented any general engagement there was hardly a night that the tramp of feet in the cold streets was not heard as weary, ragged, shivering reinforcements raced from one threatened spot to another, almost as though Grant hoped to wear them out with marching. "You would think he always knew exactly what places we have weakened in order to strengthen others as fast as we make the shift," Ransom cried in discouragement. "He must have a nearly perfect spy system right inside the city!" And Eden, hearing, felt hot with shame as though she herself, instead of Elizabeth Van Lew and others like her, had betrayed the tired grey men to Cabot Murray and his kind.

It was a bitterly cold winter too, so that Eden as she broke the ice in the pitcher on her washstand in the mornings tried to remember how it was in the old days at home when she and Sue woke to a blazing fire on the hearth and Mammy poured steaming water from a bright copper kettle into the washbowls before the two girls even left the warm bed. Coal was ninety-five dollars a ton in Richmond, and wood went up to one hundred and thirty-five dollars a cord, but the fires were kept burning in the wards all night at the Crabb house, and even then the water froze in the pitchers on the other side of the room.

But spring came early, in 1865, while the news got worse and worse. Sherman's army had left Atlanta in smoking ruins and marched south and east to the tune of *John Brown's Body*, committing theft and plunder and devastation, sometimes outrage and murder, all in the name of foraging—leaving in their wake a greater horror than anything Virginia had suffered so far as a battlefield. They came to Savannah and paused there to rest and refit before swinging northward again to teach the Carolinas that war was hell. Charleston was evacuated before them, and they burned defenceless Columbia to cinders amid terrible scenes. The back door to Richmond was forced, and Lee's supply lines could now be cut in all directions. It was supposed that he would have to evacuate Richmond. But where would he go?

At the very end of March Grafton Crabb was sent home with a wounded hand after an action on the east. He had not wanted to leave the line, but what had seemed a trifling injury got worse instead of better till blood poisoning threatened. Louise and Charlotte fussed over his dressings and persuaded him to keep quiet, but he was a bad patient and was inclined to follow Eden dolefully about the place till she almost went out of her mind.

It was a relief to her when he was well enough to go to church with Dabney and Charlotte on Sunday the second of April. The tocsin had been ringing off and on since dawn, mingling horridly with the church bells as the morning went by, and the guns were livelier than usual below the town. There were rumors of bloody fighting near Petersburg. Eden was on duty in the wards when the church party returned early, all looking rather white. President Davis had been handed a message which caused him to rise hastily and leave the church, and a few minutes later Dr. Hoge had stopped the service midway to announce that Richmond was to be evacuated that night. He advised the congregation to go home at once and make their preparations. "For what?" Eden asked grimly, and Charlotte said, "For not evacuating," and went away to take off her bonnet and hoop and help serve the patients' dinner.

During the early afternoon the streets were full of a growing confusion. Wagons were driven hurriedly towards the Capitol to be loaded with archives and sent on to the Danville railway station. People started packing again, and the demand for carriages began to be clamorous—it was like the early days of the war, when the fighting at Seven Pines and Mechanicsville had sent the timid ones scurrying southward. Richmond had become inured to alarms since then. But still a sort of panic was beginning.

Dabney and Grafton went out into the streets together, one on crutches and one with his left hand bandaged and in a sling, to see and hear what was going on. They were gone so long that anxiety rose at home. When they returned they could not conceal their knowledge that things were just about as bad as possible. Petersburg had been given up and Lee was retreating westward along the Appomattox. His message to President Davis had advised the Government to move that night, and the Government seemed to be going to pieces. Some one had ordered all the liquor stores to be destroyed, and gallons of spirits were being emptied into the gutters with the inevitable results. The same short-sighted policy had ordered the commissary stores thrown open to the public and a mob was becoming unmanageable there.

"I wish we could get Mother out of Richmond," Grafton said hopelessly, but Charlotte objected.

"She's not able to travel. She senses something in the air, and her heart is much worse today. What about Mrs. Lee?"

"The same. Bedridden, I think."

"But surely we needn't be afraid—" Eden began and stopped uncomfortably, remembering the dreadful stories about what had happened to civilians in Columbia and Atlanta and Savannah. She looked at Grafton. "Oughtn't you to get away before the Yankees come in?" she asked gently.

"That's what I've been telling him," Dabney said. "They won't bother to take me prisoner with this leg, but Grafton ought to leave while he can."

"They won't be here before tomorrow," Grafton reminded them indifferently. He didn't seem to care much whether he was taken prisoner or not.

Black Jock ran in from the rear of the house, looking scared.

"Marse Grafton—Unc' Daniel says kin he have de loan of a gun, please, suh."

"A gun? Certainly not. What for?"

"Says he got to proteck de carriages an' hosses, suh. Says somebody sure gwine take 'em by force effn we don' hire 'em out willin'."

Grafton looked at Eden doggedly.

"I hate to have you stay here. Are you sure you hadn't better——"

"Of course I'm sure. We can't all go and leave our patients, and I certainly won't leave Charlotte and Aunt Louise and Sally. What is that strange noise? Listen."

"That's the mob at the commissary. They're beginning to get drunk and fight over loot. The whole town is going to be hell by nightfall, Eden!"

"Well, *give* Uncle Daniel a gun, then!" she cried recklessly. "Lock the stables and put him on guard. We'll want the horses some day if not now!"

"If there is anything you value," Dabney was saying quietly to Charlotte, "your mother's jewelry, whatever silver is left—we'd better be thinking of a place to hide it."

"Oh, Dabney, you don't think the Yankees would dare——"

"We won't have to wait for the Yankees, Charl. There's going to be mob rule in Richmond tonight. Get your treasures together and Grafton will help me bury them in the cellar before he goes."

Eden had nothing to save but the ring. As soon as she could slip away she went up to the bedroom and locked the door, snatched the ring from its box at the back of the bureau drawer and threaded it on a ribbon which she tied around her neck with the ring hanging down inside her bodice. She had barely finished when the handle of the door turned and Sally's voice said impatiently—"Eden? Are you in there? Why is the door locked? What *are* you doing? Do you think I ought to burn my letters?" When Eden opened the door Sally grabbed her arm with a cold, shaking hand. "Eden, do you think the servants will——?"

"*Our* servants? Of course not! Dabney says the Negroes in the streets are just standing around in a daze anyway—they don't know what any of it means."

"But if they start drinking—Eden, I'm terrified, what shall we do? There goes that awful bell again! Will they bombard us before they come in?"

"Why should they, when we're evacuating? What's the matter with you, Sally, the Yankees are human beings just like us! They'll come in the same way they did at Williamsburg, there's nothing to be afraid of!"

"Look what they did at Columbia!"

"That was Sherman."

"Well, this is Grant! What's the difference? Eden, you can hear the mob now with all the doors and windows shut, it's getting louder all the time. I'd rather it was the Yankees than that mob!"

"Now, stop it, Sally, you're just working yourself up! We'll be perfectly safe here, this is a hospital. Anyway, the men have to be fed their supper. Come and help me with the trays."

By the time darkness fell there was pandemonium in the business district around the stores and banks, and looting was spreading. The local companies called up by the tocsin melted away again as fast as they came. Several small fires got started and were more or less extinguished. Everyone stayed inside behind locked doors if they cared about their own property, for anything left unguarded was subject to plunder. The excitement had penetrated Mrs. Crabb's bedroom at the top of the house, and she was much worse, and Grafton spent the evening at her bedside. About ten he came into the parlor where the others sat trying to read and talk and knit, trying not to listen to what was going on outside.

"I'm going for the doctor," he said. "Come and lock the door behind me and don't open it till I knock three times and then three times again."

When he returned, Charlotte and Louise were sitting with Mrs. Crabb. Eden recognized his signal and let him in and they locked the door again. Everything had got much worse in the streets, and the doctor said there was a rumor that the warehouses and bridges were to be blown up when the retreating army had been safely withdrawn. President Davis had fled southward to join his wife, instead of towards Appomattox and Lee. Everywhere the grim, weary men in grey were snatching a few minutes to say good-bye to their families and hurrying away to join the retreat. The doctor wanted Grafton to leave at once, but Grafton went up stairs with him and stayed till dawn, when Mrs. Crabb died.

No one had gone to bed in the house that night. Sally and Dabney and Eden were still sitting in the parlor when Grafton came in. They could tell by his face what had happened.

"I can go now," he said, and his voice was quite steady. "May I— please speak to Eden alone?"

As the others left the room Eden went to him and led him gently to Dabney's chair, by the center-table under the lamp. Before she could find words for his comfort he had collapsed across the table, his face hidden in his good arm, his thin body racked by long dry sobs.

Eden was horrified. She had never seen a man cry before, and Grafton of all men, who never had any visible emotion whatever. She hung above him, her arms around his shoulders, saying soft, incoherent soothing things as to a heartbroken child, until as suddenly as he had begun he was quiet again. Slowly he dragged himself up so that his head rested on his hand, staring down at the table cover under his elbow. The room was grey with dawn.

"I'm sorry, I—don't know what came over me," he said into the silence. "Or rather, I do know, quite well. It's not because of Mother— that was for the best. It's not being crippled and useless. It's because there is nothing left to do, Eden. We're beaten."

"Yes, I suppose we are," she whispered. And as she stood there holding him, seeing in the cold dawn which had overspread the lamplight the powder and blood stains on his shabby grey coat, the careful mending where a big jagged hole had been, the drag of the white sling across his sagging shoulders—as she stood there, he was suddenly all the grey-clad men everywhere that morning, he was the Confederacy, he was her people, at the end of the long road. A sickening wave of feeling surged through her, which was part pity for him and part her own searing sense of defeat and despair, part a lifetime of associations, common memories, and familiar scenes in both their lives, and part sheer hysteria in the dawn.

"We've lost," he was saying, motionless under her hands. "We haven't lost just the war, we've lost everything—our best men, our homes, our way of living—our world. There's nothing left. We're beaten. We're finished. It's over. We're beaten—beaten—*beaten!*"

"But some of us are still alive," she said very quietly, it seemed to her very sanely. "Some of us are still young. And we have to find something to do with our lives, don't we—what's left of them."

He turned his head a little, catching at one word she had said.

"We?" he repeated breathlessly.

"Yes, Grafton."

"Eden—you d-don't mean——"

"Yes, Grafton."

He caught at her silently with his one good hand, and she held his head against her breast as she stood beside his chair—and remembered, like a shooting pain, how once she had stood beside Cabot's chair in Libby Prison. . . .

"But I don't understand," Grafton said after a moment. "The war is over. You could—marry *him* now. You could get out of this—forget about it—be happy somewhere." He raised his face to her, still unbelieving. "You mean you're going to marry me—after all? Are you sure?"

"Yes, Grafton."

"I should have thought—well, I should have expected it to be the other way around," he persisted, begging reassurance, and she laid her hands either side of his haggard face, looking down.

"Poor Grafton—how very little you know about women, my dear."

As she spoke, a terrific explosion shook the house, followed by a moment's intense silence, which was broken by yells and shouts and running feet and the spatter of horses' hooves and soon the wild peal of the tocsin again.

Sally flung open the door of the parlor and ran in.

"Eden, they *are* bombarding us! Oh, won't this night ever end!

Grafton, you must *go,* do you want the Yankees to catch you and put you in prison?"

Grafton rose almost briskly and pulled himself to his full height, smoothing his rusty grey tunic under the sling, running a quick anxious hand over his hair, with a new air of dignity and purpose as he smiled down at Eden.

"I certainly don't intend to be caught," he said. "I'm going back to the line and stay there—as long as there is a line. That's not gunfire you hear, Sally, we're blowing up the bridges and the gunboats behind us. Good-bye, my dearest—" Eden gave him his kiss, unembarrassed, while Sally stared tactlessly from the threshold. "And whatever happens now," he whispered, his face against hers, "I've won!"

3

When Cabot said to Eden that he would be one of the first Federal officers to enter Richmond he was not guessing. His intimate knowledge of the city and the elements of coöperation inside it made certain that he would be attached to the occupation force when the time came. At the end of March Grant had withdrawn most of the troops which lay north of the James facing the elaborate defences to the southeast of the city and thrown them into the attack on Lee along the Appomattox. General Weitzel was left in command of the skeletonized Army of the James, and Cabot was with him.

They knew at Federal headquarters that the entrenchments ahead of them were two lines deep, well-gunned, and planted with torpedoes— manned largely by the local defence troops and convalescent regulars from Richmond. The front lines were so close together that the videttes of either side were within speaking distance of each other, and all day on that Sunday the Federal lookouts posted in the treetops kept the grey men under observation, waiting for the first sign of withdrawal. The sun went down in a bank of cloud, and as darkness fell a strange bluish mist settled over the ground.

With the troops held under arms all night, massed in bivouac in column behind the sallies on the New Market road, Cabot did not expect to sleep. The army was ready for the final assault on Richmond. If the entrenched defenders, most of them green or partly incapacitated, put up a fight it might come to a battle through the streets as they fell back—a possibility which left him sick with anxiety. More than once he went out alone into the still, starless night, so full of tension and uncertainty, and heard the low-voiced videttes reporting to their relief before cat-footing back to their reserve posts. Once he flung himself down with his ear against the earth—there seemed to be nothing, and yet he was sure there ought to be, not sure that he couldn't hear faint rumblings, subterranean and obscure, while the foreground remained completely quiet.

With the first gleam of dawn he was out again, straining his eyes towards where Richmond was—and then, while he looked, a column of flame flared upward above the city on the distant boom of some mighty explosion.

Instantly his immediate surroundings came to life—questions, exclamations, speculation—General Weitzel shot out of his quarters in shirt and trousers with his field glasses in his hand—they clustered round him while he peered tensely at a lowering sky tinged with red.

"Blowing up the bridges, maybe—sounded like ammunition to me— might be the arsenal, then—might be the gunboats too——"

Weitzel remarked briefly that the enemy lines in front of them were oddly quiet.

Slowly the grey light grew. The picket line was deployed as skirmishers and pushed forward cautiously towards the reddish clay banks they had confronted so long. Word soon came back from them—the Confederate front line had been withdrawn during the misty night. The order for general assault went out.

Cabot drank a cup of black coffee, standing. His eyes were on the black smoke stabbed with fire which was rolling high into a pall above Richmond as more explosions shook the dawn. His stomach was hollow and treacherous, his heart action was a disgrace to any veteran of four years' war. But this was Eden. It seemed to him that the whole Federal Army was moving in on Eden who waited, defenceless and incalculably dear to him, directly in its path. And Richmond—Richmond was already afire.

At last, when it was still barely light, he was allowed the relief of action. The headquarters cavalry was going in under a staff major to reconnoitre and Weitzel sent him with it. At last he felt the saddle under him, and was on his way to Eden. They overtook and passed jubilant columns of infantry at the double-quick, and wildly driven artillery, racing to be the first to enter the captive city. At the steamboat landing just below Richmond the Rebel ironclads lay sullenly, apparently deserted. As the cavalry came abreast of the lowest one it blew up with a terrible concussion, bits of it sailing over their heads into the fields beyond. No one was hit, and they rode on into streets thick with smoke and cinders and loud with the explosion of magazines where cartridges rattled like musketry fire above the steady, awful roar of unchecked flames and the crash of falling walls.

The arsenal had gone up, and the waterfront was blazing and the fire was spreading into the business and residential districts. The commissary stores in Cary Street had caught, driving back the drunken, brawling mob which had held carnival there all night. A little group of mounted grey-clad men waited on Mayo's Bridge at the foot of Fourteenth Street till the last of their own ambulances and cavalry rearguard had reached the Manchester side, which had already begun to catch fire too. Then in the face of the Federal cavalry galloping up Main Street they applied the torch to barrels of tar and pine knots soaked in kerosene stacked at the bridgehead and retired, leaving the north end of the bridge enveloped in flames and smoke which covered their retreat.

Richmond had been set ablaze by the reckless, crazy hands of its desperate defenders. The Federal cavalry detachment rode to the western edge of the fire, which was then about Tenth and Cary Streets and still several blocks short, to Cabot's relief, of the end of Franklin Street opposite Capitol Square. The demoralized population was doing nothing to stop its progress. As the Federal horsemen circled back through the shuttered residential district where everyone remained behind closed doors, Weitzel and his Staff were riding in past the wrecked gunboats at the landing. Not far behind them came the first infantry column, in dress formation with three bands playing Union airs.

The headquarters cavalry swept in through the gates of the Square and took possession of the Capitol building. The park was already full of people who had fled there during the night to escape the fire, and who were still strewn about the lawn in despair and exhaustion. When Weitzel's impressive arrival took place the open space inside the iron railings was further crowded by the horses and attendants of the Staff and corps commanders who accompanied him, and everyone was choking and gasping with streaming eyes in the smoky, cinder-filled air, which was stirred by a light southerly breeze carrying the fire towards them from the river front.

Weitzel lost no time in turning his victorious troops into firefighting squads to pass water from all available sources and blow up buildings in the path of the fire, and make every possible effort to save the rest of the city—so that the crash of dynamited walls was soon added to the din. Having satisfied himself on the way in that the house which sheltered Eden was still intact, though uncomfortably near the creeping edge of the fire, Cabot devoted himself to firefighting. All around the fringe of the main fire little fires caught from flying cinders and sparks, and detachments were constantly answering calls from frantic house-owners whose roofs or porches had developed menacing tongues of flame.

Towards noon, when it had begun to look as though nothing could control the conflagration and the whole city might be left in ashes, Cabot on a sweating, singed horse, himself black with smoke and dirt, was sent with his now veteran crew to the roaring block where the War Office blazed, imperilling the Spotswood Hotel and General Lee's house, just beyond which the Crabb mansion stood. A guard had been posted outside General Lee's, and an ambulance was waiting at the curb to remove Mrs. Lee if it should become necessary.

They had laid a dynamite charge and Cabot was clearing his men from the area when a small, desperate figure in a white apron and cap raced out into the street and caught at his knee. His horse, its nerves being pretty well shattered by now, shied violently and he had a horrid moment when he thought it had knocked her down.

"Get away from here, girl, we're blowing up this wall!" he shouted, trying to get the animal's forefeet on the ground again.

"Oh, please, please come and help!" she was crying. "Our stables are on fire and we can't get the horses out! Please help us to save the horses, there's only old Daniel and he——"

He controlled his horse, collected two dismounted troopers who were black in the face, dismayingly, and followed her down Franklin Street. She led him through the garden of the Crabb house and there in the stableyard a group of women were trying to throw buckets of water on the smouldering corner of the kitchen. Beyond them, the roof of the stable crackled with fire and a man on crutches stood staring at it while a black boy hovered uncertainly around the red hot doorway as though about to try a dash inside.

"Boy! Come away from that barn!" Cabot yelled, and——

"Dabney, I've got some soldiers to help!" cried Charlotte, and just then the dynamite charge went off at the War Office with a fresh shower of fiery cinders and flying flame.

Eden ran towards the grimy men in blue and caught the arm of the foremost.

"Oh, please be quick—our coachman went in for the horses—he's too old—you've *got* to get him out—!" Then she recognized Cabot.

"Well, I said I'd be here, didn't I!" His teeth gleamed white in his dirty face. "We'll get him out, give me your apron." He seized it from her. "I want another one—you, there, give this man your apron!" Charlotte handed hers to one of the troopers, who followed Cabot's example of sousing it in the half bucket of water Mammy held, and with the aprons wrapped around their faces they ran into the open stable door.

It was only a minute, or perhaps two, that she had to wait, till he came in sight again lugging old Daniel like a sack of potatoes under one arm, with the trooper just behind him grasping the halter of a plunging horse in each hand. But to Eden all eternity passed while she stood paralyzed watching the molten maw of the stable. Cabot freed himself of the steaming apron and tossed it at the second trooper who had gone to meet him.

"Look alive, son, there are two more horses in there!" he shouted, and the trooper dived in at the stable door and brought them out, all in the day's work, while Cabot stood old Daniel on his feet and made sure he was all right before Mammy led him away to restoratives. Then Cabot turned to look for Eden, and beside her stood Dabney in his worn grey uniform with a crutch under his arm. The eyes of the two men met gravely. Then Cabot said, "Well, Dabney—I'm sorry—I guess it's about over. I wish there was anything to say——"

Dabney held out his right hand.

IX OCTOBER 29, 1865

I

EDEN lay in bed in the familiar room at Williamsburg where she had always slept with Sue. It was June now, but she had lost track of time, and anyway she didn't care any more.

No one was really surprised when Eden collapsed the night of the fire in Richmond. She had gone beyond her strength so long that when at supper she said rather faintly that she would like to lie down a while Louise helped her into bed and bade her stay there, unless, of course, the fire got worse. The troops had managed to check it short of Lee's house, but not until nearly midnight could anyone be sure the city was safe.

Lying now in the big bed in the quiet room in Williamsburg, Eden was sometimes a little confused as to how she had got there—not that it mattered to her much. She remembered going to bed in Franklin Street with the roar of the fire only a few squares away—remembered the feel of the cool sheets under her shaking limbs and her own secret conviction that even if the house burned down she could not move, would not think it worth while to move to save herself. Later, Louise came back with a lamp, and tried to make her eat, but she only lay still with her eyes closed, shaking. Louise felt her head and her wrist—there was no fever, but the thin pulse raced and the quick, shallow heartbeat set the ruffles of her nightdress visibly atremble. Louise was frightened and made her drink some hot milk. They couldn't find Dr. Tracy and they had no idea how to get hold of Cabot, who had vanished into the blazing maelstrom beyond the Square. She heard them speak his name and prayed helplessly, lying motionless except for the trembling she could not control—no, no, not Cabot—don't let them—don't bring Cabot here—don't let me have to see Cabot——

But she had no words to tell them, and in the morning Louise bent over her again.

"Eden—Major Murray is here. He wants to bring a Yankee doctor he believes in—will you see him?"

"No."

"But we can't find Dr. Tracy, honey, he's been out all night long trying to help everybody at once. Won't you see Major Murray's man instead?"

"No. Tell Cabot—go away." And the effort for speech left her limp and sweating.

"Would you see Dr. Tracy if we can find him?"

There was no answer. Louise retreated to where Cabot was standing at the bottom of the stairs.

"Very well, then, we'll find this man Tracy," said Cabot, and somehow within an hour he did, and brought back with him the kindly white-haired man who had saved Lafe and tried to save Felicity, and who had tended Dabney the best he could.

Inert under Dr. Tracy's hands, Eden never knew that in the little sitting-room where Cabot waited Charlotte couldn't stand it any longer.

"Major Murray, I might as well tell you first as last," Charlotte began with an uneasy glance at Dabney, who always said she talked too much, "and it's nothing Dr. Tracy can cure—at least, she's worn herself out with work and worry, sure enough, but that's not the real trouble, you see, she got sorry for my brother Grafton and said she'd marry him, and now she knows she was wrong—at least, *I* can see she was wrong, on account of you, and she doesn't know what to do because she promised Grafton, and that's what's killing her, and you may as well know!"

Cabot looked first at Dabney as though expecting him to contradict so preposterous a story, and then turned to Charlotte slowly as though it hurt his head to move it.

"Where is your brother Grafton now?" he asked, with an effort.

"He's gone back to the line. Are they still fighting?"

"Yes. They're still fighting."

"He—Grafton has loved her all his life," Charlotte pleaded apologetically. "He's never so much as looked at another girl. Reckon he just sort of—wore her down, finally. But it wasn't his fault to love her —there's nobody like Eden, you know that yourself—Grafton wouldn't try to—I mean, you mustn't hold it against him!"

Cabot's drawn face twisted into a wry smile, and again his eyes sought Dabney's.

"I'm not blaming him," he said gently. "I'm sorry for him too. Because Grafton will have to let her go."

The doctor came back then, looking puzzled and unhappy.

"It's a form of exhaustion," he said, seeming to feel his way. "Terrible lassitude and prostration. But worst of all—she doesn't seem to care."

"Tell me what you need for her," said Cabot, and the muscles round his jaw were tight. "Write out everything that might be of any use to her, and I'll get it from our hospital stores at once."

The doctor made a modest list—he didn't really know what to do—suggested wine and tea and warm food as well, and went away, still looking doubtful and distressed, with Cabot looming beside him.

Dimly while she lay there in Franklin Street, she had been aware of Cabot's powerful hand in her affairs. Medicines, succulent bits of fresh meat such as hadn't been seen in Richmond for years, broths, fruit, wines, sweets—she turned from them all, indifferently, to lie very still with her eyes closed and listen to her own heart, which seemed to have loosed its moorings entirely to flutter somewhere in midair. Days slid by. She knew that Cabot must be there, somewhere, but relied on Louise to preserve her from seeing him. At least she would not have to see Grafton so long as the Yankees held Richmond. She didn't know which would be worse—to see Cabot or to see Grafton. But it was Grafton's right to see her now when he chose—when he could, anyway. She had promised Grafton—and by then her whole world would be a panic of wild heartbeat and cold perspiration and she would make a defensive blank of her mind again, lying very still. . . .

Finally it was Sunday once more in Franklin Street, and the church bells rang, and that was the day Louise came to tell her that Lee had surrendered at Appomattox. "They'll be coming home now at last," Louise said, with tears running down her cheeks. "They were starving at Appomattox—dropping in their tracks by the road—Grant was very generous, he fed them from his own men's rations, and they can keep their horses and side arms, and their transportation home is free—some of them are coming into Richmond already——"

Grafton. Grafton would be coming home. Lie very still. . . . Don't think at all. . . . Not yet. . . .

And so Eden was not at the window with Charlotte when the muddy caisson drew up at the curb bearing the long, rough plank coffin with the bullet-torn banner laid over it. Grafton had come home, killed on that last Sunday morning when the battle flared near Appomattox before the white flags began passing to and fro.

Tears crept out from the corners of Eden's closed eyes when they told her, and soaked into the pillow—endless, hopeless tears for Grafton, who had won after all. But it did begin to be surprising when after a few days she still got no stronger and the tears would not stop. It was not, said Charlotte frankly, as though she had ever been really in love with poor Grafton, she was only sorry for him. Dr. Tracy shook his head and muttered that dreaded word *decline,* and Cabot, who called every day and sat patiently in the parlor talking to Louise or Charlotte, made a rather sudden decision for them. Cabot got the best ambulance there was to be had in his army, and Eden was put into it and taken out of Richmond to Williamsburg. She remembered very little of the journey. And now here she was, home again, lying quite still lest she think about things she had comfortably forgotten, things it was no use thinking about any more, and besides—if she was very careful not to think at all her heart was back in the groove again and gave no trouble. . . .

She roused to find Gran sitting in the big chair by the bedside where Sue spent so much of her time. Even now, one was always glad to see Gran. Eden smiled faintly and turned her head on the pillow as a gesture of welcome.

"Hullo, Gran," she whispered.

Gran never asked how one was, nor chirped about feeling better today, nor any of the sickroom inanities so many otherwise sensible people gave way to. Gran knew by looking, how one was.

She raised one hand now and pointed to the bedside table, where the most glorious bowl of roses sat, shedding fragrance. Eden turned her head still further, to see, and sniffed appreciatively.

"Aren't they lovely," she whispered.

"Your favorite bush," said Gran. "Down by the arbor. It's blooming itself inside out for you this year."

"That's nice of it." She lay a moment looking into Gran's calm, sweet eyes, which looked back at her, unself-conscious as a child's.

"I'm taking Sue's place," said Gran, "because she has a visitor. Something she's been looking forward to. Cabot's sister Melicent has come to stay with us a while."

"N-not Cabot—?" Eden murmured, and seemed to shrink smaller into the pillows.

"He brought her here, but——"

"No—no, it's no use, Gran, I'm—too ill to see anyone."

"You won't have to see him. He started back to Washington an hour ago."

"Oh." Eden thought this over, for it seemed rather odd. And yet, after all, not even Cabot would come tramping into one's bedroom demanding an interview when one was so ill. And he had left Melicent there. He would be back.

Gran watched her with a gleam of satisfaction while she thought it over. Gran could see that she had not expected him to be gone like that. Gran knew now that she had been right to insist that Eden must not be allowed even the chance to refuse to see him. It was Gran's idea that he should go before Eden ever knew he was there.

Once more their eyes met, and Eden's were clouded.

"I suppose you're wondering why I—" she began.

"I did. But he told me what it was."

"Told you that he——?"

"That he had been a spy, yes. Working between the lines since before Sharpsburg."

"I never meant anyone to know," Eden said, fighting tears. "Not even you. I didn't want you all to hate him."

"Well, you see," said Gran, "I can remember how we felt about Nathan Hale. We thought him quite a hero."

"But he——"

"He was a spy. And he was caught and hanged. Of course he was on our side. But then there was Major André. We thought rather well of him, too, even though he was a redcoat. It's no job for a coward—spying."

"Did you say that—to him?"

"There was no need. You've talked enough now for a while, I think. Better try and take another nap."

Eden subsided obediently, but not to sleep. He had told Gran he was a spy. Wasn't he afraid of *anything?* Surely not even Cabot had had a right to expect her to take it the way she had. But he had faced up to it, the first chance he got, and Gran hadn't turned against him. Except for herself, he was still welcome here. Except for herself. . . .

"Did—does anyone else know?" she whispered.

"I didn't see fit to mention it at the dinner table, if that's what you mean."

Silence again, in the drowsy afternoon heat, sweet with roses. No one else knew. Dabney had offered Cabot his hand, that day in Richmond. Sue was friends with Melicent. The war was over. If only she wasn't so tired——

But something had happened to the hard little ball of misery which had knotted up her inside for so long. It relaxed with a slow sigh, and she fell asleep.

2

Melicent was going about in a daze of happiness.

No day was long enough to contain her delight in this new existence which stretched before her like the Elysian Fields, sunlit and laughing and full of pleasant surprises. She did not know Williamsburg well enough to notice as its homecoming residents did at every turn the added shabbiness and emptiness the war had wrought, nor to miss the faces which would never be seen in its streets again. It had been a backwater behind the lines so long that it bore no recent scars of the fighting it had seen, and its inhabitants had not starved and suffered as the people in Sherman's path had done, nor known the strain undergone by those who had lived in the comparative safety of Richmond. It was summer and the gardens still bloomed and the Negroes still sang, and there seemed always to be enough to eat in Ransom's white house at the edge of town. And in spite of the scarifying sense of defeat which lay heavy on every Southern heart, there was a kind of stealthy relief too, in places like Williamsburg—for the fighting was over, and surely nothing which was to come could be worse than that; the men that survived had come home and there were tearful, longed-for reunions, and hence a kind of happiness, even when body and spirit were damaged beyond repair. It was over. They had been beaten, they had lost beyond all calculation of love and comforts and dear accustomed ways, lost more than they could yet realize of all they held dearest—but the guns were silent at last, and those families that were left closed ranks and clung fast to what they still had, and drew breath against whatever lay ahead. It was over. . . .

Melicent had never lived among a large family before, and for her the continual to and fro between Ransom's house and the Sprague place in England Street and the Crabb house where Dabney and Charlotte had come to live was a sort of perpetual party. In no time at all Sue and Myrta were like sisters to her, and her shyness of Fauquier soon wore off under his casual friendliness. She was given Dabney's old room for her own, and this fact, along with his crutch, made her particularly fond of him. When she learned that it was also the room in which Sedgwick had recovered from his wound after the battle of Williamsburg she had to go up and look at it all over again, with new eyes.

Sedgwick, through no effort of his own, was her favorite of them all. He took no particular notice of her, not as much as Fauquier did; in fact, she saw comparatively little of him, and of course knew nothing of what lay between him and Sue. He had gone back to his reading for Law, and he took solitary rides on the little mare Jingle, who had somehow endured hard use, bad weather, and scant rations to carry her master home again when the war ended, though his war-horse, Sycamore, was in such poor shape he had to be led—they were short, gentle rides, for Jingle's sake.

Both Lafe and Sedgwick had thankfully shed the threadbare grey uniforms they wore away from Appomattox for the ruffled shirts, black stocks, bright waistcoats, skirted coats, and light trousers they had worn before the war, and they left their hair longer than the men up North. Tall and straight and slender men, oddly alike now that Sedgwick had come to maturity in the hard school of war and Lafe's perennial youthfulness was returning with rest and better food—oddly alike in their laughter, fresh and ready, in their soft Virginia speech and gentle ways with women—alike too in something in their make-up which was noticeably shining and resilient. War had not blunted or even sobered the Spragues, it had only tempered them. They were different from anything Melicent had ever seen before, and she was inclined to gaze at them silently from a respectful distance while they, assuming that she was merely shy, refrained from singling her out for any special overtures till she had had time to feel less strange among them.

Louise was mother to both households now that there was no longer a Felicity. Sally, to everyone's surprise, had suddenly married a rather middle-aged colonel and remained in Richmond as mistress of his Franklin Street mansion. Sue was doing her best to run Ransom's house as her mother had done, and at the same time be nurse to Eden. She slept on a cot in the room she and Eden had always shared, but after Melicent's arrival Eden saw less of Sue and more of Mammy. No one ever suggested that she should see Melicent, and at last curiosity stirred.

"Is she pretty, Mammy?" she enquired one day over her supper tray, after being urged to drink up a glass of the special wine their visitor had brought as a gift to the invalid.

"Pretty as can be," said Mammy promptly. "But her ma ain' got what I'd call *taste*. Mm-*mm,* her po' little clothes is fit to break yo' heart."

"What's wrong with them?"

"Plain, an' dark, an' *ugly*—ain' fit fer nobody under forty-five an' a ol' maid at that! Honest, Miss Eden, I'm sorry fer dat po' chile 'bout her clothes! You an' Miss Sue ain' nebber seen de like in all yo' born days!"

"Well, we'd better ask her brother to send her something suitable from Washington."

"Somebody sho' better—cain' get nothin' yere nowadays."

Sue looked round the door just then and came in.

"Did you think I had deserted you, Dee? Melicent and I were over at Aunt Louise's and we stayed to supper."

"I'm glad Melicent is here, I must have been rather dull company since I got home," Eden said. "Sue, Mammy's been telling me the poor girl's clothes are all wrong."

"They are." Sue came in and closed the door behind her. "I don't like to say anything to her, but she hasn't got enough thin dresses for this climate, and I've nothing fit to lend her!"

"We'll have to tell Cabot. He'll send her something."

Sue frankly stared. Eden had taken no interest whatever in anything for weeks and now here she was, eating supper without being coaxed and giving advice about clothes.

"You mean—*write* to Cabot?" Sue asked stupidly.

"Gran could do it. He'll never think of it unless he's told, but he could easily send down a couple of dresses from Washington, there must be plenty of them there."

"W-would you like to see her some time?" Sue asked cautiously, wondering if this was the opening they had been waiting for.

"Yes, I would. Maybe tomorrow."

Sue could hardly wait to get away and tell Gran.

When Melicent entered the room the next day Eden was propped up against the pillows looking frail but very much alive. Melicent thought she had never seen anyone so beautiful, and couldn't imagine how Cabot could bear to stay in Washington.

Melicent was wearing a dark green watered silk dress, with an unbecoming high neck and bulky sleeves. It was obviously new and expensive, and anything but suitable to a Virginia summer. Eden understood Mammy's horrors over the first Yankee wardrobe she had ever seen. Before the war there would have been plenty of their own thin lawns and embroidered muslins to lend her, but now everything they had was worn to shreds.

"If I were you I'd ask Cabot to send me some cooler dresses," Eden remarked soon after Melicent had settled herself in the armchair and was gazing at her with round, admiring eyes. "No one knows how hot it is here in July till they have felt it, so you naturally didn't come prepared."

"Well, I—thought he might send something," Melicent said uncertainly. "Because on the train coming down he suddenly seemed to catch sight of me as though I hadn't been there all along, and he said —you know how he is—he said, 'Oh, say, your clothes! I forgot all about them!' And when I told him I had three new dresses—this is one of them—he said, 'What good will that do!' and muttered something about getting hold of Mrs. Trimble right away. She is the Senator's wife who chose my clothes that time I was in Washington, and so I thought——"

"Maybe something is on the way, then," Eden suggested.

"Unless he forgot," said Melicent, resigned to the possibility.

"Was that you I heard singing yesterday?"

"I hope it didn't disturb you—Sue asked me to, and I tried to hold in so you wouldn't hear——"

"I wanted to hear, it sounded like an angel," said Eden. "An angel very far away. Next time I'll have my door open and you sing as loud as you can."

"I learned all that music you sent me once, thank you very much."

"Oh, yes—so long ago," said Eden, looking back.

"I sang *The Last Waltz* at the Senator's house in Washington—they liked it."

"I'd almost forgotten *The Last Waltz*—I'd like to hear it again."

"Shall I go and do it for you now?"

But before she could rise from the chair, Sue whirled into the room carrying a band-box in each hand.

"Melicent, there are *bales* of boxes arriving for you from Washington —somebody has sent you a whole trousseau!"

"Cabot! He didn't forget!" cried Melicent, shining with pride of him.

"Bonnets?" said Eden, eyeing the band-boxes, and she actually sat up away from the pillows. "Oh, let me see the bonnets! Do open them, Melicent!"

"Here?" asked Melicent doubtfully, for they had told her Eden tired very easily and no one was allowed to stay long.

"Yes, of course here!" Eden patted the coverlet impatiently. "I haven't seen a new bonnet in *years!*"

Pharaoh paused at the open door, his arms piled high with parcels adorned with a famous silver label and tied with bright red cord.

"Whereat you want all dese yere boxes?" he enquired. "All got Miss Melicent's name writ on 'em."

"Bring them in here—all of them," Eden commanded. "Do you mind, Melicent? Do you mind showing me the things as you unpack them?"

So Mammy was sent for and soon the room was aswirl with tissue paper and delighted exclamations. Cabot was not so thoughtless as to send his sister new clothes in a household where there had been no new clothes for four years, without remembering the rest of them. He had actually sent them each a summer dress, chosen by the Senator's wife and labelled with their names—and for Gran, an embroidered Chinese shawl and the most frivolous of lace caps.

Dinner was late while they admired themselves, the girls fastening each other up if Mammy was not quick enough, discussing every detail of the exquisite work and the small alterations necessary to a perfect fit, while Eden lay and watched, with her hand on the pink foulard peignoir which was her gift, and which had been laid across the bed within her reach. "Clothes," said Gran, nodding, when she heard that Eden had sat right up and asked for the bonnets. "That's a good sign." And that night she wrote Cabot a letter which made him feel roughly a hundred years younger.

Melicent was wearing her new dress, which had a white organdie guimpe and big bell sleeves gathered into wristbands made of little crystal bead bracelets, when she sat down to the piano that afternoon in the drawing-room to sing for Eden, whose door was open up stairs. Sue sat on the sofa across the room in her new white muslin and green sash, sewing a fresh lace collar into an old lawn dress for second best —but it was less discouraging to make over old clothes if you had one perfect outfit which only had to be kept nice by wearing others when it didn't matter.

They didn't hear Sedgwick come in through the hall, and he stood a minute on the threshold listening while Melicent's young voice soared through the sentimental strains of *The Long Long Weary Day.* As she came to the refrain he moved on into the room and with a mirthful glance at Sue added his own voice, so highly thought of by General Stuart and so derided by his loving family, to Melicent's. When they finished, and he struck his famous high note, he was leaning on the piano beside her and she was round-eyed and breathless, almost too surprised to keep up with him.

"That's a Southern song, honey," he said then in his gentle drawl. "Who taught you that one?"

"I have an album of Southern songs," she explained diffidently. "I got it some time ago because—because——"

"Because you thought it might come in handy some day?" He was smiling down at her, so gracefully at his ease, his dark-fringed grey eyes looking so kindly at her flushed, upturned face.

She dropped her gaze to the keyboard, and played a few sweet aimless chords.

"I didn't know you sang," she got out, and he laughed, the free Sprague laughter which had survived the war.

"I don't," he said. "It's what we call Negro tenor down here. I was just born with it. Ask Sue if I can sing!"

"Of course you can sing, Sedgie," Sue said at once, as though he was very young, and her dimple showed.

"Let's sing another," Melicent implored him, and her fingers stirred on the keys. And obligingly he began to teach her *Lorena* by rote, reaching sometimes to strike a chord himself, for he played by ear, so that their hands brushed and Melicent became aware of the somehow stinging vitality in the slim body bent above her. Her fingers stumbled and were stupid beside his, and music was not all she heard in his voice as it sang the sad, foolish words of the song.

And Sue, playing at duenna on the sofa, felt hot tears behind her eyelids, because this was how it would come some time and she must make up her mind to it. Anyone could see that Melicent had begun to love him as she herself had loved him at sixteen, with a wild, blind, unstinting devotion. And some time Sedgwick must take what he could and build the life they could not have together, so he needn't grow old alone and lacking and robbed as she had dreaded that he might.

Perhaps Melicent was the one, Sue thought. Perhaps it had come already and she must give him up all over again now that she had just got him back safe from the war. Some one had to look after him, because she could never do it herself the way they wanted. He had never once referred to that day on the riverbank, but she knew that nothing which had happened to him since had made him forget—she knew by his eyes and the tone of his voice when he spoke to her that his memory of it was as vivid as hers. He had warned her the next morning that it must be as though that day had never happened, and he kept his word. But it would never be quite the same, she knew, with something forever withheld, and guarded, and denied. The least she could do was to play up to that, and be just cousins, as he said, and never to think beyond. The least she could do was to help him all she could, by pretending to forget it too. Perhaps it would be easier if his life was filled in as it should be, perhaps the sooner he married some one else the better. And in that case, Melicent was the one. Sue felt she could bear Melicent in Sedgwick's life, because Melicent loved her too, and Melicent was lonely and rather forlorn and liked being in Williamsburg and ought never to have to go back to that dreadful place in Trenton. . . .

Sue stole a glance towards the piano, blinking away the blur. He was having a good time with Melicent. His face was relaxed and smiling, with that tight look gone from round his jaw which she so often saw there when a silence fell between them. His shoulder touched Melicent's crisp organdie, their hands moved together on the keyboard, their voices blended, and Melicent was watching his lips for the words, with a pathetic upward lift to her long lashes. Rebellion shot through Susannah like a pain and receded slowly into what she called commonsense. Poor Melicent adored him. Poor Melicent—was going to marry him. It would be best that way—easiest for everybody, if only Sedgwick could be made to see that it would be selfish and wicked to set up a headstone on Melicent's life because double first cousins couldn't marry. Melicent at least could be happy, and Sedgwick—Sedgwick could have his children.

When *Lorena* had been successfully sung from beginning to end and Melicent ran up stairs to Eden to be congratulated, Sedgwick came and sat down near the sofa and heard all about the new dresses from Washington.

"When is Cabot coming back?" he inquired then. "Eden is getting better every day—what's the matter with them, anyway?"

"I don't know. There was something besides Grafton, I'm sure, or the fact that the Yankees won the war. Gran knows, I think. Probably she'll send for him when she thinks Eden is well enough."

"She'd better. Then Eden would be provided for. The Murrays didn't lose money in the war, you can bet, if they own a steel mill! Eden had better grab him, and I'd tell her so myself."

"*Sedgie,* what a thing to say! As though Eden would marry for money!"

"Eden can marry Cabot Murray for love, we all know that. Since he's got money too, so much the better! Nobody down here will ever have any again!"

"But once Father gets the school going again, and you take your Law exams——"

He shook his head.

"We're finished, Sue. We're all gone to pieces. Nobody can afford the school as it used to be, and nobody can pay lawyer's fees any more. And with Farthingale gone, we haven't even got anything to sell."

"Isn't there *anything* left of it, after the fire?"

"The chimneys. And part of the kitchen and the quarters. And a lot of charred wood and bits of glass and china, and the stair rail."

"Do you think Butler burned it on purpose?"

"He wouldn't have to. Lots of houses caught fire just from being fought over, or being too close to the cook fires. It wouldn't have to be pure Yankee spite. I'd rather think it wasn't. But even though we never really lived there since I can remember, I hate to think of the house being gone. The Spragues have always had Farthingale, ever since Grandfather St. John married money in his day! I miss having it. So does Father."

There was a silence. Sue was thinking. She was thinking how rich the Murrays must be.

"Sedgie, what are we going to do about Melicent?"

"Do about her?"

"She oughtn't to have to go back to Trenton."

"She doesn't have to, does she? Her father doesn't seem to be the kind to care whether she's there or not."

"Sedgie. Why don't you marry her?"

"*What?*" He sat staring at her.

"Now, don't yell at me, Sedgie, it's not such a crazy idea."

"It's the craziest one *I* ever heard of!" he said, his voice still raised in bewilderment. "Are you out of your *mind,* Susannah?"

"You like her, don't you?"

"Well, yes, of course, but——"

"She's in love with you."

Her head was bent above her needle, he could not see her face, but he knew in a sweeping revelation how her thoughts were running. Once she had ridden down to the river at Jamestown, for what she conceived to be his good. And now, as on that morning, he was silent, suppressing his own emotion until he could achieve calmness for her sake.

"I'm not one of your book heroes," he said at last. "You can't just marry me off with a stroke of your pen. I can talk back to you!"

"I'd rather you didn't."

But he could not take her in his arms and kiss away the tears that dripped down, bright as the needle in her fingers, while the silence stretched between them. He rose with an angry, lithe movement like his father's, and went to stand at the window behind her, staring out into the garden. At last he spoke, and his voice was low and even.

"I'd better send Micah over here to clean out those roses," he said. "He's got our place looking pretty tidy now."

"If I were your sister, Sedgie—Melicent is the one I'd choose for you."

"You're not my sister, honey," he reminded her tonelessly from the window. "What's the matter with that cape jessamine? Something is eating the leaves."

"Yes, I know—I couldn't see anything on it, maybe soapsuds would help. Sedgie—please think about Melicent, won't you? We can't go on like this till we're old—it hurts too much——"

"It will be easier when we're old—according to what they say."

"You can't do it. I won't let you. It's not fair to her either."

"Oh, nonsense, Sue, she hardly knows me! You're just imagining that part of it."

"But I'm not. I can tell by looking at her, and she keeps asking about you—just little things—at first I thought it was just the way a girl would feel about any soldier like you, but—now I know. I *know* how she feels."

"Well, Lordy, Susannah, why did you have to go and tell me?" His flexible, revealing voice was almost querulous with embarrassment. "I don't want anything to do with it, it makes me feel like a fool, and now I won't know where to look!"

"Look at Melicent, Sedgie. She's lovely."

"No, I'm damned if I will! It doesn't make sense for you, of all people, to try and railroad me into marrying a mere child——"

"She's sixteen. When I was sixteen——"

"Now, stop it, Sue. Stop it." With another of his restless, quick movements he returned to his chair and stood with his hands on the back of it, looking down at her. His knuckles were white. "I bet you're just after more of the Murrays' money," he accused, trying to tease her out of it.

But Sue raised her head and met his eyes steadfastly and said, "I want you to marry her, Sedgie, for all our sakes."

"I can't," he said, looking back at her, the chair between them. "Don't you understand—I can't. "

Somebody ran down the stairs and Melicent's voice came from the doorway—"Gran wants to see Sedgwick before he leaves."

"Yes—I was just going up," he said quickly and was gone, without another word to either of them.

Gran saw the trouble in his face before he reached her chair and bent to receive her kiss. It came out at once.

"Gran, you'll have to talk to Sue. She's taken it into her head that I ought to marry Melicent."

Instead of laughing it off, or indignantly lining up on his side, she only looked at him thoughtfully.

"It had occurred to me too," she said.

"Is this a conspiracy?" he demanded.

"Sue is twenty, and I'm nearly a hundred—and we've both of us thought it out the same way. Sometimes people have to make do with second best, and go on living."

"That's easy to *say!*" he cried. "Especially when you yourself have had the best!"

"I was thinking of your great grandmother Dorothea," she murmured

"The one who married the Frenchman."

"Yes. You see—it was Julian she loved."

"But he chose you. It wasn't quite the same thing."

"Not quite. But they were very happy, and I'm sure Armand never dreamed he was second choice."

"I never thought *you'd* go back on me, Gran!"

She reached out a frail, compelling hand, so that he had to come and take it in both his. The line of his lips was white and hard. Softly from below came the sound of the piano and Melicent's voice repeating the lesson he had taught her—

"The years creep slowly by, Lorena,
    The snow is on the grass again,
  The sun's low down the sky, Lorena,
    The frost gleams where the flow'rs have been. . . ."

Sedgwick dropped down on the stool at his grandmother's feet, and hid his face in her lap.

3

It seemed to Gran that almost before her letter could have reached Washington Cabot was striding into her room at Williamsburg, crushing her hands in his, his eyes searching her face for encouragement in his belief that he was not too soon, that Eden would see him now, at last.

"You must have flown," she said, making no effort not to look pleased.

"I've waited five years," he reminded her. "What must I say to her now? Tell me what to do, when I see her."

"Since when have you needed help with your courting, Cabot?"

"I've never been on my knees to a woman yet," he said wryly. "But down I go, if she wants it that way!"

"I wouldn't if I were you," said Gran, thinking of Archer Crabb and how tiresome it was, really, to have to sit on a pedestal when what you wanted was love.

"Gran, I've got stage-fright," he confessed. "It's worse than a cavalry charge, walking up to her now and—well, what do I have to do, apologize because we won the war?"

"I'd forget about the war if I were you."

"Has she forgotten?"

"Not yet. But we all will, in time."

"I'm afraid that's going to be hard to do, Gran. Things are pretty bad down here."

"Yes," she nodded. "I remember. And we had George Washington."

"And we've lost Lincoln. Gran, promise me something, regardless of Eden, if either of us can think that way a minute. Promise me, no matter what happens you will let me know if—if I can do anything—for anybody—to help out. I know your grandson and the boys would die before they'd turn to me now—but you know better than that—don't you, Gran?"

For a moment, deeply touched, she sat holding to his strong hands, savoring an illusive comfort. Then she patted his fingers reassuringly and said, "Ring the bell, my dear, and we'll ask Sue if you can see Eden now."

Eden was sitting in the big chair by the window of her room when

Sue came to tell her Cabot was in the house. It took her by surprise. She was wearing the flowered peignoir he had sent from Washington, and her hair was in two loose braids on her shoulders. The late afternoon sun had nearly passed the window and shone obliquely into the room, cooling towards evening. There was the scent of roses.

"He's with Gran now," Sue said. "Wouldn't you like to see him a few minutes before supper?"

"L-like this?" asked Eden faintly.

"Yes, of course, you look very nice," said Sue, and took silence for assent, and went away to tell Cabot he might go in.

He came slowly across the threshold, and as Eden sat looking up at him from the chair she remembered how once she had thought if only he could be tamed and softened— The arrogance was gone from him now, and the mockery, and his eyes were anxious, for she looked very thin and frail, and he was long past taking anything for granted.

"Cabot, I—have so much to thank you for," she said, and held out her hand to him.

He stood holding it and looking down at her.

"Anybody could see you had to get out of Richmond. I'm glad I was able to arrange it," he heard himself saying, and wondered how he could sound so collected when there was a hammer pounding crazily inside his chest and the strangling need to lift her up and hold her forever was gripping his throat. He would never believe she was still alive and safe and getting well until he had her in his arms again. The nightmare that he had lost her would never end until once more he felt her lips, artless and yielding, under his. Her hair was so long—her neck was so small and white—her body without the hooped skirt was so pathetically slim, she would be so light and little in his arms— "You look better than you did the last time I saw you," he heard himself saying foolishly.

"I don't remember much about that."

"I'd like to forget it myself. This is much pleasanter."

"It was very brave of you to tell Gran about—about——"

"You don't think I could go round with that on my soul and her not knowing!"

"I was afraid to tell her," she admitted.

"You've lived with her all your life and you don't know her as well as I do!"

"Apparently not." Her hand was still in his and the old familiar singing of her blood had begun again. She endured it dizzily, longing for the moment when she could lean against the bulwark of his shoulder, wishing that he would simply stoop and gather her up into the crushing strength which was to her both terror and sanctuary. At the same time she felt a flicker of inward laughter—was it possible that for once he was afraid? It looked as though Cabot the conqueror did not quite dare to claim her. But one could not just say to him out of the blue, Take me, idiot, you don't have to talk— Her head was going round with weakness and excitement. If she fainted into his arms would he, she wondered, yell for help? Gran would have known what to do with him. Gran would have known how to show him that she was dying to be kissed again— "You must have wished more than once that I was as wise as Gran," she murmured wistfully.

"It will come," he promised, smiling. "If you live long enough."

"She has made up her mind to have her birthday party again this autumn."

"She will, too. You see if she doesn't!"

"Shall you be here, Cabot?"

"Shall I?" he asked gently, and felt her other hand laid on his, and saw that his ring was on her finger.

4

It was Tibby Day's hundredth birthday, and the party had gone off very well indeed, almost like old times.

Towards midnight, she lay in the big bed waiting for some one to come and see if she wanted anything more and put out the light, because she didn't. She had had her Madeira and her biscuit, and everyone had been in to say Good-night to her, and now the house was settling down, a house quite pleasantly full again.

She counted them over contentedly: Ransom, lonely and patient, without poor Felicity, but getting his school together again with Dabney to help him—it looked as though Dabney might be the next schoolmaster instead of Fauquier, who wanted to go into Law in partnership with Sedgwick and Lafe; Sue had sold her first novel to *Harper's* and had money of her own, and a future as an authoress; Myrta, passing through the romantic stage, was still not her favorite grandchild; (Barry would have been nearly nineteen now if he hadn't been killed at New Market in the Valley—she would never know how Julian might have looked at nineteen, two years before she ever saw him;) Eden and Cabot were back from their Washington honeymoon for the party, and would be off again next week to start furnishing their house there—remarkable how fast Eden had got well, once she put her mind on it, though Cabot still treated her as though she might break. Eden was happy, anyone could tell, and there would always be enough money, Cabot would see to that. There wasn't enough money in the South any more, and Sedgwick would be poor until he got his start, anyway—but Melicent wouldn't mind that, not the way she looked at him, till it brought your heart up in your throat. Perhaps something would turn up for Sue by and by—something besides writing books, though goodness knows that seemed to keep her busy and happy enough. . . .

If only Julian could have seen them all at supper tonight—she drifted, dreaming of Julian in his youth—one didn't want to live forever—one left too much behind, till finally one only wanted to get back to all that was gone. She always thought of it as getting back to Julian, wherever he was. It had never occurred to her to doubt that she would find him waiting. . . .

There were steps in the upper hall outside her open door—Mammy's ponderous tread, followed by Sue's light feet. Lying with her eyes closed, she knew that they were looking in at her from the threshold.

"Drapped off," said Mammy in her hoarse stage-whisper.

"I do hope it wasn't too much for her," Sue murmured. "I hope she won't be tired tomorrow."

"If everybody will stop whispering and put out the lamp," said Gran clearly from the bed, "I would like to go to sleep,"